Drakonian Saga:

Dragon of Darkness

(Special Edition)

Written By:

Clarence X. Johnson

&

Ali J. Baxter

Illustrations by:

María de los Ángeles Alessandra

ISBN- 979-8-218-31691-4

To my amazing friends and family. Thank you for always supporting my dreams and aspirations. I love you all and you bring so much joy into my life and I'm very grateful for each and every one of you. - Clarence

For my family, who inspire me every day to excel in everything I do. I couldn't create without having you guys behind me and supporting me. And I wouldn't create without having you beside me. Thank you for bringing light to my life, and color to my world. – Jar-mon

Table of Contents

Prologue:
The Time Before Now

There was a place. A place meant for those that could not be destroyed. A prison, devoid of life and color, where the light feared to go, and the darkness could not escape. The land where time did not flow.

In the vastness of its empty maw, a single figure resided. His torment was great, and his crimes were greater.

He led the gods to triumph, time and again, conquering all the realms that sat before them. He could never have foreseen that his greatest victory for those he held dear would be the final push towards his own demise.

He was sent screaming into the Nega-Shikari, a nexus built to house his being for all time. The God King, stripped of his power, titles, and regalia; sentenced to an eternity of abyssal torment. But his time within the void would be brief. All he had to do was wait...

There was a tremor. A smile crept onto the man's face. It was time for his release. He could feel the void shake and destabilize. White fractures surrounded the man, followed by smaller, less neat cracks in the black. Light burned through the holes of his prison. Soon the smaller cracks were followed by larger, more devastating fractures in the space. Then, in an instant, it all came crashing down, and his Nega-Shikari was no more.

The lone man, eyes still closed, refused to reject the light that now covered his body. The heat of the sun and gusts of wind attacked his body as he became free from his prison. He inhaled the salty air, and it stung his exposed sinuses. He smiled at the nostalgia he felt. The freedom.

The man could tell he was on a mountain, in a half-destroyed room plagued by age and neglect, that overlooked an ocean of darkness he had never laid eyes on before this day. The ground he stood on was made of stone, but had seals, Rites of Release, written all over it. These were common sigils used to create and destroy doorways to other realms.

As he basked in his newfound freedom, a figure approached him from behind. He could sense her rare reptilian and draconic features, purple dragon scales, without even having to look at her. He felt her uniquely shaped eyes narrow upon his godly form. She was a strong dragoness and a familiar presence.

Much to his dismay, another even more familiar presence appeared next to the dragoness. A blue ethereal being, made entirely of the black he was released from, stood unashamed, unfettered, and unbeaten with her. A Fae.

"How dare one of my own betrayers show their face to me so soon after my release." The man said as he took in his first glimpse of the world. His words completely contradicted his laid back, almost aloof, body language. "You must believe yourself immune to my wrath to be so bold."

The Fae, unmoved by his Divine command, advanced towards him. It briefly floated around the old god, and took inventory of his power and his aura, and the dragoness bowed down onto one knee.

"King of Gods." The Fae said, his voice soft and angelic. "You find yourself raised from confinement and again amongst the living. But..." The Fae briefly paused, and stopped suddenly, though no change was exhibited in their demeanor.

"This freedom comes at a price." The Fae continued as they slowly circled the god again. "Your powers have receded in your exile, usurped by the Netherworld lords and gifted to a being whose heart is more worthy."

The man, whose patience was now being tested, scoffed at the Fae.

"You waste my time with your obtuse prophecies and subtle implications, wretch." He spit at the Fae.

"Then heed this warning, sire." The Fae said, completely immune to the man's temper. "You will retain your vengeance against the Netherworld and its kings. You will receive the being that houses your power, a young dragonkin in your own domain. And you will heed our call to your true destiny when the time is right. Bear these truths close to your heart or suffer demise for your ignorance. We will be watching, King of Gods."

The Fae then disappeared without a trace. The man turned to face the dragoness, who was still down on her knee in respect, his hands behind his back.

"Tell me general." He said in a deep, commanding voice. "What has happened to my kingdom and my armies in my absence?"

"Our forces have been pushed out of the other realms and remain on Earth." She reported quickly, her head still bowed. "You have few generals left that still practice your will and conquer in your name. I, Azzaria, am among the few left within your command."

The man softly sighed. His revenge would not be an easy task to accomplish. The Fae will have to wait, for his kingdom must be brought back to its former glory. The man reached down and lifted the dragoness' head, forcing her to look him in his eyes.

"Tell me general, why has the Fae brought you to my sacred revival?" He asked, his eyes intense with curiosity. "You are a worthy fighter, I am sure. But you hold zero ties to my personal being or even possess any spells that can assist in the ritual."

"My lord." Azzaria spoke as she maintained eye contact with him. He sensed a strong, rebellious aura from her. "There is a prophecy I must fulfill for the Fae."

The man scoffed.

"You're yet another pawn in the Fae's grand scheme." The man mused as he let go of the dragoness' face and walked past her to examine the room a bit.

The room, in fact, was not a room at all; A wall and a floor with a giant window to their backside that gave access to all manner of elements. It had a stone wall in the back, its sedimentary pattern giving away its age. The room itself contained only a table, that held a few ingredients left over from the alchemical rituals that were performed there.

"So..." The man said as he turned to face Azzaria again, satisfied with his investigation. "What is this 'prophecy' the all-knowing Fae have given you?"

"I am to mother an offspring." Azzaria said as her fists tensed up just enough for the man to notice her contempt at the idea. "And he is to not only save the dragonkin from extinction... But he is foretold to destroy the Dragon of Darkness, bringing about a new age with help from the King of the Gods."

The man's face twisted up in rage at her words. How dare they, he thought. Even now, they plot devious storylines to satisfy their boredom!

"The gall of them to just plop you here in my presence..." He said lividly. “Their arrogance knows no bounds...”

"Your power is the only way to bring about the prophecy." Azzaria said firmly. "He needs the power of a god."

For a moment, there was a brief silence in the room, and the man spent that time cursing his misfortune. Then he raised his head towards the heavens and yelled at the top of his lungs.

"Fae, I grow tired of this realm and all of its jaunts." The man screamed. "Send me back to my world."

In front of the pair, a black fissure appeared in direct response to the man's request. It ripped and tore at the space that surrounded it. The man walked up and surveyed the portal, confirming its destination.

"I would be a fool to not heed the Fae's warning." The man exclaimed, knowing his intended audience was always listening. "But do know this. I will NEVER forgive the Fae, my siblings, or anyone else for my humiliation and imprisonment. You should count yourselves lucky that I cannot enact the justice I deserve."

He then turned to Azzaria, who had now arisen, and stood confidently beside him.

"Come now, ‘Azzaria’." The man commanded. "We have much work to do. The Fae have decreed that I usher in a new era. And so, they will have it. Now ALL of earth will know the wrath of King D'Merrion." D'Merrion and Azzaria then entered the portal, vanishing from sight, leaving this foreign world forever.

Chapter 1:
The Wrath of D'Merrion

Drakonis

Drakonis stood within the ruins of New York, a capital city of the Old-World. His deep black armor with its iconic spikes and white tint made him look like a ghost beneath the moonlight. He was a tall man with an athletic build, and he was larger than any average human. His dark blade sat confidently on his hip.

The night air was cold, and the sky was so clear you could make out the stars in its belly. Residing in the heart of New York, deep in 'Central Park', a giant settlement stood. It was completely made of leftover wood and rebar chunks from the nearby buildings and trees, and was surrounded by bunkers and sandbag perches, giving it much defensibility. A fruit ripe for the picking.

He caught himself marveling at the ingenuity of the humans. They always made do with the little resources they had, creating magnificent wonders that exceeded the expectations of imagination and reality. It was a feat he found admirable, even if their attempts at modern defenses were futile.

As he got closer to his destination, he could feel them. Every human within the lone fortress, panicking, coming to the realization that the invasion was upon them. He could almost taste the fear he had instilled in them, their desperation thick upon the air.

It had been almost twenty years since the Divine Accords were called off and the war between D'Merrion's forces and the Nine Divines began again. Since then, he and his men had been ordered to subjugate human settlements in the name of his lord. A mission they had completed with lethal efficiency.

His army stood behind him at the ready, thirsty for the frenzy of war. They always marched silently, per his commands, but it was hard for them to contain their excitement with the enemy in their sight. Growls escaped their lips, and minor steps became loud booms on the earth. They held their swords, spears, and mana guns eagerly. The beastkin were getting restless.

The humans, now looking a bit more organized, brandished all manner of guns and swords. They stayed silent and ready within towers that dotted the edge of the stronghold, manning mounted machine guns, ballistae and catapults. Their position was now as strong as it could be, just in time for Drakonis' forces to get in range. Another vain maneuver against his warriors but he always enjoyed the attempted effort.

He raised his hand to halt his troops. The troops let out a novel, "AHH," in acceptance. Obedience. He then raised his sword high in the air.

"Grandfather," He yelled over the growls and roars of his troops. "BURN THOSE TOWERS!"

A large mass arose from behind, amidst the ranks of the beastkin. It took off into the air, blasting rocks and dust all over the forces, and flew silently towards the stronghold. Moments later, gray flames erupted from the beast and covered the defense towers. The towers shot back feeble and ineffective bolts that missed the fast-moving dragon, but they soon crumbled and were ultimately destroyed by the flames. The screams of men and women filled the air as they painfully met their demise.

The gates of the human settlement grunted in resistance as they were pushed open and thousands of human combatants took to the makeshift cover that surrounded the fortress. It took only a few seconds for them to hunker down behind the bulwarks they constructed. Meanwhile, Drakonis roared at his beastkin soldiers.

“Charge!” He commanded as he raised his sword in the air.

The beastkin howled and growled as they barreled past Drakonis to meet their challenge and rush the fortress. Mana rounds whizzed in the beastkin force’s direction, some fell dead in the streets, but they carried on towards the stronghold all the same. As the beastkin surrounded the stronghold, they began to fire back upon the humans. Soon, humans and beastkin alike fell as gun smoke and explosions covered the ruined streets of New York.

Only one beastkin stayed behind to accompany Drakonis.

"Look at these disgusting humans, my lord." The beastkin cackled with glee. He was none other than Ashnel, a longstanding loyal servant and general to Drakonis. "They dare believe they had a chance to withstand your mighty army, blessed by King D'Merrion's will!"

Ashnel watched in silence for a moment, then started to fidget, and jostled back and forth next to Drakonis, obviously trying hard to hold in his excitement at the death that laid before him. Drakonis could see, clear as day, that he was eager to enter the battle.

"My lord..." Ashnel gestured towards the battle. "May I?".

Drakonis sighed and gave a slight nod, and Ashnel let out a mighty roar, almost exploding with excitement.

"I LOVE WATCHING HUMANS SQUIRM!" Ashnel laughed as he took off into a sprint.

He began running towards the massacre, unstrapping his double-sided scythe on his back, and leapt high into the air and right in the middle of the conflict.

Ashnel was a wolf from Clan Sunwolf, one of the many wolfkin factions around the world. Drakonis had rescued him from a group of humans that were running inhumane experiments on him. Upon trying to deliver Ashnel to the capitol, he had shown a fire in his heart that Drakonis took a liking to. This, in turn, was a gift he had to show to his King. It didn't take long for Ashnel to pledge his life and honor to D'Merrion in the end.

Ashnel was a prideful beast, and exceptionally arrogant and hot-headed. Honestly, every victory he gave Drakonis came with a headache as well, but Drakonis overlooked that as he always marveled at how efficient and gifted Ashnel was at combat.

Ashnel cleaved his way through the humans, each swing deflected bullets as well as cut through flesh and sinew. But as usual, he could tell Ashnel didn't notice the giant boulder flying towards him.

His willful ignorance of his surroundings would be his downfall one day, Drakonis thought to himself.

Drakonis rushed past Ashnel and caught the massive boulder in his hand. With a subtle flick of his hand, he sent it back to the stronghold. The massive ball slammed into the wall, creating a new window in the fort. Drakonis then turned to face the wolfkin, certain that Ashnel could feel his disapproving frown through his mask.

"Do not underestimate the humans Ashnel." Drakonis instructed. "You always get sloppy when blood fills the air."

Ashnel was breathing heavily, obviously enjoying the slaughter. He only smiled in reply. His eyes then lifted to the skies, prompting Drakonis to turn around. Perfect.

Nine bright lights shot up into the air from the stronghold and landed not even one hundred feet away from the duo. The lights then vanished as soon as they appeared and left nine knights in their place. Each was wearing heavy silver armor, crested with the symbol of the Divines on their chests.

Right on time, Drakonis thought.

"Nine... Divines." Ashnel rasped. Many beastkin didn't take notice of the lights and fought onward towards the stronghold. The ones that did rallied to their commander's aid.

Drakonis was unmoved by the entrance of the knights. While their auras were far more impressive than the human fodder, they were still nine pathetic combatants chosen by the weaker gods of D'Merrion's pantheon. Drakonis wondered if they could even withstand one of his blows.

One of the knights walked forth, a well-built man with dark hair. He was the only one of them without a helmet on.

"Drakonis!" He yelled confidently and heroically. "I challenge you to a one-on-one duel to decide the fate of this stronghold!"

Drakonis was amused by his words. What hubris could this man have to believe he was worthy of being on the same battlefield, let alone in a direct duel with him? Drakonis crossed his arms and tilted his head at the man. Meanwhile, Ashnel and the troops laughed at the poor sap.

The wolfkin stepped forward and confidently swung his scythe around.

"Poor boy!" He jeered. "You think YOU have even the slightest chance of defeating Drakonis? It'll take more than guts and valor to conquer this darkness! More than any amount of iron and steel you have! You could never fathom the strength it would take to even scratch Drakonis!"

The knight scowled, apparently irked by the jaunting and sneers of the beastkin and dashed forward with twin blades in hand. It was obvious that he intended to target Drakonis. But Ashnel was far too fast and cut him off, deflecting both of his blades with his scythe. The knight looked up at the wolfkin's face, getting a glance at the frenzy in his eyes and kicked the beast back. After sliding a distance, Ashnel stood unfazed by the blow. His eyes locked onto his prey again. And he leapt forward, his weapon at the ready, to decapitate the man.

Drakonis heard a whistling noise coming from his blind spot. Instinctively, he moved out of the way, easily dodging the projectile shot at him. A divine bullet fired from a divine weapon. Drakonis scoffed at the sad, opportunistic attack.

Pathetic.

It seemed as though not all of the knights were so honor bound. He unsheathed his sword and began deflecting the ordinance that flew in his direction while advancing upon the knight.

Drakonis' warriors began to cheer, realizing he was finally going into action. But they also cautiously moved a couple paces backwards, anticipating what destruction lay ahead.

Under his helm, Drakonis channeled his dragon eyes to see the aura of the knights. He was checking their strength, but more importantly the color of their souls.

Red, black, blue, green... All their souls seemed common and lackluster in variety. But one soul stood out to him. A golden soul concealed by all the other souls. He only knew of one other, his own father's golden soul.

Peculiar. This soul had darkness attached to it. Could this be...?

The gun wielding knight kept firing their weapon to no avail, each round bouncing off Drakonis' blade like a rubber ball. As he drew closer to the squad of knights, they readied their weapons.

Ashnel, still locked in combat with the eager knight, landed a punch that sent the knight careening towards his friends. He slammed into a pole, bending it in half, and his allies hurried to cover their friend while he dusted himself off.

"Outstanding, Ashnel!" Drakonis commended the wolfkin. Ashnel had lined them up perfectly for the dark lord. They were all right where Drakonis wanted them to be for his next attack.

He swung his sword diagonally through the air in the direction of the knights. Nothing happened at first. The air was still, and the knights held their shields up to take the brunt of any attack.

Then the space in front of Drakonis began to shiver. It shook as though it was a cage, attempting to contain a raging beast. The space vibrated furiously and crackled with power. It took on a bright red glow as it grew far larger than the swipe that created the cataclysm.

"HOLD!" The shield knights screamed as the blast grew. The attack blasted forth before they could move a muscle and slammed into the earth at their feet. The ensuing explosion sent all the knights in different directions, completely scattering and disorientating them. The smaller beastkin and humans in the immediate vicinity were either destroyed or sent flying hundreds of feet into the air. It brought debris and viscera down on the streets and the grassy earth and covered the land in a dense fog.

Ashnel landed right next to Drakonis, almost being hit by the deadly attack.

"Wow, my lord, this is the first time I've seen you exert such power." He said in awe at the chaos caused by the blast.

Drakonis didn't have time to waste gawking at his own work. He advanced upon the knights, their auras giving away any cover the fog seemingly gave them. One knight was still barely standing, his shield held high in rebellion at the power that slammed into them. The man's breathing was ragged, and he was shaking, trying his best to remain strong. He could no longer bear the weight of his giant shield, and his knee hit the ground in defeat. It took only a moment for Drakonis to stand before the weakened form in front of him. The man looked up, and Drakonis could hear the heavy beating of the man's heart. Fear.

He placed a hand on the man's shoulder.

"Your fight has come to an end, brave warrior." Drakonis said with sincerity. "Worry not, for your power now goes to a higher cause."

Drakonis then put his other hand on the man's chest, and a green light, the man's soul, was stolen from his body. Drakonis saw the shield knight's eyes deaden behind his helmet, and his body collapsed on the ground with a thud.

Drakonis looked around and spotted the gun wielding knight but a few feet away, witnessing what had happened to her ally. She screamed and raised her gun at Drakonis. Before she could pull the trigger of her weapon, Drakonis had already moved behind her, and placed his hand on her back.

"Sleep." Drakonis commanded as her red soul spilled gently out of her back and into his hand. "You are mine as well."

Drakonis looked down at the souls in his hand as they radiated with a gentle intensity. He then closed his hand, sealing them away within his being.

The thick dust started to clear from the battlefield and Drakonis saw the other knights beginning to regroup and stare in his direction.

"No," One of the knights mumbled.

"He's too strong," Another replied, as they tightly gripped their weapon.

Drakonis always wondered why these men and women threw their lives away to fight unwinnable wars. It would be easier to accept defeat, lie down their arms and be subjugated peacefully. Surely, surrender must be on their minds at this point. The One True God does not desire their destruction, only their obedience.

Five of the knights rushed Drakonis with an unforeseen resolve. So much for that thought. A large knight wielding a Warhammer let out a war cry as he led the other knights into battle.

“DO NOT WAVER!” The knight, an older man, screamed.

He brought the hammer high into the air and tried to bring it down on Drakonis' head. But Drakonis caught the head of the weapon in his hand with ease. Nonsense.

"Weak." He scoffed, before punching the man squarely in the chest. The knight coughed and gagged through his helm as he slumped down in front of Drakonis.

The other knights, almost in a frenzy, attacked from all directions. Even though their attacks were fast and meaningful, Drakonis effortlessly deflected every blow. He didn’t even attempt to move from his position. He didn’t have to.

A part of him almost felt pity for them, how futile their attempts were to win this fight. They weren’t even worth a warmup in his eyes, yet they continued to fight.

He noticed the golden souled knight in the back with another, watching the combat. He knew that the day had come to fulfill the prophecy. These were the ones he had been waiting for.

*　　　　*　　　　*

Chase

Chase watched their allies tirelessly savage the dark knight with attacks. He wanted to join in the fight, but he knew his vow. He looked over at Isobel and could see the resolve in her eyes. She was a knight, and he knew she wasn't going to stand by and watch any more of her friends be slaughtered by this demon. She put her hands together and chanted a spell.

"Divines" She called. "Give me the strength to bring my enemies to justice!"

A sigil appeared before her, glimmering with radiant energy. Then, in an instant, the other knights sensed her spell and abandoned their distraction, just in time to dodge the chains that shot from her. Even Everett, who had just received a bone-crunching punch to the chest, managed to lug his body out of the way.

The Black Knight, Drakonis, stood undaunted by the spell. Yes! It was going exactly like Isobel planned it! Chase knew the evil idiot would be foolish enough to believe he could withstand her attack, blinded by his own hubris. And when it landed, his soul would be dragged from his wretched body and a decisive victory would be won for humanity. A victory they desperately needed.

The chains were a moment from snagging the dark lord when his dragon minion landed in front of him, taking the spell head on. The chains slammed into the beast's chest and drove deep under its skin.

"How dare you, Grandfather! Your assistance was not required!" Drakonis yelled from behind the beast, disdain in his voice.

Grandfather? What a weird name for a fire breathing beast, Chase thought to himself. Shut up, you loser.

Drakonis quickly made his way to the front of the beast. The chains were pulling back now and dragged a blue soul from the dragon. The chains and the soul snapped back to the seal, before being locked in place and disappearing completely from sight.

"G-Grandfather..." Drakonis' words were stiff and uneasy.

The dragon went limp, launching dust into the air as his body slammed into the ground, and blocked Chase's view of it or Drakonis.

One of the knights, a man named Irving, had jumped in front of everyone in their group, his hands tightly gripped on his weapon.

"What's happening?" He asked. "Did we win? Is the nightmare over?"

"No..." Isobel said softly. Chase heard it in her voice

and could feel the pressure in the area change. He sensed they were in trouble now.

The skies turned blood red and the clouds blackened, causing a harrowing darkness to take the land. The earth began to shake violently, and the knights struggled to keep their footing.

"I missed. We need to retrea-" Isobel began. Then a black figure was behind her faster than anyone could react, its eyes blazing red.

Isobel yelped in pain as Drakonis grabbed her helm and began to crush it with his hand, and the sickening groan of her helmet motivated Chase into immediate action.

"ISOBEL!" Chase yelled, charging his fist with his electric aura. "LET HER GO!"

Chase then smashed his fist into the dark knight's chin. A powerful shockwave boomed through the air from the blow, shattering the street and ground around them. Drakonis stood motionless against the attack, and then he looked down at Chase as he delivered a savage backhand to the young man and sent him flying through the air. Chase slid on the ground for a few feet and grabbed his back in pain.

Chase heard two loud 'thuds' and looked up to see two other bodies, Isobel and Everett, fly towards him. Luckily, Everett guided their fall and managed to plant his feet squarely in the ground, protecting Isobel in the process. Chase looked back at Drakonis to see him scowling through his helmet and holding Isobel's now completely crushed helmet in his hand.

"Protect Isobel!" Everett commanded as he lowered Isobel to his side. "We'll cover your escape!"

"If we don't beat him now, running won't make a difference!" Chase told the older man. "I can help! Let me fight!"

"No, Chase!" Everett yelled at him. He, now annoyed, grabbed Chase by the collar of his armor. "Be a man and protect the lady. That's your vow! Now live up to it!"

The old man stared Chase down through blood-covered eyes. He was like a father to Chase and had always looked out for him. Everything in Chase's being told him to stay and fight alongside the man, but this fight was a lost cause, and Chase knew it. And if Chase knew, that meant they all knew.

He nodded to Everett, and the older man let go of him. Chase's feet felt heavier than lead anvils at that moment, and he stood there staring back at the older man. Everett gave Chase a smirk and pushed both Chase and Isobel away from himself.

"Don't make this harder than it needs to be." He said solemnly. "Go."

Everett then roared at the top of his lungs as he charged back into battle. The other knights had already begun to distract Drakonis with a savage flurry of attacks.

"Isobel..." Chase said as he turned to her. "We have to get you out of here!"

He noticed she was holding her side and wincing a bit. He guessed her ribs could be broken, or maybe she had received some sort of cut. She seemed completely out of it as blood pooled and spilled from her mouth, and mud was caked up in her hair. Chase lifted her up and put her arm around his neck. Chase lifted her up and put her arm around his neck, assisting her as best he could, and awkwardly limped away.

Sounds of flames and the screams of their allies roared out from behind them. Chase turned his head to catch a glimpse of Drakonis igniting their allies in a dense green flame. Isobel turned her head as well, and they both watched Drakonis step over the burning bodies of their friends. They were gone now. All of them. Drakonis had his eyes fixed on them, the green hue of his eyes resonating from beneath his mask. His hand was open, many small glimmering lights floating in the space above it, the souls of the Divine Knights.

Their attack was a failure, utterly and completely. Worse yet, they all died in vain. As brutally as anyone who had come before them. Without changing anything at all.

Chase understood their situation and decided that he had to do something. He laid Isobel down on her side and she looked up at him.

“What are you doing?” Isobel said with worry in her

eyes. “No… Don’t!”

“Don't worry.” Chase consoled her. "I got this."

He was lying. He absolutely did not have this, but he refused to let his last moments be anything but heroic. If he was going to die, he’d rather do it looking his opponent in the eye than being stabbed in the back like a dog.

He unsheathed his blade and assumed his stance. Drakonis would only get to Isobel over his dead body. That much was certain to Chase.

"Come boy!" Drakonis mocked him as he approached them. "How about I taste your rage and see if it can sate my hunger for your blood! I'll give you the first strike!"

Drakonis beckoned for Chase to make his move with his sword and smiled at him.

Chase's body began to conduct electricity, and bolts of energy traveled the length of his sword. He was channeling his aura into his blade, and the weapon started to glow with his red energy.

He blasted towards the dark lord with blinding speed, thrashing his sword wildly. Drakonis looked down at Chase, and blocked every blow effortlessly, unfazed by his bravado. He could tell, just by seeing his face, that Drakonis was even more annoyed than threatened by his swings, but Chase didn’t care and refused to let up. Even if it was pointless and he knew he didn’t have a chance, for Isobel’s sake, he would keep on swinging.

With every swing of his sword, he silently prayed his blade would connect with his target, but each attack seemed farther away from the mark than the last. He was far too tired and injured to make anything work.

"Your attacks are fast; I'll give you that." Drakonis said suddenly. "But you're sloppy and reckless. Worry not though, for these mistakes will be the last you make."

The dark lord then slammed his blade into Chase's sword, shattering the blade and knocking Chase to the ground.

"CHASE!" Isobel screamed.

"THIS IS FOR GRANDFATHER!" Drakonis roared as he plunged his blade deep into the young swordsman's chest, penetrating his armor and heart. Chase dropped the leftover hilt of his sword onto the street and grabbed Drakonis' hands in a futile attempt to stop the weapon from going deeper. His hands trembled as he tried to resist the stabbing.

Chase couldn't afford to lose. He tried to move but Drakonis grabbed him by his throat and leaned into the hilt. Driving the blade deeper into his chest.

Chase coughed up blood as Drakonis stared into his eyes. After a few seconds, Drakonis let go of Chase's neck and the young knight fell backwards in defeat. This was it. This was how his life ended. He could feel the tears welling in his eyes as he realized he would die a failure.

He managed to catch a glimpse of Isobel. She was crawling towards him, eyes filled with tears as well. She was saying something but for some reason, he couldn't hear her. He had let her down as well. He felt every second ticking down. His consciousness was waning and yet his mind was racing.

I'm dying. Closer. Is this it? I can't stop. Isobel. Then, in an instant, it all went black.

*　　　*　　　*

Drakonis

Drakonis stood over the man's body as a wind howled through the destroyed city. The woman, called Isobel by the other knights, was crawling at an absurdly slow pace, trying to reach her fallen ally.

Her face was completely caked in soot, mud, blood and all kinds of filth. And yet, Drakonis had a weird passing thought; even in her disheveled state, she was beautiful. Her chestnut skin matched her dazzling cinder-like hair. Her tears made her golden eyes far more magnificent, and they looked like brilliant gems in the dusty air.

She had reached her deceased ally, and blood dripped from the corner of her mouth. Tears continued to stream from her eyes as she looked over his sorry state. Drakonis could see the desperation in her actions as she put the man onto his back and tried to pry the sword from his chest.

She grasped the sword intensely with both hands. Reacting to her touch, the sword let loose a group of spikes causing her to grunt out in pain. She continued to pull through the pain, dead set on removing the sword from the man.

What was their relationship? Are they lovers? The Divines protect their own, but they are warriors at heart. Is she not afraid of being stabbed from behind? Drakonis pondered their frail existence, and in a way, was amused by them.

After what seemed like an eternity of her soft cries, she managed to dislodge the blade from the corpse's torso. Much to Drakonis' surprise, the knight was still alive. His breathing was ragged, and he was spilling blood all over the earth. Her hands started to shimmer with golden light and Drakonis knew she was slowly healing the man's wounds.

"You brought this upon yourself." Drakonis scoffed while gazing down at the man's limp body in the woman's arms.

Isobel directed a sharp gaze at Drakonis. "Lord Drakonis!" She said, "If I return the dragon's soul, would you do the same for my fallen comrades?"

Looking over the body of his fallen kin, he knew he would be betraying his king's will if he accepted the trade. The lives of his enemies or the life of his grandfather? He knew the right answer. Yet, he needed Grandfather back. He was the only family he had left. And… 'She' would never forgive him if he told her of Grandfather's demise.

"You will restore Grandfather." Drakonis commanded. "In return, I will exhume the souls I have consumed. But I will be making an amendment to our deal." He removed the armor from his hand and took the sword in his other hand. He brought the sword swiftly across his hand, drawing his own blood.

"You will be a slave to my will for the rest of your days." He said sternly. "Accept my mark and assume your new role. Do this and our contract will be complete!"

The woman stared at Drakonis for a moment, probably in disbelief at his proposition. How could she not? She would be signing her life away, all for the sake of others.

"Save them." Drakonis pressed. "Or... if you'd prefer, watch their bodies feed the buzzards."

"I-I Accept!" Isobel blurted out instantly. She was too eager to save her friends. And now, she and her golden soul belonged to Drakonis.

He placed his bloody hand on her neck and a green mark burned onto her skin. The small draconic symbol, a winged dragon, greatly contradicted her brown skin. Everything was going according to plan.

She looked up at him to see if he was done. He confirmed with a nod, then pointed to the dragon corpse not far from them. Isobel's hands returned to normal, and she lowered her ally, whose breathing had returned to normal, down to the ground. She then stood up and made her way to the dragon's body. While she was walking, Drakonis noticed an identical draconic symbol, partially covered by her collar, on the other side of her neck. It was black and had three heads instead of one.

When Isobel reached the dragon, she began whispering a hymn that Drakonis could not make out. A large seal appeared before her with a blue soul chained in its center. The chains began to slide off of the soul and release it back out into the air. It floated back to its owner and the dragon's eyes snapped open immediately.

"How do you feel Grandfather?" Drakonis inquired.

"I've felt better." The old dragon said as it rose from the dirt. He looked around and examined their immediate surroundings and stopped his eyes on the female knight before him. She had her hands by her side and refused to look up at the beast. "But it seems as though the conflict was resolved during my slumber."

"I am glad to see you in good health, Grandfather." Drakonis said. "But you will be severely punished for your thoughtless stunt."

"Yes, young master." The elderly dragon bowed his head and focused intently on the girl.

Isobel turned to Drakonis. "I have held up my end of the bargain." She reminded him. "Now you must hold up yours! Revive my allies!"

Ashnel, who had been watching the outcome of the fight from afar, approached the group.

"My Lord, your victory has encouraged the humans to surrender." He said as he bowed his head. "Let us finish their leaders off as tribute to King D'Merrion. This is a perfect time to kill her and end the Divine Knight's rebellion against our king."

He gave Isobel a snide smile and licked his lips as he tapped on his scythe.

Isobel then went wide eyed and grasped Drakonis' arm, looking up at him with pleading eyes.

"No!" She screamed at him. "We had a deal. You must honor that deal!"

Before Drakonis had a chance to reply to her plea, Grandfather spoke.

"Drakonis. We, as dragons, should honor our promises." He reminded him. "It is not the draconic way to perform dishonorable deeds, young master."

Ashnel turned and glared at the old dragon. Drakonis could feel the animosity building within his general. Ashnel and Grandfather don't see eye to eye often, although it is never a problem that needs to be managed. There was an obvious hierarchy in their relationship that solved any issue that arose because of this problem.

"Listen here, you overgrown sala-" Ashnel began, but the dragon scoffed at his interjection.

"Boy, you have many moons before you're worthy of a conversation with me." The dragon stomped his foot towards Ashnel and growled at the young wolfkin. "Do not anger me with your petulant tantrum."

Ashnel turned towards Drakonis, anger in his eyes, awaiting a statement from him. Drakonis had already made up his mind.

"I will honor my promise." He said, pushing Isobel’s hands off him. "It is not the dragonkin’s way to dishonor an agreement. Gather all the Divine Knight's bodies and bring them before me."

He could see the disbelief on Ashnel's face for a moment. Then, instinctively, Ashnel bowed his head and accepted his lord's final answer.

The troops gathered the fallen knights and lined them up before the dark lord, making sure to leave their weapons behind. He raised his hand and held it above the bodies of the knights, and each soul in his grasp gently floated back to its respective owner. Grunts and gasps arose from the knights as they awoke and rose from the ground. They shook their heads and began to piece together where they were.

"You have all been revived by my magics." Drakonis began. The knights jumped at the sound of his voice. "Thanks to the noble sacrifice of one of your soldiers."

"Who...?" The tall, old knight with short hair spoke in complete disbelief. It took him but a moment to realize who was the sacrifice. "Isobel! NO! Get away from him!"

Another knight removed his helmet, he was a young man with free form locs. The same young man that Drakonis had pinned to the dirt earlier. He began to walk towards Isobel. Before he could get too close to her and Drakonis, he was stopped by the beastmen soldiers.

"Isobel please!" The man pleaded. "What have you done? Don't tell me you actually made a deal with this monster!?"

She looked away from him.

Drakonis knew how this conversation was going to go and he did not have the time to entertain their nonsense.

"An exchange was made." He told them. "Her life for yours. You should thank her, really. If not for her, you each would be decorating the walls of our new fortress."

The warriors gritted their teeth at his words, but Drakonis could see them finally accepting their powerless position. They knew there was nothing they could do.

"Say goodbye now, for you will not see her ever again." He continued. "Do not make any attempts to save her for she is marked with my own personal seal. If I desired, I could order her to execute each one of you and she'd be forced to obey."

The young knight bent his knee and bowed his head. "PLEASE WAIT!" He yelled. "My name is Chase and I am Lady Isobel's protector. You must let me accompany her."

"Why should I care what your name is or who you are?" He said with contempt. "You were but a corpse earlier. A heap of meat ready to return to the earth. Upon what grounds do you command me!?"

"It's my mission to protect the lady..." The man pleaded loudly and desperately. "Please allow me to go with her. Whatever spell you cast on her, you can surely cast on me."

"No, Chase!" Isobel said. "Stop!"

Drakonis sighed to himself, low enough that no one heard him. The plan was going far too smoothly. He thought that he would have to work harder to get Chase to come along, but in fact, the knight threw himself on a silver platter.

Drakonis walked forward and grasped Chase's wrist. The small draconic sigil burned onto his flesh. He thrust the man's wrist down, putting on a front that he was completely annoyed at the man’s interjection.

"You are now mine." Drakonis said, not even pretending to hide his discontent with the situation. "Come."

He needed the young man to get into Isobel's good graces. But this brought about a bigger issue. How was he going to explain this to his king? He only let the thought briefly occupy him. He would have much time to think as they traveled.

"Grandfather" Drakonis called. "You will fly me and my prisoners to the Capitol."

He then turned to Ashnel. "Ashnel, you will finish capturing this fort and destroy all who resist within its walls." He said eyeing the fort. "Report the outcome to the King, and bring back any spoils you find."

The fort was extremely damaged in the battle, but the weapons it possessed may be of use to their cause. Maybe he could still offer it to his father yet, in exchange for the lives of the knights.

Drakonis turned to Grandfather, motioning for his new slaves to follow. He tossed them both onto the dragon like light luggage and mounted himself.

Drakonis took one last look at the battle. Many beastkin soldiers were rounding up human warriors and moving the captured prisoners outside of the fort. The battle was swift and decisive, just the way he liked it.

"Let's go!" He commanded the dragon. It took to the skies with amazing speed, leaving the destruction behind them.

Chapter 2:
King of Gods

Drakonis

Grandfather flew swiftly through the air, gusts of winds nudging at all his passengers. The knights, devastated at their humiliating defeat, sat silently a few feet away from their captor. This was a blessing because Drakonis needed time to think.

D'Merrion was not going to be pleased. Drakonis had not only saved their sworn nemesis from absolute defeat, but he was bringing home strays as well. Even if they were prisoners, he knew his king always preferred heads over bodies. However, he would rather deal with the reprimands of a disgraced, angry god than his foul-tempered mother.

After some time to himself, Drakonis turned around to look over his new wares. Isobel and Chase sat still on the dragon's backside, their eyes downward in shame. Their shapes were more defined against the night sky.

Isobel had a slender frame with muscular arms that rivaled many of the men that Drakonis had fought tonight. It was a shame she never got to show off her martial skill. She had natural looking hair that flowed endlessly into the night. It was rare to see one so beautiful also be so prepared for war.

Chase, on the other hand, had an athletic build. His lean physique showed his dedication to that athleticism, and yet you still would not be able to anticipate how fast he was. Contrary to Isobel's hair, his black locks hung lifelessly in the air like stable branches on a tree.

"You." Drakonis said to Chase. “Don’t talk. Don't move." He didn't wait to see if the man heard him or not. The mark would work regardless.

"Isobel." He said as he turned to face her. “Look at me."

The woman tried to resist his command and the mark faintly glowed green on her neck. Drakonis didn’t need her to comply with his requests; She would answer him even if she didn't want to.

"Look. At. Me." He commanded a second time. This time, she struggled for only a moment and then she raised her head and stared into his eyes. He could see the contempt and resentment she had for him, a feeling he knew too well.

"The Divines..." He began. "Why would they wager their greatest warriors for a lowly stronghold?"

"Is-" Chase tried to say. His mark shimmered to life and radiated with the same green hue.

Isobel looked intensely at Drakonis. He could see she had no intention of answering. Very well then, he thought. So be it.

"You will answer my questions!" He commanded, the green brand on her neck glowed with even more color than before.

She grunted and squirmed like she was trying to deny Drakonis access to her memory. Her will lasted for a few seconds but he could see she was losing the battle for control. Chase, noticing that Isobel was in pain, struggled to speak against the command again. The mark on his neck restricted his interactions with the conversation.

"Okay..." She gasped. "I'll tell you..."

Chase loudly mumbled in rejection, but his mark halted all movement and now held him hostage. Drakonis stared at Isobel in silent anticipation.

"They were not aware… That we were there..." She said quickly. She was breathing heavily. "They didn't know... We were there... As far as they know... We were somewhere else..."

"You, honestly, expect me to believe that the Divines allowed their demigod dogs to roam without being monitored?" Drakonis said with disbelief. "What kind of mutt leaves their lord unattended?"

"I speak the truth!" She yelled. "They were not informed of our actions!"

The mark stopped glowing. Drakonis looked at her neck and frowned. This was a telltale sign that she was telling the truth.

"Then why were you in the outpost!?" Drakonis interrogated.

"To kill you!" She said in a soft and intense voice. "We were there to make sure you never left the New York ruins. We were convinced that we could slay you with that spell. If not for the dragon, we might've tasted victory this day."

She looked up at Drakonis, eyes reddened by tears and frustration. Grandfather scoffed at her words. Chase was now motionless.

"Pathetic." Drakonis replied. "Your ambush was amateur, and your tactics were child's play. Answer me this... Who taught you the spell?"

Isobel's mark began to glow again. She resisted the urge to talk.

"Don't make this harder than it needs to be, Isobel..." Drakonis tried to have sincerity in his voice. He wasn't a sadist, but he needed to know. "Just give me the answers I seek. Who taught you the spell?"

She opened her mouth to talk and the brand on the other side of her neck began to shine. It was a dark purple glow, the sign of dark mana. She immediately closed her mouth. She was being restricted. She looked at Drakonis with an intense stare, her breaths deep and labored.

Chase started to get worked up again, screaming through his lips. He was trying hard to break the magic that bound him.

The black dragon mark spread over her neck and made its way down her shoulder. It was consuming her. She gripped her arm, still looking at Drakonis.

"She is bound by the Dragon of Darkness." Grandfather spoke. "The magic will continue to consume her until nothing is left if you further your inquiries."

Drakonis sighed, crossing his arms. This was a fight he wasn't going to win through force.

"You do not need to answer the question." Drakonis said, lifting the command from her.

Isobel gasped, taking in large amounts of air. She was breathing hoarsely again. The mark on her arm recoiled, shrinking to its original size. Chase was still struggling behind her, raging against the pain he was receiving. Interesting... Drakonis found himself intrigued with Chase and his pain tolerance.

"Ho... How do you know that?" Isobel wheezed.

Drakonis shot her a look, but then he slowly returned his gaze forward. He was also eager to hear the answer to her question.

"Child, I am Xinovioc." Grandfather bellowed. "I have lived through many moons and seen many wars. I am one of the last of my kin and last bearer of the old ways for my kind. The Dragon of Darkness is the sworn enemy of my people. I know of its mark. The one carried by its slaves and acolytes alike. I dare not ask your affiliation, lest I ensure today is your last."

"Enough Grandfather." Drakonis interrupted. "You've said more than I care to hear and more than they should learn. Let us finish our journey in silence."

The elderly dragon nodded in acceptance. Chase stopped struggling against the magic. Isobel was still breathing heavily but she seemed to be recovering.

A personal mission for his head, without the blessing of the Divines? This was either some desperate plan by rogue Divines or there was a greater scheme at play. Regardless, a captured Divine Knight with an acolyte branding would please D'Merrion greatly.

They were still a bit away from the capitol, but he gained what he needed to barter for the knight's lives. He just needed to find the best way to word it.

*   *   *

Chase

They had lost. Worse. They had been killed. Chase rubbed his hand over his chest, feeling the fresh scar that now branded his body. He had not only failed his vow to protect Isobel, but also allowed them to capture her. Then he sat about and allowed her to be further interrogated and have their secrets taken from her.

He felt Isobel's eyes on him as he recounted the night, the sting of his defeat worn tightly on his face.

"Sir Chase..." She whispered, reaching her hand out to console him. "It is alright."

Chase quickly rebounded from her touch. Isobel didn't have to work every day to be recognized. She was a prodigy, chosen by the gods to mete out their judgement and carry out their will. He barely made it into the ranks of the Divine. And even with all of the responsibility that sat on her shoulders, she still found time to console him. He hated it. It made him feel weak.

"I failed Isobel" Chase said, staring off into the distance to avoid her gaze. "Don't try to sugarcoat it. Just another tally to my ongoing list of failures."

They were passing over the ruins of Baltimore, deep in the heart of beastmen territory. He could see a large castle in the distance. It sat in the middle of the ruined capital of the United States. A giant gaudy ego stroke for the self-proclaimed 'King of Gods'.

Isobel turned away from Chase, lightly sniffling to herself. He knew he was being unreasonable and was punishing her for his own insecurities. He knew that their capture wasn't her fault. And he knew all the blame fell on him.

It wasn't long before they had finally arrived at the dark castle, landing right in front of the gates. The guards, a couple of Kobolds, bowed their heads as the dragon descended upon them.

"Lord Drakonis, welcome back to Zhalesh!" One of the Kobolds said. He made an obvious attempt to not make eye contact with their sovereign. "Do you desire an escort to the loading bays?"

"Yes" Drakonis exhaled, dropping from the dragon's nape. "Escort Xinovioc to the other entrance, please."

"Yes, my lord" They replied, almost eager to get out of his way.

"Down!" Drakonis said, ordering the knights to his side. Their marks glowed bright green and they obeyed without fail, jumping down from their position at the rear of the dragon. "Follow me and do not stray. Do not speak unless I permit you to do so!"

This was his life now? Bowing down to the whims of

his enemies and being led around like a dog on a leash? Chase scoffed at the command and Drakonis gave him a cold glassy stare. The dark lord walked up to his new property and removed his helmet.

Chase was completely surprised by the image in front of him and he could tell by Isobel's flinch that she was as well. The beast that was known as Drakonis had the visage of a normal man. He had warm mahogany skin that could pass for normal any day of the week. His hairline was crisp, sharp as a razor's edge and his hair was a dense afro. How could this guy be 'THE' Black Dragon Drakonis?!

"You forget your place mutt!" Drakonis spat at Chase. "You have no rights here. You have no say here. And should I demand it, you will have no life here or anywhere else! I suggest you bury any hate, disobedience, and pride you may still retain. Lest you wish for this day to be your last?"

Chase looked at the ground, anger building in his chest like fire in a furnace. He was used to being talked down to, but in his eyes beastmen were animals. A beastmen that imitated a man was no different.

Drakonis grabbed Chase by his throat, forcing the young warrior to look him in his eyes. Isobel raised her arm to try and stop Drakonis but he shot her a glare, and she found herself unable to move.

"Do not push me boy." He warned Chase. "You draw

breath because I will it to be. Should I desire, I can take those same breaths away... Do as I say."

Drakonis then threw Chase to the ground. He turned and motioned for Xinovioc to leave as he walked through the castle gates. Chase sat on the ground for a moment to regain his breath, but he felt his mark grow hot. He had to comply, there was no other choice. He got up and dusted himself off before following the dark lord into the city.

The city was the complete opposite of what he had expected. He had known his whole life that beastmen were disgusting creatures that lived barbarically. They fed on their offspring and lived in constant conflict, no order nor any structure to their lives. The violent tenacity they showed in combat was a symptom of their harsh lives. And yet here they are engaging in commerce and mercantilism. It looked like any human society.

They passed through a giant market where merchants of many species sold and spoke to others of different dialects and cultures. There was still some ruin from the city that stood before this one, a city that belonged to the Old-World, but most of the debris had been removed. Chase could see the diversity amongst the beastmen, from woolly wargs to feathered fowl. It looked peaceful and... normal. Well, except for the disgusted expressions on the faces of the local wildlife. He would be a fool to believe that the beastmen held no prejudices against mankind. They had been at war since their conception and humanity was no stranger to atrocities.

Chase realized that he had stopped moving to take in all the excitement of the market. He turned to where Drakonis was walking and noticed his captor was standing still, waiting on Chase with a grimace on his face. Chase hated this. He retook his position right behind Isobel who, oddly enough, was not as awe-stricken with her environment as Chase was. He wished he could discuss what they were seeing, he knew she also had questions.

After around an hour of walking through crowded streets and ascending the largest set of stairs he'd ever seen, the trio finally arrived at the two golden doors that served as the entrance to the palace. The palace was giant and alabaster with golden accents on the windows. The doors were massive, rivaling the walls that they were mounted on. Both doors told a story, through the engravings that sat on their face, of D'Merrion's conquest from when he was the leader of the Divines. Even more evidence of how facetious and self-righteous the King of Gods was.

Almost as sensing Drakonis' presence, the gates slowly grinded open, revealing a massive hall and two small wolfkin that manned the gate. Drakonis nodded to his subordinates and proceeded down the hall with Chase and Isobel in tow.

The hall was beyond words. Torches lit up the room

like a festival, giving the room a warm bronze hue. The bright white pillars were lined with a golden trim, much like the outside of the building. In the center of the room lay a room width set of stairs, adorned with the iconic white with golden trim. They really loved that color scheme, Chase thought to himself. Even so, he had never seen a hall so huge.

Drakonis led the knights up the steps to another large set of doors, these ones were wooden and less flashy than the ones outside. The dark lord stopped for a moment and turned around to face his prisoners.

"When we enter, you will bend the knee as I do." He began. "You do not speak. God King D'Merrion does not tolerate disrespect in any form."

Isobel exchanged a look with Chase. She gave him a grim look that he immediately reciprocated. He already understood the message. Do not test D'Merrion.

Both Isobel and Chase nodded back to Drakonis. They had resigned themselves to their fate, whatever D'Merrion had in store for them.

With that, Drakonis pushed the large wooden doors open and entered the throne room. The room was more magnificent than the last. There were lavish pillows and exquisite quilts littered all over the throne room. Bits of fabric were draped across the ceiling, giving the room an angelic feel, as though one had transcended above the clouds to the great beyond. Under the mess of cloth, you could see a giant red carpet that was lined with... Yeah, you guessed it... Golden Trim. At the neck of the carpet sat the throne, with the King of God's, King D'Merrion, sitting casually on top of it. He was holding a crystal shard in his hand, talking to it.

"It would seem you do not need to continue your report." D'Merrion sighed. "The commander has returned, but do not hesitate to inform me of its progress should any new details arise."

The deity looked delighted to see his commander. He lowered the device and motioned for them to come closer.

"Kneel." He instructed.

Drakonis walked up to the foot of the steps, head bowed, and knelt on one knee. Isobel did as Drakonis commanded and knelt right behind him and her head bowed as well. Chase stood behind Drakonis, forcing himself to resist kneeling and attempting to look D'Merrion in the eye.

The King of gods was right in front of him. The war ends right now if he falls. And yet, even with the mark hampering his actions, there was something else there. Something that was trying to command his obedience. Something that gave him silent instructions he could feel in his bones.

After a couple of moments, his eyes finally met D'Merrion's.

D'Merrion had a gaunt face with a well-trimmed goatee. His long, heavy black dreads sat wildly upon his broad shoulders, untamed by the crown that sat on them. He wore a button up shirt, with velvet golden lining, and black suit pants.

At that moment, Chase saw it. D'Merrion's eyes were sharp, golden, and piercing like a dagger. The Dragon Sigil on his throne was the last stamp in his royal aura. This room was drenched in D'Merrion's Divine aura.

They only looked at each other for a few seconds before Chase broke eye contact and knelt as he was commanded. D'Merrion's Divine command was almost unbearable. He found himself wanting to kneel, to avoid the god's scorn.

"Hmmm..." The king said. "Curious. You have brought me an interesting set of trophies, my son. Most humans find themselves compelled immediately by my visage, demigod or not. And yet, this one was... Disobedient."

Chase heard the god lean forward.

"I wonder what power lay hidden in your chest." He continued, his tone sounding lower and more sinister. "Perhaps I should have you dismantled by my researchers. Or maybe I should dirty my hand and pull that repulsive Divine essence from you myself."

Chase started sweating, his eyes shaking from fear. He couldn't resist. He didn't want to. The longer they were in the room, the less control he had over his actions or even his thoughts. He couldn't even will himself to look at the other two to see if they had the same reaction he did.

His heart started racing. He had never felt this before. Not even his death could match this new emotion, a different kind of dread hanging upon him.

"Hah." The god scoffed. "I jest, young knight. Cease your rapid, obnoxious heartbeats or I'll quell them for you."

Chase felt the pressure in his chest subside, the Divine command becoming less dense. One minute in the throne room and he found himself more powerless now than any other moment in his life.

"Drakonis, my son!" D'Merrion's tone changing again. "News of your exploits have confidently reached my ear! You have struck a grand blow to the Divines and achieved a massive feat in my name!"

Chase could hear him standing and walking, his steps echoing in the chamber as he approached them.

"Or..." He began. "That's the phrase I would have said, had you not revived my enemies and set them free!"

There was rage in his voice. Chase felt the air in the throne room change drastically. The king was livid.

"And then you dare bring their ilk into my sacred chamber!" He continued, his words like a whip, cracking at their backsides. "These pathetic creatures pollute all that they touch, painstakingly choosing the abyss time and again. They only desire war and chaos and refuse to be enlightened; to seek true Divine interaction. They settled for the weak Nine Divines instead of their true lord and savior. I, God King D'Merrion!"

He was right on top of them now.

"Drakonis." He said, lowering his tone a bit. "Stand and let me gaze upon your pathetic face."

Chase could see the dark lord slowly rise out the corner of his eye.

"Give me one reason why I should allow these vermin, these pests, to remain on my side of the veil any longer!?" D'Merrion questioned. "Of what worth could you have possibly believed these specks contained that was greater than the joy of their eradication? Let alone the revival of the other seven?"

There was a brief silence in the room.

"Father." Drakonis began. "I made the decision-"

A loud smack echoed through the room. Drakonis fell right in front of Chase. He could see blood dripping from the lord's lip. Drakonis wiped his mouth and stood again.

"I have already discovered who made the decision." D'Merrion hissed. "I asked... Why?"

"Grandfather had been slain." Drakonis began, not showing any pain in his voice. "I made the trade because he was a valuable asset. Losing a dragon would have hampered the war effort. And it would have made mother... Problematic."

Another loud smack echoed above Chase's head. He waited to see Drakonis hit the ground and was surprised to hear his body land with a thud a few feet behind him. After a couple of moments, he heard footsteps approach them again. From how Drakonis acted, Chase surmised this wasn't the first time he had been struck by the God King; He knew all too well what it felt like to be beaten and not show weakness.

"I can handle Azzaria." The king whispered. "Command them to rise."

Chase began to sweat again. What he would do to not have to look the king in his invasive eyes again.

"Knight Isobel, stand!" He instructed. "Knight Chase, stand!"

The marks on their necks glowed and they did as they were bid. As Chase's eyes rose, he saw the dark god staring directly into his eyes. D'Merrion then looked over at Isobel.

"Answer his questions honestly." Drakonis told them.

D'Merrion walked up to Isobel. He put his hand around her neck, almost benevolently.

"Oh, you are the spitting image of my battle sister." D'Merrion said tenderly, before his tone grew menacing and violent. "She and her kin took everything from me, seeing fit for me to be trapped for all eternity. But I'm out and about now. So... No hard feelings, huh?"

His grip tightened around her neck. Isobel gasped for

air and grabbed at the god's fingers, trying to release his grip. Chase could feel the rage build in his chest. 'Move, come on, move' Chase thought. But he could not will even a single muscle into action.

Drakonis' hand then tightly grasped the king's wrist. D'Merrion shot him a violent gaze, his eyes bright and orange.

"Release me, boy!" D'Merrion commanded. Drakonis did not oblige.

After a moment, D'Merrion let go of Isobel and she fell to her knees. She coughed a few times, her body fighting to receive as much air as it could hold.

"That is the reason I love you, my son." D'Merrion said as he ripped his arm away from Drakonis. "That fire in your eye that burns hotter than any sun I have seen. The way, even when I beat you into submission, you still try to resist my control."

D'Merrion then walked over to Chase. He stood a few feet taller than Chase, and the young knight felt the overwhelming difference in their aura. The god looked him up and down before putting his hand on the knight's chest.

D'Merrion then smirked.

Chase went flying back into the wall, making a crater in its ornate design. He felt like a boulder had smashed into his chest. He was confused. He didn't see the god move at all.

He stood up, gasping for breath, fighting against the

urge to just lie there and accept defeat.

"Impressive." D'Merrion applauded from the other side of the room. "He will last long in the crucible. A true treat for me and the masses. A Divine Knight fighting for his life against the strongest beasts of Zhalesh."

Crucible? Chase didn't like the sound of that. He looked up to see D'Merrion was sitting down on his throne again.

"Send them to the dungeons." D'Merrion told Drakonis. "Let them be moderately fed and bathed until the day of the next Crucible."

"But Father-" Drakonis interrupted.

"My verdict is final, son." D'Merrion said firmly. "Do not incite my rage with further insubordination. You have done enough this day. And I believe allowing your pets to live is lenient enough."

"Yes, father." Drakonis conceded. "I will escort them to their cells, and make sure arrangements are in order for their treatment."

"Thank you, my son." D'Merrion said, obviously pleased with his son's acceptance. "Return to my chamber tomorrow to receive my gospel. We have much to discuss when your temper has subsided."

Drakonis nodded.

"Follow me." Drakonis ordered. The marks on the knight's necks glowed in response. Isobel and Chase both lumbered over to Drakonis' side and accompanied him out of the throne room. Chase had never experienced anything like that. That kind of control. The pressure that existed in that room was one of a kind. It was beyond explanation.

He gave a glance to Isobel, her eyes glazed over. He reached over to her and held her hand. She snapped out of her stupor and simply gazed over at Chase with pain filled eyes. This was their lives now, for however many moons they had to spend as prisoners, for however many moons they continued to draw breath.

They walked for only a few moments before Drakonis stopped right in front of the prisoners.

"Halt." Drakonis commanded.

Isobel and Chase both looked around. They hadn't paid any attention to their surroundings since the encounter with the King of Gods. They were in a dimly lit room, with a Stoney floor that had a mustiness to it and smelled of feces. The ceiling was extremely low and had chains hanging from it every couple of feet. There were a couple rough cots on the ground.

"This is where you will be sleeping." Drakonis said, letting his prisoners pass him into the room. "Get in and do not try to escape or cast spells. I know you have many questions. So... you may speak freely until your food arrives."

"How can you serve a king as sadistic as D'Merrion!?"

Isobel blurted out. "He beats you! His own son. What kind of god behaves so cruelly?"

Drakonis sighed and leaned against the doorway.

"That god is my father, and you will not slander his name." Drakonis hissed. "You've wasted my time and your question, woman. Ask your inquiry, Chase. I have a feeling I know what it is."

"What is the Crucible?" Chase said.

"The Crucible is my father's way of providing entertainment for the great city of Zhalesh, and all of its inhabitants." Drakonis began. "It is a brutal show invented to be the pride of the mid-year festival and a proving ground for those that seek the glory of the God King. It is also for those that refuse to show fealty to our 'One True God'."

Chase squinted his eyes a bit. Was that a bit of sarcasm in his voice?

"It will have 20 combatants, each one of the lands strongest warriors, and a special exhibition." Drakonis went on, a little less enthusiastic than when he began. "It is an honor to be selected for its ranks. Only one participant has made it to the final round, much to the chagrin of the God King. As for the 'special event' in the last crucible, the winner had to face Ashnel without a single weapon. You can piece together how that may have played out..."

At that moment, a servant arrived in the cell bearing a

basket filled with fruit.

"That is the end of our conversation for now." Drakonis said as he walked towards the door. "Rest now, I will retrieve you after I receive the gospel."

Drakonis then left the cell. The servant unloaded the food baskets onto the ground in front of the prisoners.

Chase glanced at the door, longing for freedom, but he knew there was no escape. At least not tonight. He grabbed his food and began to eat to his heart's content. If they were going to feed him lavishly, he was going to indulge when he could. He looked up, mouth completely stuffed with food, and saw Isobel not eating. She looked distraught, and after what they went through in the throne room, he was surprised she wasn't swearing revenge or punching the walls. She hated losing almost as much as he did.

"Starving isn't going to make escaping any easier." Chase exclaimed, jamming more food into his mouth. "Just go ahead and eat. It won't kill you. Or maybe it will. Then they will have done what they wanted from the beginning."

Isobel just sighed and shrugged.

"You go from self-deprecation to cheerful so frequently I have no choice but to assume you're insane." She joked. "We are in the worst predicament we have ever been in and you're stuffing your face like any other day. Are you THAT confident in our escape?"

"No." He answered. "But I am sure dying on an empty stomach isn't on my bucket list. So just eat. We can worry about our lives after we rest."

That did the job. It had to; he couldn't muster anymore confidence. Maybe after some sleep he would have a bright idea? Who knows...?

Chase and Isobel both finished their meals. Then they laid down and looked at the ceiling, waiting for sleep to take them.

"We're not getting out of here, are we?" Isobel asked.

"You worry too much, princess." Chase answered back as he turned over and away from her. "Get some sleep now." Chase closed his eyes, waiting for the darkness to calm his racing mind.

Chapter 3:
The Mad Maj

Drakonis

Drakonis' eyes flickered open, struggling against the sunlight. He let out a casual yawn, his breath visible in the air as he looked up at the tree he slept under. It afforded him no cover from the sun on the horizon. It was morning, and the kingdom was already wide awake with bustle.

He stood up and got a minor stretch in. The royal grotto was his favorite sleeping spot, and everyone knew not to bother him when he slept there. The old tree always calmed his heart and made him feel at home. The Fae never tried to remove him either, so he assumed that his presence was ordained by fate itself. He looked around and noticed that no one was around to disturb him.

“Where are those little troublemakers?” Drakonis mumbled to himself. He was used to them waking him up early, but he guessed they must be busy somewhere else or still sleeping.

He reached down and picked up his armor, which had been delicately laid next to him.

He let out a deep sigh. Another day, another new challenge to conquer. He had to get himself ready for the trials ahead. If he were to get his way and convince his father, he had to make sure everything was in place. Nothing could be left to chance.

Drakonis carefully redressed himself. A black knight can't really walk around without his black armor now, can he? He made sure that his armor appropriately fitted, using the nearby ponds that surrounded the tree to see his own visage.

"Great." He said to himself, content with his appearance.

He turned to the nearby doors and made his way through the palace. The first stop in his itinerary was the prisoners. He had to take them to King Maj. And if he were fast enough, he could get them there and get to the throne room in time to receive the gospel.

He was speed walking now, whilst still trying to be as intimidating as possible. A couple more rooms. Just a few more doors.

"You look like you're in a hurry!" A familiar, gruff voice suggested.

Curses Ashnel, Drakonis thought. Go away!

Drakonis couldn't believe his luck. This was not what he needed. Ashnel was hard to deceive and was even harder to get rid of. Drakonis did not need this hound on his backside right now.

"I am in the middle of important business general."

Drakonis bellowed. “For what purpose have you halted my duties?”

“Duties!?” Ashnel scoffed. “Is that what you call going to play with your little 'toys'? Surely you can make a better excuse than that, my lord?”

“As your lord, I need no excuses.” Drakonis retorted, raising his voice and advancing upon the wolfkin. “I do all for the glory of the God King. Where do you get the gall to even question my purpose?”

Ashnel raised his hands, slightly retreating from the conflict.

“No gall or cause, my lord” The wolfkin said quickly. “I was just making sure Drakonis had not been replaced by a milk maiden! You know only the strong thrive amongst the One True God's ranks. Do not let those wretches tarnish your-”

He didn't even let the wolfkin finish. He grasped Ashnel by the scruff of his neck, intent on not wasting any more time.

“Remember your place wolf.” Drakonis said, his tone growing intense and violent. “The next time you see fit to address my actions, remember your station, and keep your counsel to yourself. I'll let you know when I desire advice from my lesser.”

He then threw Ashnel backwards a few feet. The wolfkin was able to land upright, he was always agile and limber.

"My apologies, lord Drakonis" Ashnel said as he knelt to one knee. "I will resume my duties and stop hampering yours. Oh, and don't forget your helmet my liege."

Ashnel then retreated backwards out of the main doors with haste.

Drakonis turned and started walking towards the palace dungeons. He forgot his helmet in his rush, but there was no time. That little conversation was going to cost him.

* * *

Isobel

"Fifty-Seven. Fifty-Eight. Fifty-nine. Sixty." Chase counted out as he finished his set. He did a spectacular flip upright and landed on his feet.

Isobel had been watching Chase do handstand pushups for the last hour since they had awoken. There wasn't really much else to do in the dark, disgusting cells. The imprisonment lifestyle was not for them. There wasn't workout equipment or books for them to read, and she couldn't believe how bored she was.

Her back was also aching due to the lack of accommodating furniture. Never had she had a night more uncomfortable. Even when she and Chase lived…

Her ears pricked up a bit. She saw Chase react to the pressure as well. She could sense an aura approaching them. It wasn't too hard to imagine who it might be. Drakonis.

His pressure was followed by the thunderous stamps of his footsteps as he made his way to their tiny, cramped cell. He stopped right at the door and peered into the space. His silver eyes glared at them through the bars of the cell. She could see he wasn't wearing his black helmet to hide his face either. He had some human qualities and if she wasn't so hellbent on killing him, she might have considered him handsome.

"Rise." He commanded. "Do not stray from me or attempt escape."

They both silently obeyed and rose to their feet. Isobel hated this; she couldn't stand it. Her worst enemy, her arch-nemesis, commanding them like dogs and having no say in her actions.

Drakonis opened the cell and led them out of the dungeons. They made their way through the same halls that they passed on their way in. The walkways were well lit now, and their imperfections were easier to notice now. The rooms leading to the dungeon had a layer of dust on them, as though they hadn't been used for some time.

Drakonis then stopped them abruptly and lowered his pressure.

"Wait." He told them, ushering them out of sight near

the corner of the hallway. “Stupid mutt, what are you doing?”

Isobel looked past Drakonis to see his wolfkin general standing in the main atrium. He looked like he was waiting on something. He patiently waited around for a couple of minutes, looking up and around.

Drakonis stayed his hand and all movement for a couple of moments. The wolfkin then huffed a bit and left the access way. He looked disappointed.

“Let's go” Drakonis marched them onward.

They quickly walked past the area and went through a series of very similar hallways and rooms before they were standing outside of a large metal door. There was a chorus of impacts and chimes from the other side of the door. It sounded like an armory of some sort. Music to Isobel's ears. She missed the hum of metal and the sizzle of molten ore as it was treated in the White Forge's waters. Maybe she could steal some secrets from the smiths while she was here.

Drakonis lifted his hand to open the huge doors, but the doors popped open before he could touch them.

A large man, almost seven or eight feet tall with a muscular build, held his arms out towards the dark lord. He had a bald head and a large beard with almost human features, except that his teeth were so rigid they resembled the teeth of a buzzsaw. Isobel could tell by his blackened fingertips that this man had seen many days in service of the anvil.

"Drakonis!" The man exclaimed. "You forgot your mask at home, and I see you've brought company!"

He reached his hands out to shake Chase's hand, his tanned skin so much shinier than the young knights.

"Do not fraternize with my prisoners, Maj." Drakonis warned. "They are my entourage for the day, and we are not here for your hospitality. Also, I did not forget my mask. I left it. I decided I didn't need it for my affairs."

"Oh ho ho hooooooo!" The man guffawed. "You are just a right stick in the mud, ain't ya?"

Then the man pointed to Isobel.

"Can't you see this darling flower doesn't deserve to be trapped inside." He said as he made eye contact with her. He had round, soft brown eyes that looked very sincere. "And what is your name, pretty lady?"

Isobel looked at Drakonis. He turned to meet her eyes. He let out a light sigh.

"You both may speak freely." He said, showing little to no enthusiasm. "But answer his questions quickly and without chaff. We are in a hurry."

Isobel could feel the intensity of her mark lessen. She looked to Chase to see if he had the same effect.

"That's more like it!" Chase said. "You ever get tired of being a slave driver?"

Drakonis immediately turned to Chase, a light intensity

in his eyes.

"Sit down and shut up." Drakonis commanded.

Chase sat down immediately, and he looked up at Drakonis with an angry glare on his face. The Maj laughed out loud.

He really knew the right words to piss someone off, Isobel thought to herself. She wasn't going to make the same mistake.

"I am Isobel, of the Nine Divine Knights." She introduced herself. "And this fellow to my right is Chase, my trusted protector and guardian. We are prisoners of Lord Drakonis. Nice to make the acquaintance of an individual with common decency."

The chorus of impacts colliding with metal and the shaving of swords ceased. It was hard to see past the giant man, but Isobel could feel the whole room looking at them.

"A pleasure'ta meet ya as well!" The man jauntily replied. "I am King Maj, King of the Majes. They call me king because'a my great exploits with iron and stone, and my superior craftsmanship. Please Drakonis, bring'ya friends into my forge."

"Come on" Drakonis commanded.

Chase got up and dusted himself off, and the duo followed him into the forge.

The area was mostly outside, half of the room was

uncovered and open to the elements. The other half, which housed an obsidian hearth in the shape of a man's face, was mostly tiled with white pearl flooring. The hearth had a constant flow of magma that was chambered and cycled over and over from the mouth of the face. The kinds of beastkin that worked in the forge were a mix of pigkin and humans. Some of the humans looked as tall as the man they were talking to. Maybe they were giants?

Each smith was working on different weapons and working hard to complete their orders. Or... They were. Now they were standing around gawking at the new additions to the room, light gossip and banter filling the air.

They act as though they've never seen humans before, Isobel thought.

“Did’Ah tell you mites to stop workin?” The giant man yelled, spinning around to get a glimpse of all his workers. “Get on with it!”

With that the workers returned to their projects, occupying themselves with their tools instead.

“King Maj.” Drakonis yelled over the crafting. “You know why I've come. Let's not waste any more time.”

“Ah yes, your lordship!” King Maj replied, bowing before Drakonis. “How best can I do your bidding? Should I simply stop everything I'm doing at the moment or just the most important jobs?”

“Cease your jests, smith!” Drakonis snapped. “You are wearing my patience thin!”

“I kid, young lord!” The man apologized. “I kid. Soooo... These are the ones, huh?”

“Yes.” Drakonis replied.

“Well, well, well.” King Maj said, rubbing his chin and turning to the knights. “Beautiful Isobel and brawny Chase. Ya stand here before me and my fellow smith's criminals of the state, evil creatures that commit atrocities against our kind.”

Isobel shook her head and felt her blood begin to boil. What!? What manner of trial is this!? They dare accuse them of atrocities. Humanity did not choose this war! She felt her hands clench at the man's words.

“HOLD UP!” Chase interjected before Isobel could speak. “Atrocities…? Against you? What in the world are you talking about!? Your ancestors attacked our predecessors long ago! You started this war and you even spat on the Divine Accords that were in place to protect the realm!”

Isobel could see a vein appearing in Chase's head. He was about to blow up. His face was reddening.

“Yeah, yeah, yeah.” King Maj began, but he was cut off by Chase.

“You killed our friends!” Chase said, his voice getting louder for all the beastkin to hear. “You slaughtered us by the thousands and forced us to go into hiding! You've taken our quality of life and denied us peace! YOU ARE THE CRIMINALS! YOU ARE THE EVIL ONES!"

Boos and jeers started coming from the smiths in the room. They left their work again and made a crowd around the group.

Isobel raised her hand towards Chase, letting him know he had lost control of his emotions. She turned around and looked King Maj directly in his eye.

"We have worked tirelessly to end the war and spread the influence of the Nine Divines across the world." She said, never breaking eye contact with the man. "We do not wish to destroy your homes. We have sought peace time and again. The beastkin refuse to accept. This war is a result of your constant desire for conquest. You mock us with this 'trial' when the aggressors are yourselves!?"

"So we're at fault, huh, girl?" King Maj retorted, his voice still calm and collected. "Humans have grown all ova our green earth and taken from her without penance. They steal, lie, cheat, and slaughter ta get what they want. They constantly destroy the homes of any animals that refuse to be domesticated and eat the rest. Should'an 'animal' rise up and defend the land they grew up on, they are purged."

The smiths all nodded their heads in agreement with the speech and some even cheered a bit.

"We have lost our families." King Maj continued, his

voice growing louder. The beastkin in the room started uttering 'yeahs' and 'uh huhs' as King Maj spoke. "Our loved ones lost in'a life-long exchange of bullets and blades. Humans always believe that they sufferin' is above all others. Who deemed you so special? Huh? You? We deserve life too! A life free of war and death. A life free from the terror of the human race and their archaic beliefs. A world where we can all live'in peace!"

Isobel felt her chest tighten. The man wasn't wrong. Humans weren't perfect. But she couldn't help but feel rage for their words. She didn't like being framed as the villain in this scenario. She didn't have a family because of the Divine War, but she would be lying if she said she couldn't also see the effects of the war on the beastkin as well.

King Maj closed the distance between him and Isobel. Chase looked as though he regretted speaking up. He, in fact, had a sort of guilty look on his face.

"We are Majes, child. Kin to the dwarves, and sons and daughters of Earth and the King of Gods." He said, placing his hand over his heart. "And we fight for the greater good of all life in this realm. Our weapons are for beasts. No others."

The 'Yeahs' were getting louder now. It was almost like a rally for beastkin.

"The God King allows all, humans included, to live peacefully in his kingdom." He continued. "He'sa JUST ruler. No one is scrutinized here. We all bleed the same here. AIN'T

THAT RIGHT, BOYS!?"

There was a chorus of cheers that rang out of the room. Isobel realized this wasn't a battle that they had a chance of winning. And in a way, she felt as though they may not have deserved to.

"See now, you've gone and got me all political." King Maj scoffed, sweat dripping from his brow. "SETTLE DOWN EVERYONE! We're not here to compare and prattle on about our experiences regarding the war. Drakonis... Ya'know I need the orb."

Drakonis walked forward with an annoyed expression towards the Majes and balled his hand into a fist. When it was opened, it revealed a large golden orb.

"Ha HAH!" King Maj exclaimed; his excitement could hardly be contained. "You really brought it, my lord!"

A gold soul. But where did Drakonis get a gold soul? Had he had it the whole time? Isobel's mind raced with questions, many she knew would not be answered right this moment.

The Maj grabbed the soul with fervor, and turned towards a machine that was etched into the wall. He pulled open the shaft and it exposed a dozen more souls, each of varied color and aura strength.

Isobel had heard rumors of this kind of metallurgy, but she never thought she would see it firsthand. Soul-infusion was a concept that they had discussed within The Barracks. But it was taboo, completely off the table due to the nature in which the souls were procured... You had to take the soul of a living individual. But here, the rules were different. They were stacking souls like loaves of bread.

"So now, Lord Drakonis, only one question remains." King Maj said, as he closed the shaft. "What weapon do'ya desire? You know I can have whatever you want ready in'a few weeks. Just name the product and its quality is assured."

"You will be making a weapon..." Drakonis began, turning to point at Chase. "For him."

The room went silent once again. Everyone's eyes grew wide with bewilderment. Then King Maj laughed in the silence, his hearty guffaws the only noise in the forge. He kept laughing all alone for a while. Then caught his breath.

"I didn't know you were capable of humor, lad" he said, wiping his eyes a bit. That's when he noticed the serious look on Drakonis' face.

"Wait... Are you serious?" King Maj started. "Ya can't expect me to believe that you would collect such powerful souls for an equally powerful weapon and waste its potential on this pissant? The same pissant that just a moment ago questioned our very honor!?"

"I don't jest." Drakonis said, crossing his arms. "You will construct the weapon with his arm in mind, and I will return to retrieve it. A simple direction. Do not let me down."

Drakonis turned towards the door and walked out, beckoning Isobel and Chase to follow.

"They could betray us, my lord." King Maj argued as he followed Drakonis. "They have not sworn fealty to D'Merrion. Do you realize what ya doing...?"

Drakonis turned back again, looking King Maj in his eyes.

"They would never betray me," he said sternly. "Construct the weapon."

Isobel and Chase both exchanged a look, one filled with confusion. What did he mean by that? Isobel felt like her head was going to explode. So much had been said and revealed in so little time. She felt a slight headache begin to form.

King Maj looked over the pair and gave them a smile. He then turned to face his guild of smiths.

"HEY!" He yelled. "Did'ah say you sloths could sit around and gawk!? GET BACK TO WORK!"

With that command, his subordinates returned to their duties. The forge went back to business as usual as the trio left through the entrance.

"Isobel." Drakonis said as he stopped right outside the door. "What did you think of the Majes?"

Isobel just shook her head. Too much was happening at once. She was exhausted from the emotions in the room and honestly, she was questioning her own sensibilities. The Majes seemed honor bound, but they also engaged in soul-infusion. King Maj's words resonated with her, and yet she resented them. And the peace in the kingdom was not what she had expected when they were captured. The stories the Divines told of D'Merrion may be true, she'd seen it firsthand the day before, but his loyalty to his people seemed unquestionable, at least to his subjects. She was at a loss for words.

"They seem to be honorable people, on the wrong side of the war." She finally replied, looking up to meet his eyes.

The sun was hitting his face at an angle, which showed off his attractive qualities. His eyes were like deep lagoons with dragon-like slits down the middle. They stared into each other's eyes for a moment before Drakonis nodded his head, seemingly content with this answer, and turned back towards the hallway.

"Thank you for being honest." Drakonis said. This was the first time he showed any kind of consideration or concern for their thoughts. It was almost sincere. But the feeling only lasted but a moment, because Isobel felt a tap on her shoulder.

She turned to look at Chase and he was staring back at her with a very disgusted look on his face.

"Isobel, what in the Divines was that?" Chase said, his eyes judging her profoundly.

"It was nothing." She said, walking past him. "Come

Chase, we are lagging behind and I do not wish to suffer unnecessarily."

"Whatever." Chase replied while shrugging his shoulders.

Isobel and Chase followed Drakonis through the palace hallways until they were back at the main atrium. He looked around, searching for something, and then turned to them.

"Wait here." He said as he walked off. "Do not move from these positions or even speak. If you do, I cannot guarantee your safety."

"So now you want us safe?" Chase said, purposely trying to antagonize the dark lord.

"Close your mouth, both of you." Drakonis commanded, silencing Chase before he could say another word. "I will return in a moment."

Drakonis then turned to the throne room doors and entered.

Isobel and Chase had no choice but to stand there, completely motionless, watching the doors. The room was silent. More silent than they believed a palace could be. There weren't even any guards guarding the throne room.

A few minutes later, Drakonis came out of the throne room with a new cut around his brow.

"Follow me." He said, walking past them. He led them to a large set of stairs, in the opposite direction of the prisons.

She wanted to ask where they were going, but the mark would not allow her curiosity to be sated.

They walked up the stairs and followed the lantern lit hallways to a giant room. It was filled with heirlooms and relics from different cultures from across the world. Do these guys ever get tired of these colors?

Drakonis then turned to Isobel and Chase.

"Welcome to the Royal Quarters."

Chapter 4:
Three Stars

Isobel

Isobel and Chase followed slowly behind Drakonis, marveling at the exotic wonders. The room had elegant braziers hanging from the marble pillars, covering the room in a warm and comfortable light. Exotic paintings from different parts of the Old-World and banners of D'Merrion littered the walls of the royal chambers. The floors and walls were white and kempt, almost unnaturally clean, with Persian rugs in the hallways leading to the rooms. The windows were stained with intricate carvings of the King of Gods and golden curtains outlined them. There was a concierge desk in the center of the room where a beastkin waited to be addressed.

Drakonis turned and raised his hand to them.

"Do not speak." He commanded them, the humble lighting hiding his draconic features. "Stand there and listen."

Immediately the marks on Chase and Isobel glowed their familiar hue.

"There will be no inquiries into why I have brought you here." He began, walking towards them. "You will do as I say, and no harm will come to you. If either of you fail to comply with this command, your judgment and punishment will be swift."

Drakonis now stood right in-between the pair, his eyes moving back and forth amongst them. He tilted his head towards them.

"You both do understand, correct?" He quizzed them.

They nodded in response.

"Now that you both have been properly addressed, we have another matter to discuss." Drakonis said, his demeanor becoming more somber. "My father has dictated that you Knight Chase, be subject to the crucible. As it stands now you would not last a day in the competition." Drakonis ran his hand through his hair, undoing his afro's perfect form.

"So, I will be training you Chase, to help increase your survivability in the coming battles." Drakonis said, turning to the concierge desk.

Isobel turned to see Chase's eyes wide with shock. He turned and looked at her, his chest pumping as he tried to contain his anger. She could tell he wanted to burst out in a fit, to give the young dragonkin a piece of his mind. The marks restricted all unnecessary gestures.

"Concierge!" Drakonis yelled at the receptionist. "Escort these two to their rooms. Do not worry, they will not attempt to escape or harm you. See fit that they receive a new set of clothes and have food prepared for when I return."

Drakonis turned around and walked past the pair of knights towards the open staircase.

"Stay here and get situated with your new rooms." He commanded them. Isobel shook her head in disbelief. "I have some things that I need to address. So, I will leave you in the servant's care. You will listen to their commands and will not usher harm or judgement on them. You will have your voices back when I leave, I hope you do not waste them scorning my commands."

Drakonis then turned and left the room, his cape waving around in his wake.

Isobel was in as much awe as she was anxious. The night prior, the dungeon was set to be their home. So why were they here in the Royal Quarters? What change of heart could inspire such an improvement in their conditions? What were the evil lords planning?

Isobel and Chase felt their movements become less rigid and controlled the farther away Drakonis got. The concierge ran up to the pair as they flexed their limbs, testing their movement.

"This way please!" He spoke as he hopped away. The beastkin was a small foxkin. He had orange fur with an adorable little outfit on but seemed a bit on the nervous side.

Isobel noticed he was smaller than most foxkin they had seen, and she thought the small creature was quite cute in comparison.

He led them up the center stairwell.

What did Drakonis mean by 'training'? Why would they want to train their enemies? The more she remained in the keep, the less she understood. The questions were stacking, and their helpless predicament meant they were never afforded answers. What is going on in this palace?

When they reached the top of the stairs, there was a branching pathway with giant troll-sized doors at the end of the hallways. They took the right path, a narrow hallway with more D'Merrion propaganda and clean white walls.

These hallways were just as gaudy and self-serving as the rest of the palace, filled with effigies of the vain god. Does D'Merrion ever get tired of looking at himself? How many busts of his own face does he have!?

They passed a window that overlooked a small garden. Isobel stopped to take a look at the tree that sat in the center. It was beautiful, its snow-white leaves glistening in the sun's light. The aura the tree gave off calmed her anxious heart. She felt as though her problems were millions of miles away and she could feel a kind of peace building in her. She wondered 'what species of tree had this kind of power?'

She turned to see if Chase was looking with her, maybe he had found his own peace in the storm brewing in his heart. But he had kept walking towards the room, oblivious to the serene scene behind him. Isobel sighed softly.

He must still be preoccupied with his thoughts on his supposed training. This moment would have greatly benefited him, she thought. If she could take but a piece of the tree, she might find a way to calm his fiery spirit.

She took one last glance at the wonder, before she turned and regrouped with Chase and the foxkin at the giant doors.

The little foxkin surprisingly pushed open the doors, revealing a huge suite with a massive living room filled with very expensive looking furniture. The room resembled an elegant hotel room, with soft lighting and an open terrace that overlooked the capital. It had the same familiar, and unsettling, decor that they had become accustomed to. There was a fridge, and nice black furniture dotting the room. It was very welcoming, which completely contradicted their predicament. She had only seen rooms like this in books. Isobel laughed lightly to herself, it felt like they were on vacation.

"Please make yourselves at home." The beastkin said. He had a very accommodating air to him. Suddenly, he gasped and rushed towards the sink a few feet away, his tail rigid from shock.

"Oh no!" He cried. "Drakonis will not like this one bit! I must remove this before he gets back!"

The little foxkin then pulled some cleaning supplies

from below the sink and scrubbed fiercely at a spot on the counter with a rag. Isobel and Chase watched blankly as the foxkin continued to scrub, humming while he worked. After a few moments, he stood up and wiped his brow.

"There!" He exhaled. "It is done, and he will be none the wiser!"

Chase and Isobel just stared at the foxkin, waiting for him to leave the room. He stood like a deer in headlights, staring back at them. The room now had an air of awkwardness, and it became very still.

"I-I'll be on my way then!" The foxkin declared. He replaced the cleaning kit under the sink and rushed out of the room, closing the door behind him.

Chase immediately let out a roar and kicked one of the elegant end tables in the center of the room.

"He's going to train me!?" Chase scoffed, his voice slowly rising in volume as he spoke. "TRAIN ME? LIKE I'M SOME SORT OF DOG!? HOW DARE HE BELIEVE THAT I WOULD JUST... SILENTLY BE INSTRUCTED AND GO ALONG WITH THIS... THIS... CHARADE!"

Isobel softly grasped his shoulder hoping to reign-in his anger, but he forced her hand off his shoulder.

"Isobel." Chase said, beginning to stomp around the room. "This is no better than slavery! These marks... They control our every move, and he commands us like pawns. Why have they not just dealt away with us? Why do they toy with us in this manner!? I am a warrior, Isobel! Not someone's squire or apprentice! I have been trained in over a dozen different martial arts...!"

She couldn't dispute anything that he was saying because he wasn't wrong. Chase, realistically, was one of the strongest amongst the Divine Knights. If not for his hot-temper and propensity to leap before gauging how deep the hole, he would be an elite amongst their ranks. Well, that, and his... humble beginning.

Chase was rambling now, a tell sign that his mood was subsiding, and he was coming to terms with his situation. He walked over to the sofa in the middle of the room and plopped himself right onto it. Isobel walked over to Chase to join him on the couch.

"Chase." She said as she put her hand on his. "I am so sorry that this has happened. This is all my fault. I was so sure... I had convinced everyone to follow my lead and look where it has landed us..."

Her words trailed off. Isobel's vision began to blur. She reached out to Chase.

"Isobel?" Chase said, concern replacing his former rage. "Isobel, what's wrong? Isobel?"

She didn't get a chance to answer. The room started spinning and she felt herself falling forward. Her head was pounding and felt as though she had thousands of bells ringing in her ears. Her neck had a burning sensation, like the sun was boiling her skin. Then she felt the soft of the sofa and the world faded to nothingness.

*   *   *

Isobel

She was here again. Back in the endless black. She opened her eyes and saw nothing. She spoke and heard nothing. She reached out to grab something, anything, to anchor herself. But she felt nothing. She was in the darkness again and she was lost, another piece of the void.

I know you're here. I know you're here. I know you're here. I know you're here.

She kept speaking the thought in her mind. She knew these words would attract the old god. She couldn't last in the depths for too much longer.

"I know you're here!" She heard herself yell. She was screaming at the top of her lungs. She felt beads of sweat on her forehead and her voice was hoarse and ragged.

A pair of giant green eyes appeared in front of her, illuminating the immediate space around her. The area was still black and endless, but she regained her solidarity and senses.

She felt the Divine pressure still her movements. She

hated this aura, one that commanded without words. It was unholy and sinister, evil by all means.

"You lied to me!" She screamed. "You said I would be the one to kill Drakonis! You said that he was going to die by my hand!"

Isobel felt herself pulled closer to the glowing orbs. She couldn't resist. Here, she had no power.

She felt the dark essence creep into her mind, peeling apart her thoughts, pervading her memories. The beast now knew what she knew. Almost as though it was repulsed by what it saw, it tossed her backwards out of its space. Isobel attempted to speak, to renounce her exile, but the darkness took her again.

She felt her skin grow cold, and her breathing grow short. She couldn't take it. The madness was setting in.

"*Failure*!" She heard someone scream. "*Pathetic*!"

"*You let them down*!" Another said. "*They'll never trust you.*"

More and more insults began to hit her, some from voices she recognized, some she didn't.

You lied to us! Isobel! It's all your fault Isobel! You will never save them! How could you let us die!

She couldn't reply. Her voice was strangled and lost its will. She had no defense against the onslaught.

She began to curl up in a ball and cover her ears. *SHUT*

UP SHUT UP SHUT UP SHUT UP SHUT UP SHUT UP SHUT UP SHUT UP SHUT UP SHUT UP SHUT UP SHUT UP SHUT UP SHUT UP SHUT UP SHUT UP... Silence.

She felt her senses return and the voices died down. She felt her heart racing and her skin had goosebumps all over it.

"How brave of you to addressss one as old as I in sssuch a way..." The beast whispered into her mind. "You would do well to remember who... Is masssster... and who is ssservant."

The being pulled her closer to its space. She could make out more of the old god now, seeing its maw and snout clear as day. The blackened scales of its face were illuminated by the intensity of its eyes. She never would be able to guess the true size of the beast. It was greater than the space they were in, and its face was as big as any statue she had seen. This was 'THE' Dragon of Darkness after all.

She was right in front of its sickly green eyes when it decided to speak.

"The termsss of our agreement..." The dragon began. "Have changed... There are now more watchersss... They will try to obssscure... Your path..."

Isobel felt a clawed hand move her around and the eyes were looking up and down her body.

"You are lucky to be alive..." The dragon began again, shifting her farther from his eyes. "However... We will use...

This to our advantage... Your goal... is to gain the young dragonkin'sss... Trussst... Succcceed... And your dreamsss will come true. You and your companions... will be...reunited and free... Now... Begone!"

Isobel was cast out into the darkness and silence grasped her. She felt the emptiness clamoring at her, pulling her deeper into the void. Then she felt the familiar weariness take her, softly guiding her from this realm and she blacked out once again.

*　　　　*　　　　*

Chase

“Isobel!?” Chase said, frantically shaking Isobel's lifeless body. “Isobel!? I can't believe this is happening now!”

Her skin was growing cold to the touch, becoming pale and sickly blue. She had been unconscious for more than three minutes, the longest her call had ever lasted. But this time was unlike any other, she had never been called away while awake before.

He raised his hand and began to channel his aura. His mark burned, restricting his movement, but he fought through the pain and stiffness. He needed to call her soul back.

“Ket.” He started, making the hand gestures needed to cast the spell. “Et. Maen.”

Chase was a second from bringing his hand down on her chest when Isobel gasped loudly, rising from her coma. She was struggling to breathe, and she cradled her head. Chase started patting her back and holding her, hoping his efforts would help her recover.

Thank the gods! That spell was a one-time ordeal, and honestly, there was no guarantee it would work, only that it would hurt both of them.

Isobel's eyes opened but they were still foggy, like the lifeless eyes of a corpse. Chase couldn't stand looking at her like this.

"Isobel..." Chase said, putting his hand on her shoulder. "Are you okay?"

Her mouth opened but her words refused to leave her body. She was coughing violently and in response, Chase stood up and searched the kitchen for glasses. He found a collection of glasses in one of the cupboards and filled one up with water, rushing to get back to Isobel's side.

When he sat down, Isobel's coughs were lessening, and her eyes started to become less foggy.

"Ch-Chase..." She started to say, her voice weak from her ordeal.

"Hush now, Isobel..." Chase replied, putting the glass to her lips so she could drink. She grabbed the glass from him and began to chug the water, her eyes squeezed tightly shut. After she finished the drink, she opened her eyes again, and the fog was almost gone.

She groaned in pain, sweat still falling freely from her forehead.

"You were awake this time." Chase said, turning her to face him. "That was too dangerous! What if I weren't around to aid you, to stop you from a more severe injury!?"

"But you were around," she said confidently. "And I have no doubt that you will make every attempt to be around always."

Chase stared at her, holding her hand firmly. She was really testing his patience. She could try to play it off and act like this was just a regular part of their day, but he knew better. Something had changed.

“You're an idiot.” Chase said, softly smiling at her.

“Glad you finally noticed.” Isobel rebutted, smiling wryly, and hugging him. She pulled away and took a deep sigh. She seemed to be back to normal.

“The dragon gave me a different prophecy...” she said, looking Chase directly in his eye.

“And you would believe it?” Chase said angrily. “After what happened to us in New York? Our defeat was sound and absolute, Isobel. We listened to your “visions” once before and look what it got us. Chained and enslaved.”

He dreaded hearing about her dreams. She told no one else that she received dark whispers as she slept, and he had held her terrible secret with him for years. A secret that had cost him sleep and even his life. He wondered if it was even worth keeping any longer.

“No.” She said as she got up onto the couch. “I don't believe it. Not one bit. But... He told me we could be free. That we could find a way to freedom... Through...”

Isobel hesitated for a moment. Chase felt a chill run down his spine. He didn't like where this conversation was going. Isobel rarely lied and never hesitated to let anyone know what her true thoughts were. If she did, it was because she knew that it would light his fuse. He braced himself.

“Isobel.” Chase said, grasping her hand again and smiling softly. “I swear I won't be mad for but a moment, but if you say that we have to work with that undergrown draconic wannabe, I will punch this table in half and then huff it out of the window.”

“Then I won't.” She spoke. “Though I am surprised you figured it out so quickly.”

*   *   *

Isobel

Isobel wrung out her hair in the sink. She looked up at herself in the mirror. It had been a while since she had a nice bath. The amenities of the suite were a luxury they weren't regularly afforded so they decided that if they were going to be trapped here, they might as well relax when they can.

She rubbed her face a bit, looking over some of the new scars that she received from their previous battle.

“I guess you're not the most beautiful woman at the ball anymore, Isobel” she said to herself. “I wonder if Everett and the rest of the Divines are okay.”

She was the only one to not be killed. The sole survivor of an expedition she convinced the rest to go on. If she and Chase returned home... When they returned... She would have much to answer for.

After a couple more moments mulling over her new face, she grabbed a robe from the hamper in the bathroom and made her way to the living area.

Chase was sitting on the couch, in a robe identical to hers, looking at the ceiling.

“The clothes still haven't arrived yet?” Isobel asked.

“No-pe” Chase said back to her, sighing deeply.

They weren't expecting punctual service, but the wait

seemed unbearable. It had been a few hours since Drakonis had left them in the chambers. Seconds later, there were a couple light taps on the door.

Chase and Isobel looked at each other, and then the large doors slide slowly open. A small girl, undeniably human, walked into the room. She looked around, then noticed the pair sitting on the couch.

"I FOUND IT!" she said, obviously proud of herself. "Bring it in here, Dior!"

The little girl left the room for a moment, and returned with a giant rolling rack, filled to the brim with women's clothes. Another rack soon followed, held by another girl who could only be assumed to be Dior. This rack held many men's outfits, each seemed to be exquisitely tailored and nicely sewn.

The second girl then ran out and pulled in yet another rack, with just as many clothes as the first two.

Little girls were the ones they had been waiting all this time for? No wonder it took a long time for them to get here, Isobel thought. She couldn't believe these were the servants they were waiting on.

The pair of girls approached Chase and Isobel, skipping over to them.

"Hi, my name is Mahogany!" The first began, a huge smile brandishing her face as she pointed to herself. "AAAAAAAAAANNNNNND this is Dior!"

She pointed to the second girl, putting her hands obnoxiously close to her face. Dior was not as excited to meet them as Mahogany was, nor was she super ecstatic to have her face jabbed at either. In fact, she seemed almost anxious and on edge.

Now that they were close, Isobel could make out their features quite distinctly. Mahogany was a small child with soft brown skin, her hair tied into a fluffy ponytail. She had a little button nose and soft hazel eyes that melted Isobel's heart. She was so cute.

Dior shared an identical frame and features, but slightly taller with her hair braided into two fluffy pigtails held together with golden bands. They both had on green dresses, with nice golden satin woven into the creases. These outfits were more refined than what common slaves wore. Who were these kids?

"SEMAJ!" Mahogany yelled back at the door. "GET IN HERE!"

A small, slim boy poked his head into the room. He obviously wasn't trying to be called in or even noticed. He had very short hair, but it was long enough to be seen from the door.

"What do you want, Mahogany?" Semaj yelled back. "I'm busy doing important things in the hallway!"

"Greet the new guests or I'll tell!" She threatened him.

Semaj let out a groan and looked at the ceiling. He then

proceeded to stomp all the way to the other girls. When he reached them, he crossed his arms and looked out the window. He was wearing a similarly refined outfit. He had a blue shirt on, made in a style of garb she had never seen before, and red pants that looked like they were only made for this shirt.

"Hello, my name is Semaj." He said unenthused as he huffed and puffed immaturely. "I am King Maj's son and the next successor to the throne. Blah, blah, blah, can I go now?"

Mahogany gave him a stern look. She was obviously the mature one in the group, and she didn't seem to be any older than eight or nine years old.

"Be nice for one minute!" She rasped at the boy, before turning back to Chase and Isobel.

"I don't think I will." Semaj said under his breath.

Mahogany gave him a bit of side eye. Then she proceeded with her greeting.

"Drakonis ordered us to bring you clothes and supplies for the room." Mahogany said as she motioned towards the outfits. She had a soft accent that was appealing to the ears, one that Isobel had never heard before.

"We have scrubs, shorts, jeans, cleaning stuff... Uhhh..." she continued, trailing off at the end of her sentence.

"We brought you a lot of stuff!" Semaj blurted out, now impatient and fed up with Mahogany. "Just put some clothes on because we have to meet up with big bro."

"We're already late for that." Mahogany interjected. "Thanks to SOMEONE not helping push the carts or find the room!"

"You guys always laugh at me when I push the carts!" Semaj shot back. "You always laugh at me when I struggle. IT AIN'T THAT FUNNY."

Isobel giggled a bit at the exchange. She was reminded of her and Chase when they were children. Like looking into a mirror of their past.

Semaj noticed that Isobel had laughed at him, and now he was pouting heavily. He crossed his arms tightly and balled his fists in a small tantrum.

"NOW SHE'S LAUGHING AT ME!" he said, his eyes fiery and full of anger.

"Now, now, little man." Chase said walking over the children. "She wasn't laughing at you. She was laughing because you reminded her of us. When we were children, we argued all the time. Now we're best friends."

He then put on a big goofy smile for the kids. Mahogany and Dior chuckled while Semaj still pouted, not convinced he wasn't the butt of the joke.

"Umm, thank you for the clothes and supplies." Isobel said, trying to bring some order back to the room. "We haven't decided on the rooms yet, you can leave them the carts here and we'll sort through them later."

"Yes ma'am" Mahogany replied. "I implore you to hurry and get dressed. Drakonis is waiting and we are already SUUUUUPEEERRR late in meeting him. So, hurry and get dressed!"

The marks on the knight's necks glowed a bit; they knew that they weren't allowed to sit any longer. Isobel and Chase both stood up and began to sift through the clothes.

There was an abundance of outfits of different cultural styles. Some were from the humble and unrefined beastkin clans of the south. Others were regal attire that Isobel had never even seen before. She was overwhelmed by the options before her. A lofty blue dress with velvet purple out seams and golden trim? Humble unattractive brown garb, with nice black pants and a soft linen under shirt? The options were endless, and Isobel's mouth was close to watering over the choices.

"This will do me fine." Chase said as he grabbed a bundle of clothes. He carried the heap to one of the rooms. "I'll return in a moment."

Isobel cursed her luck and Chase's lack of love for the sophisticated, exotic tailoring before them! She continued to sift through the clothes, trying to find something fitting for personality but with a bit of maneuverability. They were all so beautiful and well-maintained. The craftsmanship of each outfit was almost too fascinating to put down. She really wanted a dress, but she knew that a fight could be around any corner and opted for something a bit more mundane.

Chase returned with his new ensemble. He had chosen a soft white shirt, with daring black pants and a pair of nice running shoes. A little of home; a little of Rome, Isobel thought. She heard a traveling merchant say it once. Apparently, it meant the best of both worlds or something of the like.

She followed his example and grabbed a soft brown shirt, some decorative black pants, and brown sneakers.

"Lookin' nice, lady killer." Isobel teased Chase. "I'll be right back."

She walked back to the room she showered in and quickly put the new clothes on. As she made her way towards the door, she marveled at her appearance in a nearby mirror.

"That's it, Isobel." She said to herself.

She adjusted her hair and rejoined Chase and the children in the room.

"Okay." She said to the children, then turned to confirm with Chase. "Ready when you are."

"Not sure what I'm getting ready for, but we can leave now." He replied, a little disdain in his voice. He probably realized that his "training" was going to begin today. Who knew what that entailed?

The leader, Mahogany, then turned towards the door.

"Let's make haste then!" She bellowed. "We can't allow

Drakonis to wait a second longer! Let's hurry!”

Then the group left through the doors, shutting them tightly behind them

Chapter 5: Might Makes Right

Ashnel

Ashnel never liked the Royal Districts. Too much bureaucracy and capitalism. The soft, domesticated merchants made immoral deals with each other, and forced the less fortunate to labor in their name with menial tasks and worthless jobs.

He was making his way up to the quarter, walking up the large stairwell that led to the "Illustrious" sector.

He had been tasked by another commander of D'Merrion, to deliver his daily insults to Drakonis. Ashnel grabbed the small paper in his pocket, recalling the unpleasant memory.

He was in the barracks sparring, if you could even call it that, with one of his lessers, Ophog.

Ophog was a large and hardy boarkin that Ashnel decided to keep as an underling. He joined the beastkin Army before Ashnel, but his meek nature made him easy to manipulate. When courage and conviction failed, Ashnel used fear to get what he wanted.

The wolfkin had been using him as target practice for some new equipment they had received from the Majes, a personal delight he undertook in his free time. His minions made the best targets.

"Ashnel..." Ophog began to plead. "We have many targets, explicitly designed for target practice. Could we not simply use those for testing the crossbows and mana guns?"

Ashnel stood around twenty feet away and he could smell the pig's fear, clear as day.

"Oh, Ophog." Ashnel said, raising the crossbow to the sky. "Stationary targets only show that the weapon works. We need to ensure they are accurate and powerful! How best to ensure that they hurt our enemies and hit moving targets than by using his as a moving, living target?"

A bead of sweat slid slowly down Ophog's face as he prepared to dodge the next bolt.

Ashnel lowered the gun, taking the aim at the giant boar.

"Ahh!" A familiar voice said from behind Ashnel. "Here you are, toying with your subordinates as usual?"

A large black phoenix was crouched down behind

Ashnel, ripping the meat off a leg of a fowl. From the smell, it seemed like a fresh kill. He was wearing a ritual headdress, filled with feathers that complimented his blood red feathers.

"You are aware that's cannibalism, right?" Ashnel asked, lowering the crossbow again. Ophog sighed in relief, but his respite was short-lived. Ashnel, without looking, raised the crossbow and fired a bolt.

"YEEEEEEEEEEEEEEEEOOOOOOOOOOOWWWWCH!" Ophog yelped in pain, putting a smile on Ashnel's face.

"I share no relations with lesser birds and common fowl." The phoenix began, chomping away at the limp meat in his claws. "You're wondering why I, the wise and mighty Addurog, have come to you during my lunch break? Well, let me answer all of your inquiries with haste and great fervor before you lose interest, and begin to chase your tail or whatever it is you do for fun."

The smile on Ashnel's face faded and was replaced with annoyance and disgust.

"Now, now, Ashnel." Addurog said, tossing the bony remains of his meal to the ground. "I heard Drakonis has returned to the kingdom, and I have no time to make his acquaintance. So thus, I need an able-bodied warrior to deliver my insults. As his second-in-command, you are the best candidate. Please do not make me beg, wolf."

Addurog made puppy eyes at Ashnel, which immediately put the wolfkin in an even fouler mood than before. This is no way for a warrior of Addurog's caliber to act! He hated the infantile grudges between the commanders, mostly because it never amounted to any kind of actual fighting. Just big words and puffed chests. The complete opposite of what it means to be in beastkin society.

"Don't you have other subordinates to handle your chores for you?" Ashnel questioned, taking the paper from Addurog's claw.

"Aww Ashnel, don't be that way!" Addurog said standing up. He towered over Ashnel, almost two times the size of the wolfkin. "I have many tasks today, and I never use subpar tools. My magnificence dictates that I must have only the best. Go on this quest for me, Ashnel. It will be worth your time! FAREWELL!"

Before Ashnel could gripe more to the phoenix, he leapt from the barracks and laughed all the way to his destination. It was a scene that Ashnel always found unsettling and annoying.

Ashnel turned and looked at Ophog. Ophog stared back, blank faced.

"Well..." Ashnel began, almost completely unenthused. "We still have good bolts left to test. Assume the position."

Ophog tensed up and readied himself.

* * *

Ashnel

The royal chambers were empty during the midday, most of its tenants out and about on 'important business'. Ashnel walked up to the empty receptionist desk and pressed the bell, hoping to get immediate attention.

He looked around and noticed not a soul in sight. Empty seats and lonely couches. He was already annoyed, but now he was mad. Where was Tejari? Out frolicking, picking flowers, or some other pathetic task?

"TEJARI!" Ashnel screamed out, but his words did not meet anyone's ears. Now he had to walk up to Drakonis' room and handle the delivery himself. What was the use of servants if they found themselves unavailable for work?

He walked past the desk and began to ascend the stairs. He had almost made it to the top when he spotted a familiar orange foxkin.

"SIR ASHNEL!" Tejari squeaked at the top of the stairs. "I heard your call-"

Ashnel had already leapt up to the young beastkin and taken hold of his nape.

“You disappoint me, Tej.” Ashnel said, sniffing the foxkin. “You smell of cleaning detergents, but you know that when I call, you come. No excuses.”

“I'm sorry, Sir Ashnel.” Tejari choked out, Ashnel's large hands constricting all of his movement. “I was preoccupied and I couldn-”

Ashnel turned him around and slammed him against the wall in the hallway, knocking loose one of the D’Merrion banners.

“No, no, no, this won't do at all.” Ashnel said, waving a finger in front of Tejari. “I was having THE MOST ANNOYING afternoon and seeing one of my favorite chew toys really lightened the mood.”

Tejari gulped loudly as Ashnel cracked a sinister smile.

“Let's see...” Ashnel whispered. “I could... Toss you around a bit. Or maybe I should take out Executioner and show you why it's the sharpest scythe in Zhalesh. Or maybe I could pluck each individual strand of fur from your tail for hours... How does that sound?”

Ashnel was so caught up in antagonizing the little foxkin that he barely heard the murmurs down one of the hallways.

"Maybe we should just wait back in the room." One of the voices whispered. If not for his amazing senses, he might have missed the remark.

Ashnel turned to see the three Maj whelps accompanied by...

He couldn't believe his eyes. There they stood. The knights, fully dressed in regal attire, were well-kempt and rested. What was the meaning of this!?

He felt his blood begin to boil again. This time he was beyond angry. His rage felt like a molten volcano, bubbling beneath the surface. He dropped Tejari at his feet, the young foxkin coughing and struggling for air.

"Well... Well... Well..." Ashnel began walking towards the group. "If it isn't the orphans and their inept prince. Oh, and I see you have a matching pair of pathetic knights with you. How fun!"

Ashnel broke out into laughter. But this was a ruse for he wasn't happy, not for one second. These humans experimented on him, humiliated him. Now here they are, walking around without a single worry in the world. Along with Dior, Mahogany, and Semaj, three Majen children that annoyed him to no end. This is the perfect time to rend them all. He could just say that they tried to escape. He licked his lips, anticipating wiping their blood from his weapon.

“Honestly.” Ashnel began, advancing on the group. “I assumed D’Merrion would have killed you both, as he tends to do when he is displeased. But instead, he decides to send you to the Crucible! Imagine my surprise when I hear that I, the great and mighty Ashnel, will have the honor of gutting a Divine Knight? How beautiful is that? What have I achieved to be allotted such an honor?”

The knights jumped in front of the children and began to slowly recede back towards the large doors behind them. There was fear in the air, Ashnel could smell it.

“Do you really have time to be talking to us? “Dior said mockingly, peeking out from behind the female knight. “Don't you have to go smell someone's butt or something!”

She immediately stuck out her tongue, but Ashnel was already behind the group and grabbing the young girl before anyone could react.

“Your tongue was always sharp.” He said in a low growl. “It would be a shame if you lost it. How about you air those insults again?”

“Shut up!” Dior spit back. “You're a house pet and Drakonis will always own you!”

She started kicking him in the chest, but they were like rain droplets against his powerful muscles and dense fur. The others had turned around and stared in horror as Ashnel then readied his hand for the killing blow.

“Do say hello to your mother for me when you see her in the afterlife.” Ashnel said as he brought his hand to the child's chest. It stopped a few feet from her body, but not because Ashnel stopped. He had a hand on his arm, strong strands of lightning jumping from it.

“You're fast, I'll give you that.” The male knight began. “But I can't just sit around and let you bully anyone that walks into your path. How about you put her down and we settle this like gentleman, huh?”

Ashnel let out a giant laugh. This human was not only bold but was actually quite skilled. He didn't even sense the man's presence when he invaded his space, let alone feel him when he grabbed his arm. He might have a bit of fun with this one.

“Well I would like to accept your proposition, human.” Ashnel said as he let go of the child. “But I have never been gentle.”

Ashnel then threw a jab, smashing the man in the face. The knight did a backflip and landed next to the window. Ashnel leapt after him, grabbing his trusted scythe off his back.

“Or a man.” He snarled as he charged the stunned knight, bloodlust in his eyes.

* * *

Chase

Chase could see it in the wolf's eyes. He was trying to cleave him in two. So much for the diplomatic route. Chase leapt high into the air, his hands pressed against the ceiling, to avoid the large swing of the wolf's massive scythe.

Ashnel then reached up and grabbed him by his ankle. Chase, anticipating this action pushed himself from the ceiling into the large wolf, knocking him off balance. Ashnel was only stunned for a second though, and he began to swing his weapon wildly.

"You can't dodge forever!" Ashnel grunted, attempting to chop Chase to bits. He was laughing as he narrowly missed Chase, each slash getting closer and closer to the mark. This guy has a screw loose, Chase thought to himself. He didn't know how to tip the odds in his favor. He was without a weapon or any decent armor, and he was getting increasingly fatigued the longer this went on.

"Come on, Knight" Ashnel taunted. "At least put up a fight!"

Then the wolf began to channel a sickly yellow aura into his scythe, spinning it around his body, building momentum. He then lunged forward towards Chase, with frightening speed. Chase just barely managed to leap high enough to vault over the scythe, aiming a kick for the wolf's head.

Chase felt his foot connect with the wolfkin. A direct hit, and with that kind of impact, he had to feel something.

“Fool.” Ashnel spit out, grabbing Chase's leg. He slammed the knight into the floor. “You're more durable and a little more skilled than I gave you credit for. But let's put those traits to the test, shall we?”

Chase felt himself being slammed repeatedly.

“Chase!” He heard someone yell. It was probably Isobel. He could feel himself losing consciousness between each slam.

No, he thought. Not like this.

There was a shattering of glass around him and then a thud. He looked around and didn't recognize any of his surroundings. There was a tree, and some bushes. Did he fall from somewhere? He tilted his head back and saw Drakonis a few feet away before he was overcome with a serene and calming peace.

Then all of the lights turned off.

* * *

Isobel

Isobel stood in front of the children as the large wolfkin turned to face them. He started to laugh maniacally into his palm.

"To think I was here just to oversee a menial task." Ashnel rasped, excited and breathing heavily. "Now I get to kill some humans and scratch a couple of loud-mouth orphans off my hit list!"

Isobel was done with his jests and taunts. A beast like this did not deserve to live. What monster torments children and laughs at death? Only a vassal of D'Merrion was capable of such villainy.

She channeled her aura, her golden hue brightening the room. Ashnel shielded his eyes with his scythe, steadying himself for her attack. She knew she could be faster than Chase though, even if it was for half of the time.

She propelled herself forward, hand cranked back to avenge the beating her friend received. The wolfkin had a surprised look on his face when she entered his aura. She slammed her fist into his nose with all her might, sending him flying right out the window.

"GYAAAAAAAAAH!!" Ashnel yelled as he flew from the window. Isobel wasn't done with him, she jumped out the window and mounted the wolf midair. She pummeled him with blows, his pained snarls leaving his mouth with each impactful blow.

"I'll make you-" Isobel started to say as Ashnel grabbed her by the mouth.

"BE QUIET!" He yelled as he reversed their position right before they hit the ground, landing on top of her. The breath was knocked right out of her.

Ashnel raised his scythe above his head and tried to bring it down on her skull, but she kicked his leg out from under him and leaned away from the attack, narrowly escaping death. Isobel rolled from under the wolf swiftly.

He was strong, but she still had golden time left and she wasn't going to waste it.

Ashnel roared loudly and charged Isobel, completely lost to bloodlust and rage. He looked like a wild beast. She readied her stance, sure she could survive anything he threw at her.

He swung his scythe at her midsection, and she grabbed it confidently. The wolfkin had a look of surprise for a moment and spun around to kick her in the face. Checkmate.

She hopped over his kick, flipping above his head and head-butted him into the earth. His scythe flew upwards and lodged itself into one of the grassy patches a few feet away.

Isobel faltered a bit afterwards, trying to regain focus. No one wins with a headbutt, she thought. She had hit the wolf for a decisive blow, and he struggled to get to his feet.

As Ashnel slowly lumbered to his feet, Isobel tried to catch her breath. Her golden time was running thin, she couldn't keep fighting at peak potential for too much longer. He grabbed his head, shrugging off the blow she had dealt him.

He reached to the side and grabbed a tree with one hand. Yes, a tree! Isobel couldn't believe the stamina this wolfkin had. He was otherworldly.

He lifted the tree and threw it in her direction. In retaliation, Isobel took a stance and channeled her aura into a forward strike, smashing the tree to smithereens with her fist. She failed to notice the wolfkin had used the plant as a distraction and was now behind her, preparing his final attack.

“Die.” He said in a soft, sinister voice. She couldn't react to the blow, her golden time was over, and she awaited the impact of his strike.

One second. Two seconds. Three. She was confused, she wasn't dead. She turned to see the wolf locked in place, his eyes turned to the side, beads of sweat dropping down his face. He was completely motionless, almost like he was paralyzed. She turned to see what had the wolf so terrified.

There stood Drakonis, leaning against the giant snow-white tree that sat in the middle of the orchard.

"Oh." He spoke. "Don't mind me, I'm just waiting to see what happens next."

Isobel stared in disbelief. Had he been there the whole time? She was so locked into ending the wolf, she didn't even recognize where she was. She hadn't even looked for Chase.

There they stood inside of the calming garden she had noticed earlier. There were multiple large trees and dull blue bushes dotting the courtyard. Chase was next to Drakonis, completely battered, with his clothes partially torn. He also had shards of glass sticking out of his back.

Isobel felt a gust of wind blow by her. Ashnel had already rushed to kneel in front of Drakonis.

"I have a letter from Addurog, My lord." He said in between labored breaths. "I swear I came to deliver this message when I was-"

"You are dismissed, Ashnel." Drakonis said. "Do not tarry and I will not seek retribution for this disrespect."

The wolf then bowed deeply and rushed over to grab his scythe. He then ran down the pathway back to the building and disappeared from sight.

Isobel looked over at Chase and quickly examined his body. He was in bad shape. He had broken bones, too many shards of glass to simply remove, and had a collapsed lung. Maybe she could remove the glass and heal the wounds before he bleeds out?

She raised her hands to chant a healing spell, when Drakonis grabbed her hand.

"I failed to inform you that using magic anywhere inside the castle is strictly forbidden." Drakonis said as he picked Chase up. "Do not worry, I have a means of healing him. We need him ready for his training."

Drakonis then looked up above Isobel's head. She followed his eyes to see the three children staring down at them.

"Come and explain what happened to me." Drakonis commanded. "Do not waste time, we have limited light and I still have errands.

The children popped their heads back into the window, assumingly doing as they were told. Drakonis then looked down at Isobel.

"Follow me." He said, now throwing Chase over his shoulder.

The mark on her neck left her no choice. She was lightly fatigued but she had to follow.

Isobel walked a few feet behind Drakonis towards the large tree in the middle. The powerful, potent mana was thick in the air, tightly keeping her emotions under control. The garden itself looked nothing like the ones she had seen or read about in her books, the plants were a dull blue with a pearlescent aura around them. The leaves of the trees were white, and still like a lonely forest.

Drakonis put Chase down at the base of the tree. Fairy-like creatures then descended upon them, examining his body.

"What is this place?" Isobel asked awestruck by the sheer beauty of the garden. "It's so... calm."

Drakonis reached up and rubbed the tree softly, with a tenderness that she didn't even know existed in the dark lord. There was love in his strokes.

"This is the Garden of Amity." he said softly. "And this is the Tree of Life."

Chapter 6:
The Others

Chase

There was smoke, the kind of smoke that accompanies a long burning fire, so thick that it was impossible to see past it. The air had a chill, a brisk cold that would warrant a hardened adventurer to reconsider his decision to continue. There were sounds of explosions and destruction all around, but none of that was visible amidst the dense cloud that covered the area.

Chase could feel the dirt caked on his face as he forced himself from the mud. His knightly cuirass was battered, and almost completely destroyed. He looked down at his blade, which had been blunted from the impacts of his foes. His breaths were labored and course from the smog that hung in the air.

He looked around and saw no one was with him. Where were his allies? Why did he feel so disconnected from the gods?

He didn't have much time to search for answers as a growl from behind him prompted him to respond.

Chase whirled around to narrowly block an axe swing meant to pierce his skull. A beastmen snarled back at him, murder in his eyes.

"Curse you, human!" He spat. He pulled his axe back and lunged at Chase again. This time, however, Chase saw his opening.

He lunged toward the beastmen, stabbing him in the abdomen, stopping the soldier's motion dead in its tracks. The beastmen coughed horrendously through gurgled growls. Blood began to fall down and patter on Chase's arm as he felt the beastmen attempt to move.

Chase pulled the sword back out of the beastmen and stabbed him again, aiming directly for the soldier's heart. This time, the beastmen dropped his weapon.

Chase looked up to meet the beast's eyes. The murder and anger that had consumed his eyes was now replaced with peace and sadness. The soldier fell backwards off Chase's blade, turning to dust before him.

"YOU PATHETIC, WORTHLESS LOUT!" A ragged voice from behind him screamed.

He tried to turn around, but he was fatigued. His body had given all it could give. He clenched his eyes shut and braced for impact.

A loud clang rang out from behind him, and Chase turned to see Everett, a senior Divine Knight, standing over him.

"Don't give up." He instructed Chase, reaching down to

help him up.

All of this was familiar. Chase couldn't place it, but he had lived these moments before.

A squad of Divine Knights then pushed through the dense mist, right behind Chase's aggressor.

The middle knight drew his weapon and impaled the beastmen before he could react to their intrusion. He let out a soft gurgle as the knight dislodged his weapon from its body.

Everett lowered his weapon, and untensed his shoulders as the group advanced upon them. As they got closer, Chase could see Jerak, Mirela, and some of the other usual knights of the team...

They looked younger, almost ten years younger. This didn't feel right. Why couldn't he remember what had happened?

Everett turned around and reached his hand out to Chase. Chase reached up and realized his hand was slightly smaller than he expected it to be. Wait... Why did he expect his hand to be bigger?

He was confused and fatigued beyond belief. Maybe things would make more sense after he rested.

Everett, who saw him ogling his hand, reached down, and pulled Chase up to his feet. Chase felt as though he should be taller, as though he wasn't quite right.

The group of knights stopped a few feet away, and the

middle knight moved to talk to him. He could make out her body, it had feminine qualities, and he looked up at her face. The face was a blur, rubbed out from existence. It had no distinguishable qualities and made his skin crawl.

Then the being began to talk to him. But he couldn't make out any of what it was saying... Its visage was muddy. Encrypted. Completely incomprehensible.

Chase stood there petrified, at a loss for words.

“He's fine.” Everett replied to the faceless knight, patting the boy on his back. “You -Stzzz- are pretty durable.”

The faceless knight then turned around, addressing the other knights in her cryptic speech, and the dense fog began to thicken. Chase covered his eyes as the wind picked up, shielding them from the changing elements.

When he lowered his hand, he was startled by the sun. It was at its highest point in the sky, its warmth a welcome change to the cold and dirty mud of the battlefield. He looked around, realizing he was now in the courtyard of the Ascended Heights, near the Tower of the Divines.

Chase looked around, marveling at the old Divine statues, as though it were his first time seeing them. He missed its high walls and it had felt like he hadn't seen it in a long time.

He was standing behind his allies, the Divine Knights, but he was far too small to see where exactly they were heading. Then the group stopped, so abruptly that Chase smacked into one of the knights in front of him and fell backwards.

"You can't change -Stzzz-" A voice angrily yelled from ahead. "You think you can just -Stzzzzz- this is a -Stzzz-. I trusted you!"

Two of the knights went flying into nearby buildings, caving the front half of the building in. Chase shielded his eyes from the debris.

The knights assumed the subjugation formation, moving to form a circle around the voice.

The faceless individual stood in the middle of the circle across from a young man with short dreads. He was wearing the knight's garb and had a single sword in his hand.

Chase stood up and reached for his weapon, but he felt nothing. He looked down and realized that he had no weapon.

"-Stzzz-" The faceless body jerked forward, readying her weapon. It moved its arms in a way that indicated it was talking to the man.

"I should have known you'd -Stzzz-" The man rebutted. "You thought I would sit in your -Stzzz- and be -Stzzz- with -Stzzz-! I AM WHO I AM!"

At the utterance of those words, Chase felt his head began to throb and ache. He wobbled a bit on his legs, trying to maintain his balance. There was shouting all around him, but he couldn't concentrate.

He heard the clanging of blades while he fought to control his headache. He looked at the commotion with a pained expression to try and make sense of the noise.

The dreaded man was fighting off all the knights single-handedly, a red electric aura following all his movements. Two spear wielding knights rushed him from opposing sides, intending to end his life. He spun quickly, chopping the heads of their weapons off, and kicking one of the knights in the chest before he could process his weapons destruction. The other threw his weapon to the ground and pulled out a dagger. The dreaded man was already behind him, punching the knight to the ground.

Chase's head had recovered in the meantime. He could see that most of the knights had been decimated. The faceless knight was still standing, visibly injured and on her last leg.

"-Stzzz-" The man said gasping for breath, sweat dripping from his brow. "They turned you against me. My only -Stzzz-. Every last one of you are -Stzzz- of -Stzzz-."

The man rushed the faceless figure, slamming his shoulder into her. She fell down, her armor loudly smashing into rocky road.

Chase felt it in his core. He needed to stop the dreaded man and save the faceless figure. He was still off balance from his fit, but he willed his entire being to move.

The skies turned gray with overcast and began to roar as rain began to pour. In almost an instant, it was down-pouring. The wind picked up, swallowing the warmth the sun had created.

The dreaded man raised his blade high, readying it for its final destination. Chase lunged forward in an attempt to tackle the man, but he didn't feel the impact of his body connecting with the man. Instead, he landed face first in the mud, the wind knocked out of him as he slammed into the earth.

He turned over and looked in horror as the man, unfazed by Chase's attempt, drove the blade deep into the woman's chest. She reached up towards him, uttering something incoherently, then she slumped backwards into the mud lifeless.

Chase realized two things as he watched her die.

The first was that the man had his hair, his body, but his face was blurred. Who was he? He felt as though he knew the man. But where? Who could this be?

The second was that he couldn't do anything. His attempt to stop what was transpiring was futile. This had to be a dream. Or was this a premonition? Something yet to happen?

His mind was racing as the man turned to him.
A bright flash of light from a lightning bolt in the sky, caused Chase to raise his arms in defense. When he lowered his hands,

the dreaded man had a different appearance.

He had eyes now, red and burning, with black armor. His sword and parts of his arms were drenched in blood as he took slow, powerful steps towards Chase.

"Chase!" He heard a voice cry from behind. He looked back to see Isobel, armor worn and destroyed, reaching for him a couple feet away.

Then he felt the pain, something penetrating his sternum. He looked back towards the man, to see he had lodged his blade deep into Chase.

Chase gasped in pain and tried to push the sword back, but it was no use. He was done.

Chase felt himself losing consciousness, and his vision was slowly fading to black. He felt the darkness consume him and take him deep into its heart.

"Chase!" Isobel called again. This time she seemed so far away, almost as though she was trapped behind a wall.

He wanted to call back, but he didn't have the strength.

"Chase!" Isobel called again. This time she was closer, like she was pushing through the darkness to him. The world was shaking now. He could feel it in the calm darkness, but his eyes wouldn't open.

Then the shaking became more violent.

"Chase!" Isobel called a third time. His eyes flung open, letting all the light in. He felt her holding him as he fought to sit upright, tears burning his eyes. The nightmare had ended.

*　　　*　　　*

Isobel

Peace and tranquility. These were the only emotions that Isobel could feel while her friend lay motionless on the earth, fairies tirelessly at work to mend his injuries.

They were in the heart of the mystical sanctuary, surrounded by blue flora and white trees of an otherworldly nature. A brisk chill filled the air as the sun began to recede behind the horizon. The white aura of the largest tree created a small mist around it and covered most of the small plant life.

"This tree acts as a gateway, of sorts, to the greater gods." Drakonis explained, leaning against the tree. "It has stood here, against the test of time, for many millennia as the first true wonder of the world."

Isobel took a seat on one of the large roots right next to him. She was winded from her fight with the wolfkin, and the deficit of furniture had limited her resting options.

"And what species of beastkin are these... Fairies?" Isobel asked.

"No." Drakonis replied, wagging his finger through the air. "Not beastkin. They are The Fae. They are the protectors of the tree, and oracles of fate and time. They may seem like tiny beastkin now, but they have untold magical ability. A single Fae could cause much trouble for both of our armies. That is, if they actually cared for the wars of lesser gods."

"What? Do they not desire conflict and conquest like the rest of your kind?" Isobel said, inflecting her words with a bit of sarcasm towards the dragonkin.

Drakonis shook his head.

"Believe it or not, not all of those that reside behind the walls of Zhalesh are bloodthirsty warlords." Drakonis said, his eyes glimmering with a sadness Isobel hadn't seen before. "We chose D'Merrion because he chose us. He has never abandoned his people or his cause. Those that choose The One True God are embraced like lost brothers. They are not discriminated against or segregated. He is a merciful and benevolent ruler."

Isobel scoffed a bit and then looked away. The sun was almost gone over the horizon, and the wind had picked up a bit, rustling the leaves of the tree.

"Benevolent?" She said sourly as she turned back to face him. "Is that what we're calling that savage beating he gave us? Merciful? How he orders every village his armies come across to burn in his name?"

"That is the way of war." Drakonis replied.

Isobel knew that, but she hated hearing similar anecdotes from her enemies. They were not the same. They couldn't be. She had spent a lifetime desensitizing her empathy for warriors that opposed the Divines and humanity. Yet, they all seemed so human, more than she would admit openly. For some reason, she was having a particularly hard time hiding her sympathy for them.

"I do not take pleasure in the ugliness of war." Drakonis said somberly. "But war is where I thrive. I was born for combat, and as long as I serve D'Merrion..."

Drakonis took a deep breath and ceased talking for a moment, looking away from Isobel. She noticed the sun always had a habit of hitting his face perfectly, lighting his most attractive features. Or maybe he just had more perfect angles that she loved to look at him from.

Isobel then widened her eyes.

What was that? She thought. Loved to look at him from? What kind of thoughts were these? She knew she had to win his trust somehow, but was she unconsciously drawn to him? She looked up and noticed Drakonis looking back at her again.

"The tree has a very calming aura that I am sure you have noticed." Drakonis began. "It stills the storms in men's hearts and uncovers their true desires, bringing them to the surface. Or at least, that's how Grandfather describes it. You cannot lie to the tree. Or the Fae."

She didn't like the sound of that. He knew of her pact

with the dragon, but she had to keep the details of that pact a secret. Or suffer catastrophic consequences.

One of the small Fae hovered over to them, pointing to Chase. Isobel stood up and walked over to him. His wounds were healed, and he seemed in good health.

She was exceptionally glad. He was a demigod so the wounds he received wouldn't have killed him, but she never liked seeing her friends be injured.

Isobel felt a hand on her shoulder and turned to see a large ethereal like individual. It was like she was staring at a ghost or the outline of a person. She turned around and looked at Drakonis, but he just stared at her.

"We are the only ones here, young Isobel." The being behind her said. "This moment exists within one second of your conceivable timeline."

Drakonis still didn't move, confirmation that the being was not lying. Isobel quickly turned back to the being and stood up to face it.

"What... are you?" Isobel asked, backing away from it.

"Do not fear me, child." The Fae said, raising his hand to her. "We are Fae. We do not place worth in titles or monikers. But you can pronounce me, Fae, if that would please you. Please. Come closer."

Isobel untensed her shoulders. She couldn't maintain her apprehension for too long, the tree still calmed her nerves.

She sensed no ill-will from the Fae. She slowly walked up to be near it.

"Your trust is well-placed." The Fae assured her, reaching his hand out to her. "Please take my hand."

"Before I do, why have you reached out to me?" Isobel asked, still unsure of the consequences of this meeting.

"We, The Fae, exist above the call of this realm or any realm." It said lowering its hand. "We are one and many, and we answer only to the greater gods numbered in three. The Fae are messengers between worlds, oracles of time and space. We exist in the past, present and future. Our existence is based within our mission of maintaining order and balance in every instance of reality. When that balance is threatened, we have been tasked by the gods above gods to correct the anomalies. To receive personal audience with the Fae is no small occurrence, we do not waste our energy on meaningless visitation."

Isobel didn't know how to respond. She felt like she should be overwhelmed, but her heart was at ease. Its monologue didn't exactly answer her question. Actually, as usual, she had more questions than she cared to ask.

The Fae reached his hand out again.

"Please take my hand, child." Fae instructed. "I know you have many questions, but I cannot answer them at this time."

Isobel stared at his hand a bit, then took it confidently. She wasn't in a position to argue. They stood there; their hands joined for a moment. Then the Fae released his grasp.

“It is done.” It replied. “We know of your bondage and your plight. We have seen how it all unfolds. Hold dear to your resolve child, and you shall receive true resolution.”

The Fae waved his hands and then faded away before her eyes. Isobel stood there motionless.

“I see the Fae have gifted you a visit.” Drakonis said from behind her, a little closer than she expected. “It would be wise to not divulge what transpired. The Fae are more powerful than you or I could ever imagine.”

Isobel turned and looked at the dragonkin, his silver eyes now illuminated by the light of the setting sun. She took a step back.

“How could you tell?” She asked, sure he was frozen during the visit.

“You're completely healed, and you went from sitting to standing in less than a second.” He told her as he picked up Chase. “Since you both have recovered from your ordeal with my dim-witted subordinate, I guess we can conclude today’s activities.”

Drakonis began to walk towards a small entrance that led back to the royal quarter.

Isobel stood still for a bit. Drakonis continued to walk.

"Are you not ordering me to follow you?" She asked, still slightly confused by her oppressor's actions.

Drakonis stopped a few feet from the door. He turned and looked at her, his expression going from stoic and collected to sincere and playful.

"You can try to escape." He said calmly with a smirk. "But I don't think you're the kind of person to leave her friend behind. Plus, it would wound me to toss you back into the muck of the dungeons when you could have a nice bed here."

He was smiling and having a jest. Her sworn enemy was smiling at her, not with a smug look but with content happiness. Or maybe he was simply trying to be hospitable. He was making it too easy to get close to him. She wasn't complaining but it felt... wrong somehow.

His actions confused her. His body language and demeanor didn't give up any answers either. Since arriving in the capital, she never sensed any malice from Drakonis. Even when he threatened them. His aura was never malevolent. Why?

"I can see you're still processing my actions." Drakonis said, completely turning to face her. "I told you. While the mark does restrict your actions, it is not the reason I have confidence against complicit behavior. Your hearts are what give me ease."

He then turned to continue walking towards the door.

How could he turn his back on her so confidently? How could he trust so willingly? She felt at ease by his words, but it wasn't her will; it was the tree and its stupid aura! She felt the flames of rage burn in her heart, her calm, collected spirit beginning to ignite

"We are not allies, Drakonis!" Isobel yelled at him. "I could kill you while you sleep"

"You won't." Drakonis yelled over his shoulder.

"We could escape in the middle of the night, be gone before anyone would notice." She continued. "Maybe assassinate all of the generals in the night. Go on a complete rampage."

"Not really a smart idea, seeing as we have beaten you back before." Drakonis said, stopping for a second. "But you won't do that. Because your heart won't allow it. Divine Knights are honor driven. Despicable, underhanded tactics like that are beneath you."

"I really could kill you." Isobel said, her expression becoming darker. "And you would deserve it, for all the cowardice and evil you have committed in your lord's name."

Drakonis stood still for a moment, facing away from her. Then he walked through the doorway, out of sight into the hallway.

It was hard for Isobel to keep herself in the mood to be angry, due in part to the tree that calmed all who walked near it. She wanted to be mad. How dare he walk around with such a smug face, in control and powerful, like he knew who they were.

She wanted to stay infuriated, but the tree's aura calmed her spirit. She sighed in response. Being mad wasn't going to get them anywhere. She was annoyed he had gotten under her skin the way he had. He did have control over them, but he didn't have to be so cocky about it.

She looked towards the door and walked towards it. Hopefully, Chase would wake up soon. She was tired of looking at Drakonis.

Chapter 7:
Consequence

Drakonis

Drakonis dropped the knight down on the sofa. He was tired of carrying the man, and he still had much to do before night was done. He positioned himself against the counter of the kitchen, giving Isobel a chance to look her friend over.

"He should be returning to consciousness soon." Drakonis said to her, reaching for a glass that lay on the counter. "I'll leave you both to rest for the night. When I return in the morning, it will be to train your colleague for the battles ahead."

Drakonis filled the glass with water and drank it quickly. After finishing it, he walked towards the door.

"Wait." Isobel said, standing up.

"Ha." Drakonis scoffed, turning to look at her. "How brazen are you to order me, your sovereign, to do anything. What do you want?"

"Why?" Isobel asked, her face stern. "Why are you doing this? Why have you brought us here? Why have you kept us alive, fed us, given us sanctuary? What do you gain? Why have you done any of this?"

Drakonis chuckled lightly to himself and turned back around, looking her in her eyes.

"One day, I will be able to answer that and all your questions." He began, his voice low but still confident. "But the answer for today is because I can. We all have a role to play and a story to fulfill. Do your best to follow The Fae's orders, and things may work out for us."

Without delay, Drakonis turned around and exited the room. There was a visit that needed to be made to ensure his plans didn't fail. A certain wolf needed to be put in his place.

He made his way to the front of the palace, making sure to avoid most of the servants that populated the keep. He didn't want any interruptions or for them to be involved with his personal matters.

When he reached the main gate, he used his draconic eyes to sense out the wolf's aura. Nothing...

"Where are you, Ashnel?" Drakonis muttered to himself. "Give me a sign... I know you do not want to evoke the Rule of the Wilds. Where are you hiding, mutt?"

Almost on cue, a small aura sparked for a moment in the marketplace quarter, almost a mile from Drakonis.

"Found you." Drakonis said, jumping over the gate towards the spark.

* * *

Chase

Chase sat up gasping for air, sweat dotting his brow. Isobel was holding him closely, trying to console him.

He was breathing heavily and was coming to terms with his environment. Where had he been? Grey dusty battlefield? Home? That weird garden? He could feel Isobel grab his face. He realized that he had been muttering to himself, saying his thoughts aloud.

“Chase...?” Isobel said, holding him still. “It's okay now, you're fine now.”

“Wh-Where am I?” Chase questioned. He needed to be anchored. Everything felt unreal. Almost like a lie, or fake in some way. He rubbed his face to clear the tears from his eyes.

“We are back in the Royal Quarter.” She spoke. “You're in one of the beds of the suite. I moved you after we returned. You weren't severely injured, but Drakonis saw to it that we were properly healed after our fight with the wolfkin.”

“The wolf!” Chase yelled as he jumped up from the bed. “What happened to the kids!?”

He was staring at Isobel intensely. She was wide-eyed in surprise. Hopefully, he hadn't failed the kids as well.

Isobel looked away from him, her eyes hitting the floor. He felt his personal pit of dread build in his chest.

She then pointed to the foot of the bed. Chase's eyes jerked toward where her hand pointed. At the base of the bed, three small round heads sat staring back at him, obscured by the railing of the bed.

He looked back at Isobel, who now had a sly smile on her face.

“Not funny, Isobel.” He sneered.

The kids then jumped onto the black bed sheets, extremely excited.

“You're finally awake!” Mahogany said. “That was really cool how you hit Ashnel!”

Dior and Semaj nodded in agreement.

Chase could see the excitement brewing especially in young Semaj. He looked like he was about to burst.

“YOU ARE SO COOL!” The boy screamed. “The way you went ZOOM! Then you had all those blue lights around you and then you kicked him! And then... And then...”

The boy stopped, noticing everyone was looking at him. This was the complete opposite of his dissented and disinterested demeanor from earlier that day, Chase noted.

“I mean... You were cool.” Semaj said calmly, sticking his hands in his pockets.

“No one was hurt, right?” Chase said, looking back at Isobel. “We all seem healthy.”

“No more than you were.” She confirmed. “And don't

worry, they already badgered me to death as well."

Chase felt relieved as Isobel stood up.

"Okay guys." She addressed them. "I told you that I would allow you to stay only until he awoke. Now it's time to go!"

There was a chorus of "Awwws" that erupted from the children, but they stood and began to leave the room. Dior lagged behind a bit. As she was leaving the room, she turned to the knights.

"Thank you for protecting my friends and me." She said, bowing and then closing the door to the room.

"Cute kids." Chase remarked. "This place is some and none of what I expected it to be. It almost reminds me of home."

Chase felt Isobel's hand on his. He looked up at her, her eyes filled with concern.

"You were crying, Chase." Isobel said. "Was it the dream again?"

"No." He responded, looking away. "This one was different, more real than any of the others."

"Tell me." She said.

Chase looked back at her, a lump forming in his throat as he relived the nightmare.

"I was alone and yet surrounded." He began. "There was fighting. The booms of armaments and cannon fire. I was fighting for my life. Everett was there. You... weren't."

Isobel nodded as she listened to his story.

"But then I wasn't fighting anymore." He went on. "There was a man. Strong and loud. He was a Divine Knight, and the others had surrounded him. He fought against them. I can't remember the words. I am who I am maybe? He fought them and killed some of them. Are these memories? Or maybe a premonition?"

Chase looked towards Isobel, hoping to gain some sort of insight from her reaction. Maybe she could make sense of the cloud of confusion in his heart. Her face was blank, but she looked to be thinking.

"I don't know." Isobel finally said. "It could be just a dream. Or maybe it is a Divine premonition. And the events you describe don't seem too familiar. We should see the Divines when we return home."

Chase felt at ease by her words. She was right. It was just a dream, and the Divines would be able to alleviate any confusion that he may have. They always had.

Chase looked around the room. The same old, facetious furniture with D'Merrion insignias all over. Ugh. He was never going to get over how ugly this palace was.

Isobel stood up.

"You should get some rest, Chase." Isobel said, making her way for the exit. "I know you just got up, but you need to get as much rest as you can for tomorrow."

"Yeah..." Chase responded with disdain. "Drakonis' special training. Thank you, Isobel. We'll talk more tomorrow."

She turned and exited from the room, closing the door behind her.

Chase took a huge breath and laid back on the bed. These dreams were getting increasingly vivid. They had to mean something... He just couldn't figure out what. He laid over in the bed. He resigned himself to rest. Maybe the dreams would make more sense in the morning.

* * *

Ashnel

Ashnel couldn't believe that the humans had survived. Just a few more minutes was all he needed to eliminate them.

He had walked down to the marketplace quarters to lick his wounds. The market was dark now, and many vendors were picking up their tents. He didn't want anyone to see him in his sorry state, and he needed a few moments to heal his wounds. If the whelps in the barracks saw him, they might try to test the Rule of the Wilds. Ashnel was confident that he could eliminate any of the barracks combatants, but he was not willing to lose underlings to ignorance.

He walked into a small alleyway behind one of the market buildings and sat next to a small abandoned wooden booth. There was a set of palettes, moldy and forgotten, next to it. It would make a perfect chair while he recovered.

As he sat down, he reached up and felt his head. His head was throbbing from the blows he had been dealt today, and welts had begun to bulge on his forehead. The knights were stronger than he thought, and had he not braced for some of their attacks, he certainly would have been knocked unconsciousness. He would be ready next time though; they would not surprise him again.

Ashnel began to softly chant a healing incantation he had learned, a secret gift from one of his subordinates. They weren't happy about it at first, but they were eager to be of service to him once he withdrew his scythe. He could be quite 'persuasive' when he wanted to be.

"Gro. Mend." he said, closing his eyes and resting his elbow in the window of the booth. Today was more stressful than he had anticipated, but at least he would be able to heal and come back stronger tomorrow.

He closed his eyes and felt the soft sensations of the healing magics as they continued their work. A loud boom rang out from in front of him, sending debris up into the air.

Ashnel, surprised, threw his hands up to shield his eyes from the blast of sand and dirt that flew his way. He could not make out what or who had caused the impact.

"So I see that an old dog can learn new tricks." A voice said from the smoke, and destruction. "A healing incantation AND disobedience, Ashnel? You never cease to surprise me!"

Ashnel's eyes grew wide as he realized who beckoned from the smoke. He leapt down off the boxes to bend his knee towards his superior.

Drakonis.

"Rise, Ashnel." Drakonis said, the dust dissipating enough to make out his face and torso. "Meet me eye to eye."

Ashnel stood up to face his fate, looking the young dragonkin in his glowing green eyes. Drakonis was making a face that Ashnel hadn't seen in a long time, one distorted by anger and rage.

"My Lo-" Ashnel began.

Drakonis grabbed Ashnel by the snout and rammed his hand into the wolfkin's chest, sending him flying through the wall of the building. Ashnel smashed through store shelves and non-perishables before coming to rest in the center of the building. He was dazed but tried to focus his thoughts to make some plan of escape.

He couldn't beat Drakonis. That much was readily apparent, especially not when he was in such ragged shape. The store was dark and filled with aisles of bread and frozen produce. Maybe he could appeal to the lord? He would have to come up with a plan soon or Drakonis would end his life tonight.

Drakonis stepped over the rubble, his cape lightly gliding behind him, and walked over to the fallen beastkin. His eyes illuminated his face, his scowl brightened by their green radiance.

“Have I not given you a modest life, Ashnel?” Drakonis said in a soft, menacing voice. “A position of respect and power? Allowed you to behave and revel in almost any manner you saw fit? Given you endless battlefields to fight on and adversaries to wet your blade with? Why do you plot against me, Ashnel?”

“My Lo-” Ashnel tried to start again. As soon as he spoke, Drakonis dropped his heel on Ashnel's chest. The wolfkin grunted loudly, a bit of blood spilling from his lips.

“Did I say speak?” Drakonis questioned. “You seem to have forgotten who is master and who is subordinate. Worry not, for I do enjoy a good lecture.”

“My Lord!” Ashnel yelped out from under Drakonis' foot.

Drakonis let out a deep sigh, removing his foot from the wolfkin. He crouched down next to him, eliminating the space between them.

“What, mutt?” Drakonis said, the words emotionless and biting.

"I was doing you a favor!" Ashnel spat. "You brought the Divine dogs to the heart of our home and treated them as kin! They stay in luxury, wearing the finest of Zhaleshian garments! This goes against the decree and his testament!"

Drakonis stared at the Ashnel for a few moments. He then rose back up to his feet and turned away from the wolfkin.

"You know not of God King D'Merrion's plans." Drakonis said, his voice slowly rising in volume as he spoke. "Do not act as though you perceive the word and presume to dictate it to me! I am the right hand of The One True God, his greatest warrior and confidante! I am second in power only to Azzaria, the high dragon and Queen of Zhalesh. All my actions have been to perpetuate his rule and extend his light to those misguided by the Nine Divines."

Ashnel coughed again, blood escaping with every breath of air he choked up. He was in bad shape. He tried to move, but his limbs could generate no will, a side effect of the wolfkin battle trance. While most of his senses were fading, his sense of smell was still sharp enough to sense it. A scent he had become familiar with, one he could pinpoint from a mile away... Fear.

"You plot against our God, Drakonis!" Ashnel shot at him. "You speak of loyalty and yet you bring rodents to our home! You poison the marrow of our city with their presence. I noticed your changes since your last visit to The Fae!

D'Merrion demands our enemies be razed to the ground, and yet you offer mercy and sanctuary to our enemies!"

Ashnel had no intention of escaping anymore. His only objective was to make Drakonis see reason, to denounce his allegiance to the worthless human louts. He couldn't muster the strength to fight or run.

"I told you, Ashnel." Drakonis boomed as he turned back to look at the wolfkin. "They are a part of D'Merrion's plans. Your petulant meddling will only end in your demise. That is your warning, Ashnel. Be a good dog and do not bite the hand that feeds you."

Drakonis stared at the downed beastkin for a moment. He then turned to walk back through the hole he had created.

Ashnel felt a slight chuckle escape his lips. He began to laugh lightly then loudly at the lord as he walked away.

"What could you possibly be laughing about, Ashnel?" Drakonis yelled back, turning to face him.

Ashnel kept laughing, becoming overjoyed with himself.

"The 'old' Drakonis would have killed me where I stood for insubordination." The wolfkin cackled, his voice sinister and low. "Deceit doesn't suit you my lord, and you'll pay for your transgressions. That is assured...."

"Foolish." Drakonis said, the word drenched in sadness.

Drakonis then waved his hand through the air and

walked away. Ashnel tried to move again, but to no avail.

He managed to live, he thought. Drakonis had become weak. He was changed by the Fae and he even plotted against their god. And now he threatened Ashnel, trying to swear him to secrecy.

Ashnel sighed softly, looking up at the ceiling. Drakonis would pay for this humiliation and his arrogance. Ashnel would see to it.

He heard a crackle from in front of him and redirected his eyes towards the noise. A red fissure had formed near the hole in the wall, building in power. A bead of sweat formed on his head.

"Oh no." Ashnel said. The fissure then erupted forward, exploding inside of the store.

Chapter 8:
It Begins

Chase

Chase sleepily rubbed his eyes as the sun peered through his window. It seemed to be around noon, the sun was close to its highest point.

He lifted his arms and yawned, groaning as he pulled himself from the bed. It had been a while since he had slept so soundly; dirty cots and rocky grass patches his usual spots for rest. He had become accustomed to the hardships of knighthood, but he couldn't deny the appeal of the royal living arrangements.

It was especially startling because only hours before, he had experienced one of the worst nightmares he'd had in a long time.

He readily put on one of the royal outfits that had been provided to him. They were itchy, and honestly really uncomfortable but it was all he had. Someone had taken his armor, much to his chagrin, but it wasn't worth much in its current state.

As he was getting dressed, he could hear conversation in the other room. It sounded like Isobel and some younger voices.

"Guess we made a good first impression." Chase said to himself. "I should join them in a bit."

He finished buttoning up his shirt and ruffling his hair to get its usual unruly look.

He opened the door to his room and saw Isobel sitting on the couch, the children playing around in the living area. Everyone turned to look at him, smiles on their faces, but Semaj's smile was the largest as Chase entered the room.

"Chase!" He shouted from the other side of the room. He ran towards the man, brimming with excitement.

"It's Knight Chase, SEMAJ!" Mahogany yelled as he ran past her. "Acknowledge their titles. You HAVE to practice that if you're going to be King Maj one day!"

Semaj turned and made a gesture that Chase couldn't see before continuing to run up to him.

"We were waiting for you to wake up!" Semaj said. "You sure must've been tired. That fight had to have taken a lot out of you! You also flew out a window and lived! You're really tough, you know that?"

"Woah kid." Chase said, putting his hands up to calm the boy. "I have only just awoken, and I need time to get my bearings. Why is everyone up so early?"

Isobel laughed softly.

"They arrived only a few minutes ago." She said as she

repositioned herself on the couch. “Drakonis sent them to retrieve you, but I don't think they needed much convincing to come and see you. They have been talking my ears off about yesterday. I think you have some new fans.”

Chase made a face, grabbing his chin. He couldn't hide his smile as he flexed his biceps.

“Well, I am pretty awesome.” Chase bellowed confidently. “That big, bad wolf didn't know what hit him!”

“Okay, Schwarzenegger.” Isobel sighed, rolling her eyes at him. “You should take a couple of moments to be mentally prepared. Who knows what Drakonis has in store for you?”

“Ahhh, I'll be fine!” Chase reassured her. “I am the most persistent and toughest knight the Academy has ever produced. I'll be more than fine.”

“If you say so.” Isobel shrugged.

“What will you do while I'm gone?” Chase asked her as he walked to take a seat in one of the chairs, Semaj following closely behind him.

“We have many errands we need to run today.” Mahogany chimed in. “Drakonis has asked her to accompany us today. She is going to be our chaperone.”

Simple shopping in the market, Chase thought. Hardly seemed fair, but they had little to no control over their days now that they were slaves to the Drakonis.

"Then I hope you have fun." Chase said, smiling at the children.

"Finally!" Semaj yelled, skipping over to the door. "We should leave now, or the marketplace is going to be crowded! It's hard to move when all the beastkin start bidding!"

Semaj then bolted out of the room, not waiting for anyone to respond to him. Mahogany and Dior rolled their eyes. They both stood up and made their way towards the door.

"Knight Isobel." Mahogany said as she turned back to the knights. "We will wait for you both in the lobby. We are in no rush, but please do not delay."

She bowed to them and then turned to walk away. Dior waved at them, then closed the door behind her.

"This feels like a bad dream." Chase said as the door closed. "A couple of days ago, we were in the trenches, fighting for what we believed. We watched over our brothers and sisters, routing D'Merrion's forces when we could. Now we're in the belly of the beast, lounging in the royal quarter of D'Merrion's palace. We sleep in the same beds as our enemies, and honestly, we've even befriended some of them.

Isobel had a surprised look on her face, that soon brandished a sad smile in reception to his words.

"Yeah." She replied. "I thought the same when we arrived, but I believe there is a reason we are here. As much as I hate D'Merrion, there is something I can't understand. How could a god so violent and ruthless reign over a land with such peace? How was he able to unite the beastkin and humans under one banner without any in-fighting?"

Chase gave her a puzzled look.

"Who said there wasn't any infighting?" He said sternly.

"No one, but you can't deny the evidence." She replied.

He could understand her curiosity. They had been there for two days, and they had learned so much about the beastmen capitol. Chase still very much wanted to destroy D'Merrion and Drakonis, but it wasn't hard to become empathetic to the plight of the people who lived there. They resembled the people the Divine Knights strove to protect.

Isobel stood and stretched a bit, sighing in relief. She had a different outfit than the one she had worn yesterday. Chase assumed it had been destroyed in the scuffle with the wolf, but it reminded him that she had taken care of him when he recovered.

"Chase..." Isobel began, her voice low and soft. "I understand all too well what the war with D'Merrion has cost us, but we have always been fighting a losing battle. The one opportunity we have NEVER had was candid intel on our opposition. This is a chance we cannot pass up."

She walked around the table, approaching Chase, prompting him to get up as well.

"As much as I hate to admit it, you're right." Chase said

standing up. "We will win this war, and then we'll focus on you. You are my only family, and I will work tirelessly to nullify your pact."

"I appreciate the words, Chase." She sighed. "But we can never forget about the reason we joined the Divine Knights. To do good. To defend those that cannot defend themselves and rid the world of D'Merrion's evil."

She put her hand on Chase's shoulder, looking at him with that motherly look that all of the Divine Knights fell in love with.

"I want to see what the city is like, to be around the people, and maybe learn more about them." Isobel began. "I want peace for all of us. When this war is over and we beat D'Merrion, I want us to never have to fight again. We need to learn how humans and beastkin co-exist without conflict, even if it means having to cooperate with Drakonis."

Chase grinded his teeth a bit at the sound of that. He loathed the beastmen, and the generals that commanded them. He wasn't completely under the control of the mark, but he knew that disobedience would be met with swift annihilation. That was a fact he hated but had to accept.

"I know that you speak the truth." Chase spat through his teeth. "But I wish you didn't look so content with the notion. He is still the enemy."

"Yes, he is." Isobel replied. "But according to the other,

we may be able to earn his trust. We could do so much good for the world if a warrior like Drako-"

Chase put his hand up to halt her words. No, he thought. He wasn't ready to even consider this route.

He quickly turned towards the door, trying his best to hide his annoyance from her.

She always had the best of intentions, willing to dream big and hope to save everyone, putting the world before herself and thinking about the future. It was something he always admired and hated about her. It was the reason he always wanted to help her.

"We shouldn't keep our attendants waiting." Chase said as he gestured towards the door. "We'll talk more later, I promise. I just can't handle the thought of even considering that low life an ally. Let's go."

Chase opened the door to the hallway and left swiftly before Isobel could try to convince him. He already had to deal with being his pupil, but being his ALLY? Highly unlikely and not a thought he even wanted to entertain.

* * *

Isobel

The palace was just as still and organized as it was the day they had arrived. Isobel was almost surprised that they were never jeered or hassled in its wall.

The group was walking through a section of the palace that the knights hadn't seen before, enjoying a conversation about the different shenanigans the kids loved in the palace.

"That seems kind of mean-spirited, Dior." Isobel said trying to hide her amusement with their mischief. "And they never go looking for the eggs?"

Semaj jumped in front of the group, particularly proud about this prank.

"NEVER!" Semaj said happily. "Cockatrices are always angry, so no one cares about them. And their eggs smell AWFUL!"

"Yeah..." Mahogany and Dior said in unison.

"Jinx, you owe me some lemon juice!" Dior said with excitement while Mahogany fumbled with her words. "HA, HA, GOT YOU!"

Mahogany began to pout heavily.

"No fair!" She blurted, crossing her arms.

Isobel exchanged a glance with Chase, laughing with the children as they walked. They reminded her of their youth, before they joined the Knights. When they were carefree and without responsibility.

Mahogany stopped abruptly in front of a large door with two large beastkin standing guard with giant halberds in their hands. They sat in the cool shade of the building, a small sliver of sunlight sneaking its way into the covered courtyard.

It had been a while since Isobel had seen such large creatures. She surmised that these HAD to be giants. She couldn't make out any more physical details due to the giant plate mail that they wore; their helmets completely covered their faces and left their identities to the imagination. The armor itself had no dents or damage. One could argue that they had never seen a day of battle or even a small skirmish. *Were they even awake*, Isobel thought to herself as Semaj approached the giant soldiers.

"Voar! Vexir!" The young boy proclaimed with a dignified manner Isobel wasn't aware the boy could project. "We're on strict orders to bring Chase and Isobel to Drakonis."

Isobel could hear Mahogany scoff, obviously annoyed with Semaj's continued objection to using their titles.

"KNIGHT CHASE AND KNIGHT ISOBEL, SEMAJ." Mahogany said sternly. Dior snickered under her breathe.

Semaj turned to look at the group, he had an embarrassed look on his face. He then coughed and looked back at the soldiers.

"Knight Chase and Knight Isobel, sirs." Semaj corrected himself. "Would you please allow us to pass through your checkpoint?"

One of the giants leaned down, onto one knee to speak to the young Maj prince.

"General Drakonis is currently speaking to Queen Azzaria, young lord." He whispered in his deep voice. "He has asked that they not be bothered while inside the War Room. I am sure you have urgent arrangements, but we are not permitted to let you inside."

"Oh Joy." Mahogany huffed. "Now we have to wait for D'Merrion knows how long."

"We apologize for the inconvenience, young ones." The second giant said, gesturing to the benched area in front of them. "It won't be too long now."

The young boy guided the knights to a nearby resting area, with small stone benches that sat underneath the sun's warmth.

"Hey." Chase exclaimed as he sat down, trying to get the attention of the young prince. "I know I have heard the name Azzaria before. Semaj, who is this, Azzaria?"

Semaj opened his mouth to answer but Dior immediately jumped in front of him.

There was a loud clang from the direction of the soldiers. They had readied their weapons as though they were going to charge.

"It is QUEEN AZZARRIA to you, welp!" One of the soldiers roared.

Then a terrifying pressure began to exude from the door. It was so strong, the soldiers were prompted to retake their positions, stand upright at the sides of the door. Isobel looked at the children and noticed each of them were still as stone, their eyes wide with either terror or anticipation.

The pressure persisted for only a few moments until it faded behind the door. Everyone in the courtyard let out a sigh of relief.

"Please, Knight Chase." Dior said, turning to Chase. "You may not care for beastkin, but titles are especially important in our culture. To not mention one's title is to spit on their career and their accolades. You may not know who she is, but it would be detrimental to your health not to acknowledge her title."

Chase nodded back at her in reply, although he seemed quite annoyed with her words.

"Now to explain." Dior said, whispering to the knights. "Queen Azzaria is the current wife of the One True God, D'Merrion. She is second only to God King D'Merrion but also the mother of Drakonis. All beastkin answer to her. She's currently unbeaten in mortal combat and D'Merrion's strongest warlord."

"I wasn't aware that D'Merr- God King D'Merrion..." Isobel said, struggling with the thought of respectfully acknowledging D'Merrion's status. She will never respect the fallen deity, but she didn't need unwarranted trouble. "I wasn't aware that he had taken a wife. How come we have never seen her before?"

The three children exchanged a look that veiled a hidden meaning, almost like they were speaking telepathically.

"Well..." Mahogany began. "The One True God has tasks and matters that only his Queen can settle. She is usually needed elsewhere."

Isobel was unsatisfied with that answer.

"You wouldn't happen to know what these "tasks and matters" are, would you?" Isobel said quizzically.

"Even if I did, I would not tell you." Mahogany said in a very pale tone. "You are our guests and while we may have no ill will towards you, you were once and may still be enemies of our God. You may inquire about our history and culture, but matters of state are off limits, Knight Isobel."

Mahogany then turned away from them, her shoulders slouched a bit. Isobel wasn't ready for the serious tone in Mahogany's voice. She could tell neither was Chase nor the other children. The group fell silent for a bit.

Semaj, sensing the energy in the area change, spoke up.

"All of that is boring anyway!" He said trying to lighten

the mood. “Have you guys played “Scissors, Paper, Rock” before? My dad taught me it a long time ago when we used to play.”

“I'll have you know.” Chase spoke up eagerly. “I was there when that game was made. I'm a three-time world champion!”

“NO WAY!” Semaj exclaimed, unable to hide his excitement.

Isobel was lost in her own thoughts, as Dior sat beside her sister trying to console her.

Azzaria. Who are you? Isobel thought. She knew she wasn't getting more answers from the children. Maybe she could squeeze some information out of Drakonis. She crossed her legs trying to get comfortable.

“Three-time world champion?” Isobel playfully mocked. “Let me show you a thing or two about this game!”

* * *

Drakonis

"Incompetent." A voice spat at Drakonis from across the room. "Absolutely pathetic."

He was in the center of the War Room, alongside the communications board. The room was filled with beastkin of all races, operating sending crystals that could communicate sensitive information to any officer of the beastkin army. Unlike the other areas of the palace, this room was not filled with vain effigies and regal cloth. The room was designed to be functional and optimal, the brightly lit rooms and the computers that lined the walls assisted to that effect.

At the back of the War Room sat a master shard, its crimson exterior adorned with magical runes as it sat inside of a golden circlet. It was dubbed "The Divine Conduit" and only God King D'Merrion and Queen Azzaria were allowed to ever operate it.

"It is not wise to zone out while I converse with you, Drakonis." The voice said, this time angrier than before. "You will lend me your senses, or I will take them from you."

"Apologies, Queen Azzaria." Drakonis said in a low tone. "The calibration seems to be in working condition and optimized for your use."

Drakonis had spent the past hour being berated by one

of the only people he couldn't assert his authority over. The Queen was taking time to re-evaluate some of the equipment, as well as scold Drakonis for his failures as of late. This wasn't an isolated incident, and it was one of the rituals that Drakonis would prefer to not keep practicing.

Azzaria walked down from the alter, the different shards illuminating her dragon scales. As she made her way down to Drakonis, many beastkin hustled to get out of her way.

“I will let you know when the calibrations are sufficient, lest we add this to your bloated list of failures.” Azzaria hissed from a few feet away. “I've known you to be a mediocre warrior at best, my son. How about we leave matters of sophistication to those qualified, hmm?”

Drakonis nodded and bowed his head. He could hear her feet pounding the ground as she stomped her way to him.

King Maj explained how useful the shard map and the Divine Conduit would be once they were operational. Most, if not all, of D’Merrion's generals were briefed on the capabilities of the shards. It would be able to communicate with any shard, no matter the distance. It even had the ability to communicate with shards in other dimensions, or realms.

The Queen didn't need Drakonis' help to calibrate or evaluate the shards at all, they had already done that. He knew his mother just used this as an excuse to summon and insult him when she had an opportunity. It was almost as if she reveled in his failures.

"Drakonis, raise your head." Azzaria commanded.

Drakonis did as he was told and lifted his eyes. He was met by eyes of sheer rage. Azzaria's eyes were smoldering amber braziers in her skull. He could tell... She was in a bad mood.

"Tell me." She began. "How is it a distinguished general of the One True God's army managed to get one of the last breathing dragons slaughtered by mere common folk?"

Drakonis stayed silent. He knew that silence was better than excuses when it came to Azzaria.

"It seems as though my confidence in your limited ability was greatly misplaced." Azzaria continued, pacing back and forth in front of the younger dragonkin. "If I were in the capitol, I would have wrung your neck for such a blunder. Be grateful. Not only because I am on assignment, but that father lived."

Drakonis nodded once more.

"Good." Azzaria said. "There will be consequences for your ill handled campaign in New York. I suggest you ready yourself for my return."

"Yes, Ma'am." Drakonis replied, silently accepting his fate.

There was a moment of silence as Drakonis awaited his mother's self-dismissal from their call.

"You don't have any questions for your mother, Drakonis?" Azzaria said, trying to sound hurt. "We haven't seen each other in almost eleven years. Has your love for me soured with time?"

"It has only been two years in this realm, Queen Azzaria." Drakonis said stalely.

"You have gall to correct me now, Drakonis?" Azzaria sneered. "I thought we already agreed, your acumen was for swinging swords wildly. I would watch my tone if I were you, child."

"Yes, My Queen." Drakonis replied again. He was beyond annoyed with her teasing and insults.

"I can see you have questions." Azzaria sighed. "Ask them. I have already grown bored of your presence."

"You left suddenly." Drakonis said. "Why has the One True God commanded you beyond the veil? Why has he prioritized the subjugation of other worlds when his nemesis lies in plain sight in this realm?"

"Watch your tongue." Azzaria hissed at him. "You speak travesty. You do not presume to know his plans."

She stared at him for a while, before taking a deep breath.

"If you must have some knowledge to ease your already overburdened mind, then allow me to give you some relief."

Azzaria began. “I have been stationed in the land of Agarion at the capital city of Arundi to seek the Divines. There is a chance that they have spread lies about D’Merrion and their whereabouts, and I have been tasked with finding the truth. Let The God King know that the Divine Conduit is fully functional and give him my report and regards.”

“Wait!” Drakonis yelled.

“Azzaria out.” Azzaria exclaimed before the shard shuddered and powered down. Her silhouette faded to nothing, and the shard went dark.

“Aargh!” Drakonis groaned. Annoyance. His mother always operated within her own rules and getting information out of her was never worth it. Her excuse for her departure didn’t even make sense! The Divines were in THIS realm. Why is she looking for them in other realms?

He rubbed his face in frustration and turned to see some of the beastkin looking at him, awaiting his commands. He took a moment to recollect himself.

“Soldiers.” Drakonis said, his voice booming, loud enough for all of them in the room to hear. “Congratulations on a job well done. It was almost as though she was here with us. Very amazing work. Be sure to send the Queen's report to The God King and make a copy of the report for the archives. Dismissed.”

“Yes, Drakonis!” The beastkin of the room replied

before shuffling back to work amongst the shards and computer screens.

Drakonis let out a deep sigh. If she were here, he thought, he would not be leaving with his sanity intact. Dealing with her was a chore in itself, but he was awfully glad for it to be behind him, for now.

Drakonis turned to open the large doors that belonged to the War Room. As the doors opened, he had to readjust his eyes to the outside. He was only a few steps out of the room when he heard his name.

"Drakonis!" A familiar voice yelled.

He'd almost forgot. There was a certain knight he needed to train.

Chapter 9:
Fights and Flights

Chase

Chase walked next to Isobel and the children, following behind the dark lord silently. Unlike their peaceful walk earlier, this one was more organized, and a bit stricter.

They were on their way to 'The Grindstone', a place where Chase was to be trained in beastmen combat. He was already uneasy about the training and didn't know what to expect.

As they passed a large lake, Semaj picked up his pace to walk alongside Drakonis.

“Drakonis.” Semaj said, tilting his head down shyly. “Did you perchance... Were you able to speak to my mother in the War Room?”

“No, young prince.” Drakonis replied. “She wasn't included in the call, and we had more pressing matters to attend to. But do not despair. When there is time, I will ask about her well-being.”

Semaj, obviously saddened by the news, slowed his pace to walk back amongst the group.

“It's not too far now.” Drakonis said, leading them towards a giant set of doors of a wooden fort.

The fort was surrounded by a deep moat, filled to the brim with all kinds of fish and beast vermin. They had to go through a gate that exited the city to reach it, and it was larger than Chase expected. He also happened to notice a small sign in the grass that read "Constitution Gardens." Much of the sign was eroded away from years of decline and neglect. He wondered what possibly could have been held in there in the years before the war.

Drakonis raised his hand and the doors of the fort groaned as they slowly opened.

"Woah!" The children gasped loudly. Chase even found himself marvel a bit at what they saw.

Drakonis turned to the group.

"This is where we part ways." Drakonis said sternly. "You remember your tasks in the market, correct?"

Like a chorus of busted brass instruments, the children groaned in response to his words. They wore their displeasure on their sleeves.

"We never get to go in!" Semaj yelled, obviously over excited about the complex and its contents.

"Take Isobel and handle your errands." Drakonis ordered, crossing his arms at the young prince. "You'll earn your chance to enter soon enough."

The children turned, disappointment forcing their feet to drag. Chase turned to look at Isobel.

"Good luck." She mouthed, as she turned to follow the children. They stayed on the path leading to the market and Chase turned to see Drakonis watching him.

"Follow me." Drakonis commanded. Chase could feel his mark glowing, and rather than make a fuss, he followed obediently.

As they entered through the large doors, Chase immediately noticed the many rows of beastmen archers firing into the archery targets. The arrows already in the targets were centered in the bullseyes. Chase was actually kind of impressed with their accuracy.

The organization of the camp was also resemblant of The Academy. There were many practice swords, runes, and dummies lined neatly along the walls of the fort. The ground was a bit overgrown and had a concrete path that ran down the middle. The path was slightly overrun with patches of grass, showing that the soldiers and trainees had not maintained its appearance. Many beastmen were hard at work, improving their craft, and sparring in different combat pits.

"This is The Grindstone." Drakonis said, raising his voice above the clatter of blades and grunts of the beastmen. "This is one of the strictest and most arduous training camps in all of D'Merrion's Kingdom. You and I will be spending quite a lot of time here."

Chase could see that his presence had already drawn

attention from the beastmen. They didn't stop what they were doing, but he was aware everyone was watching him intensely. Even the beastmen instructors were wary of him.

"Yay..." Chase replied dryly.

"Stop." Drakonis said, turning quickly to meet Chase's eyes.

Chase felt his mark compelling him to obey the command and stopped in his tracks.

Great, he thought. Another long-winded lecture about importance and respect. He really was growing tired of Drakonis' snobby, uptight personality.

"We have no time for your sarcasm." Drakonis said calmly, surprising Chase. "If you wish to survive The Crucible, you need to not only be the strongest combatant but the smartest combatant. These warriors risk everything in The Crucible. Name, title, clan, rank, all of it, to be in the tournament. They will be brutal, violent, and cunning in their attempts to sever your head."

Chase saw Drakonis' hand twitch and jumped back in reaction. Drakonis had his sword in hand, slicing the air. If Chase had been one second slower, his head would be rolling on the floor.

Chase could feel his neck burning again. He looked at Drakonis, the angriest he had been since being taken prisoner.

"Yes." Drakonis said. "You will need to always be on

your toes and be faster than the others. You passed the first test."

Drakonis sheathed his blade as he walked on the path again.

"Follow me." Drakonis commanded, not turning to confirm if his order was being heeded. Chase had no choice but to obey and follow his tormentor.

"You fiend." Chase said. "You're so full of yourself. What would you have done if I hadn't been able to dodge that attack?"

"Had you died from that." Drakonis replied. "Then you would be unworthy of the Divine Knight title and would have been of little worth to anyone's plans, let alone my own."

"And what are your plans?" Chase said, his voice becoming rigid. "For me, and for Isobel-?"

Drakonis raised his hand, signaling Chase to stop talking.

"A dog does not question its master." Drakonis said, still leading him. "You and Isobel will receive answers when I deign to do so. Now..."

Drakonis' words made Chase grit his teeth in rebellion. *You will get your day, Drakonis*, Chase thought to himself. *It's only a matter of time...*

Drakonis stopped walking in front of a giant pit of sand. Many beastmen were lined up along its edge. They were eager, almost expectant of something. The question was... why?

There was a bench at the end of the sandy bunker, one that Drakonis was making his way to. It held many different items on top of it, from swords to clothes, which seemed to be designed to aid in training. Much of the equipment seemed like lining for clothes, each with ropes to tighten around joints and the abdomen. A boar beastmen stood watch over the bench, and eyed Drakonis as he approached.

"Give him the runic garb and a runic sword as well." Drakonis commanded. "Make sure that it is tied as tight as possible."

"But sir-" The beastmen tried to reply, but he was interrupted by Drakonis grabbing him by the face. This, in turn, caused some of the beastmen to erupt with grunts.

"I did not ask for lip." Drakonis said slowly. "Do as I say."

Drakonis released the beastmen, and he stumbled backwards a bit. After regaining his senses, he gulped and then proceeded to gather the aforementioned items.

"Do you just enjoy bullying everyone you come across?" Chase said, making sure to imply he was still furious.

The boar beastmen snorted at Chase, starting to put the armor on him.

"Do not speak to the High General, welp." The beastmen grunted. "You are pathetic and serve lesser gods."

"I WAS DEFENDING YOU!" Chase yelled, pointing at the beastmen.

"ENOUGH!" Drakonis roared at the both of them. "We are not here to prattle on like housewives."

The beastmen stopped and nodded at Drakonis. He then continued to tie the garb and pants on Chase.

"Yell at me again..." Chase taunted. "Your spell won't stop me from coming for you. You already know your time is limited."

Drakonis ignored the jeers and began to remove his armor, his afro bursting from his helm.

"Getting naked for me too?" Chase continued. "I didn't know you cared for me-"

The beastmen tightened a loop tighter than he needed to, which made Chase grunt in response. Afterward, the beastmen jammed the sword into Chase's hand. He then turned to Drakonis and bowed.

"It is done." He spoke. He then rushed out of the pit to join the ranks of beastmen on the side.

There was a subtle rumbling of the ground. Chase looked around to see all the beastmen stomping their feet. They began to bark and howl, making all kinds of noise around him and Drakonis. He returned his eyes back to the dark lord.

"THIS…" Drakonis yelled at Chase. "IS THE PIT! THIS IS WHERE YOU WILL LEARN TO LIVE OR YOU

WILL DIE! HERE IS YOUR CHANCE, BOY! COME AT ME WITH THE INTENT TO KILL!"

Drakonis didn't have to tell him twice. Chase lunged forward with all his will and being, intent on stabbing the man through his heart.

"But first…" Drakonis said, raising his hand towards Chase. "To help you a bit."

Chase was about a foot away from Drakonis' chest when he felt himself become unbearably heavy. He slammed face first into the sand, filling his mouth to the brim with it. He sputtered and coughed a bit.

"What was that!?" Chase exclaimed, trying to lift his body. He was barely able to stand, and he started to sweat profusely.

"Just a bit of magic." Drakonis said nonchalantly.

Chase grunted and groaned as he tried to lift himself from the sand. Not only was his body heavy but his sword was just as heavy and even harder to wield.

"You're wearing weighted clothes." Drakonis taunted him. "I assumed someone as mighty as yourself had seen such equipment before. Maybe you're not as fierce or smart as you say."

The beastmen started to point and laugh. They stomped even louder than before, kicking up dirt all around them.

Chase felt his chest burning with rage. He was being

demeaned for their entertainment. This wasn't training, this was a spectacle.

"Graaaaaaaaah!" He roared, lifting himself up. He gripped the sword confidently, the veins in his forearm bulging as he grasped it with both of his hands.

"YOU'RE DEAD!" Chase yelled as he pulsed forward, completely covered in electricity. He held the sword high above his head, attempting to bring it down on the dark lord.

For a moment, they were eye to eye. Chase could see it in Drakonis' face. Chase was faster than Drakonis had expected. He screamed as he brought the blade down, sand kicking high into the air.

Chase was breathing heavily. He did it. He ended him. The dragonkin had underestimated him and paid for it dearly. Or at least that's what Chase thought for a second. He heard clapping coming from behind him.

"That's it." Drakonis applauded. "That's the ferocity that you'll need to live. That's the ferocity of the beastkin."

All the beastmen were now grunting, howling, and roaring at the battle. They couldn't contain their excitement.

"I let you attack first." Drakonis said, readying his blade. "Now... It is my turn."

Drakonis then appeared right in front of Chase, sword high above his head. Chase turned and took a defensive stance as best he could. That one strike greatly tired him out. He had let his emotions ruin his breathing and fatigued himself too soon.

Drakonis then began to savage Chase with blows.

* * *

Isobel

Isobel followed the children down the tattered path. They were surrounded by large bushes and trees filled with fruits and berries, and ruins of the Old-World as they made their way to the market. The sun was beating at their backs from its highest point, ready to begin its final descent for the day. The walk was peaceful and less tense than the authoritative march they endured with Drakonis, and they took it as an opportunity to enjoy themselves once again.

"Man!" Semaj said pouting, his hands drooped by his side. "We never get to see the inside of the barracks! But one day, I'll get in! Drakonis won't be able to deny me access forever!"

"Semaj..." Mahogany sighed. "There is a responsibility that comes-"

"Responsible blah, blah, bl-blah!" Semaj mocked. "Stop being such a stick in the mud. I just want to see the warriors spar and see how the soldiers train! You always want to bring up 'RESPONSIBILITIES', Maho."

"Don't call me that." Mahogany said far too quickly.

"Someone has to remind you, Semaj." Dior chimed in. "One day, you will surpass King Maj. You would do well to acknowledge and treat that honor with reverence."

"You too!?" Semaj shrieked comically, grasping his head.

Their repartee prompted a laugh from Isobel. She found their giddiness and exaggerated personalities very uplifting. The kids laughed in response to her.

"You're very amusing, Semaj." Isobel complimented. "I'm sure you will be a just king, one worthy of praise and the love of his subjects."

"Ah!" Semaj said raising one brow, and his face formed a very creepy smile. "Someone that recognizes how great I am! Don't worry, Knight Isobel. Keep your eyes on the shining jewel in front of you and you'll never be lost!"

Isobel rolled her eyes as Semaj turned, strutting out in front of everyone. He was obnoxiously guffawing, completely overjoyed with Isobel's acknowledgement.

He has much to learn, Isobel thought to herself, but he is a kind and gentle young man. Only time will tell whether these characteristics will mold him into a wise and noble king. Maybe, if fate persists, they won't find themselves on opposing sides of the war. Her heart ached at the revelation. If... When...

She returned to her people, these children would be her enemies... And as royalty, their deaths were almost certain.

Isobel shrugged off the gut-wrenching thoughts. Here and now was all she needed to worry about.

The group found themselves at a large gate at the end of the path, as big as the gate to the barracks. Two large beastkin, both clad in heavy plated armor with giant halberds in hand, stood watch over the door.

"Guards!" Semaj yelled confidently at the towering soldiers. "Let us through, post haste!"

Both of the soldiers snorted as they crossed their weapons over the door.

"Let you through?" The guard on the right snorted. "We should imprison you for your last escapade!"

"Let you through?" The left guard continued. "We should report your exploits to the King Maj and Lord D'Merrion!"

"Report me to my father and the One True God?" Semaj rebutted, unfazed by their threats. "Of what adventure could I, the humble Semaj, have engaged in to warrant such behavior?"

The guard on the right chuckled a bit.

"None that a wise warrior would ever speak of a young prince." The right responded, bowing his head.

"None that a loyal servant of the Maj's would ever

repeat, gracious prince." The second said, bowing his head. "Although I must warn you, my liege. Your entourage's recent... activities... were not well received. The butcher may seek reparations for that disaster."

"I am well-aware of my misconduct." Semaj replied. "Mahogany has made that painfully aware. I only seek passage for but a moment, so that I can receive wares that were purchased by my ente... intour...."

"Entourage, Semaj." Mahogany interjected. She then covered her mouth, as though she made some kind of folly.

"Apologies, young prince." Mahogany said, in a more reserved tone. "The word you seek... is entourage."

"Thank you, confidante Maho." Semaj said, giving her a broad smile.

"Don't call me that." Mahogany said, even quicker than last time.

Both of the guards replaced their halberds at their hips, standing high and alert. The guard on the right tapped the gate two times very loudly and it slowly crept open. The door moaned loudly as though it hadn't been opened in a thousand years.

"May your visit to our humble district proceed without encumbrance." The guard on the right said, sliding out of the way so the group could pass.

"May your errands in the market yield fortune, young

prince." The guard on the left said, elegantly sliding out of the way.

"And may you both have an uneventful shift today." Semaj said leading everyone inside. "Good day and praise the One True God."

Isobel was awestruck by the children. She had only really seen them in their playful manner. They were very mature for their age... When they wanted to be.

The gate slowly opened to reveal buildings made of brick and stone. Some of the buildings had obvious signs of decay, their walls were crumbling, and some vines were bursting from the recesses. There were tarps connecting every other building, creating makeshift shaded areas for the people to hide away from the elements. These buildings were far better than anything Isobel had ever lived in.

Men and women walked around, feet dragging as they lived their lives. Some others were hanging around in the tarped areas, just smoking Old-World cigarettes, sharing meaningful conversation, or overseeing some chores. Children covered in soot and dirt ran around chasing a basketball, playing to their hearts' content. A woman could be seen beating the dust from her rug, coughing as she though she had never breathed clean air in her life.

This was a surprise to Isobel. The quality of their homes was actually less than what she expected.

The human settlements were made from the desolate ruins of burned-out buildings and destroyed military compounds from the past. They lacked any kind of electricity now, but still provided some shelter. Anything greater than a hut or small cavern was noticed by the beastmen and razed to the ground. Her people were dirty and lacked many necessities such as food and water, a problem that left a schism between the different human tribes. But the beastkin and people here... They looked exactly the same as her people, just as dirty and just as downtrodden.

Isobel felt a tug at her pants leg and looked down to meet Mahogany's eyes.

"Is something the matter, Knight Isobel?" She said with concern in her eyes. "You have a very scary look on your face. Are you okay?"

Isobel looked around to see the other children staring at her. She had realized she had been frowning awfully hard and even had grimaced a bit in her moment to herself.

"No children." She said, taking a deep breath. "All is well. Just surprised is all..."

The children eased up a bit, looking at each other to confirm they were fine.

That's right, Isobel remembered. She was not home, and she was not amongst friends. She was a slave and she needed to keep her guard up.

“Now that you're done making that hideous face...” Semaj began. Isobel gave him a dry look in response, unamused by his joke.

“We can get back to the greatest city in the world!” Semaj continued, raising his hands in the air. “ZHALESH! There's always something to do in this town!”

“Voraken has boar fights and a traveling circus.” Dior said.

“Voraken!?” Semaj said, his face twisted in repulse at her statement. “Voraken is a war zone. An eyesore in comparison to the capitol, Dior.”

The two children started squabbling about which cities in the beastkin kingdom were better, speaking quickly and naming locations that Isobel had never heard of. The conversation was far too fast for her to follow really.

Luckily for Isobel, Mahogany stepped forward and put a hand on both of their shoulders.

“We have something we came here to do, do we not?” Mahogany said. “Maybe we should save debating for our free time?”

Semaj looked up at her, still worked up from the argument. He then turned away and began to walk down the dusty road. Mahogany sighed and then motioned for Isobel and Dior to follow him.

Semaj, whether he was aware of it or not, led the group

silently through the district. The citizens barely paid the group any mind, occupied by their day-to-day activities and the stress of life.

As they walked through the busy and dusty streets, Isobel could hear a soft rumbling coming from down the road. Shouting and animal noises were becoming more recognizable as they came closer to the end of the street. They stood at the edge of the street as carts rolled by carrying miscellaneous goods.

“Okay guys.” Semaj began. “We're almost at the market. Maho, don't embarrass me.”

“Don't call me that.” Mahogany said in an almost record-breaking pace.

“Dior and Isobel.” He went on, ignoring her. “Just stick by me, I know the area like the back of my hand!”

“We come here all the time with you, Semaj.” Dior chimed in. “If anything, we should be worried about yo-.”

“Shh, shh, shhhhhhhh!” Semaj replied, putting his finger up to his lip. “Hold your tongue for a second, Dior. I've got this. And I promise on the One True God... I will be on my best behavior.”

Semaj then trudged forward with a walk of confidence and dignity.

The two young girls exchanged a look that Isobel could only perceive to be disbelief and annoyance before they shrugged their shoulders and followed closely behind the young prince.

As they moved down the side of the road, the walkway became more and more crowded. Many beastmen of different origin populated the path. Isobel also noted that the quality of the buildings began to improve as they came closer to their destination. beastmen and humans alike shouted from their storefronts and booths, advertising their wares.

“Fresh fruits!” A lizardkin yelled from his wooden shack. “Dimaberries, and Lax Corns for sale. The best of quality available!”

“Fine clothes!” A man yelled. He had a fan blowing on him as he sat by his store. “Clothes of all kinds, available here!”

“Ah.” Semaj sighed, satisfied. “The market of the kingdom.”

The group walked past, ignoring the vendors, and stopped right next to a giant statue. A young beastkin, a small Fowlkin of some kind, stood with paper under his wings on a box next to the statue.

Isobel took a moment to look at the plaque that was at the foot of the statue. The message 'May the One True God guide all that stand in his visage and save all that avoid it' was carved into it.

Another self-righteous message, Isobel sighed to

herself. D'Merrion's constant desire to grandstand at every single corner of every single street was beginning to annoy her. She didn't bother looking up. She already knew it was some self-serving D'Merrion effigy that 'watched' over the market.

"News of the war front!" The Fowlkin yelled, loud enough to startle Isobel a bit. "Prince Drakonis subdues evil knights, whilst saving tortured, imprisoned beastkin from savage humans. Another strong victory for The One True God!"

This made Isobel turn her head. The citizens began to form around the crier, grabbing a copy as they walked by.

There were no prisoners, Isobel thought to herself. They were defending themselves and they weren't in the wrong. Is this what passes for new in the capital? Outright lies and propaganda. She had to tell them the truth.

She broke away suddenly from the kids, walking directly towards the crier.

"Hey Isobel!" One of the kids called after her. Isobel didn't hear them; she was dead set on correcting the beastkin.

She was around five feet away when a large beastkin jumped in front of her. He was a Tigerkin, and he wore a fine purple shirt, his chest partially exposed, and soft brown pants.

"Cutting in line?" He said quizzically, his arms crossed. His voice was deep, like a soft roar against the crowd. "I know the news is tantalizing, but don't you think you're a little 'too' excited?"

She looked up at him. He was almost three feet taller than her, and he seemed to be in shape.

"That information is wrong." She spoke. "It's not accurate."

"Huh?" The Tigerkin said in reply. "You're gonna have to speak up if you want to be heard. This is the market, after all!"

"THAT INFORMAT-" Isobel began to yell, before she was cut off by a small hand hitting her stomach.

Semaj jumped in front of her, followed by Dior and Mahogany standing behind him. Isobel could feel the girls pulling her away from the Tigerkin.

"Targus, my man!" Semaj spoke coolly. "We were just passing by. Nice article by the way!"

Isobel let herself be pulled away. She wanted to right the injustice, but she began to see her folly. She let her emotions escape her and was about to make a scene.

"One of your friends, I presume?" Targus said. "You always find a way to have the most beautiful women at your side! Being royalty does have its perks, I guess."

"Don't get too jealous of me, Targus." Semaj said jokingly. "I'm just well-liked is all. I'm showing my new friend around town, so I must be on my way."

"Well in that case, bring her by the office sometime!"

Targus laughed a bit. “Let me show her around and introduce her to the radiant charm of Targus!”

“Uhhh... Sure thing, Targus!” Semaj said, backing up from the Tigerkin. He then turned to meet with Isobel, Dior, and Mahogany. Targus turned and walked over to the crier, continuing to watch over the stand.

“That was close.” Semaj said, sighing loudly.

“Knight Isobel...” Mahogany said, a stern look brandishing her face. “That was extremely irresponsible. I know the news of the war may startle you, but should you create havoc within the capital by revealing who you are, we will not assist you. In fact, we would alert the guards to detain you.”

“Yeah.” Semaj said, a slightly guilty look now covering his face. “We know you're not here because you want to be. You are a prisoner, and you would do well to remember that you will be KILLED if you do not obey.”

Isobel took a deep breath and smiled.

“I'm sorry children,” she said softly. “I lost myself for a bit, but I am fine now. Your world... It is foreign to me. It honestly surprises me how different and yet so similar our people are. “

“Good.” Semaj said. “I would hate for my friend to meet a distasteful and avoidable end.”

He walked to her side and took her hand.

"I know this is overwhelming for you." Mahogany consoled her, taking her other hand. "But you have to remember that you are not the heroes here. Do not worry, we're almost at our destination. Please bear with us for a while longer."

Isobel knew the children weren't trying to threaten her with death and incarceration. They were warning her because they were worried about her.

"Yes." Isobel replied, trying to calm the storm in her heart. "Thank you, for coming to my rescue."

Semaj looked up at her, his face bore a smile that was larger than life.

"What honorable and noble prince wouldn't save a damsel in distress?" Semaj replied. "It was my honor... Knight Isobel."

"Well then." Isobel said. "Lead the way."

* * *

Isobel

"We'll take four please." Semaj said, his face bright with excitement. "Two vanilla and two Dimaberry, please."

They stopped at a wooden booth, and a silver wolfkin knelt behind it awaiting their order. The booth had the words "Ice Cream" in bright yellow letters at the top and had an otherworldly chill coming from inside the stand.

Isobel and the children had walked for some time through the crowded marketplace, avoiding the overcrowded areas altogether. They had to scale a large, open staircase just to reach that part of the district. They weren't as steep as the steps to the palace, but they still left the group a little fatigued.

Isobel was surprised at how huge the district actually was. The roads were so long it felt as though, if she kept walking, they would go on forever. She had seen all manner of stores, from mana guns and armor to masonry and relics, in the marketplace. No item was too dangerous or too taboo to sell here. She marveled at the accessibility of goods that were available here.

The overall quality of the district was better the farther the group walked as well. The decayed, and crumbling buildings were all but gone by this point, replaced by buildings that resembled the magnificence of the palace. They were adorned with fine tapestry and elegant sigils of the One True God. There were doors on every building now, and even though the exterior was still a bit run down, the buildings looked sturdier. It was almost like the marketplace was a kingdom of its own.

There were less people and beastkin as well. The area felt more exclusive and was higher up than the rest of the district.

“That will be six deedees.” The wolfkin said, opening his stand up and releasing a brisk breeze. The air made Isobel shudder a bit, and she wondered what could create such a cold.

Mahogany pulled out a small sack and pulled out six rough looking coins from the bag. The wolfkin nodded and then took the coins from her and began to prepare something from deep within the booth.

Isobel couldn't make out any distinguishable features on the coins from where she was, but the muddy appearance made the little slits of metal uninteresting and repulsive.

“Is that what they call, 'Currency'?” She asked Mahogany. “I've only seen it in books.”

Mahogany gave her a startled look.

“You don't have money where you come from?” She said, unable to mask her surprise.

“Well... No?” Isobel replied. “In my home, we barter for goods.”

“Here you go!” The wolfkin said, interrupting their conversation, as he handed each of them different colored balls on a weird chunk of wood.

When the wolfkin reached out to give Isobel one, she was hesitant. What in the Nine Divines, she thought. The vendor stood there, eyeing her hands, implying she should take it from him. She grasped the wooded portion of the object.

“Have a nice day!” The wolfkin said, giving them a giant toothy smile, before going back to resting at the back of the booth.

Mahogany then led the group a couple of feet away from the shop and stood by a bench. Semaj was so enamored by the tiny object in his hands, that he hadn't realized his role had been usurped for the moment.

Isobel took a moment to examine the small thing in her hands. The top of it was cold and rough, while the bottom of it felt hollow an-

“Isobel...?” She heard a voice say from her side. It was Dior.

“Oh, yes?” She said cautiously, looking around to make sure she hadn't made a scene or was in anyone's way. “Sorry, I was preoccupied with... whatever this is?”

The children shared a look.

“YOU'VE NEVER HAD ICE CREAM!?” Semaj shrieked. “It is beyond delicious!”

Semaj then took a giant bite of the ball, seemingly drinking it off the wood. The other children then started to eat their "Ice Cream" as well. Isobel shrugged her shoulders before deciding to take a bite out of the ice cream.

Her senses were overwhelmed. The course ball on top was not rigid or hard at all! It was soft and fluffy, with a light vanilla taste. It slid down her throat with ease and even though it was chilling, it didn't hurt to consume. She couldn't tell if it was more like hard water or soft ice. If those things actually existed, that is! She took bite after bite of the small delicacy, ravaging it without mercy.

"I-Isobel..." Semaj said, a bit of worry in his voice. "Maybe you should slow down..."

Isobel felt it before Semaj could finish his words. A sharp pain inside of her skull, almost like a knife stabbing her directly in her brain. She grabbed her forehead and grunted as the jarring pain completely stopped her from consuming anymore.

"We really should have warned her." Mahogany sighed softly. "That is a brain freeze, Isobel. You have to eat it slowly to avoid that."

As the pain slowly began to subside, Isobel was having reservations about the frozen delight.

"These things should really come with a warning label..." She said, now eating the treat slowly, deliberately debating every bite.

"Ok." Mahogany said, looking at the sky. "We really need to finish our errands. Luckily for us, the tailor is across the street."

Mahogany checked both sides of the road, a habit they hadn't had to exercise since coming to the center of the district, and then made her way to walk towards a building across the street while everyone finished their treats.

The building had a giant arch with multi-colored banners on each side. There was also a marble sign in the middle that had 'Couture and Modiste, Elegance Beyond Request' carved into it. The front had steel doors that slid to the side, much to Isobel's surprise, when Mahogany approached.

Semaj, Dior, and Isobel each bit the last of their ice cream cones and followed Mahogany into the building.

As they entered, Isobel noticed many fine gowns and elegant suits of many assorted styles floated above their heads. Assembly lines of fine outfits flowed endlessly throughout the store, sending the clothes into appropriately shaped holes in the wall. It was like a river of fabric, seamlessly traveling through the store, creating a beautiful mixture of bright and reflective colors. There were racks of clothes sitting in the lobby of the building that Isobel managed to get a chance to examine as they approached the front counter. She could tell each and every outfit was made with great care and precise stitching.

As she ogled the fine fabric that floated around her, she noticed a small, frail old man approaching them slowly from behind a very unappealing counter. In fact, it was so dull, it seemed almost out of place amongst the vibrant cloth that floated about. Behind it lay a large burgundy curtain that hid the back end of the store.

"Why if it isn't the young prince..." The old man said as he rubbed his tattered and pale beard. His skin was pale and a bit yellow, and he had a very peculiar piece of glass over his right eye. His hair was wild and untamed, almost the opposite of the precise and careful work that flowed through the shop. As if that wasn't weird enough, he also wore a thick blue mage's robe with many ragged holes in the side. If he wore the outfit for protection, then this was poor judgment on his part.

"Oh." The man continued. "And he has brought along his loyal subjects? Excellent. I just finished the order and need but a few moments to retrieve it."

"Sir Therron!" Semaj said eagerly rushing to greet the old gentleman. "Always a few steps in front of everyone else. This is why you are the greatest tailor in the kingdom!"

He stopped and bowed respectfully. Mahogany and Dior followed closely behind Semaj, bowing to Sir Therron as well. Isobel followed closely behind them, stopping, and bowing along with them.

"Oh dear, young Semaj." Sir Therron said, letting a soft

cackle escape his lips. “You don't need to be so formal with me, you troublemaker!”

Therron put his old, wrinkled hand on the Semaj's shoulder. They both reflected a smile that was larger than life. Then Therron grabbed the boy by the shoulder and turned both of their backs to the rest of the group.

There were a couple of moments of whispers, then Semaj shrugged his shoulders.

“Ah, you're no fun.” Therron said dejectedly. “Why do I even bother with you?”

“And you're just a weird old guy.” Semaj rebutted, not dropping his radiant smile for a second.

“I have the order in the back.” He said, turning to the back of the shop. “Give me a moment to retrieve it for you.”

The man proceeded to walk so unbelievably slow it could only be perceived as comical and intentional. The group watched him for a few moments, before Mahogany walked forward and stopped him mid-trek.

“Be at ease, Therron.” Mahogany said, smiling at him. “I will retrieve the order. Where can I find it?”

“Oh!” Therron jumped a bit, seemingly surprised by her eagerness to help. “Well... It's on the shelf in the back, and next to the workshop. It's a moderately sized package, so you should take help.”

“I will grab it with haste!” Mahogany said, ignoring the

man's recommendation. She then turned and left through the curtain that guarded the details of the back.

Therron then turned and swiftly slid over to Isobel. She raised her hands and shrieked in response. The old man was within spitting distance in mere seconds.

“Oh!” The old man said gleefully as he stroked his beard... “And who might this be young, gorgeous specimen be?”

Four arms burst from the holes in Therron's robe, each with a piece of rubber that had weird lines drawn on it. The hands began to place the rubbery tool around Isobel's body, pawing at her furiously. She tried to jump back but found herself unable to move, powerless to resist his onslaught. He then pulled the band back, before repeating the process a few more times.

“Hmm?” The man said inquisitively. “Thirty-eight. Twenty-eight. Forty. You have a nice figure... Miss?”

“Knight Isobel, you lecher.” Isobel rebutted angrily. “You can't just touch me whenever you please!”

“Lecher!” The man scoffed, ignoring her complaints. “Burning hair. A fiery personality. Bronze skin. I have a perfect masterpiece in mind.”

“Therron?” Semaj said, a little worry in his voice. “Please stop being weird...”

“Ah!” Therron said, giving attention back to the group.

"Let me fetch that order for you!"

He made a gesture with his hand, as though he was pushing an invisible curtain.

Mahogany screamed from the other room. She then suddenly came flying back into the room with a giant box in her arms, into the hands of the tailor. She had a look of surprise on her face as he caught her.

"You were taking too long, my dear." Therron said dryly, easing her to the ground. "I swear. You young'ns are always talking about 'post haste'. Yet, you move like molasses."

Isobel felt a soft tug in her mind. A series of images of herself wearing a dress flowed into her thoughts. The dress was a sparkling white gown, with gold trimmings expertly sown down the sides, completely fitted to her form. It was mesmerizing and even though she knew it was herself, it was almost uncanny how much she resembled her mother.

"This will be ready for you in a few days, Miss Isobel." Therron said. "A beauty such as yourself should not wear such drab clothes. Your current choice of garments just doesn't honor your looks. In fact, they are quite repulsive."

"How much would such a dress cost for the fair maiden?" Semaj chimed in.

"Oh..." The old man said, rubbing his beard again. He started to scratch his balding head. "To make such a magnificent piece, I'll need to convene with my fellow tailors... This one will be truly inspired! A cacophony of ideals and style that will transcend the-"

"THERRON PLEASE!" Semaj said impatiently. "We just want to know the price!"

"One thousand DeeDee's." He said plainly. "Novelty is dead, I guess..."

The group was silent for a moment. The children then looked at each other with meaningful glares.

"Drakonis will pay for it!" The children said in unison.

"Splendid!" He said exuberantly. "I'll get to working on it right away."

The old man slid to the back of the store, vanishing behind the curtain, and leaving the group to their own devices.

"That was awkward." Isobel exclaimed, still feeling confused and annoyed by the old man's antics. "Could you not have just warned me about his plan?"

"I knew you were safe." Semaj replied. "Therron means well. He's just excited to share his craft. I wouldn't worry about him."

Suddenly, a loud horn bellowed from outside of the shop.

Isobel looked around to see if she should be alarmed by the noise. Mahogany and Dior had a hopeful, almost excited look amongst their faces. Semaj seemed mostly uninterested.

"Is anyone going to inform me about the horn?" She said curiously.

Unfortunately, this came too late as the kids rushed out of the store, leaving her alone. They had also forgotten their package. She walked over to the soft brown box and picked it up easily.

"I guess this is my job now." She said as she walked back through the doors, hoping the kids weren't too far ahead of her.

* * *

Isobel

Isobel was down on one knee, using all of her might to keep her barrier up. She was the only thing keeping her and the kids alive, but the Barrier of Faith was failing. Her assailants leered at her from beyond her magic field, licking their lips, as they realized she was growing weaker. They pressed their hands deeper into the barrier, draining more of her power.

There was blood everywhere. A horse and its rider lay in the middle of the streets eviscerated and deceased. The massacre had left many fleeing, trampled, and otherwise dead. Smoke and dust covered the previously occupied booths and stands, while sand was kicked high into the air as everyone ran for safety. The sun setting over the horizon made the fires more vibrant and seemingly more destructive than they were.

Giant mechanical guards slashed at the hooded figures, but to no avail. Their attacks could not hit the swift assassins. One by one, the machines were disabled by a few seconds of touch from the warriors.

The clanging of blades and swords was vibrant in Isobel's ears. She could hear metal meeting flesh, followed by the screams of the slain. The thuds of bodies as they fell lifelessly to the earth, fodder in a conflict they didn't understand. As the last of populace escaped the gruesome brawl, Isobel felt her situation grow dire. The assassins advanced upon her, their hands glowing as they readied their next attack.

Isobel's mind raced. Where did they come from? Who were they? How can they manipulate and steal mana so effortlessly? She knew she would never receive these answers.

A tall lean man, with skin white as alabaster and hair like thin blond silk, stood in the middle of the attackers with a huge grin on his face. He was the only one with his face exposed and the only one who spared words.

"Your mana by far trumps any that I have ever tasted!" He laughed, tilting his head back at a sickening angle. "Keep struggling, my love! It brings me pleasure when my food fights back!"

"Why are you doing this!?" Isobel yelled in retaliation. Her will was at its end and her breathing was wild and uneven. "We don't even know who you are!"

"Tsk, tsk, tsk." The man said, wagging his unnaturally thin fingers. "Cattle aren't supposed to talk back to the butcher! Close your mouth swine and recognize your role as sustenance!"

Mahogany, Dior, and Semaj whimpered from behind Isobel. This man... He was a monster in every sense of the word. Isobel had seen him rend a few beastkin to shreds in seconds and siphon off their life-force only moments later. She would not let the same fate befall the children.

Isobel knew that the only way to ensure their survival was to use it. She had to use the Mark of the Black Dragon.

"The Black Dragon..." Isobel said slowly, grunting between breaths. She felt the mark glow, attempting to restrict her actions and words.

"The Black Dragon..." She said again, louder than last time. She felt the darkness expand from her neck to her shoulder. The familiar cold began to cover her.

She heard one of the children shriek from behind her, probably at the sight of her mark expanding.

"ISOBEL, WHAT ARE YOU DOING!?" Mahogany yelled from behind her.

"THE BLACK DRAGON!" Isobel yelled, the mark

now covering most of her upper body and beginning to restrict her eyesight and deafening her ears. She felt the world leaving her, fading to nothingness. She didn't need to hear or see to finish what she had to do. She just needed to stall for someone to rescue them, for someone to come and even the odds.

She then channeled her aura and released her Golden Time. She fueled the barrier with the mark's energy, using her body as a catalyst to channel the dark power. When her golden time ended, her body would not be sufficient to withstand the darkness. She knew that she could only hold this state for about two minutes before her body would give out from exhaustion. She prayed that would be enough.

She looked up with her right eye, the last eye that wasn't covered in darkness. She met eyes with the unhooded man, his white and blue retinas illuminated by the barrier's newfound strength.

"BRILLIANT!" He roared. "Magnificent. Marvelous. Amazing. Beautiful! The way you struggle against certain death, your brutal desire for life. The symphony of your struggle resonates with my heart!"

He raised a hand and all of the hooded beings let go of the barrier. Much to Isobel's surprise, but she knew she would be foolish to see this as a sign of retreat.

"Release her!" He commanded. "THIS MEAL IS MINE!"

He then slammed his hands into the barrier.

Isobel felt the Black Dragon's Power fight violently against his mana, struggling to resist subjugation. It hesitantly was siphoned by the man, slowly being drained from her. Her will waned; she couldn't fight against the man's power. Somehow, him alone had a stronger effect than all of the warriors around him.

The man laughed, knowing she had no way to fight against him. He started walking slowly through the barrier, taking more of her and the marks mana as he progressed.

Her other knee dropped. She had given all she had, and more than she could. The man continued to laugh, placing his hand on her shoulder.

"You..." He said slowly. "You broadened my palate and piqued my interests... You..."

Isobel couldn't hear anymore. Her golden time had ended. She fell forward into the silent void, the abyss swallowing her whole. Its depth was already strangling her, taking her consciousness. She was losing herself.

"*Pathetic woman...*" The Black Dragon whispered in her mind. "*You dare endanger the pact and use my power for your own gain!? And insult me by losing your life, my vessel, for worthless specks? You shall suffer for the inconvenience. You shall suffer for the ignorance. You shall suffer for my delight, and because I shall have pleasure from your continued torture. I will never release you from my prison.*"

Isobel tried to respond, but the darkness was too strong. She was helpless to resist, and powerless to fight back.

The familiar voices began to plead and shout at her.

You let us down. You could have saved us. We were allies, ISOBEL!

The voices were louder than she could bear. This was her fate. She was doomed to an eternity of endless darkness, and misery. She lamented her weakness and inability to complete her destiny. And worst of all, that she couldn't save the children from such a fate.

You left us to die Isobel. We're never going to see our parents again. I'm scared Isobel.

She could feel them, somewhere in the darkness. The voices of the children calling out to her, forever reminding her of failure.

She was already losing her mind. She screamed. Even if no one could hear her. She screamed. Even if no one would ever find her. She screamed. Her mind would be forever lost in the darkness of the dragon's realm. And no one would ever save her.

The voices continued to beat her mind into submission. And she continued to scream into the blackness, silent as a mouse and lost as a lamb.

Chapter 10:
Boiling Point

Chase

The corridor of the cathedral was dark, save for some torches silently flickering from subtle breezes in the hall. The walls were slick with moisture of some kind, although closer inspection would be needed to dictate what the paste really was. It was hard to tell that this was the pathway preceding to the throne of the Divines; that this was the Cathedral of the Nine.

The building's interior itself was completely overrun with bits of nature, untouched by the hands of man, which invaded every inch and every corner of its insides. This was particularly odd because it was constantly surrounded by the Chosen Devout, the priests that walked the grounds. No one was allowed to enter the inner sanctum most days, except for a select few individuals.

The building was deep within the city of Karia-Novim, in a hollow cave underground. Karia was the largest human settlement on Earth; it was divided into nine different districts, and it sat deep in the belly of a large cavern. If you stood at the top of the cavern, looking into its black maw, it would be almost impossible to tell that most of humanity lived at its core.

Only the humans that lived or had lived there knew there was a refuge that lay hidden inside of the darkness. This was how the Divines stayed hidden from D'Merrion and his beastmen army. Well, that and the massive barrier that hid all mana usage inside.

Chase walked silently amongst his fellow Divine Knights as they made their way to the antechamber for the ceremony. He wore his ceremonial garb, a soft green hooded cloak that covered most of his physical features. Around him, every other knight was dressed the same. He looked up at the figure in front of him, a slightly shorter individual than him, who was none other than Isobel.

She had two strong elder knights by her side, Everett and Moranson. Both of them were indistinguishable with the hoods on, but Moranson was far paler than Everett was on a good day. Also... Moranson had white, thinning hair while Everett was completely bald.

Behind him, Chase could hear Jerak, Mirela, Xeilani and some other younger knights-in-training whispering. He couldn't make out the conversation at all, but he could not care less about their chatter. He was only worried about the ceremony.

Isobel had been chosen to be the next High Priestess of the Divines. Actually, she hadn't been chosen yet, but everyone knew it was her. She showed the most promise in the academy.

She had the highest affinity with Divine arts, magical conjuration and was a leader by nature. There was no better choice for the role. Isobel would be promoted far up the ranks of the knights and be forced to the front lines of the war, far from him and Xeilani, in the war-torn battlefields.

This fact sickened Chase. She and Xeilani were his only family. They were good friends beforehand, but after the Black Dragon had destroyed their homes, they had become inseparable. He couldn't imagine either being away from them.

Everett raised his hand, prompting the troops to stop in front of a large gate. Light spilled from its cracks like a treasure ready to be pillaged.

"Young knights..." He began, turning to look over the group. "You have trained hard for this day. For many of you... This will be your first-time laying eyes on the Divines. Remember, do not speak unless spoken to, and bow when you are addressed. They are the protectors of this realm and deserve your sincere respect."

There was a chorus of shuffles in the group, most likely the knights nodding in agreement. Chase didn't dare look behind him, he'd gotten scolded enough as is. It wouldn't do well to bring unnecessary attention to himself.

Moranson then turned as well and stood beside Everett. He looked over the group, the light from behind them made him seem more stern than normal, almost little menacing as well.

"You would all do well to remember your place inside the antechamber." Moranson warned. "The Divines do not tolerate impertinence and effrontery. Mind your tongues and your actions. Beyond this door, your fate is up to the gods. Remember that."

Moranson glared at Chase.

"It is an honor for you to be here." He said, squinting his eyes at the boy. "Do not embarrass the Divine Knights with any unworthy outbursts or acts of disobedience."

Chase and his peers then saluted back at their elder.

"Yes Elder!" They said in unison.

"Excellent" Everett said. He took a moment to glance at Chase. He had a firm, but sad expression on his face. Chase understood his grimace. Everett was like a father to him, and sometimes it felt like he could read the old man's mind.

You're going to have to grow up, Chase thought to himself. *You're going to have to be alone and be okay with that.*

Light rushed out into the hall as Everett opened the giant doors. Chase had to cover his eyes to keep from being blinded by the brilliant rays that washed over the knights. He opened his eyes, giving them a chance to become adjusted to the light of the room.

Slowly he started to make out the room they stood

before... Or maybe room wasn't the right word for what this was. It was more like a realm, or space that he could only describe as heaven. It was the only conclusion his mind could come up with to explain the expanse that lay before him. More and more, he was able to take in the grandeur that laid before him.

There were golden pillars, or maybe beams of light that went high into the ceiling. And the ceiling, or what he perceived to be the ceiling, was really just endless sky that stretched far beyond his sight. The ground, which resembled golden clouds, flowed endlessly forever in all directions. It seemed that if you walked in any direction in the room, you'd walk for all eternity.

The knights marched a few paces. Chase was in awe at the possibility of such a place existing. As he looked around, he noticed the other knights-in-training were in as much awe as he was.

He looked for Isobel and noticed her still staring ahead.

That's right, he thought. Isobel has been here many times before. Her latent talent for channeling Divine energy allotted her such experiences.

“Hold.” Everett commanded, raising his hand again to stop the knights.

They came to an abrupt stop. Chase looked around with his eyes, searching for any indication of the gods, but he found only more sky. More... Emptiness.

Then suddenly, he heard a loud footstep. Then another booming footstep, just as loud as the first. Each step came one after the other, getting closer and louder with each stomp. Then Chase saw it.

Someone was walking from the heavens... Or the ceiling... Or whatever it was that was above them. They were descending on the group of knights, slowly and calmly. Their body was surrounded by a white aura, like a beacon even in the golden paradise. They also had the figure of a tall and slender woman, far too tall to be human, and wore a white gown or cloak draped in see-through scarves as well.

Chase felt himself immediately calmed by the sight of the being; it was as if his woes had simply vanished into thin air, dissipating like smoke. He felt drawn to its side, an invisible string linking between them.

"My children..." The being said in a soft and sincere voice. "Please... Avert your eyes, my kin... Lest my enchantment overtake your heart and seal your fate here in paradise."

Chase bowed his head, making sure to stare straight at the ground. He didn't know what fate lay for those that peered too hard, but he knew he did not want to find out. He tried to catch a glimpse of how the others were reacting, but he couldn't see anything without having to stand upright.

“My liege.” Everett said, his words slightly muffled from bowing. “We have come for the...”

“The Ceremony of Ascension...” The being said, her voice getting closer. “Yes... I am Divine Karia, one of the nine Divines and teacher to the nine legendary heroes; Adel, Novim, Eris, Argathion, Zeke, Garredan, Aphermia, Rajmon, and Herra were the precursors for the Divine Knights. They were the first generation of Divine Knights that saved the world from calamity. The first demi-gods to ever walk the earth.”

Chase held his head low, listening to the Divine's words. He had heard stories of the hero’s exploits but to hear it from a Divine, in person no less, was assuring. It filled him with hope.

“But...” Karia said, pausing for a bit. “I loathed the day I had to lower my blood back to the Earth. Their sacrifice sealed the Black Dragon into the abyss, but it cost them their bodies and souls. Since their demise, we have continued to gift humans with the blessings of the Divines to combat our dreaded foe... D’Merrion the Deceiver...”

The Divine's voice was close now, Chase could tell that she was around ten feet away.

“Which brings us to the reason for our parley...” She continued, her voice switching to a more commanding tone. “Raise thy head, knights.”

Chase did not know if he was being tested or not. He

kept his head lowered, not willing to risk being enchanted for the rest of his days.

"Ahhh..." Karia said softly. "You are wise to not trust that which you don't understand, young knights. But this will be your first lesson in true faith. Raise thine heads..."

Chase looked up at the Divine. She was smiling back at the knights, her hands out in front of her.

"The power of the Divines comes from faith in the unseen." Karia said as she raised her hands to the heavens. "I apologize for the deception, young ones. Obedience and faultless faith are our strongest weapons against the beasts of D'Merrion. We must train ourselves to advance even in the face of death if we are to win against his hordes."

Chase took a deep breath and wiped the sweat from his face.

"Now." Karia said, standing in front of Isobel. "Let us continue with the ceremony..."

*　　　　　*　　　　　*

Chase

"So how are you feeling today?" The doctor asked as she sat down.

Chase gritted his teeth as he looked up from the rusted, blotched table that separated him, and his interrogator. The woman had on a white lab coat; it was eerily clean and had an unnecessary number of pockets. She had honey brown hair that ended below her waist.

"How do you think I feel?" He said not even attempting to mask his anger. "Day in and day out I receive the same line of questioning..."

"And as long as you continue to shy away from progress and perpetuate your own misery, it will continue." She replied in a very lax and monotone voice. "If you're going to be a complete drag today and, y'know, clam up, then we'll be done sooner than usual."

Chase sighed heavily as he looked up at the off-white lights in the pale, broken ceiling. He lifted his arms onto the table, slamming the heavy chain restraints against its surface.

This had been his life since that day. The day chaos and death erupted from the center of the market. The day he couldn't protect Isobel.

There was a moment of awkward silence, the only noise

was the mild rumbling from outside of the room. Chase simply stared back at her, in a silent rebellion.

The doctor sighed in response.

“Do you want to go back to the dungeon?” The doctor said finally. “I can just have you sent back. It wouldn't be a problem and I'm sure you've become accustomed to the smell by now. Home sweet home, correct?”

Chase looked away from her. He didn't want to go back. He refused to go back. The last thing he needed was to be left alone with his thoughts. The past two weeks had been torture enough. The silent, lonely nights followed by grueling training during the day. He was at his limit, and he needed to buy himself some time.

The doctor stood up, gathering her belongings.

“Then I guess that's it then.” She said putting her pen in her coat pocket and shuffling her clipboard under her arm.

“Wait...” Chase stopped her. “I will... I'll talk.”

The woman looked at him with a blank stare, her eyes not betraying any of her emotions.

“Okay...” She said as she sat down again. “How about... We take it from the top then. How are you feeling today?”

“Angry.” Chase said sharply.

“Why do you feel angry, Knight Chase?” She said, staring at her clipboard as she twirled her pen around in her hand.

"Why do you really care?" Chase snapped back at her. "You're just some beastmen shaman. What do you possibly hope to gain from interacting with me?"

"I could not care less about you." She said, still calm and composed. "But someone of high relevance values your well-being and saw fit to enlist my help in maintaining your mental health. So can we skip the useless repartee and just get to the part where you willingly answer my questions with meaningful answers?"

Chase stared at her hard for a few moments, before sighing again and nodding his head.

"Good." She said, flipping a page on her clipboard. "Now. Why are you angry, Knight Chase?"

"The food tastes terrible." Chase said. "The lighting in the dungeon doesn't give me that familiar 'home' feeling. The walls have just a tad bit too much slime on them..."

The woman smiled softly in response to his gripes.

"All contributing factors to your attitude, I'm sure." She said with a light chuckle. But her elated mood only lasted for a second. She leaned forward and stared at Chase with a serious expression.

"But why are you angry...?" She said.

"Well, I guess..." Chase began. "My woes began..." Chase leaned forward into the table, staring hard into the doctor's eyes.

"They began when my friend was savagely killed." He said, breathing heavily. "Attacked in the heart of the city, and no one will even tell me what happened..."

"And why would we?" She asked dryly, placing her clipboard down on the partially rusted table. "Let me ask you this; would a lord hold a meeting to console his mutt? To explain to him why one of his most beloved hounds won't be seen around the kennel again? No. He wouldn't. Because it's physically impossible for mutts to articulate or engage in meaningful conversation. And because explaining to the mutt won't make it feel better. Thus, it's not even worthy of the notion to begin with."

Chase leapt up, slamming his hands into the ragged table.

"Don't talk about her like that!" He screamed; his voice shook the walls of the tiny room.

"Or what?" The woman said, unamused. "You'll go on another rampage? Do you believe your little fit in The Grindstone would warrant any emotion outside of pity from anyone with actual power? You should be happy Drakonis didn't behead you and parade your corpse around town."

Chase was breathing heavy now. He slammed back down into the seat, causing a sickening screech to vibrate through the room.

"You don't know what I'm capable of..." He said under

his breath.

“I know very much what you're capable of.” The woman said confidently. “That's my job. I can analyze the strengths and weaknesses of anyone within these walls. I knew who you were and what you could do the moment I laid eyes on you. I am a beast general, you worm. And you are a slave to a slave.”

“You look human and yet have no humanity.” Chase interjected, slamming his hands on the table again. “How is that even possible?”

“Because I am human, fool.” She retorted.

“And you would stand with them!?” Chase shot back. He couldn't believe this. There was no way she was human. “Stand alongside the beastmen, the mortal enemies to humankind!?”

“The humans abandoned me.” She said calmly. “They left me for dead after taking what they wanted from me. D’Merrion and his beastkin have treated me far better than any human has. With respect. With dignity. So, when you call them “beastmen,” you're insulting my friends.”

Chase saw a tail creep from behind the woman. It resembled the tail of a scorpion or a snake. He couldn't figure out how she managed to hide something that large in her coat.

“I am a Chimera.” The woman stated. “I have DNA from the strongest beastkin races combined into my anatomy. I am stronger than you in almost every way. But I'll let you in on a little secret... I was smarter than you without the augmentations."

Chase looked away from her, a scoff escaping his pursed lips. He had heard enough. This conversation was only aggravating his bad mood. If he heard more, he was going to try and kill her.

"I'm done." He said.

"Oh." She said with a shocked look on her face. "Is sharing time over? I thought you wanted to try and throw your weight around some more? Maybe attempt to strangle me with those chains? I'd let you get the first move."

She was mocking him now. He knew better. He was in no position to threaten anyone. He still had the dragon mark on his wrist. He was still enslaved and powerless as ever.

"I will speak no more." He said sullenly, refusing to look at her.

The woman stood up and began to write furiously onto the clipboard. She continued for over a minute then put her pen in her pocket as she walked to the door. Before she left, she turned back to the restrained man.

"Today was... productive to say the least." She said, maintaining the calm expression she had the entire time. "It may have felt like you've told me nothing, but I've learned so much from you today. So as a reward, I'll tell you, my name. I am Cyarah, the lead medical professional of D'Merrion's kingdom, and one of the Beastlord Generals in his retainer. Today, the pleasure was all mine, Knight Chase. I pray you continue to be as forthcoming in the future."

She smiled at him for a moment, a glint in her eye. And it wasn't the warm glint of a woman seeing an old friend. No, this was the glint of someone who had just found their next project to work on. Something akin to a madness.

She then left out the door, closing it shut behind her.

* * *

Drakonis

Drakonis stood on the balcony overlooking the city. He was in the Garden of Amity, healing from his latest scolding from The God King. The past couple of weeks had been hectic. But none of it was unexpected. Everything was happening just as the Fae foretold.

He was beginning to settle into his favorite bend on the tree when he heard feet rushing towards him. The fairies that were healing him scattered in response.

"Drakonis!" Semaj, Mahogany, and Dior said all at once.

"Greetings, young ones." He replied, adjusting himself against the tree.

"Drakonis..." Semaj said again, this time with a look of sadness in his eyes.

"How may I help you, Semaj?" Drakonis said, looking at the boy weirdly.

"Why are you always shirtless when we see you around the tree?" Semaj said, prompting Dior and Mahogany to burst into a frenzy of laughter. "You're always wearing the same black pants, and always naked under this tree. That's kind of suspect, big brother."

"What!?" Drakonis said completely surprised. "What are you talking about!? I'm a dragon! My natural state is without clothing or armor! I'm about to rest so of course I would remove my armor!"

"Seems like a convenient excuse for an exhibitorist?" Semaj said, putting his thumb under his chin snobbishly.

"It's exhibitionist, Semaj." Mahogany corrected him.

"THANKS MAHO!" Semaj said quickly.

"Don't call me that." Mahogany said even faster.

Drakonis laughed heartily in response to their nonsense. The children laughed right along with him. Drakonis never found a dull moment when the kids were around. He always appreciated their honesty and liveliness.

They all sat down around the tree and chuckled for a bit longer.

"So Drakonis, how are the knights?" Mahogany asked

after the laughter died down a bit.

Drakonis looked at her with a smile as he tried to hide his agitation at her question.

“They're just fine.” Drakonis said, staring up at the sky. “In fact, as we trained, Knight Chase asked about you today. You made such a big impression on him; he'd like to hangout again.”

“Really!?” Dior said, extremely excited.

“Absolutely.” Drakonis replied with a smile.

“And what of Knight Isobel?” Semaj said, rubbing his thumbs together. “Her body was... charred. Almost completely when she was taken away. Is she okay?”

“Don't worry, Semaj.” Drakonis replied quickly. “She is being taken care of by Cyarah. She's in good hands.”

He didn't want to tarnish their evening with talk of the Knights.

“How about you head to your quarters for the evening, young ones?” Drakonis suggested. “The sun will find it's home behind the hill shortly and you have chores to complete, no?”

“Bunk chores!” Semaj yelled loudly. “I just want us to have fun, all the time!”

“Well perhaps when you become King Maj, you'll decree every day to be fun day.” Drakonis said, trying to alleviate the boy's aggravation.

“Drakonis...” Semaj said lowly. “That sounds so

dumb!"

"What did you say, you little brat!?" Drakonis yelled at him, making a grab for the young prince.

Semaj managed to get away and poked his tongue out at Drakonis.

"Too slow!" Semaj yelled before running down the stairwell.

Drakonis sighed and leaned back against the tree.

"You can't let him win forever." Mahogany said, dusting off her dress and standing up.

"Shut up and go be a kid, Mahogany." Drakonis replied to her as he closed his eyes.

He heard the girls shuffle back towards the stairs.

"Bye, Drakonis!" Dior said, as she and Mahogany left the way they came.

The Dragon Lord laid for a moment before he heard a soft sigh from above him.

"What do you want, Cyarah?" He said dryly, now agitated because he knew he had lost his chance for a nap.

"Oh." She said with some amusement. "Is that how you treat your veterinarian? Especially when she comes bearing good news?"

"Spit it out already." Drakonis said distastefully. "I don't have the time or energy to deal with your cryptic messages. Be candid."

“Okay... Rude.” She said as she jumped down from the tree. “Your pet project just bore fruit. Knight Chase spoke his first words today...”

Cyarah trailed off, seemingly waiting for a response from the dark lord.

“Go on...” Drakonis ordered.

“He's very agitated.” She continued. “In fact, he's in so much emotional distress, I can't believe he's not attempted escape or to kill me.”

“We knew this already...” Drakonis said, annoyed with her for dragging out the results. “WHAT DID YOU LEARN?”

“I took a few moments to really pick away at him today.” She said pulling out her a mana crystal. She held it out in front of her and many graphs and bars began to protrude from it.

“Look... I don't care to see your findings or personal musings.” Drakonis interrupted, getting up from his sleeping spot. “You're getting on my last nerve.”

“Jeez.” She snapped back. “How impatient are you? Alright. Knight Chase has a limiter of some sort on his power. There. Happy? You really know how to take the mystery away from discovery, Drakonis. Would it kill you to show a little interest in expression and science? There's a method to all this!”

“So... Why?” Drakonis said puzzled, ignoring her.

"What's so special about this man?"

"I don't know." Cyarah sighed. "We analyzed his aura readings after interrogating him. When he was most emotional, his aura spiked to an alarmingly elevated level. Way stronger than any normal demi-god or human. But then his power drastically dropped, and he calmed down immediately afterwards. He believes that he's in full control of his emotions but he's being manipulated. Someone doesn't want him mad."

Drakonis began to ponder the new information.

So anger is his weapon, Drakonis thought to himself. They needed to find some way to harness that power if they were to help him survive the crucible. And if Chase was to be of use to Drakonis in the future, he needed to be able to go all out.

"Thank you Cyarah." Drakonis said. "You can go."

"Hold on, my fair scaled friend." Cyarah said as she placed a hand up to him. "You and I have a deal and I desire compensation for my findings. I believe one dragon scale is in need of a new mommy."

She turned her hand over expectantly.

"You'll receive the scale when we finish our tests." Drakonis said, grabbing his armor. "I am heading down to the infirmary. While I'm down there, you should think of apt ways to progress Chase's training."

Cyarah made a face as Drakonis walked past her.

"You're really going to be like that." She said with a giant frown on her face.

"You're asking for one of the most precious items a dragon can give." Drakonis said as he got dressed. "Of course, I won't part with it so easily."

He left her there next to the tree, heading down the stairwell and entering the palace. There was someone he had to see, now that he had the information he needed. All he had to do was ask the right questions, and the first phase of his plan would be complete.

He only walked for a couple of minutes until he arrived at his destination. The door slid open in front of him, revealing the unnaturally white and clean walls of the infirmary. He walked past the front desk of the ward, which was empty this time of night. He followed the halls all the way to a wall in the back. He pressed his hand on the wall and it revealed another room hidden behind it. He walked into the room and the wall slid back into place.

There was a woman sitting on the only bed in the room, hooked up to multiple machines. She was half covered in the blackness of the abyss, but she was fully lucid. Her recovery was going nicely from what Drakonis could see. She looked up at Drakonis as he approached her.

"Drakonis." She said softly, her strength had not quite returned yet.

“Isobel.” He said in reply. He grabbed a chair and sat it down next to her bed.

“We have much to talk about.” He said, looking into her eyes. “And today, I don't plan to leave without the answers I seek. So, I hope you're prepared to enlighten me on everything that happened that day.”

“Drakonis... I don't think I have enough energy.” Isobel tried to protest, staring at the floor.

“No excuses this time Isobel.” Drakonis replied, pressing onward. “You did something that day, something no one should ever do. Anyone proficient in magic could feel that energy coming from the market. That overwhelming darkness that feeds on death in the atmosphere. I'm giving you a chance here, Isobel.”

She looked up at him, her eyes filled with regret and pain.

“Isobel...” Drakonis said, leaning towards her. “What did you do?”

Chapter 11:
Watchful Eyes

D'Merrion

D'Merrion sat upon his throne, thinking over his next move. Every action had a consequence, every piece had its place, and for every push, there was an equivalent pull in the opposite direction.

These philosophies of war were taught to him long ago by a former brother-in-arms. Remembering such lessons brought a smile to his face for a moment... Before it turned into a hideous grin as he realized what he'd do to that man if he ever saw him again. He could practically feel the pleasure he'd receive as he imagined ripping the man's head from his shoulders with his bare hands.

"I can see that you've become quite occupied with your thoughts, God King." The Fae said to him in the same monotone voice all the other Fae used. "If you'd like, I can return after you've reminisced a bit."

D'Merrion scoffed at the Fae that floated across from him. He detested their lax demeanors. Quite honestly, the absolute lack of vigor was enough to make him sick. A being with no drive of their own was worthless in his eyes, below the dirt of the earth and the bugs that infested it.

"Then would you allow us to continue our game then, King D'Merrion?" The Fae questioned, its eyes lifelessly staring into his.

"I don't appreciate your familiar tone, Fae." D'Merrion said gruffly. "You may reside here, taking sanctuary in the Garden of Amity, but you are no friend of mine. Certainly not an ally, or blood brother. Mind your tongue, before I mind it for you."

The Fae retained its same neutral mood, and simply motioned toward the chessboard that was suspended in the air between them. The game was half finished, in the Fae's favor.

"Do not rush me." The God King spat at the Fae.

"I couldn't fathom the point of an invitation into the God King's Grand Hall, if he only wished to berate us and delay the inevitable." The Fae said. "Or perhaps... Your absence from the world has inspired a bit of docile behavior? Has the God King... learned civility in his incarceration? Reformation is unheard of within the Nega Shikari..."

D'Merrion felt a familiar burning sensation in the pit of his stomach, and his blood began to boil at the Fae's insults. He angrily grabbed one of his pieces and eliminated one of the Fae's pieces from the game. The Fae then moved his piece to eliminate D'Merrion's piece from play, prompting the God to stare at the board for a second. D'Merrion then began to rub his face in frustration, baring his teeth at the Fae.

"You do know that future sight takes the enjoyment out of the game, correct?" D'Merrion said, trying hard to make his distaste apparent. He continued playing, moving another piece into play, but he had lost all interest in the game. He hated losing in all its forms, even if the situation was unwinnable to begin with.

"Future Sight...?" The Fae replied, its words implying confusion. "We, Fae, don't rely on magics and incantations for our duties. We exist in all instances of time and reality, beyond their touch, knowing all within its reach. I am not "seeing" into the future God King. I am already there. But you..."

"Cease babbling to yourself, Fae." D'Merrion interrupted. "I didn't command your attendance to be bored with a history lesson, or to play this wretched game. We have important business to attend to!"

"Sore loser." The Fae said quickly under his breath.

"WHAT WAS THAT!?" D'Merrion replied, furiously jumping up from his seat.

"Nothing, God King." The Fae said, his face not betraying his emotions. "Please... Ask your questions, my lord."

D'Merrion took a deep breath, organizing his thoughts, and trying to get over his searing rage. He turned and stared at the windowpane behind his throne, the light of the moon showing off the magnificent white-gold, and red details of the image. It always calmed him a bit. He loved staring at the mural of himself, holding the disembodied head of a wolf while blood pooled at his feet as he roared in victory. It reminded him of his glory days, when his only thoughts were of conquest and combat... Simpler times.

"Answer me this..." D'Merrion said, his tone dead serious. "How is it that I, the Great Conqueror of the Realms, Hero of the War of Darkness, Savior of Mankind, and all of creation... How is it that I cannot find the haven where my blood kin hide? How have these vermin so effectively eluded my attempts to subjugate them, when I am the greatest war mind to ever draw breath within this realm? What aid did you give them to cease my revenge, to halt my retribution for years of unjust and highly irregular imprisonment?"

"Great and noble God King." The Fae answered. "We have not gifted the Divines with any more assistance than we have given you."

D'Merrion turned to face the Fae again, with a large grin.

"I wasn't talking to you, Fae." He said, his grin becoming a frown saturated with rage as he walked up to the chess table. He leaned forward onto the boardgame, the magic tethers wavering under his weight, game pieces falling to the ground and shattering upon impact. "I was talking to your masters..."

The Fae's eyes widened a bit at his words, but its expression didn't change.

D'Merrion knew what he was doing. He had interacted with the Fae for many eons. He knew what to say and how to say it to get the attention of the old gods, the beings above the Primordials. When he spoke, the old gods answered. Simple as that. The Fae was just a pawn, a mouthpiece, at best.

The two sat staring at each other for a couple of seconds, not breaking eye contact for even a moment.

"Watch your words, lesser god." The Fae warned. "The three exist in a state of being beyond our realm of perception. You have never been in a position to demand from that which crafts the thread of existence. The thought of you being more than mere entertainment in the three's eyes is a fantasy only you could have envisioned. To be frank, you are a punchline in a long list of jokes, and your life has no meaning other than to sate the Greater God's boredom."

D'Merrion's frown turned back into a smile. It was working. He only needed to press a bit farther, to egg the gods on more.

"They deem me, the god king, as a joke?" D'Merrion questioned, his voice low but slowly gaining volume. "Then remove my restrictions! Give me back my power and allow me to show them what a proper 'joke' looks like!"

The Fae's eyes rolled backwards into its head and its

mouth opened slightly.

“D’Merrion...” The Fae boomed. But this time, its voice was not its own.

The god king could feel it in his bones. His very atoms shook at the utterance. Three voices spoke to him through the Fae, their absolute pressure attempting to smash his determination, to force him to bend his knee to their will. He resisted their demand with all his might, his hands clenching the chess board, smashing its sides. His body felt as though it was on fire, as though all of his skin was being peeled away from him, as this single word tried to strip away all of his strength.

The Fae’s eyes rolled back to their original position and its mouth closed just as slowly. As just as soon as the assault had begun, it was over.

“You will continue with what you have.” The Fae began to speak normally again. “And if you want to have any hope of your wish being granted, you must win the game.”

D’Merrion was uninterested in the Fae’s guidance. He was too busy laughing to himself. Even at a tenth of his original might, the gods still could not break him. They would NEVER break his will. He was the greatest warrior, the strongest combatant to ever form thought. His path had never been so clear.

“D’Merrion.” The Fae said, interrupting the god king's

epiphany. “As much as I hate to interrupt your delusions of grandeur... You have a servant seeking your wisdom.”

D’Merrion gathered himself, taking another deep breath and stood up right.

“Our conversation is not over, Fae.” D’Merrion said, staring directly at the Fae’s eyes. “I hope the gods become more social at our next parley. I would hate for words to go... Un-said...”

The Fae bowed and disappeared from sight.

“Enter!” D’Merrion commanded as he walked back to his throne. He already knew who wished to speak to him. A particular disappointment had come to tattletale on his plotting son. Too bad for him, D’Merrion had spies all around the capitol. He knew everything that happened within his walls and not even his strongest generals could elude his gaze.

The giant throne room doors creaked open, and a figure walked into the throne room.

* * *

Ashnel

The sun burned Ashnel's eyes as it crawled over the horizon, he raised his hand to block the rays. The restless beastkin gathered all around the wolfkin in the courtyard in front of the palace. They howled in anticipation, shaking like wild weeds in a windy meadow.

"Wilds." They chanted rhythmically again and again. They stomped their feet, kicking up dust all around them, creating a thin haze over the area.

Ashnel loosened the straps on his armor, which clattered as it hit the ground. The chants of the crowd grew in volume as the chorus of voices became more in-sync with each other.

"Wilds." The beasts continued to chant. The crowd was growing restless and couldn't contain their bloodlust any longer. The wolfkin could see it in their eyes... They hungered for blood.

Ashnel walked forward, his fur free of restriction. He stared intensely at the giant boarkin across from him.

The boar was heavy set, as boarkin tend to be, and carried himself arrogantly. Ashnel had only just left his quarters in the grindstone when the boar flanked him. He made proper boasts of power and made a giant speech about "weak wolves" before challenging Ashnel's position. From the spectacle he made in front of the other beast kin, Ashnel could tell he was eager for victory... Too eager...

The boar smirked at him while he removed his armor. He huffed as he approached Ashnel, never breaking eye contact with the wolfkin.

Ashnel scoffed and rolled his eyes.

A free kill, the wolf thought. Another weakling whose name he would take, and toss to the wayside, to be forgotten and lost in obscurity.

Ashnel stared at the boarkin again, this time with murder in his eyes. He was already imagining bashing the boar's skull against the pavement, the fresh smell of blood in the air, as he raised his hand in triumph. He wouldn't enjoy the fight, his opponent was far too weak for that, but he could at least relish in his guaranteed victory.

"Rule of the Wilds." Ashnel said as he hunched over.

"Rule of the Wilds." The Boar Kin replied, smirking back at the wolf.

The boarkin charged forward, his arms outstretched, and slammed his weight into Ashnel. The wolf kin didn't falter against the blow, he barely felt it, and chuckled softly to himself.

The beasts of the circle cheered and howled at the impact, delighted that they would finally be sated, and that blood was on the verge of being spilled...

"I am going to smash your skull and eat your brains through the hole!" The boar roared as he tilted his head down, attempting to stab Ashnel in the eye with his tusk.

The wolf had fought many boars before, and this tactic was not unknown to him. Ashnel managed to easily grab the tusk before any damage was done. He then grappled the boar by his waist, digging his claws into the fat of the beast.

The boarkin roared out in pain right before he was tossed over the large wolfkin's shoulder, head-first into the ground, and was rendered unconscious. Ashnel then knelt down next to the boarkin, growling in his face, and repeatedly slammed his fists into the boarkin's face. This caused an uproar amongst the beasts, excited by the savagery. The wolfkin then grabbed the boarkin by his throat and lifted the defeated beast up, like a champion holding a trophy. He howled, parading the body around for all of the beastkin to see. The other beast howled with him, chanting his name.

"ASHNEL! ASHNEL! ASHNEL! ASHNEL! ASHNEL!" They roared, loud enough that maybe the gods could hear their chants.

Ashnel savored his victory a bit, closing his eyes as his fellow beast marveled at his power. This was what it meant to be the strongest amongst the beasts.

"I AM ASHNEL OF THE SUN CLAN!" He yelled

powerfully. “And this pathetic excuse for a warrior...”

Ashnel dropped the boar, his body slamming into the ground with a heavy thud.

“Needs a healer.” He finished. “Beaten beastkin have no value to the cause. Get him out of my sight.”

A couple of small wolfkin moved over to the boar's body and lifted him, struggling to hoist him onto their shoulders. When they had a firm enough grip on him, they retreated in the direction of the nearest doctor.

“Is there anyone else that wishes to test their mettle in the wilds today!?” Ashnel said, turning around, searching the crowd for more contenders. No one bit the bait. Many simply grumbled to themselves and walked away from the palace gates.

“Ophog, my armor.” Ashnel snapped. “Make haste, we're already late.”

Ophog rushed over with the armor Ashnel had dropped on the ground and replaced it on the wolf's person.

Loyal Ophog, Ashnel thought. If only you were a capable warrior, not a cowering wimp. Maybe you would have a chance to obtain a name worthy of remembrance.

Ashnel chuckled to himself. Who was he kidding? If Ophog was strong or had any kind of backbone, he wouldn't waste his time being ordered around like a wretch. Maybe then, he'd be a meal worth eating...

Ophog finished lacing up the last of the armor. He seemed to be taking extra care not to tie anything too tight or leave anything too loose. Ashnel stared hard at the boarkin, who was raising his head to look the wolfkin in his eyes. Soon beads of sweat were dripping down Ophog's face.

Ashnel licked his lips at the boar kin, certain Ophog could see the hunger in his eyes. The constant bloodlust was admittedly hard to control at times. But this time, he only wanted to toy with his subordinate.

Ophog rushed behind the wolf, visibly disturbed by what he had seen.

“Y-y-your armor is ready, and y-y-you are equipped for combat, S-sir!” Ophog said with satisfying distress in his voice.

“Thank you, peon.” Ashnel said snidely, looking over his shoulder. “Rest easy, Ophog. I have a larger quarry than a boar with a soft hide and even softer tusks.

“Th-Thank you, Lord Ashnel.” Ophog replied, his voice cracking as he tried to maintain his composure.

“Come.” Ashnel commanded. “To the Grand Hall, we go. And don't linger. We're already behind and I have a busy day ahead.”

Ashnel began walking to the giant doors of the palace, not waiting to see if his subordinate was following or not. He needed to speak urgently with the God King, to lend his tongue to the court... He only wanted to pursue the capitol's best interests, even if revenge was the only thought on his mind.

He passed through the large palace doors, nodding to the guards as he entered the grand hall. The guards nodded in return, confirming his entry into the palace.

He walked in silence for the next couple of minutes, sweating a bit as he tried to formulate his argument in his head. He had to get it right. He was never good with words, always focusing on his swordsmanship and martial arts. He chose the straightforward approach because it offered the least resistance, and it alleviated him of the mental strain of having to actually think. Actions create change, not thoughts. He always told himself that, but he knew that to sway a god amongst gods, he'd have to come up with a compelling argument.

Before he knew it, he was a few feet from the main doors of the Hall of the God King. He took a deep breath, closing his eyes to collect his thoughts one last time. Then he realized he had forgotten about Ophog. He turned to see the boarkin was still at the entrance of the Hall.

Good boy, the wolf kin thought to himself. Ophog wasn't strong enough to handle the pressure of the God King and would probably faint or have some other embarrassing mishap. The situation was already stressful enough without his lesser making a complete buffoon of himself.

He turned back towards the door, his nerves now steeled for the conversation ahead.

“Then remove my restrictions! Give me back my power and allow me to show them what a proper 'joke' looks like!” A voice boomed from beyond the door.

Ashnel felt his ears deafen at the words. His body shuddered and his hand locked in place as he reached for the door. He felt sick to his stomach, his head sweating and his mouth beginning to slack. His vision began to blur, and he felt his equilibrium falter. He was losing control of his body and he was almost powerless to stop it.

The voice could be no other than the God King. It HAD to be the God King pushing this massive pressure from the other room. There was no one else in the world who could promote such power...

Ashnel managed to regain some of his will, planting his hand on the door for stability. He closed his eyes and gritted his teeth against the pain, hoping to survive the ordeal.

The pressure was intense, but it began to subside after a couple of minutes. He had never felt the God King's aura before, never on this level. It was... Inspiring. To know there was a level of strength where just fueling your aura with frustration or anger could cause nausea and completely incapacitate an individual. He smiled at the thought of such power, envy filling his heart. There was only one way to acquire strength of that caliber for beastkin... And as much as he hated to admit it, he wasn't strong enough to gain the blessing of the Sun Clan.

He took a few deep breaths as he gathered his strength.

“Enter!” The God King beckoned from the other room.

Ashnel was too fatigued to be immediately startled by the King's call, but he was surprised to know the God King already sensed his presence.

The doors creaked loudly as he pushed his way past them. There was a soft golden hue spilling into the room from the windowpanes along the walls, murals of D’Merrion's previous exploits. Ashnel enjoyed marveling at himself and his own strengths all the time, but he had to admit that even for his tastes, the panes were unsightly to say the least. Especially the pane that portrayed the God King slaying a large wolf, a sight that he can say truly unnerved him.

Ashnel walked along the red carpet that led to the throne room's steps, making sure to never look up directly at the God King. There were rumors that should you even see his face without his permission, his radiance would destroy you wholly; you'd burst into flames and have your existence completely erased. He placed zero stock in outlandish stories, but he would be a fool if he just strolled in casually gazing at the lord of the known universe. He finally reached the throne, and he knelt down on one knee.

He noticed there were bits of broken glass and shards of splintered wood littered upon the steps to the throne. He couldn't tell if anyone else was in the room, but some kind of heated argument took place here. That was certain.

“Ahhh...” The God King sighed. “Young Ashnel. Why... You've never graced me with an exclusive audience before... To whom do I owe the pleasure for gifting me your attention?”

“My liege.” Ashnel began, sweat building on the fur of his brow. “I apologize for my inconsideration. My time is yours, and I hope your penance is most merciful for my indiscretion.”

King D’Merrion chuckled at the wolfkin.

“Please War Lieutenant, your victories in my son's campaign are worthy of much renown, and award... some... respect from me.” The God King said, almost completely aloof.

Ashnel could hear The God King shuffle in his seat a bit, probably changing his position. Sitting in the throne for most of the day... Ashnel couldn't imagine the immeasurable boredom he must suffer every day.

“Ahem... With that being said...” King D’Merrion said, his tone becoming deeper and more serious. “I don't remember my royal secretary scheduling you for an audience with your Great and Powerful God King. So, with respect, I presume you understand that I may just beat you for simply walking into my court unannounced, correct?”

“S-sire!” Ashnel replied, realizing that the conversation

had already soured. He knew that punishment from the God King meant execution, physical smiting, and possible torture for the King's amusement.

"My liege!" Ashnel continued. "Drakonis is the reason I stand before you! He trains those Divine dogs in hopes of them overcoming your crucible! He has met in secret with the Fae, using your will as an excuse for these parleys. And the Fae! The Fae... They... They plot against your Kingdom and your reign... They..."

Ashnel stopped talking, sweat now pooling at his feet. He had to. There was a hand on his shoulder, one that seemed to be heavier than anything he had ever tried to lift. It planted itself solidly on his shoulder and he felt himself being smashed into the earth. Every bone in his body seemed to groan in a futile resistance against the hand's pressure, but he continued to will them to push against the force.

"Ashnel..." The God King said calmly from behind the wolfkin. "I don't remember giving you permission to speak. In fact, I believe that you're overdue for proper etiquette training. I guess gallivanting in the wilds with the lost, wayward souls misguided by my traitorous brethren has had a lingering impression on you. You're being just as disrespectful as those vagrants. So, you must be punished."

Ashnel's thoughts were wild. Ashnel didn't even hear him move. He couldn't sense the God King's steps. Did he walk? Was he faster than light itself? Did he use some kind of magic, invisible to even his trained eye?

His thoughts were interrupted by a searing in his shoulder, almost like he was being branded like cattle. He grunted as the pain persisted, but he refused to yield to the pain... Then the nausea came back. He felt the edges of his vision begin to blur again, and his legs began to shake. He felt his mouth lose its strength and start to slack. Just when he thought he couldn't take anymore punishment, all of the pain subsided so fast that he couldn't tell if the experience had even been real.

"That was impressive, wolfkin." The God King said, satisfied. He was back on his throne. "You're stronger than I remember, Ashnel. Worthy of an audience with me and some discretion within these halls."

Ashnel grabbed parts of his face and body, trying to see if he suffered any damage. He felt his shoulder, which he had forgotten, had been completely covered with a pauldron. It was smashed with a hand-shaped impact, the only indication that The God King had invaded his personal space.

"Don't worry yourself, Warg." King D'Merrion "You'll find that the only lasting effect of this meeting will be my judgement on my son, and your gained favor. Now... To resolve this little meet up. Raise your head and meet my gaze."

Ashnel raised his head slowly, unsure if it was wise to

blindly follow the order. He saw The God King's face, half shown by the light of the panes in the room. Half of his body was covered in the shadows of the pillars that littered the room, making him look more ominous than he already was.

"I know ALL that happens within the walls of Zhalesh." The God King said, staring directly into Ashnel's eyes. The wolfkin felt as though they stood right next to each other, no gap between them. "You have done well, bringing this to my attention and I commend you for your patriotism and dedication to Zhalesh and her people. I have seen my son and his little... pet project. He has strayed from my path, the true path of benevolence I have laid before him and must be shown that even his actions have dire consequences."

The God King then smirked.

"EVERYONE must be shown that there are consequences for their actions." King D'Merrion continued, his smile fading to a grimace. "And I have the perfect mission for you, my proud, powerful lieutenant. There is only one individual fit to mete out a reprimand that Drakonis will remember..."

Ashnel stared at the King for a moment. He opened his mouth then immediately closed it. The God King raised a finger at him, and then waved his hand.

"Can I ask who will receive this honor, my lord?" Ashnel said, a little uncertain of how to proceed.

"Ah." The god King said with what seemed like hope and satisfaction in his voice. "See? What's the human saying? Old dog, and new tricks? Cliche and yet aptly appropriate."

The God King stood up and turned to look at the windowpane that sat behind his throne.

"Bring me Addurog." King D'Merrion declared. "And do tell him to leave that detestable notebook behind."

Chapter 12: Preparation

Drakonis

"Tragic." Drakonis said to himself, scowling as he walked through what was left of the market. Most of the road was covered with debris from collapsed buildings, and a dusty haze blanketed the area while beastkin were hard at work repairing the damage. The clangs of hammers meeting steel and the whirring of flame torches made a mechanical symphony that Drakonis was not particularly fond of either. Even though the beastkin were preoccupied with their miscellaneous tasks, they made sure to not hinder his progress.

Drakonis walked, completely burdened by his thoughts, towards a tower in the far reaches of the Market. He needed help with Isobel, who had shown an extreme resistance to his interrogation techniques. He couldn't even use his own mark to command the answers to the surface; his own power paled in comparison to that of the Black Dragon. So, he decided to ask for assistance from someone who was a little more persuasive than he was.

It didn't take him too long to reach the tower.

Looking up, he noticed the familiar eroded walls of the

old, decrepit structure. No, old was an understatement. This tower was close to prehistoric by this point, a relic of a time long before the modern age. There was a small layer of moss overtaking the base of the tower, almost artistically lining each stone that made up its exterior. Gargoyle statues overwatched the entrance to the tower, standing guard on both sides of the door.

"Sir Mordeus." Drakonis said as he walked by the stone guardians, nodding at them. "Sir Balthios."

The statues didn't reply. How could they? They were statues, after all. Drakonis pushed through the door to the tower, but it was more of a hassle to keep it on its hinges versus opening it. The door was as decayed as the walls it sat within and it barely aligned within its frame.

As he passed through the door, Drakonis was greeted by the familiar warmth of the library. He sighed and breathed in the crisp library air, smiling a bit. The room was filled with large bookshelves that housed many different tomes from all over the globe. Black curtains littered the walls and covered the windows, making the room feel dark and isolated. There were many beastkin studying, reading, and organizing books around the room, each wearing a silver cloak to guard their appearance. Torches weren't allowed here so much of the lighting came from magically charged artificial orbs that sat throughout the room. In the center of the room sat a large golden door, big enough for a dragon to fit through.

The layout of the tower was remarkably simple, there were only two rooms in its entirety. The giant library that sat at the base of the monument, and the inner sanctum that could only be reached with the giant door.

Drakonis spent time in this tower as a boy. He'd conducted much of his studies in the arcane arts here. This place was a sanctuary for him at one point and sometimes he'd even call it home when his mother was away on conquests.

As Drakonis let down his guard and walk towards the door, he felt a large group of beastkin walking towards him.

Here we go, he thought to himself.

He looked around, but he couldn't make out where they were coming from. He could feel their heart beats approaching from right in front of him, but he could not see the group.

“Really?” Drakonis said aloud. “Do we have to do this every time I enter?”

The group was circling around him now, barring his movement.

“C'mon, dear Drakonissssssssss” A raspy voice replied from directly in front of him. “You know we have to insssssspect everyone who enters the Hold of Knowledge. This isssss a formalityyyyyyy!”

The group of beastkin slowly faded into existence, like a group of assassins ready to pounce on their quarry. They all wore silver cloaks with silver lining around their hoods, a slight improvement on the regular silver garb being worn by everyone else. The ringleader was taller than the others but was a little shorter than Drakonis.

"Lilian..." Drakonis said dryly with a puzzled look on his face. "WHY ARE YOU TALKING LIKE THAT!?"

"Don't break character, Drakonis." The tall beastkin whispered back. "We're trying something here! Play along!"

"Look, I REALLY don't have time for theatrics right now." He said bluntly. "If we could just hurry this along, I need to see the master."

The beastkin pulled down her hood, revealing her beautiful blue scales and her sharp emerald eyes. She stomped over to Drakonis, huffing the entire way.

"You're no fun!" Lilian said with what looked like genuine hurt in her eyes. "We're practicing a routine for checking new visitors. Just walking up to each other gets boring."

"Quiet!" One of the beastkin from the circle chimed in.

"Quiet!" Another echoed.

A giant voice boomed throughout the library, one that rattled the walls and shook the shelves.

"LET HIM BE!" The voice commanded.

This prompted all of the beastkin except for Drakonis to jump in reaction. Lilian's shoulders dropped and she moved out

Drakonis' way, bowing her head, as did all the other beastkin of the circle.

“Master Xinovioc awaits...” She said, disappointment blanketing her words.

“We'll talk later, Lilian.” Drakonis said, placing a hand on her shoulder.

All the beastkin kept their heads bowed as Drakonis turned towards the golden door. Many other scholars were walking around but the door remained closed as they passed. As Drakonis drew closer, the door slowly began to open.

On the other side of the door, he could see a room. It was filled with magical objects and books floating around, each on their own personal journey. Each of these books floated around a giant, silver bearded dragon who was sitting motionlessly. He was surrounded by piles of books, sitting directly under a magical lamp that illuminated his body in a mysterious light.

“Aaaaaaahhh.... Drakonis, my boy.” The giant dragon greeted him. “It warms me to see you here in my home. I had begun to wonder if you'd forgotten about an old dragon.”

“Grandfather...” Drakonis said, approaching the aging giant. “I apologize for waiting so long to see you. The capitol has had many issues as of late.”

The Elder Dragon readjusted his body to properly face his grandson, knocking some books over as he got into place.

"Don't worry, young prince." Xinovioc reassured. "I have my tomes to keep me occupied. Have you come to listen to an old man bicker about history and magic?"

"Not this time." Drakonis replied. "I've actually come for guidance. Do you remember the attack on the market a few weeks back?"

The dragon reached out his hand, prompting Drakonis to sit on it.

"Yes." Xinovioc said, lifting Drakonis close to his face so that he didn't have to roar at him. "The one that involved the wards and those detestable Lorins? Ah. You want to understand the magics that the priestess used?"

"Absolutely." Drakonis said. He was never surprised that it felt like Xinovioc could read his mind. The old dragon was extremely wise, and his insight and wisdom had helped Drakonis overcome many dilemmas.

"She was able to channel the power of the Black Dragon..." Xinovioc said, stroking his beard. "And yet she lives, almost unscathed."

"And her mark has grown significantly..." Drakonis continued.

"And you can't tell the nature of her deal." Xinovioc finished. "Her mark probably has grown exponentially, and that means your mark has no power over her."

"Exactly." Drakonis replied, satisfied with Xinovioc's

understanding. "I need you to gain insight as to what she did to not only harness the power, but to survive the ordeal. Her body should have been disintegrated by the Black Dragon's pressure..."

Drakonis watched as the dragon narrowed his eyes at him.

"Surely you understand the severity of the situation..." Xinovioc questioned. "This is not something to take lightly and as soon as we gather the information we need, her life will be in danger. The gravity of The Black Dragon's Deal has WORLD ALTERING effects."

"I understand... to an extent." Drakonis said honestly. He didn't have first-hand experience with the dragon's influence, only information he had read or heard from acolytes of the Dark God.

"Good." Xinovioc said, satisfaction in his voice, as he lowered Drakonis back to the floor. "Then you'll have no problems looking after my library!"

"Huh!?" Drakonis said in a weirdly high-pitched yelp. "Wait..."

"And while you're at it..." Xinovioc continued, smoke falling from his body. He was shrinking down in size, disappearing into the smoke. "You should really refresh your knowledge of draconic magic and your Dragon Transformation. Best not regret tomorrow what can be learned today, my son!"

Drakonis pinched the bridge of his nose in frustration, sighing deeply.

"Can we talk about this?" He said as he put his finger on his temple. "Information on draconic morphing is scarce! I doubt I'll find any book in here without... Aaaaand he's gone..."

The smoke dissipated and Xinovioc was nowhere to be found. All that he left behind was a dragon-shaped arch in the books that sat behind him.

"I didn't even tell you where she was..." Drakonis said annoyed.

Drakonis turned and looked at the books that littered the room, piled high to the ceiling. This was his grandfather's personal collection, a hobby the dragon dedicated his life to retrieving. So, he knew that every single book in the room was going to be a giant bore.

"Frustrating..." Drakonis said to himself, walking over to a pillar of books. "This will not be enjoyable."

*   *   *

Isobel

Isobel laid in the bed in the back of the hospital room, staring blankly at the wall. She was in pain. Her skin was burning... All the time. Or it felt as though she was in a constant inferno. Everyday... Every minute that she continued to live was the most painful minute of her life, but she knew calling on his power would cost her.

The room was small and had sinks and beds all around. Only... She was the only patient in the room. There was a sink across from her, surrounded with sutures, syringes, and all kinds of bandages and antibiotics that they used on her. There weren't any windows in the room, so it had been a few weeks since she'd seen the sun. She really missed the sun... Missed Chase. Missed her life before the pain.

She sighed and sunk deeper into the bed, staring at the artificial lighting in the ceiling. Her agitated skin wasn't even the worst of her worries. Her mana was out of whack because her core was damaged and drained of mana. She was broken. Through and through, she probably wouldn't be able to cast another spell again... Her magic was gone.

The entranceway slid open, making her jump and turn away from the door. They were back again, coming to try and pry the thoughts from her mind, she thought frantically. She'd been resilient against their attacks before, but she didn't know how long she would last against them. They wanted the secrets of the Black Dragon, and they were willing to torture her to get them. Constantly asking questions that would set her body ablaze.

She heard footsteps approach from the door, each step bringing her oppressor closer and closer. She cowered away from the noise, holding her head.

"Please go away." She whispered into the wall behind the bed. She didn't want the questions to burn her skin anymore. She was tired of being confined to a room alone, separated from her friend and anyone else she cared about.

"You're shivering..." An old man's voice said behind her.

Isobel didn't recognize the voice. Who was he? Some specialists, with new means of extracting information. A mind sweeper? Was he going to harm her?

She felt a hand on her shoulder, and she recoiled from its touch, her back hitting the wall behind the bed.

"Don't touch me." She said in a dark, grim tone.

"Poor thing..." The man said. It was Drakonis. But then she realized it wasn't. He was way older, with graying dreadlocks that covered his face, and a massive beard, which was surprisingly well-trimmed, that ran down to his chest. He had a small frame, his build was tinier than Drakonis', but it wasn't frail or weak; his giant silver gown was just huge in comparison to his body. His most striking feature was his eyes. The room was dimly lit, but somehow, his soft topaz eyes glowed like gems; it was as though someone had a tiny flashlight and had illuminated them from somewhere.

The man pulled a chair from the wall over to her bed and sat down next to her.

“Hello, Divine Knight Isobel.” The man began. “It seems we have been fated to meet each other once again. For the accommodations, I must apologize. I can see they have done nothing to aid in your recovery.”

Isobel didn't reply. Talking never solved anything, it only brought more pain for her. The man would not trick her, she knew what he wanted.

“Hmmm...” The man sighed. “This is worse than I thought. The mark has consumed most of your body.”

He began to move his hands in a weird way through the air chanting a small incantation. It took her awhile to realize he was casting a magic sigil. She could tell by his hand strokes and the chants that it was a silencing symbol. What unholy interrogation tactic was he going to employ!?

There was a small burst in the room, indicating the spell was complete. Now the room was a small shade brighter due to the spell. The darkness peeled away from her mind. Her heart felt at ease, and the burning was gone. It was finally gone!

“There... Now we can speak freely.” The man said as he brandished a huge smile. Something about it was confident, and almost welcoming. She kept her guard up. She knew this relief was momentary, and he could drop the spell at any moment to bring the pain back.

The man pulled out a tea set from his cloak and set up a table next to the bed.

“Can I interest you in some lemonade?” He asked, sounding extremely genuine. “Water, bread, and bits of pork soup can only help your bones so much.”

Isobel stayed silent. She would not be won over. She didn't want to be won over.

“I can see you're interested.” The man continued. “There's a glimmer in your eyes and... Saliva. You're drooling. Here.”

She wiped her lips, and he pulled a napkin from his gown. He noticed it was gone so he just set the napkin down on his table.

How the heck was he hiding all this stuff in his gown, she thought. Where were these things coming from? She was burning with questions, and... She wanted that lemonade. She wanted so bad to drink just a cup, maybe eight. Just enough to get a taste of lemonade. She was tired of water.

He poured two cups, filling each to the brim. He handed her a glass of lemonade. Isobel inspected the lemonade, seeing if there were any enchantments or hidden poisons. The man drank his lemonade and gave a satisfying "ahh" when he had finished.

She gulped hard... She really wanted to drink the lemonade. Her throat was dry from all the days in the bed, just drinking water and eating bread twice a day, for weeks. She couldn't hold back anymore; she downed the lemonade with reckless abandon. The drink was sweet; the lemony taste was savory and appealed to all ten thousand of her tastebuds. The immaculate taste was enough to...

"I can see you're enjoying the lemonade, Knight Isobel." The man said as he reached for her glass. "So, Isobel, I know you have questions. Feel free to ask me anything."

"Who are you?" She asked quickly.

"I brought you here, to our lovely city, Knight Isobel." He replied, pouring her next cup. "You don't know me in this form but if I were to perhaps... transform into a giant dragon... Maybe you would recognize me...?"

"You're... Grandfather." Isobel guessed.

"Yes child." The man replied. "I am Xinovioc, one of the last pure-blooded dragons and honored to make your acquaintance. It actually warms my heart that you remember me. You may ask your next question."

Xinovioc handed her a freshly poured cup of lemonade and took a sip of his. Isobel noticed he had scars all over his body. He had seen many battles, this she was sure, and she wondered how old he was.

"Did Drakonis send you here to get information from me?" She asked, staring right into the old dragon's eyes as she downed the sweet drink.

"Yes." He replied bluntly.

"I knew it." She said, defeat in her voice. "You're all the same. You only care about your desire to destroy, your interests piqued by even just a whiff of power. What makes you think that I would tell you? That I would suffer more of the Black Dragon's torment and invite his wrath?"

"Hmm..." Xinovioc sighed, putting down his teacup and rubbing his beard. "I suppose you've seen the ward I cast?"

Isobel nodded. How could she not?

"And have you felt any pain?" Xinovioc questioned, his eyes glowing radiantly.

"No." Isobel replied. "In fact, I haven't heard whispers either. What... What have you done?"

Isobel grabbed her neck. The mark stayed still, unfazed by their conversation. She looked down and realized that her body was hers again. It was untainted by the Mark, save for its original sigil branded on her neck. This gave her a euphoric amount of relief, to not be under the gaze of the Dragon of Darkness for even a moment was a blessing she didn't believe she would experience again.

"Child, I am well-aware of the stipulations in the Dragon of Darkness' deal." Xinovioc stated calmly as he reached for her cup. "However, there are ways to get around such limitations. All I have done is made a safe space for us to communicate. No one that isn't in this room can hear us. For instance, you don't have to relinquish the deal you agreed upon. I can clearly understand to what lengths you would travel to achieve victory simply by the spell you were willing to cast on my grandson. A spell of that nature is not of this or any world for that matter..."

Isobel narrowed her eyes at the dragon. There's no way he could know of the spell's origin. Not even the Divines speak casually of that place. Even mentioning it was taboo and an act of chaos.

"The Divine Athenaeum has many curiosities that an old mind like me takes an interest in." He continued, a smile creeping onto his face. "You know as well as I, that the dragon can make anything happen when it forms a deal."

Isobel knew. He didn't have to say it, but she knew. This old dragon made a deal, probably decades ago. But dragonkin are the strongest and most gifted in the arcane arts outside of the gods. What could he possibly have wanted so bad that he shackled himself to such an abomination? She felt she couldn't trust him and yet felt he was very trustworthy. This was a hard conundrum.

“Xinovioc...” She said, her voice low.

“Yes?” Xinovioc replied, handing her the cup again.

“What kind of deal did you make with him?” She asked, unable to control her curiosity. She hastily drank this cup of lemonade as well, and instinctively held the cup out for it to be refilled.

The smile on Xinovioc's face faded away, giving way to an expression Isobel could only describe as grief.

“That's a bit personal, don't you think, Knight Isobel?” Xinovioc said, not breaking eye contact with her. His expression wasn't cold... It was just... Sad.

“I will tell you this.” He continued, grabbing the cup back from her. “I understand all too well the toll it takes to submit oneself to the demands of another. To be seen and abused as a pawn, disposable at any moment. But in exchange, you receive knowledge and power unknown to this realm, that only the gods can see. We will not exchange the reason for our deals or the terms. Allow me that respect.”

“I'm... Sorry, Xinovioc.” Isobel said regretfully. “I didn't mean...”

“Think nothing of it.” Xinovioc interrupted, pausing for a brief moment. “Instead, I want to offer you a trade, Knight Isobel.”

“A trade?” Isobel replied unamused. He was going to ask about the market. He held out the cup to her and she took it again, this time waiting a bit to drink.

"I want to know about the market." Xinovioc stated. "In return, I will continue to answer all your questions and visit you until you're able to leave this room."

"That deal... Hardly seems fair to you." Isobel said honestly.

"I find it appealing." Xinovioc said, his welcoming smile returning. "I hear that you have quite the acumen in the arcane and have a well-traveled intellect. You might even gift me with a surprise for a change and teach me a lesson. How about it?"

Isobel was tired. She didn't want to just give in to his demands, but she was exhausted. She couldn't handle another wave of torture from Drakonis. She didn't want to go back to being alone in the room either, to go back to listening to the darkness eating away at her will. And speaking with Xinovioc was like chatting with an old friend. She would do anything to not have to be alone anymore... To get back to Chase.

"Yes." She said swiftly. "But I want to add an additional amendment to the deal..."

"And that is?" Xinovioc asked.

"You must find a way to bring Chase here." She said firmly. "He... He needs me."

"Child... I don't know if..." Xinovioc tried to argue.

"You must!" She yelled back. "He has a rage in him

that never stops burning. And the longer we are apart, the more the kettle stirs. He needs me."

"I can't guarantee that I can bring him here." The old dragon said solemnly. "But I can give you a Dragon's Oath that you will be reunited with him before you know it. A dragon never forgets his promises."

"I guess I have no choice but to just trust you then?" Isobel said. She didn't have much hope left, but Xinovioc seemed to be an honorable being. She drank the cup of lemonade she had been holding and held it out for Xinovioc to retrieve.

"Brilliant." The dragon said, a hint of excitement in his voice. "A few guidelines if you will... Never state the nature of your deal. That will break the ward and make us susceptible to the dragon's curse. This will be especially relevant when you reveal the events at the market. For your safety, do not break this rule. And more importantly, do not repeatedly say his name. That will compel him to enter this conversation."

"Ok." Isobel agreed. These were the general terms of the deal, so she was already familiar with the rules.

"Alright then let us begin." Xinovioc said, giving her cup back. He then proceeded to drink some lemonade himself. "I will be blunt. How could you, a mortal woman, somehow subjugate the power of an immortal deity without repercussion?"

"Without repercussion!?" Isobel said, disgusted at his words. Her sudden outburst almost caused her to spill the lemonade in her hand. "I died! I was destined for eternal suffering. No hope of rescue, no hope of redemption. There WERE repercussions, and I am still suffering! What could you possibly know of that, to be trapped in the miasma of the Dragon of Darkness for the rest of existence!?"

"And yet, you are not." Xinovioc calmly rebutted. "Here you stand, free of responsibility. To only answer for your ignorance of execution. That power... could be felt by even the weakest of the magically inclined. I can see you, Isobel. You understand the gravity of a deal with The Dragon of Darkness. So why would you tempt fate, his anger, and the wrath of all who scorn him?"

"There was no other way..." Isobel replied leaning her back against the wall. "Dying face down in the mud is not my fate. And there was so much death... I had to stop it. Chaos overtook the market quicker than anyone could react. Those... things... were surrounding us. If I was going to die, I would die a proud warrior fighting till my last breath for what I believe... Saving innocent lives and fighting evil."

"How naive of you." Xinovioc said, reaching for her cup again. It sounded like he was pitying her. She didn't care. She knew in her heart that her actions were just. She handed her cup back to him.

"Well, in a sense, you did buy many citizens enough time to escape." He continued. "But I'm not interested in the details of the attack. How did you use that power, Isobel?"

"Our arrangement." Isobel said grimly. "You understand that everyone that creates a pact with the Dragon of Darkness has their mana core linked to him. Usually, he only allows himself to have access to your core, so that he may grant you, his blessing. But for my deal, in particular, he has opened access to his core."

Xinovioc's eyes widened.

"You... can channel his mana freely?" He said with bewilderment. Much to her chagrin, he placed her cup of lemonade on the table in front of him. She could see a bead of sweat fall from his brow.

"Not freely." She replied. "I have only attempted to use it on three separate occasions, each with their own brand of torture as a reward for my reliance. The first experience was beyond excruciating... But there was worth in my pain. I created my first spell using the will of the dragon."

"Spell Crafting?" Xinovioc scoffed. She could tell he was surprised, and maybe even in disbelief. "You crafted a spell? Creating a spell can take decades, sometimes entire lifetimes. Many spend the first half of their life studying and understanding the Weave of Magic. The danger of even thinking you can manipulate the weave is astronomical, and yet you believed you could?"

"I had to." Isobel replied. "I wanted... No... I needed power to fulfill my goals. There are things that only I can do, and I have to continue to grow if I want them to come true. Believe it or not, Chase actually was the one who showed me it was possible."

"THAT HOT-HEADED PUNK CRAFTED A SPELL AS WELL?" Xinovioc said with complete disbelief in his voice, throwing his hands on his head. "Surely you, as you humans say, are pulling my leg. Creating a spell with the dragon's influence is a grand reach, but that little ape actually managed to make a spell!? Even if it was a little one, the thought that he made it with his own core? Unfathomable!"

"It's true." Isobel said, a light smile lighting her face. "He's actually quite amazing. I couldn't even make the spell perfectly with the dragon's assistance, I was almost killed. If not for the dark mana, I would have ceased to be. I can't even cast that spell anymore, but it allowed me to make something greater."

"Something greater?" Xinovioc said. Isobel could see how intrigued he was by the conversation. "I know it isn't part of our deal, but would you let an old fool live a little? I am deeply intrigued by the magical world, and sometimes, my love for magic overtakes my interests. You do not have to share, if you do not wish it."

Isobel was torn. Even if he'd only wished to learn about her to manipulate her, to take advantage of her and Chase... She'd missed this. Socializing. Talking with someone, reminiscing, and theorizing. She missed home.

"It's... an enchantment I made." She started, fiddling with her hands nervously. "I call it Golden Time. It allows me to increase the size of my core, to channel more mana and be able to withstand more physical abuse. It can even amplify spells that I use."

"Marvelous!" Xinovioc said, seeing her hands out and giving her the cup of lemonade. "And what inspired such a spell?"

Isobel thought for a moment. That was a personal question that she couldn't reveal to him. An insecurity that she hadn't overcome yet.

"I wasn't adept at swordplay or magic." Isobel replied. "And so, I made the spell as a counterbalance."

Xinovioc rubbed his beard for a moment, and frowned, thinking on her words. A part of her told her that he didn't fully buy that excuse but even if he asked for more, she wouldn't reveal it.

"Interesting." The old dragon said slowly. He suddenly blurted out. "Have you considered making levels to it?"

"Levels?" Isobel said, taken aback by his enthusiasm. She took a sip of her lemonade.

“Yes!” He replied. “With that, you can amplify the strength of the spell. You could even train your body to withstand even more duress. You could also...”

Xinovioc paused for a moment, crocking his head to the side.

“You could use the spell to move through time as though it stood still.” He said, staring back at her.

Isobel gagged a bit, her mouth barely stopping the lemonade from erupting all over Xinovioc. She had revealed too much. She realized the kind of individual she was dealing with. He was able to piece together her plan with breadcrumbs. She didn't know what he'd do now that he knew. She slowly forced the lemonade down.

“Ahhh...” Xinovioc sighed, grinning and shaking his head. “You're quite the genius, aren't you? Precocious, arrogant, and naive. You remind me so much of my grandson. To think, that someone would attempt a spell like that... Brilliant.”

“I'm nothing like Drakonis.” Isobel shot back sharply.

“Nonsense child.” He said jauntily. “You both are two sides of the same coin. I can tell that you are masking an unforgivable amount of pain. In these same ways, you both are alike.”

“I would never torture someone for information.” Isobel said coldly.

"Aren't you being a tad bit dramatic?" Xinovioc said with a puzzled look. "I know my grandson. He is one of the most honorable dragons I have ever met. You may not have realized it, but your actions have gained you new enemies who would do anything to enslave you."

"Because I'm not enslaved already?" She rebutted sternly.

"No child, you are not." Xinovioc said with a grimace. "These reprobates would warp your mind and lock away your heart. Corrupt your core and use you for their wicked doings. Right now, they pose no threat to us, D'Merrion, or the kingdom. But with you in their ranks, with your power? They could very well upset the balance of the war and destroy humans and beastkin alike."

"The likes of D'Merrion and these "enemies" you talk of are one and the same." Isobel snapped back. "There is no EVIL worse than D'Merrion."

"Child..." Xinovioc said with a soft sigh. "I don't wish to sully the sweet lemonade we've shared today. So, I'll be brief. This world and any other is not black and white. There isn't GOOD or BAD, Right or Wrong, Left or Right. There is a giant gray abyss that we all reside in. You may see The One True God..."

Isobel scoffed loudly at the mention of his name to which Xinovioc smiled back at her. She slammed her cup on the table. She had her fill of lemonade for the day.

"You may see The One True God as a menace, a tyrant." Xinovioc continued. "But before his existence, beastkin were hunted. As you may have surmised, all of mythology was crafted around humanity's fear of the beastkin. We were hunted to near extinction with your god's approval, with no chance of unity or peace. With D'Merrion's return, beastkin and humans can live in peace in self-sustaining and beautiful cities."

"I guess the genocide of humanity is a reasonable cost for that peace." Isobel replied.

"Resistance has brought on the humanity's destruction." Xinovioc stated bluntly. "Ask yourself... How have you been treated since entering this city? You and your friend were among the highest-ranking adversaries to D'Merrion's cause, and yet you were spared complete imprisonment and execution. You've even been treated akin to royalty, spending most of your days within the castle walls, gifted clothes for your backsides, given proper food, and comfortable sleeping arrangements. Our goal has never been extinction..."

"Don't give me that bull." Isobel interrupted, now fed up with the dragon's words. "We may have broken bread here and shared common interests, but you won't fool me. The only reason Chase and I still draw breath is due to Drakonis having some sort of need for us. Otherwise, we'd have returned to the earth by now. Don't pretend that you're on some tour of philanthropy when I have personally seen Drakonis burn towns to the ground."

Xinovioc grimaced again, this time looking down solemnly and taking a sip of lemonade. She could see it in his eyes, some regret to his actions.

That regret won't revive any of the humans they have slain, she thought. They have been on a non-stop murder spree since the war began and she would not be swayed by their propaganda.

"I... can't apologize for my actions, Knight Isobel." Xinovioc said softly. "I do not regret what I have done. But I can say that I am sorry for how they have affected you. I do not enjoy war and death. Actually, it is because of war that I have spent over three centuries with my mark. But my time with the mark has been a moment, a blink in my life."

Even though Isobel was angry with him, she also couldn't help feeling sorry for him. She could sense the pain in his words. Maybe he was genuinely trying to bond with her, but with their history... It would just be wise to keep him at arm's length. One day, he would be her enemy again. She would rather not grow close to him.

Xinovioc reached out and grabbed her hand, turning it over in his hand.

"It has been my pleasure, Knight Isobel." He said as he

stood up, letting her hand go. “But I must take my leave.”

The dragonkin began to pick up the tea set. Isobel quickly drank the rest of her lemonade and handed the cup back to the man.

“Thank you.” Xinovioc said as he bowed his head.

He then stacked the cups on his table and put the whole set back in his cloak.

“Wait.” Isobel said abruptly. “Where does it all go? I can't pretend I'm not curious.”

The old dragon smiled wryly at her.

“Ah, this old spell?” He said proudly. “I made this a while ago among others. I call it 'inventory' and yes, it can be quite convenient. Especially for a dragon who spends most of his time naked.”

He let out a hearty laugh, which put a smile on Isobel's face.

“There we go.” Xinovioc said. “That smile is worth a thousand words. I will return again. I also want to put your mind at ease. I won't inform Drakonis of your personal history or of your personal spell. I'll only let him know of your 'arrangement' with you know who.”

“Thank you, but... Why?” Isobel asked, a little confused. It only seemed natural to tell him of everything that transpired. He had nothing to gain from keeping secrets from his grandson.

"I want you to believe me when I say we have no ill intentions against you or the boy." Xinovioc replied. "Regardless of what you believe, we are NOT evil beings."

He was really good at making you feel guilty for not believing as he does, Isobel thought. She just couldn't help it. She really appreciated her conversation with Xinovioc. He was genuine and caring. Drakonis could learn a thing or two from him.

"Xinovioc... Thank you." Isobel said politely, standing up and bowing to him. "Thank you so much for this reprieve."

"You are quite welcome, child." He said, heading towards the door. "Now get back in bed. You have a harrowing ordeal ahead."

"I know." She said, teary eyed. Isobel was prepared for what came next. It was like she had been holding her breath for a long time and now she could finally breathe easy. It was depressing to know those breaths were going to get choked again.

"You'll let me see Chase, soon?" She asked as she walked to the corner of the room.

"Dragon's Oath." Xinovioc said as he closed the door behind him.

She winced as the Mark of the Black Dragon on her neck began to burn and expand. The pain was back, every part of her body on fire again. She felt the darkness grip at her heart, reach into her mind, and a familiar, menacing voice whispered to her.

"Little Knight." The voice hissed. "You're back..."

Chapter 13:
Adversary

Addurog

Hmmm... So how does one even begin to recount a chapter of their life? Does he simply start with "I am here" and begin to rabble? Could we not skip to the part where I dramatically thrash and humiliate my quarry, accomplishing all I set out to do...? What? Spoiling? What carbon, silicone, hydrogen, or calcium-based life form believed otherwise?

Oh... You're wondering who has commandeered this little tale and imported their relevant perspective into the narrative? Well cease all inquiries for I will reveal the answer to all your burning questions! I am the humble, generous, and admirable ink feathered Addurog of the First Pantheon of the Rising Phoenix. Formerly...

We were a proud and zealous few... Oh... It seems like it's not that chapter quite yet. Hmm... I can't seem to remember where we are in the vastness of time and space... Oh, right. Well then...

The room was dimly lit, only a few sources of light penetrated the damp and stuffy darkness. Torches flickered as they were licked by a brisk breeze that entered through tiled windows. The flames danced elegantly, casting shadows on the armor stands and antique treasures that littered the room. This room was one of many treasure troves hidden away by the gracious God King, a tower far above watchful eyes and away from prying fingers of the dreadful dreary. I, the gallant Addurog, sat upon a fickle, decaying chair, reviewing the latest of my brilliantly articulate insults for one undergrown sea lizard.

"Ahh... I do hope you stub your toe upon the mightiest of Majen furniture." I concluded as I closed my prized book of pejoratives. It's 'bashful bull' brown leather case looked marvelous in the soft lighting of the room, a treasure far greater than the archaic trash that littered the room, and I strapped it to my waist after admiring its quality.

I was not alone in the dimly lit prison for forgotten goods, accompanied by a table of which two incorrigible wretches sat uncomfortably. The table held but my sword and a few pieces of text that were strewn across its surface. Soon the individuals opened their unsavory orifices in my direction, speaking of plans and what not. One of them, a pet of my nemesis, sat on a chair of equally poor quality and squalor.

His name was Ashnel of the Sun Wolf Clan. He was a complete lout, a burden to his troop commander, and his voice could scrape rust from rotten metal. If his rugged and nasty growl couldn't scare you away, his odor and offensive personality would. While Ashnel was generally undesirable most days, I did have a fondness for the wolfkin.

"Addurog..." The smelly wolf growled at me. "Put away that wretched journal! We have urgent business and there is no time for your usual insanity."

"I don't expect you to understand the complexities of my text, wolf." I rebutted, holding back my laughter at the dog's ignorance. "But please cease to dictate errands to me as though you're someone of repute. You're here to assist me, not the other way around. Now be a dear and fetch me some water. You mutts do love wagging your tail, searching for trinkets and such."

He didn't reply immediately so I looked across the table to see how scalded his ego was. His eyes were almost bloodshot, smoldering with rage, shooting a glare of extreme aggravation right in my direction. If a stare could kill, I would be in bits across the wall by now, a new decoration for all the antiques in the room. And it is precisely that killing intent that makes Ashnel such an appealing creature. He was a beast in its primal form, an apex predator in his respective food chain... Well... When he wasn't following his or someone else's tail. Many beastkin have adapted their lives to the acceptable societal standard we maintain within this capital, but not Ashnel. And neither I.

“We're not here for idle chit-chat, Addurog.” The other stated, a woman, as she broke my concentration. Her voice was grating on my ears, like a fork dragged across a blackboard. “You know the consequences for failing the One True God. Let's not allow incompetence to defeat our objective. Especially when it's so easily avoidable.”

The woman was Cyarah the Chimera, and she was an abomination against all that was keenly and tenderly crafted by the gods. This roach decided instead of living her days like the pathetic shaved ape she is, she would graft the better qualities of beastkin onto her rotten bones. Now she is a morbid freak, a complete pariah with no friends or family in this realm or the next. I understand the desire to emulate the ferocity and elegance of beastkin, but some sciences are better left unexplored.

“Hold your tongue wench!” I shot sharply at the mutant. “You are only here because the One True God deemed your services a necessity, but I can't for the life of me even fathom why. Don't waste your words for I have already compiled a scheme worthy of praise and glory. No need to fry that little peanut-shaped brain with any half-sparked plans, dear.”

Cyarah stared blankly back at me, almost as though she couldn't fathom pejoratives inhabiting her immediate vicinity. After relishing her expression for a few seconds, I noticed that the little bug had a folder clutched under her arm.

“Anyway...” Cyarah said rolling her eyes and opening her folder. “After reviewing your medical profile, I couldn't find any way to increase your power short of modifying your...”

“No.” I interjected before she could finish. I would not even allow her to suggest the notion of changing my pure phoenix blood.

“... Modifying your sword.” She quickly finished. “You would never allow anyone to change your DNA and there is no one of your lineage to name you and augment your aura, so we have only the option of attaining physically superior gear at our disposal. In fact, your file says that you're inferior to the dark lord in every way.”

I scoffed at her revelations.

“I AM BETTER than that ape.” I said, turning my beak up at the mention of my nemesis. “The sweaty kobold should feel honored I have allowed his stench to occupy my thoughts this long. His power is barely worth reverence, let alone mention...”

“Then why haven't you won yet, Lord Addurog?” She said quizzingly. “It says here that you've incited Rule of the Wilds against Drakonis countless times without success. If 'inferior' isn't a term you would use, then what should we call it? Pathetic? Sad?”

Before she had even finished her sentence, I had already

unsheathed my blade, made my way to her, and swung down upon her with enough force to separate well-bonded steel. Much to my chagrin, there was no satisfying destruction of flesh and crunch of bone or even a deathly wail to signify her demise. My hand had never reached its true destination.

The woman had stopped my strike completely with her tail and was rubbing the blade, examining it.

"Unhand my sword, cur." I said bluntly, insulted that she still drew breathe.

In response, she brought her hand down on the blade, quickly smashing the blade to pieces. The shards rained all over the room, covering the ground.

"What have you done to Severance?" I growled. "How could you destroy my prized sword, made by the finest blacksmith in Zhalesh!?"

Cyarah tilted her head for a moment, confusion covering her face.

"You and I both know that Killian is the WORST blacksmith in town!" Cyarah said, half smiling. "That sword is poorly crafted, and even worse, beneath the military's standard. You should be ashamed of such a blade."

"ASHAMED!?" I gawked back at her, eyeing her intensely. "I SUPPORT LOCAL BUSINESSES, YOU PUTZ!

I ran over to the window of the tower and yelled at the top of my lungs.

“KILLIAN!” I screamed. “Some wench destroyed your black-hilted steel blade!”

“What!?” Killian's voice rang back. “Not the black-hilted steel blade!”

“She also said you're the worst blacksmith in Zhalesh!” I replied.

“Rude...” Killian yelled back. “But she ain't lying.”

“KILLIAN, YOU HUMBLE IDIOT!” I yelled angrily.

I turned from the window to see the atrocity once again furrowing her brow. My distaste for the brat was growing ever so deep, and I could see that she couldn't see the significance of a humble weapon like mine. Admittedly, Killian's style was iconically bad. The weapons were unnecessarily flimsy, sure, but they looked nice. Who was she to ridicule a beastmen's craftsmanship?

The atrocity sighed again and turned to the mutt, who had been watching the altercation unfold. He seemed annoyed and mildly amused by the repartee.

“Addurog...” Cyarah begins glumly. “You do realize... That this is supposed to be a secret meeting, yes?”

“No one knows or cares what we're doing up here!” I stated bluntly. “Those brainless plebs are most likely assuming I'm up here to collect my thoughts. Speaking of thoughts, did I tell you that you're a monstrosity? An actual affliction on my eyesight? If I had to measure my discomfort from looking at you on a scale from one to Cyarah, I would say two Cyarah's."

"Ashnel..." Cyarah said, her discontent unhidden in her words. "Show him...PLEASE!"

Ashnel nodded and then turned to a giant cloth leaning on the wall. I had assumed it was another one of the worthless relics, forgotten by its owner. Now that I had properly examined the object, it did seem sword shaped.

The dog pulled the cloth away from the wall to reveal a massive sheath. It was silver with different colored runes attached to the hilt of the sword hidden within. There was a soft blue aura that radiated and buzzed with power. I had trouble placing the craftsmen's smithing style. Was it Majen in origin? Oranikan? Dwarven? I couldn't help but be taken by its appearance. It was beautiful. Marvelous. Exotic. Extravagant. Sublime. Splendid. Wonderful....

*　　　　*　　　　*

Cyarah

"Glorious." Addurog continued to speak to himself, obviously taken by the sword's appearance. "Delightful. Goodly and gorgeous steel."

Cyarah rubbed her temple in frustration. It was one thing that she had to work with the brutish thug, Ashnel. But she almost couldn't stand having to even share the same air with Addurog. He and his antics were insufferable. Even worse, he despised her for absolutely no reason!

"Enrapturing." Addurog continued, lifting the sword.

"Addurog!" Cyarah yelled, tired of his delusion. "Please cease your bumbling!"

The phoenix looked startled for a bit. He turned around and stared back at her, tears in his eyes. She didn't see him often but when she did, Addurog always had a goofy, half-cranked smile. It was a weird sight to see from a phoenixkin.

"I-Is this sword mine?" He asked meekly, the tears beginning to flow. "Have the Majes constructed a blade for my use alone?"

"Not the Majes..." Cyarah replied, walking over to Addurog. "This sword was a collaborative prototype. You may notice some of the Maje's crafting style in the hilt, but there is Arcian and beastkin influence within the metalwork."

"It is truly... "Addurog began, closing his eyes and letting his tears flow freely. He hugged the sword, completely ignoring the fact that it was a very, very sharp sword. "Lovely... I shall name you Severance"

"The sword's anatomy..." Cyarah continued, ignoring his meaningless comments. She was tired of the buffoon's comical behavior. "Is a combination of Zhaleshian steel and a new element, gifted to our cause by the One True God himself. Let me ask you something Addurog... Are you familiar with Dark Mana?"

"The First Poison?" He said, rubbing his eyes dry. "When the substance was used to subjugate the Old God, I was indeed present. It was unlike anything I had ever seen. An entire army was brought to its knees in a matter of moments. It was a debilitating affliction that corrupted a man's very spirit before rendering him feeble and powerless. In fact, I'd like to see you take a bath in some. An abomination like you could benefit from a change in perspective."

"I'm baffled you even know what a bath is, considering you smell like a week-old cadaver!" Cyarah scoffed back at him.

"ENOUGH!" Ashnel roared, slamming his fist on the table. There was a fist shaped impact where his hand was. "We did not come here to share insults, and chatter like hens. Our lord has entrusted us with the punishment of my lord. Cyarah!

Regain yourself!"

Cyarah blushed in embarrassment. It was rare that she let someone's insults get to her, but there was something about Addurog that really got under your skin. He had a way of dragging your insecurities to the surface. She had never had any real conversation with him, and now she knew why. He was insufferable, and all around loathsome.

"Well if you've grown tired of trying to match wits with my superior intellect, I'll be off to route our mutual annoyance." Addurog said, unsheathing the blade and eyeing it intensely. "If I based my plan's outcome off this sword's appearance alone, I'd surmise only victory in my immediate future. I could..."

"Addurog, you idiot." Ashnel said, standing up, interrupting the bird's monologue. "We have a plan! One you'd best resort to if you don't want to doom us to the One True God's wrath."

Addurog continued to eye the sword, ignoring Ashnel's warnings.

"Yes." Cyarah said after taking a few moments to compose herself. "Our window for opportunity is dwindling and if we wish to route Drakonis, we need to be swift. Ashnel, you know the plan. Please report to your station and await further orders."

"No." Addurog replied to her, sheathing the giant blade.

“The rat dog will not fetch cheese this time. No. He will be the cheese. I'm going to make an amendment to the plan.”

“Amendment?” Ashnel and Cyarah said in unison. They looked at each other with worry on their faces. Cyarah had no hope in Addurog's madness.

“I suggest that if you wish to maintain your neutrality, wench.” Addurog leered at Cyarah. “Then you make your exit here. Your presence, while dreadful, was at least not a complete bore. Since this is our first interaction, cherish the thought that you've earned favor with a true warrior.”

Cyarah was already making her way towards the door. She couldn't stand his hubris.

“Oh, and Cyarah...” Addurog said softly. This was the first time he'd called her by her name and it made her skin crawl. “I had believed you to be somewhat of a weakling, and I didn't apply even a fraction of my strength to that blow. I won't make that mistake again should you use that tongue to even utter my name in my presence.”

She turned to meet Addurog's eyes. The aloof and mildly jovial expression on his face was gone. They stood there, eyes locked, for a few moments before Cyarah turned towards the door.

“I wish you both the best of luck.” She said flatly before leaving the room.

She never wanted any part of their buffoonery. She

wanted even less to tangle with Drakonis. Being at D'Merrion's mercy was rare because he was constantly looking at the big fish and hardly bothered with menial affairs and commoners. But Drakonis would make time for anyone who wronged him, making his rage far more terrifying than either of his parents. Staying in Drakonis' good graces was in her best interests.

She raised her wrist to access her crystal, which was inlaid into her watch.

“Ermes.” Cyarah called into the crystal, her wrist glowing a bright blue.

“Yes, ma'am?” A voice from the crystal replied.

“Prep the lab, a canister of B45, and let my bae-bee out, please.” She said, walking down the steps to leave the tower. “There's a possibility that there will be injuries today and we need to have the infirmary and lab ready to receive patients.”

“At once.” Ermes stated back. “Should we... stop our 'Project'?”

“No.” Cyarah said calmly. “Let the Maj continue his work. Just take a moment and do as I ask, okay? I'll be returning to the lab soon.”

“Understood.” Ermes said as he moved about. Cyarah could hear a door closing in the call, confirming Ermes was in the kennel. “See you soon.”

Before she ended the call, a soft roar could be heard.

Chapter 14:
Laying the Cheese

Isobel

Isobel awoke the same way she always did and rubbed her eyes as she sat up in her bed. She sighed as her body recognized the familiar, uncomfortable pricks of the IVs and the coarseness of her gown. She groggily turned and placed her feet on the cold stone floor. She willed herself to stand up but felt slightly weak and a little dizzy, so she sat down quickly.

She took a deep breath and closed her eyes. She searched her being for her mana core, trying as hard as she could to will some power from it. But nothing happened.

Between the Black Dragon's mental assaults and her interrogations by Drakonis, she had spent much of her time alone recovering just to repeat the torture again the next day. She hadn't been able to focus on her core's recovery or her physical rehabilitation.

And yet, she was relieved. Today was the day she would be released from her imprisonment and would finally be reunited with her brother. She couldn't stop herself from smiling at the thought of feeling the sun's warmth again, to have the wind pet her skin and smell the nuances of nature. She had felt herself drop so far into the pit of depression and had endured so much mental pain and suffering that she believed that she would never see the light of day again. So, in all honesty, to say she was relieved was an understatement. She was ecstatic.

"*Do not forget your purpose and oath to me, Isobel.*" The Black Dragon whispered to her. *"Your life is mine. Remember that as you enjoy your false freedoms. You can never escape my grasp."*

"Yes, My lord." Isobel replied, clutching her fists. She was punished for even small respites from her bondage. Would she ever be free?

The door to the room slid open suddenly, pulling Isobel from her meditation. A small woman, carrying a clipboard and pushing a cart of various medical tools, entered the room. She had honey blonde hair that contradicted her brown skin, but what was more jarring was that she had a tail! She wore a pristine and well kempt lab coat, that she dug into searching for something.

"Alright, Knight Isobel!" The woman exclaimed. "It seems as though you're scheduled for immediate release, regardless of if you're physically able or not. Let me take a couple of measurements and we can work on getting you discharged from our care."

Isobel only nodded in response.

The woman walked over to the bed, dragging the cart behind her. She grabbed various limbs and joints on Isobel's body and counted softly to herself while scribbling something down on her clipboard. She then reached onto the cart and lifted an awkward device from its surface.

“Please stand up and turn around.” The woman instructed.

Isobel turned to face the wall behind the bed, even though she felt a little embarrassed revealing her back to the woman.

For a moment, there was nothing. She almost turned to look at the woman in confusion, when she felt a soft jolt on her spine.

“Nothing has changed, I see.” The women said with an unsurprised tone. “Your core is still crippled. Thanks, love. You can sit down.”

The information wasn't new or unknown to Isobel, but that didn't stop her from being saddened at hearing someone else confirm the fact. She didn't know how she was going to fix her core. She didn't even know if she could.

The woman began pulling the IVs from Isobel's body. After a few minutes, the knight was completely free from the medical equipment.

“There!” The woman proclaimed. “I would say good as new, but that's reserved for those that have actually recovered in our care. Your body was never in any real danger, I assume from years of physical training. But your core, as hardened as it was, is cracked. It's a miracle you're even alive with the type of damage you sustained."

Isobel just kept staring towards the wall. She didn't want to turn to face the woman, to have to look at the woman's eyes as they judged her decisions.

"And even with the unsurmountable damage you've done to your core, somehow your condition has worsened..." The woman continued. "I don't know what you and Drakonis have been doing, but if it continues, you will die."

Isobel turned around to face the woman.

"Thank you, doctor." Isobel said sitting back on the bed. "I will keep that in mind."

The woman looked at her with a thoughtful expression, then she just shrugged and placed the tool on the cart. She bent down and pulled some fabric from the lower shelf of the cart and handed them to Isobel.

"Here's some pants and a fresh shirt." The woman said smiling. "Good luck today, they say the first steps are always the hardest."

The woman seemed expectant of a reply to this statement, but Isobel just took the clothes and turned towards the bed. From behind her, she could hear the woman sigh and roll the cart out of the room.

"Drakonis will be here shortly." The woman said. Then there was a soft thud as the door closed shut.

Isobel took off her gown and put on the new clothes she received. Something about the woman felt... off. And it wasn't her weird appearance or the words she chose. The woman just gave Isobel the creeps. She pushed the negative thoughts away.

After putting on her new outfit, she sat on the bed again. Even that small act of changing clothes was exhausting. But if she could survive weeks of isolation and beration, then she could survive this...

She had almost gotten comfortable on the bed when the door slid open again, revealing a familiar dark figure.

*　　　　*　　　　*

Drakonis

Drakonis walked down the narrow hallway, past some examination rooms towards the wall that held the hidden room. As he rounded the corner, Cyarah was walking away from the room with her cart of trinkets and gadgets.

"How is she?" Drakonis asked.

"Miserable and depressed." The chimera said, not looking up from the cart. "She's as good as dead in her current state."

“Regrettable.” Drakonis replied with a grimace on his face.

“Very.” Cyarah said back as she rounded the corner. “Good Luck, Drakonis!”

He turned back to the wall and took a deep breath. He didn't have any clue what was going to happen once he let Isobel out. But he knew that he couldn't keep her trapped in the room anymore.

He looked down at his outfit. He was in a black T-shirt, and with equally black dress pants. He had hoped that his casual appearance would be more welcoming, a sign that he was here to not do harm, but he felt ridiculous. He already missed his cloak and armor. Casual clothes always made him feel... Vulnerable.

He opened the door to the hidden room. Isobel sat on the bed, dressed in the clothes he had sent to her. Even with the worn look in her eyes, she still was easy on the eyes. The velvet red dress shirt went well with her skin and the black slacks were a nice touch.

“Are you ready?” He asked, remaining in the doorway.

Isobel nodded back to him and stood up from the bed, making her way to the door. He stood aside so she could walk out of the room and followed her out.

“Come on then.” Drakonis instructed. “It is time to reintegrate you into society.”

Isobel didn't reply. They continued walking out of the medical ward, navigating the maze of halls back to the front desk.

"There are beings..." Drakonis continued. "Strong beings that still remember the Black Dragon's betrayal. To the best of my ability, I have tried to hide your presence. It's why I had you moved to the Beastlord's ward in the Research Center, but those that covet the dragon's power are watching now."

From behind him, he didn't hear any reply from Isobel. He turned to face her, rubbing the bridge of his nose.

"Isobel." He said sternly. "I need verbal confirmation that you understand the predicament that you are in. And I need you to give me a chance to mend the damage to our... companionship?"

Technically, he enslaved her and her brother-in-arms, but he didn't feel like he treated them any less than guests of the capitol.

"I understand." Isobel said with a dry and sullen voice.

Drakonis gritted his teeth at her words. This was going to be a lot harder than he thought. It had only been five minutes and he could see that she was beyond emotionally distancing herself. He knew she would do her best to not acknowledge him if she didn't have to.

He resumed leading her out of the ward. When they reached the front desk, he bent over to write his sign out time on a clipboard.

"My weapon." Drakonis stated in a more aggravated tone than he intended.

"At once, my lord." The large horned beastkin stated as he reached down behind the desk and pulled out Drakonis' famed black blade. "I wish you and your companion a wonderful morning."

Drakonis simply nodded and headed towards the last of the doors. A set of silver knights guarded the door closely. When they noticed the Dark Lord, they reached over and opened the door instinctively.

"Lord Drakonis." The Knights sounded.

"At ease." Drakonis replied.

He walked Isobel out into the courtyard where Semaj, Mahogany, and Dior awaited the duo.

They were bickering amongst themselves, not really paying attention to their surroundings. As Isobel and Drakonis closed in on the children, their faces lit up in excitement.

"Isobel!" The kids yelled before jumping off the bench to greet her. They hugged at her side while Drakonis stood aside and let them be lost in the moment. They held onto her for some time, speaking over each other in a gleeful frenzy, and Isobel reciprocated the hugs. But she seemed... Preoccupied.

She stared up at the sky and closed her eyes. Drakonis could tell that her breathing was steady and deep, as though she was savoring every breath. Tears began to fall from her eyes, and she then looked down at the kids once again. They were crying now, obviously overwhelmed by emotion. And she finally spoke to them.

"It has been far too long." She said with a large smile on her face.

This gave Drakonis a sense of relief. He had feared that his actions may have taken her ability to express happiness. Or even pretend to express it within his presence at the very least.

"Alright, you gremlins." Drakonis said, approaching the group. "Give her some room to breathe."

"NO!" Dior yelled out loud.

"Yeah!" Semaj replied, just as loud.

"You said you were taking care of her, but Isobel looks like an old grape!" Mahogany said angrily. "See!?"

Mahogany then grabbed Isobel's cheeks. Isobel smiled at her in response, but then her expression hardened as she looked at Drakonis with accusatory eyes.

Drakonis frowned. He could understand Isobel's discontent, but now the children were against him as well. Was this the price to pay for his arrogance?

He didn't have much time to think about how to win their favor. He smelled something in the wind. A horrid smell that only a few creatures could produce on this side of the Mississippi. The smell was so dense that Drakonis' sensitive nose couldn't pinpoint where it was coming from. He turned to look at Isobel and the kids to see if they were bothered by the scent. They were all grabbing their noses and gagging as well.

"My lord!" Drakonis heard a voice rasp from behind him. He turned to see a small ratkin bowing before him. It was no larger than Semaj and had a horribly arched back. He immediately recognized the rodent.

"Krat." Drakonis said unamused. "To whom do I owe the displeasure of your presence on my day off?

"Clearly, you know that I only serve the One True God, My Lord." Krat said staring up at Drakonis. "I apologize for being an affront to your morning, but the Great and Mighty God King has requested your presence immediately."

"Curious." Drakonis said, rubbing his chin. "Since when has your responsibility been liaison and messenger of the king? I could have sworn you were too disgusting and repugnant to even be allowed above ground in the kingdom?"

Krat chuckled at the dark lord's words, and a thin, yellow mucus-like liquid fell from the corners of his mouth. This was the kind of gurgled laughter that would incite gagging from all that heard it. Drakonis never had a weak stomach, but the stench mixed with Krat's nasty appearance would make most people nauseous. Drakonis was no exception.

"I have many services that I offer to our master." Krat said as he stood up. "Please allow me the honor of escorting you to the throne."

"Please tell my father that I will receive my audience once I have finished my responsibilities here." Drakonis said glaring at the Ratkin.

"Surely, you are not asking the God King to wait?" Krat replied as he narrowed his eyes at Drakonis. "Certainly, you do not desire reprimand from Lord D'Merrion? Whom would openly seek his punishment?"

"I tire of your jests, rat." Drakonis said, looking back at Isobel. "I have important tasks that need care and attention today. Let my father know that he can punish me to his discretion when the day is done. Now leave us."

Drakonis had grown weary of this pest. The rodent wasn't particularly strong, but his appearance and smell were used in the same way a Venus flytrap traps its prey. More often than not, beings would rather comply with him or run away than deal with any of his assaults on their senses.

Drakonis bent down to talk to the kids, ignoring Krat behind him.

"Let us head over to the Grind-" Drakonis started to say. But a small whisper behind his back stopped him dead in his tracks. His muscles stiffened, and he felt a chill roll through his spine. He turned to Krat again, their eyes locking in fierce engagement.

The Ratkin was staring back, a smile on his face and

awaiting Drakonis' response. Drakonis turned back to Semaj.

“Remember the stone I gave you?” Drakonis said, trying to hide his worry. “If trouble should find you, do not hesitate Semaj.”

“Yes, Drakonis.” Semaj replied. The boy's eyes were wide and Drakonis could tell that he heard the rat as well. And if Semaj heard, then the girls did as well.

Drakonis looked at Isobel and smiled.

“Head over to the Grindstone, I won't be long.” He said, hoping that she could sense his good intentions. Isobel simply stared at him blankly and nodded.

He stood and walked past Krat towards the castle.

“We will head to the throne room at once.” Drakonis said in a very agitated tone. “But once we're done, me and you will discuss at length how we're going to deal with that foul mouth of yours.”

“Yes, My lord.” Krat replied. He couldn't see the Ratkin, but he knew that he was smiling.

*　　　*　　　*

Addurog

Oh, is it my turn already? Good grief. I don't think I'm prepared... Hahahaha! I kid. Of course, I'm ready for the chapter of my life that ends in the debilitating defeat of Drakonis. How could I not be ready to watch myself end my nemesis in front of all he holds dear? Then humiliate and torture him for sheer sadistic enjoyment. No, I am absolutely ready. Now... Where to begin?

I was sitting, as most individuals that lie-in-wait comfortably do when they're getting ready for a pristine ambush, in the guardhouse's lounge area just outside of the medical quarter. I very well can't be seen just strolling about in broad daylight. Our favorite pensively skeptical dragonkin would see that ploy coming a mile away, and I need him to be blissfully surprised by the gift I have lined up for him.

As I waited in the backroom of the guardhouse, I took time to engage in my favorite pastime: writing Insults for Drakonis.

Hmmm... Overgrown shelled roach? Jaundiced foot-callus? Ulcerous back detritus? I don't know. None of these seem viable as suitable monikers for our foolishly chosen and misunderstood young hero. In fact, they weren't disgusting enough. I had almost two hundred pages of derogatory slurs for that failure of a dragon, and I was suffering from a bit of writer's block. I wrote my newest insults into my journal, but I eyed the device on the table constantly. The communication shard that would signal the beginning of our glorious plan.

As I sat in intense thought, awaiting the call, I began to wonder what was taking the rat so long to act. It doesn't take more than a few moments to deliver a message to a buffoon. Just walk up, tell him, and get on with it! Maybe my anticipation of boiling that tail-less salamander was making me highly impatient, and a little unagreeable. Or maybe the world was moving slower than normal, and my highly developed brain was moving at six thousand miles per hour. I could never really understand the complexities of my intense thoughts.

The device, buzzing to life with a blue glow, awoke me from my deep and meaningful thought.

"Drakonis has taken the bait." A voice growled from the other side. "He is on his way to the palace."

"It's time, gentle beasts." I replied excitedly. "Move in on the targets. Peacefully. For now."

I stood up and stretched a bit, getting a good 'crack' from my neck and arm joints. It was better to let my men get a head start, apprehend the children and that hideous woman, and doll them up for me. That way they can get that sense of achievement for doing an excellent job, and I can make my grand entrance.

I exited the guardhouse, the warm air of the outside world was a welcome change to the cold interior, and I made my way into the courtyard. I didn't have to move too far before I saw a gaggle of beastkin surrounding the four whimpering humans. They were dressed in casual clothes, far more casual than *ones* of their ranks should be dressing, and the kids were particularly ugly with their faces covered in boogers. The priestess even looked worn and impoverished, and her hair was disheveled and nasty to boot. They had been moved up against one of the benches and were yelling in protest.

"Well if it isn't the 'Drakonis' cheer squad', and his shriveled harlot." I exclaimed loudly. "Who would have guessed I would stumble upon four perfectly wrapped gifts. Is it my birthday? Has Christmas come early!?"

I laughed heartily and some of my men joined me. Bullying them wasn't part of the plan, but it would bring me much joy to watch them squirm. I could see their insecurities getting the better of them, and one of the kids yelled, "Bully!"

I walked over to the prince's attendee, whose eyes were now red from the crying. She tried to inch away from me, but I knelt down next to her.

"A bully?" I said accusingly. "Me? I don't waste time on the weak, darling. And if you believe that all this is just to antagonize a group of privileged little rodents, then you aren't as bright as everyone says you are. Idiot."

The girl dropped her head in what I could only assume was defeat and shame. I could see that she was aptly intimidated and didn't wish to talk anymore. Good. It disgusted me to even converse with these brats, especially when they were covered in mucus.

I had just stood up to issue orders to my men when I felt a soft magical presence coming from the prince a few feet from me. Then the priestess whispered, “Please don't resist.”

Everything was going all according to plan now. One more push and all the cogs would turn naturally.

“You and you.” I said pointing at some of my men. “Grab these fine ladies and escort them to the staging area.”

I then turned to the prince. His eyes were red from crying as well, but he had the fiercest look in his eyes. They were smoldering like brimstone, and I could tell he had a fighting spirit.

“Let this one go.” I said, smugly raising my head to him. “Go back to your handler, boy. Tell him to meet us at the Grindstone. And don't tarry. Not unless you're ready to play Hide-and-Go-Seek with your friend’s body parts.”

With that, I turned to address my men. That is... until I felt it. The rage behind me. I turned to see the boy, hands balled into cute little fists, staring at me as though he wanted to HARM me.

“What?” I asked casually, crossing my arms. “Do you

wish to fight me, child? Or do you have a problem comprehending orders?"

"Drakonis..." The prince started to say, not breaking eye contact with me. "Drakonis said that you should always stand up to protect those close to you. I will not leave Dior, Mahogany, or Isobel behind."

I scoffed at his words before replying, "I feel as though he gave you that guidance without context."

Me and my men shared a light chuckle at the expense of the young prince. This brat was being cheeky, much to my annoyance, but I respected his bravery in the face of the Great Addurog. I'll let it slide, just this once.

"Boy." I said sternly. "I'm in an exceptionally good mood because this is a great, and momentous day. But don't take my jovial demeanor for granted. Leave my perfectly maintained space before I grow tired of your insubordination, child."

He stared at me for a second, his shoulders pumping up and down. He was extremely worked up and his attitude was now testing my patience. I moved a muscle to approach the boy and really make an example out of him, when the knight spoke up.

"Please go, Semaj." She pleaded with him through weary eyes. "We'll be fine. I will protect Mahogany and Dior. Just go get Drakonis."

I could hear the boy gritting his teeth, and he finally unballed his hands. He began to walk towards me. As he walked past me, I felt a small impact on my perfectly shaped foot. Did he... DID HE JUST STRIKE ME?

The boy attempted to keep walking, but I reached down and lifted him up by his hair.

"You pathetic wretch." I yelled at the rat in my hands. "I sympathetically allow you to leave unharmed and you DARE ATTACK ME!?"

"Let me go!" The prince cried in my fist.

"Please don't hurt him!" The knight pleaded. The servants next to her yelped incoherently.

But we were far past pleas and begging. This roach had tested all lengths of my patience when I didn't ask for much other than obedience. What happens next is the culmination of his bad actions and his unfortunate luck to be associated with Drakonis.

"Sometimes!" I croaked loudly, breathing harshly in my anger. "Sometimes, there are times when baring your fangs will get you hurt, boy! MEN! SHOW HIM THAT THIS IS ONE OF THOSE TIMES!"

I punched the child in his stomach and then threw him into a pack of my men. He hit the ground with a hard thud and yelped like a pup as he hit the ground. He would learn respect today. We would make sure of that.

The boy looked up at the beastkin around him, and I could see the regret in his eyes. I savored his expression as the beastkin began to kick and claw at him. He tried to protect himself, covering his face and protecting his head, but it was to no avail. The soldiers swarmed the boy like flies to dung.

"NO!" I heard from behind my head. I turned to see the knight fighting against her enforcers. The young servant girls were screaming at the top of their lungs for their friend. I raised my ear to the scramble in front of me and was delighted to hear a 'snap' and the 'crack' of bones. Music to my ears. The women continued screaming at the pack of beastkin ravaging their friend for a few minutes then the group dispersed.

The boy was limp, with a small pool of blood around him. The sad females called out the boy's name, but no response. I don't think I have ever had a greater smile in my life than now. It was so beautiful. I danced and moved my hands like a conductor for an orchestra, savoring the screaming. The Prince of Wyrms can't ignore this. If this didn't set him off, nothing would.

Chapter 15:
Hurricane

Chase

"This was such a waste of time." Chase sighed as he dislodged his sword from the beastman's back. "You guys should have just given up and left when I asked you to leave me alone."

He was in the heart of the Grindstone, the inner Arena, where he spent most of his days these past few weeks, finishing his training regime and waiting for Drakonis. Unfortunately, a small group of beastmen tried to remove him from the training grounds, and he was feeling particularly sour this morning.

"W-w-w-what are you!?" Once of the beastmen stammered as he fell over his own feet, his face dripping with the blood of his allies. "We couldn't even see you! No human moves that fast!" He tried to retreat backwards towards the entrance, but Chase couldn't allow that. He threw his sword right next to the beastmen, its blade lodged in the dirty sand. The beastmen yelped and cowered on the floor, shaking incredibly.

"I strictly remember a certain beastmen stating 'We will remove you by force if you refuse', and then that SAME

BEASTMAN..." Chase said as he advanced up on the last of his foes. He grabbed the beastmen by the scruff of his coat, lifting him to eye level. He immediately regretted his decision to even touch the animal. "The same... Ugh... Nasty, filthy, rank beastmen then started running his mouth about 'filthy humans knowing their place'. That ring any bells?"

The beastmen shivered violently in his hand. He was a Jackal or Rat or something... Some kind of terrible smelling beastmen that felt around the same weight as a decent dog.

"What?" Chase shouted at the beastmen. "Cat got your tongue all of a sudden!? No witty remarks now? Where'd all that bark go, huh!?" Beating the group of beastmen and mocking them was amusing... At first. But it didn't take a genius to recognize that this beastmen was thoroughly defeated.

No point in prolonging the inevitable, he thought.

He lifted the beastmen into the air, an action that prompted a quick yelp from the beastmen, then drove him into the sand headfirst. A giant cloud of sand lifted high into the air, blotting out the sun. The cloud only lasted for a moment before it dissipated and revealed the legs of the beastmen, twitching above the earth. Then that, too, ceased after a few seconds and the Grindstone was silent.

Chase took a deep breath. He really needed that. The past few weeks have been miserable. Isobel's death still weighed heavy on his mind. Not only had he allowed harm to come unto his friend, but he had allowed the High Priestess to be slain. This was a cardinal sin that could not be undone. Should he return home, he would be a pariah, and never allowed to set foot within the Halls of the Divines again. He had no home anymore.

Chase walked over to the nearest bench that looked over this section of the Grindstone, shaking away the daily self-pity party. He marveled at his work, bodies of beastmen laid strewn all over the place, chuckling to himself.

Whether he wanted to admit it or not, his training with Drakonis over these past weeks was paying off. He trained everyday back home in Karia, sure, under the strict tutelage of older Divine Knights. Every action he was trained to take was methodical, well calculated, and precise.

But the beastmen Generals were always better than the Knights. Divine Knights almost never opposed a beastmen General in a one - on - one scenario. The power disparity was just too high.

It was always assumed that due to the beastmen Ascension Ceremonies, their powers were less diluted, and the transfer of mana was more potent than the Divine's Blessing. And because the Divines blessed Divine Knights with their power instead of passing it down, the knights needed teamwork to defeat even one general.

But that isn't the only reason the generals are stronger. Their training is more violent, and less organized... But it isn't disorganized either. They lecture strength, prioritizing overpowering your opponent instead of utilizing strong movements, tactical footing, and exploiting weaknesses in your opponent’s defense and posture. It's a simple concept that Chase has come to learn... The Rule of the Wilds. The strongest beastmen will be the strongest. He will be blessed with the strength of his ancestors, and with all the benefits and consequences that come with that. To that end, every day is competition. The beastmen are constantly not only at war with humanity, but amongst themselves. You're never safe, and someone is always looking to conquer and take what's yours.

As much as beastmen disgusted Chase, he couldn't help but admire the system. He had been training under Drakonis, constantly fighting against him and other beastmen. He was always either outnumbered or under-equipped, forced to use whatever was on hand at the time. He felt more mentally alert, stronger and faster than he had ever felt. Almost like... His inner beast had been unlocked and he felt more in-tune with his aura.

Well, most of the time... The daily psyche evaluations from Cyarah put him on edge. They were exhausting and every day he wished the meetings would end. She only asked about Isobel. Every day, he was reminded how losing her felt. How it still feels. It was torture and even recounting the sessions brought a familiar cold to his heart. An emptiness that he just couldn't shake.

Chase sighed and stood up.

"I guess it's time to clean up this mess." He said walking over and picking up the nearest beastmen by his leg. "Can't have you guys stinking up the place. Hope you don't mind me dragging your hides out to the pyres. Nameless beastmen don't deserve funerals."

As he started to drag the corpse to the gates, he could hear the first set of gates to the fort open. Wild laughter could be heard on the other side of the wall, and he was so preoccupied with his thoughts that he didn't realize the massive aura that accompanied it.

"Ah!" The giant voice bellowed. "What happened to my wonderful soldiers? Beastkin A? Beastkin F? Where have you misplaced yourselves!?"

Chase looked around for a moment. *Beastkin A*, he thought puzzled. Any one of the animals he killed could have been those guys... He assumed by the voice that this must be their leader, but it didn't seem like the beastmen cared about their well-being, not like his words implied.

"Sir!" Another, smaller voice yelled. "They've been decimated! They're all dead!"

"How observational!" The giant voice replied. "Was it

the toasted sinew on the ground that gave it away? Maybe this... SEVERED HEAD was a key clue in your investigation? Could it be the sliced fur bodies lying about!? You're working hard for a promotion, aren't you?"

Chase could sense the annoyance in the giant beastman's voice. He was actually surprised at how loud the beastmen were. It's a wonder the whole capital didn't know a massacre had just taken place.

"Alright." The large beastmen said in a calm tone. "Whoever decided to turn my soldiers into fresh giblets, show yourself and the GREAT ADDUROG will be merciful. Your death will be quick and painless, I assure you! How could you have known you stepped on the mighty foot of Lord Addurog? How could you foresee your pathetic life coming to its abrupt conclusion, its final chapter, and immediate close because of a simple folly? Will you not grace me with your presence? Are you going to-".

Chase couldn't take any more of the nonsense being spouted from the beastmen. He was grating on the ears and Chase sought to shut him up as soon as possible. He kicked the Inner Arena's doors open, dragging the body behind him. There were a couple beastmen checking the bodies while a large beastmen, presumably the 'Addurog' fellow, stood with several of his soldiers watching the door Chase had just come from. Addurog himself resembled a bird of some kind, wearing a headdress that was a bit too large for his head.

"You know, I wager your soldiers wanted to die." Chase yelled at the group of beastmen troops. "Especially if you're their leader. Your mouth must run on some kind of motor or something..."

"A wretched human did this?" Addurog replied perplexed. "Oh wait... You're the Divine Knight, aren't you? Oh well. How unfortunate for those fellows." Addurog shrugged his shoulders nonchalantly, completely apathetic to the deaths of his men.

The large bird began to walk towards Chase, rubbing his beak a bit. Chase could tell the beastmen was sizing him up and was taking stock of his strength.

As Addurog closed the distance between them, Chase could tell the birdkin was a bit larger than your average beastmen, and he towered over Chase. He also carried a large golden sword that resonated with some kind of 'dark' energy. He was probably overcompensating for something.

"I guess you're Addurog?" Chase said trying to mimic the confused look Addurog had. "These guys said I would regret not heeding their orders. I'm assuming you'll put up a better fight?"

"Oh!" Addurog said, his eyes widening. "I can tell you might be worth your weight in salt. I assumed that with their numbers those beastmen could overpower anyone foolish enough to not heed an edict from Lord Addurog. But it seems I was mistaken. An occurrence that does not happen often, I swear."

"Blah, Blah, Blah!" Chase mocked the general. "There you go with all that talking again... Are we going to do this or what?"

Chase then felt it. It was faint, but he felt something behind Addurog. The large beastmen pulled out his sword and started to say something boring, but Chase ignored him. He felt a familiar aura, one he thought was lost. He took a step to the side and took notice of the beastmen surrounding a woman and some children. He immediately recognized Dior, and Mahogany. But there was a woman with pale orange hair and common street attire. Even with disheveled hair, he knew. That was Isobel's aura.

"Isobel..." He said in disbelief.

There was a bit of silence for a second, then Addurog spoke up.

"No, I'm Addurog." He stated plainly.

"Not you, ya giant turkey." Chase growled at the beastmen before quickly returning his attention towards the woman. "Isobel... Is that you?"

The woman shuffled out from behind Addurog. He noticed that she and the children had been bound with rope. She looked in his direction, shaking her head to remove the hair from her face so he could see her.

“Yes.” Isobel replied in a raspy and weak voice. She looked worn out, a bit dried up, and paler than he had ever seen her but... It looked like Isobel. But he had to make sure this wasn't some sort of illusion or trick.

“What's my real name?” He said quizzingly.

“What?” The woman replied quickly with a very confused expression.

“What's my real name?” He repeated again, sterner this time.

“It's Chasel-” She began.

“STOP.” Chase said abruptly cutting Isobel off. It was her and she was in trouble. She had been missing for weeks and everyone had told him she was dead. And now Addurog has her, bound and in tow. Whatever Addurog had done or was attempting to do to her, Chase would make him pay for his transgressions.

Chase exchanged a smile with Isobel, but her expression changed when Addurog suddenly grabbed Isobel by the throat.

“Oh, I'm sorry!” He interjected. “Am I interrupting this heartwarming reunion? My perfect plan didn't account for-”

Chase exploded towards Addurog, aiming a mighty punch at the beastman’s stomach. He slammed his fist into the beastmen, a mighty clap rang out from the impact. But to

Chase's surprise Addurog had caught the young knight's fist easily.

"It's rude to interrupt!" Addurog grunted as he lifted Chase into the air by his captured fist. He then swung the man down into the dirt. Chase gritted as he landed in the dirt, and looked up at the beastmen just in time to see Addurog was bringing his foot down on top of him. Chase channeled his aura and leapt safely a few feet away.

"Now that I have your attention!" Addurog roared as he threw Isobel to the dirt. She coughed loudly as she gasped for air. "I didn't account for the other dog to be here."

Chase wasn't going to waste any more time listening to this overgrown chicken's nonsense. He began to channel his aura, letting his emotions become one with his core. He took a deep breath and felt his heart beating rapidly in his chest. Every muscle in his body tensed and he felt energy coursing through his blood. A violent torrent of red lightning began to flow around Chase and shoot the earth with blasts of energy. He let his anger flow and used it to power his aura.

"Ohhhhh..." Addurog said rubbing his beak.

Chase's chest was pumping erratically. He crouched down and lowered his stance. He spread his hands out in front of him and lowered his head. The beastmen that stood behind Addurog mumbled amongst themselves. Dior and Mahogany watched wide-eyed.

“Rule of the Wilds...” Addurog said with surprise in his tone. “How dare you step to I, The Great and Mighty Addurog!”

Addurog turned to one of his subordinates.

“Hold my weapon!” He yelled as he tossed his sword to a beastmen. The weapon slammed into the beastman’s chest, and he fell on the ground. The beastmen struggled to get to his feet and a few beastmen had to help him while lifting the sword.

Addurog then turned back to Chase and reciprocated his stance. The two began to slowly circle each other. The rest of the beastmen stomped their feet and chanted 'Wilds' rhythmically. Chase took a moment to look towards Isobel, who had recovered from her coughing fit. She had her eyes locked on the battle unfolding in front of her.

“I respect your courage, human.” Addurog said as he stared into Chase's eyes. “I could only hope that your strength lives up to your mind's ambitions... Maybe you'll make a decent warm-up...”

Chase exploded forward towards Addurog, leaving a large cloud of dust and dirt behind him. He drew his hand back, putting all of his energy into this one blow, and brought it forward with the intent to remove Addurog's head from his body. Addurog never broke eye contact with him and stared down the blow. At the last moment, as Chase's fist was a few inches from Addurog's face, Addurog stood up and took the blow right to the center of his abdomen. Lightning crackles and smolders against Addurog's feathers, and dust flies back into the crowd behind him. Chase looked up at Addurog to see his expression and was surprised to see Addurog was emotionless and unfazed.

Chase drew his other fist back and began to savage the birdkin's chest with blow after blow of lightning charged impacts. The beastmen crowd roared when each hit connected, not hiding their excitement as they watched the brutal onslaught. After he felt he had dealt sufficient punishment to his opponent, he leapt away to see the extent of the damage. He knew that he had landed solid and strong hits. Even a beastmen general had to have felt that.

“I will admit.” Addurog said breathing outwardly. “You have some bite. But I'm a little disappointed in you. That laser light show was really just for show.”

Chase was in disbelief. He looked down at his hands and saw that they were visibly bruised. He had landed so many hits and aimed for vital organs. And yet the beastmen was shrugging off the hits like he had finished a minor workout!

“I actually am ashamed I got into ceremonial stance for this.” Addurog continued as he rubbed his neck. His soldiers began to snicker amidst that chant. “Let me show you how a true beastkin fights. Do keep up.”

Addurog leapt towards Chase, raising his claw high into the air. Addurog brought a fist down towards Chase, but the man managed to narrowly jump out of the way. Chase's feet hadn't properly planted yet before Addurog was at his new location, claws exposed, swung wildly at the Chase.

Chase was relieved that he hadn't underestimated the general and channeled his aura beforehand. His training was paying off, he was able to see each blow clearly, but he still was struggling to keep up with Addurog. He started to move backwards and make attempts to separate himself from the birdkin's attacks, but each attempt to disengage ended in failure.

"Come now, human." Addurog said in between his flurry strikes. "Surely you can do more than just dodge and run!"

Chase kept trying to move away from Addurog while looking for some sort of weakness in his form, some kind of opening to exploit. But Addurog's attacks were becoming faster and more precise, and he was getting closer to the mark with each strike that flew by. At this rate, he was going to connect sooner rather than later.

Addurog took a massive swing at Chase's head, forcing him to duck under the blow, but as he lowered himself, Chase saw it. Addurog had already readied another thrusting strike aimed for the knight's head, and there was no way to dodge it.

At that moment, Chase embraced his aura and used it to dash away a few feet. He was breathing heavily, glad that he had saved this technique for this moment.

"I see." Addurog said intrigued, his arm still locked in place. "You're blessed. That blow should have ended you. But you're faster than you've led me to believe. You... sparked away."

Addurog cackled a bit to himself, obviously amused with himself. Now that he had a moment to breathe, Chase realized that the chanting of the beastmen had died down. Everyone was intently watching now. He had revealed his aura and the beastmen were taking notice of him now.

He wasn't unaccustomed to this reaction from the crowd. In fact, all the beastmen reacted the same when they found out about his aura.

"We don't have much time to play anymore, it seems." Addurog said reaching his arm out towards the crowd behind him. The beastmen holding Addurog's large blade began to hobble over to their leader. "I can sense him coming and you'll only be a pain in my side once he gets here. I planned on only drawing this blade against Drakonis, but I guess you've earned an audience with its edge."

Addurog began to draw his giant blade from its sheathe. Bright blue flames seem to tumble out from the open sheath, like a waterfall spilling over a cliff. The flames fell from the blade and rested softly on the ground creating a soft blue fog at Addurog's feet.

A slight chill hit the air, and even with Chase being over a dozen feet away, he could feel the cold of the flames sending shivers up his spine. Chase knew that no matter what, he must not let it hit him. That was no normal blade.

Addurog took a stance with the giant great sword, but not the stance that Chase expected. He held his blade like a rapier and widened his stance. The sword looked silly and unbalanced being held in that nature. But Addurog's stance looked solid and driven.

This was it. This moment would decide the winner. Chase had managed to keep up, hiding his abilities till he needed them most, and was certain that he could use his aura to win.

His aura allowed him to move faster than ever before and shift into a state of intangibility, while moving from one location to the next. He could travel in any direction at great speeds, and its greatest strength was that there was a special 'Road' that only he could see that allowed him to move even faster. It was almost like a current or river that was exclusive to him. Most wouldn't even notice that he had passed by without training to sense auras. And even to them, they've described it as watching a "lightning bolt" move from one place to another. With his new level of mastery, he was going to bet everything on this strength, speed, and precision.

Chase got into his stance, searching the environment for weapons. He felt a bead of sweat fall from his brow, he couldn't help but be nervous. If he were going to stand a chance, he would need to steady his nerves and find as many weapons as possible. Luckily for him, the grindstone had been littered with swords and spears from fallen beastmen. More than enough to defeat Addurog.

“Come now, human.” Addurog said with seriousness in his tone. “Show me the extent of your abilities, and or are you giving me free reign to kill the woman and children now? It's perfectly natural for an inferior human to be overcome by immense fear at this moment, the pinnacle of Battle-”

Chase dashed over to a nearby sword on the ground. He lifted it, gripping it and charging it with his aura, and leapt over to Addurog and swung down with all his might.

“SHUT UP!” He screamed as he dashed away, not waiting to see if the blade connected. He went and grabbed another blade and leapt back to Addurog trying to impale the beastman’s opposing hip.

Chase's plan was simple. He would overwhelm Addurog with attacks until he found an opening. This was a battle of attrition and Chase was confident in his stamina. He shifted and dashed over to a spear and threw it towards Addurog's stomach, and then dashed for another sword. Chase only looked at Addurog to keep track of his target, but his main focus was more attacks. The loud 'clang' of weapons could be heard as Addurog deflected each attack, but Chase didn't worry about it. He was going to wear the beastmen down with this attack.

Chase's speed kicked up lots of dirt and sand, creating a small tornado around Addurog. And since Chase had his aura fully channeled, the tornado even became electrically charged, making it easier for Chase to move around and attack from all directions. He continued to grab weapons from all around and toss them at Addurog. Then he saw the road and felt his speed increase as he traveled along its edges.

But even as he gained speed and increased the frequency of his attacks, it seemed that Addurog was unfazed by any of the strikes. He simply deflected each weapon back into the tornado and held his ground. This was exactly what Chase wanted, but something about the confidence of Addurog's defense unnerved him. It made him wary, but he couldn't give up.

Faster, Chase thought. He had to go faster and keep up the pressure. He dashed by Addurog, weapon in hand, ready to make another attack when suddenly he felt something go through him. Something cold, and evil passed through his being and siphoned his mana.

He went flying through the air as his shifted state

disappeared, and he was tangible again. He looked towards Addurog as he fell from the air, and saw the beastmen following his flight path, driving his sword forward for the kill. Chase could sense Addurog's weapon had the same polarity as his body and used the rest of his mana to supercharge his weapon. Chase raised the blade to block Addurog's stab, but just as he had hoped, a repulsive force caused Chase to be launched out of range of Addurog's attack. Chase landed a few feet away on his stomach, kicking dust up into the air upon landing. He tried to stand immediately but found that his body couldn't muster the strength. His mana was exhausted, and his core was empty.

“Not bad, human.” Addurog said without a hint of sarcasm this time. He sheathed the blade and stood upright. “Given a few more decades, you could be an admirable warrior... For human scum, that is. I did have fun, but I do believe it's time for the main course.”

Chase laid there in the dirt, feeling the familiar sting of defeat. He struggled to will his arms to lift his body, to pull himself from the dirt. He had just managed to lift himself up onto one knee when a loud boom came from outside of the Grindstone's entrance. He looked up and saw a giant cloud lift into the sky, blotting out the sun. The sky grew dark, and a fierce wind began to blow. He felt a significant pressure outside of the gate and saw multiple beastmen fall down to their hands and knees. He looked over at Isobel and the children, and even they were forced to bow in the presence of such a strong aura. Chase felt himself being pulled back to the earth and resisted with all his might. The only one that wasn't affected was Addurog, who turned to watch the door of the Grindstone.

Then Chase felt it. Deep in his heart, it slowly crept into him, like a silent infection of the flesh. A sense of dread that he had only felt when he was in the presence of a Divine. Who could give off such a violent and oppressive aura!?

At that moment, the doors of the Grindstone were torn apart, wood splintering into the courtyard. Black mist covered the door and began to seep into the courtyard hiding the one creating it. But Chase didn't need to see who it was to confirm the owner. He could tell who it was. He had only seen this sort of aura one other time. When a group of Divine Knights foolishly killed his grandfather. It was none other than Drakonis. And this was the angriest that Chase had ever seen him.

“I see you have finally joined us, Your Worminess.” Addurog said smugly. “That's quite all right, though! Punctuality has never been your strong suit!”

“Addurog!” Drakonis yelled, his eyes blood red. “You've gone too far this time!”

* * *

Drakonis

The giant doors of the throne room creaked loudly as they were closed behind Drakonis. He walked down the red carpet towards the throne where a very unhappy-looking D'Merrion sat. He felt the pressure in the room increase as The One True God laid eyes upon him.

Drakonis had grown accustomed to the antics of his father. Even though D'Merrion knew Drakonis was not immensely affected by his aura, he still attempted to use it to oppress him.

"Thank you, my loyal subject." D'Merrion said as he leaned back on his throne. He placed his hand on his knee and slouched a bit, as though he was already bored with the meeting. "Please, leave us so that I may speak with my son."

The hooded beastmen that had led Drakonis into the throne room bowed and left quickly. Drakonis bowed his head and took a knee at the steps of the throne.

"Raise your head, my son." D'Merrion bellowed. "We don't have time for pleasantries."

Drakonis looked up at the King. Something didn't feel right about their meeting. He had the feeling when he was approached out of the blue in the courtyard of the medical ward, and he was getting the same feeling now. He felt a sense of uneasiness as he stood up.

“My son.” D’Merrion continued. “Have I not given you the best life any being could ask for within these walls? Have you not been given a proper education, and trained to be one of the most effective tacticians this Earth has ever seen?”

Drakonis remained silent. He knew this routine and what to expect. All questions asked are rhetorical, and only silence and obedience were acceptable answers. Any deviation from this behavior would lead to immediate punishment. He was used to it.

“My son, you must tell me what I should do to help you understand the effort that I use to make sure you are well-equipped for your reign as king.” D’Merrion stated as he bent forward. He had a look of disappointment and disgust on his face, expressions that seemed to be reserved for Drakonis. “Time and again, I have forgiven your transgressions, no matter how severe. You take my soldiers, and use your rank to do as you please, completely ignoring your responsibility to the kingdom. It seems as though your Dragon-Blood compels you to want for more. I know you've talked to the Fae! What did they offer you? Power? Complete Dragon-Shifting?”

D’Merrion's expression then changed into a soft smile.

“Don't tell me it was something as pathetic as freedom?” He said mockingly as he stood up. “You're such a simple creature, my son."

D'Merrion began to descend the stairs from his throne. With each step, Drakonis felt the pressure increase around him. He struggled to withstand it, but it was growing far too fast. Drakonis fell down to his knees, his head being forced to stare at the floor.

"You pretend to do my bidding while indulging your own desires." D'Merrion said, his tone becoming angrier. "I cannot- will not forgive you this time."

The pressure was now ten times the strength that it was when Drakonis entered the throne room. He fell down to his hands and was being crushed under the weight of D'Merrion's aura.

"Dearest Drakonis." D'Merrion said now standing over the dragonkin. "I cannot allow my most loyal warriors to forget their place. So thus, I must deliver judgement swiftly to ensure constant control. I know you believe that you can take anything that I give you. But what of your friends? What of those children that you've grown so fond of? How would they fair, standing here in your stead?"

Drakonis felt like he was being smashed against the earth and being grinded to a pulp. He was losing the fight against the pressure. He heard bells ringing in his ears and he knew what was happening. While D'Merrion trapped him here in the throne room, someone had attacked the children and

Isobel. He needed to leave, to ensure that they were not harmed. But he couldn't even stand. How could he escape the strongest being in this realm?

As soon as he had the thought, the pressure disappeared in an instant. Drakonis looked up to see that D'Merrion had returned to his throne and was sitting once again.

"You have my permission to see your little 'pets'." D'Merrion said with his usual tone of derision. "Let this moment be a reminder that I know everything that goes on within this kingdom. You would do well to remember that fact."

Drakonis didn't waste any time. He turned and sped out of the throne room, their safety the only thing on his mind. The ringing in his ears was from the emergency device that he gave Semaj to alert Drakonis if the young boy felt he was in danger. Drakonis rushed out into the palace courtyard as fast as he could, not worrying about the destruction he was causing along the way. As he moved, the ringing became louder and more frequent; this was a sign that he was closing in on Semaj's position.

He stopped at the top of the stairs leading to the palace and felt his heart drop. Panic. The ringing was beyond unbearable, a piercing ringing noise throttled his brain and made him unable to hear much anything else. But what was more unbearable was the sight of a small, bloody child hobbling up the steps.

“Semaj!” Drakonis cried as he leapt to the boy. He landed right next to him and grasped his shoulders.

Semaj looked up at Drakonis, but his eyes were unfocused and cloudy. He was barely conscious. As Drakonis examined the boy’s body, he noticed that he was brutally wounded. He had gashes on his arms and legs, blood practically leaking from his injuries and his right arm was swollen. The limb had to have been broken.

“Semaj! Drakonis said a second time, trying to get the child to focus. Semaj smiled lightly and collapsed into Drakonis' arms. Drakonis turned Semaj over so he could see his face.

“What happened!?” Drakonis said with urgency. “Where are the others?”

Semaj just looked at Drakonis for a moment, his breath was ragged and hoarse. He wasn't responding to any of his words.

Drakonis picked Semaj up and held him in his arms. He needed to get him medical help. Then he would find who did this to him... And rend them... Limb from limb. He turned back to the palace, to rush Semaj to the royal medical chambers, when he spotted Cyarah walking over to him.

“They're at the Grindstone, Drakonis.” She said quickly. “If you wish to save them, you should leave now.”

Drakonis closed his eyes for a second. He felt his chest burning with rage and he immediately was frustrated. More betrayal. Everyone in the capital was plotting against him. Admittedly, he never trusted Cyarah. It would be foolish to place any eggs in that basket, for she was only loyal to D'Merrion. But this level of brutality was unheard of.

"Who..." Drakonis said softly trying to control his emotions. "Who did this?"

Cyarah paused for a moment, then reached out for Semaj. Drakonis hesitated, looking down at the poor, beaten child in his arms, then gave him to the woman.

"Addurog." She said as she looked away. Drakonis turned away from her, balling his fists.

"Help him, Cyarah." Drakonis said through gritted teeth. "And for your sake, you'd better hope that boy lives. Because if he doesn't...."

"I know." She replied. Drakonis heard her walk away with the boy.

He felt despair creep into his heart and the pain of seeing Semaj began to take its toll. He walked down the stairs until he was far enough away from Cyarah to use his aura. If he had used it in his current state, that close to Semaj, he would have killed him.

A black cloud formed at his feet as he channeled his aura, and his heart became still. When his aura was channeled, his focus was driven and guided. His heart slowed down, and he felt calm. But even if he calmed his heart, his mind was still a torrential storm.

The air around him began to heat up and the ground crumbled under each of his steps. He stopped and bent his knees, readying himself for a great leap, then he launched himself in the direction of the Grindstone. From where he was and how strong the leap was, he guessed he would be there in four minutes. Far too much time to have to himself.

He didn't have anything on his mind but smashing Addurog's face into the concrete. And for every second that drew by, he felt that desire build.

As he drew closer, he felt Chase's and Addurog's auras emitting pressure. Drakonis knew Chase would be emotional when he saw Isobel, but the situation was probably worse with him seeing her as Addurog's captive. There was a massive tornado inside the grindstone, which meant that Chase must've activated his aura. Drakonis landed right outside of the gates, a large cloud surrounded his area of impact.

He walked up to the gate and pulled both doors backwards, not regulating his strength. The doors went flying back into the field behind him. He saw Addurog standing next to Chase, who was struggling to lift himself.

“I see you have finally joined us, Your Worminess.” Addurog said with a smug little grin on his face. “That's quite alright, though! Punctuality has never been your strong suit!"

The sight of Addurog made his anger swell, and he channeled his aura completely. He wasn't going to listen to any of his 'I AM ADDUROG' drivel today. Today, his goose was going to be cooked.

"ADDUROG!" He bellowed as he walked forward. "You've gone too far this time!"

* * *

Addurog

As Drakonis came closer, I could see his face twisted and warped into a grimace of rage and anguish. My plan had worked like a charm! The proud and stoic Drakonis brought low by his personal pet collection being threatened.

This was it. The moment that I had been waiting for! The feeling I felt was... It had to be what true bliss felt like! To be in the advent of retribution, to have your revenge on the tip of your beak, was a feeling I wished that I could savor for years to come. But I must not get ahead of myself.

Wind swirled around Drakonis as he lumbered over to me. All of my beastmen troop were crippled by his pressure. I even spied the pathetic humans Drakonis loved so much bending at the knee due to his aura. The Maj girls were huddled next to the knightess, probably due to being unable to withstand the pressure that plagued the area.

"Too far?" I scoffed at Drakonis. I could not help but laugh at his words. "I haven't gone far enough! Maybe I should have targeted the shrimps sooner!"

Drakonis did not reply to my jests, and simply kept advancing upon me. That menacing glare in his eye brought shivers down my spine. Yes! He was ready. He had come with the right mindset. I could tell he wanted nothing more than to rip my head from my shoulders and blast my remains into oblivion.

I had written so many things to say but I must admit, I was at a loss for words. So many insults were racing through my brain that I had forgotten my book of insults laid neatly on my hip. Then my mind gave me this amazing idea...

I slammed my new prized sword into the dirt and swung my arms open to the half-lizard in a friendly gesture for a hug.

"Ahh Drakonis!" I said mockingly. "Did I hurt your feelings by crippling one of your wards? If that only made you cry, then maybe I should cripple one of these humans to get you REALLY motivated? How does that sound?"

"D...Drak...Onis!" The knight next to Addurog grunted under the pressure. "Do...n't let..."

I quickly slammed my foot on the back of the knight at my feet, causing him to yelp in pain. The children and the other knight grunted, possibly calling his name or whatever. In response, I grinded my heel deeper into his back and he cried out in pain. His pained grunts brought a familiar elation to my heart.

"Shhh...." I whispered to the knight. "Don't ruin the surprise now."

The pressure in the area increased and I looked up to see Drakonis pick up his pace a bit. Now we're talking. I needed him mad. Mad and driven towards my demise. The more he concentrated on my destruction and the safety of these mongrels, the easier it would be to destroy him.

As Drakonis ran towards me, he released his aura completely and a dome of concentrated mana surrounded us. I had felt this mana before, a long time ago in a different time and realm. This was a dome of Dark Mana.

The dome surrounded all of the grindstone, small orbs of black energy dotted the area, but it did no harm to anyone I could see. I moved my hand through the air to try and get a feel for the aura that surrounded us, and I noticed that the mana reacted to my movements, almost gluing themselves to my body as I moved. I quickly picked up my blade and dropped into my stance. The sword began to resonate with a soft hum as it glowed the familiar soft blue.

"So, this is the Legendary Dark Mana Field that I've heard so much about!?" I asked jokingly. I still needed to egg the vermin on if all my hard work were to pay off. "You've never used this in any of our previous encounters! What makes today so special? Oh, let me guess? Is it because you changed your hair? New outfit and accoutrements? Big promotion at the job?"

Drakonis didn't budge one bit. He was letting his mana core align and finishing his dome placement. I knew as much. This level of mana involvement was taxing on even the strongest warriors, but once it was complete, he would be able to move and monitor my reactions at the peak of beastkin potential. This was humorous at first, but now his dedication was making me a little sick.

"All this..." I said as my face became stern and serious. "All this for humans. How pathetic."

The knight was still struggling to escape from underneath my foot. I decided to release him and placed my foot by his side. As he looked up at me with a surprised look, I raised my leg again to kick him with a nefarious smile on my face.

"Catch." I yelled at Drakonis. "I was growing bored with that one anyway. You need to train-"

I didn't even get a chance to finish that sentence. As I brought my leg forward to kick the knight, Drakonis was already between us. I winced in pain as he caught my leg, gripping it intensely.

"Don't talk." He said in a low, menacing voice. "Shut up and fight."

Drakonis flipped over my leg and slammed a ferocious kick into me. I parried it with the side of my blade easily, but it was a lot stronger than any blow I had ever received from him. I slid backwards a few feet and readied myself again.

"You've always talked too much." Drakonis said, readying his hands. He had forgotten his blade in his haste to come see me. This fight was going to be easier than I thought. He was like an eagle with no talons or a shark with no teeth. Still moderately dangerous, but nothing a true hunter like me couldn't handle.

He dashed over to me again, kicking up a large cloud of dirt, and slammed another kick into me. I blocked it with my blade and was lifted a few feet off the ground. Then twisted off of his attack and spun another kick into my sword, launching me a few feet backwards. My claws tingled from the impact, but I wouldn't allow myself to be staggered by these blows and I took my stance again. It was my turn now.

I launched myself forward, thrusting at his midsection with my sword, hoping he would be sloppy enough to let my blade even scratch him. But as expected, he dodged the blows with ease. His dark mana field made his detection skills impeccable and allowed him to trace my movements with little to no effort. He was at a disadvantage, sure, coming here unequipped, but the mana field made him that much harder to hit.

"CURSE THIS MANA FIELD!" I yelled as I continued my attack.

I then unfurled my glorious wings and rose above Drakonis' head, making sure to blow dust into his eyes. He raised his arms to block the thrusts of air I had caused. I flapped furiously trying to escape the field, but Drakonis was not going to let me go so easily. He leapt up to me, aiming a punch right at my sternum. But his attempt was predictable, and I grabbed his arm. I spun around and threw him back towards the earth with all my might and continued to ascend towards the edge of the dome. I felt myself pass by the threshold of the dome and heard a loud boom as Drakonis landed back at the Earth. I stayed and waited for the dust to clear so I could see what his current state was. He stood unharmed as the cloud cleared beneath me.

We both watched each other for a second. I'm sure he was wondering what I was up to at this moment. Since we've fought before, he knows that I can only use close range attacks. Or so he thinks. I've never used any other form of attack on him. It was time to unveil my secret art to him. I channeled my aura.

* * *

Drakonis

Great Phoenixes and Grand Dragons are natural born enemies. So much so that their hatred of each other spreads to their lesser offspring. Each race was designed by their gods for combat and destruction. To fight each other was innate. It was destiny. But Addurog's rivalry with Drakonis was more than that. This was a deep obsession that Drakonis could never understand. He had always rationalized it as a desire to usurp his position, or to expose his weakness. But this latest plan was far grimmer, and more sinister than just a simple duel. To boot, Addurog was near silent as they exchanged assaults. Drakonis could tell that this time, Addurog meant to kill him. And he was willing to do whatever it took to make it happen.

Drakonis stared up at Addurog. The phoenix was channeling his aura and preparing something up above. But as far as Drakonis had seen, Addurog specialized in sword arts and aura abilities. He wondered what he could be preparing up there.

Drakonis took a moment to look around and make sure his allies were okay. Chase laid a few feet away, still coughing from being stepped on. For someone that had been beaten by Addurog, he wasn't extremely injured. But he looked extremely exhausted and unable to move. What had Addurog done to Chase?

As he checked back at the entrance, Isobel, Mahogany, and Dior were all watching from their stomachs. In fact, all of the beastkin were watching in awe at the giant spectacle before them.

Drakonis knew that his and Addurog's auras colliding would create an extreme amount of pressure, but he couldn't afford to let up. For now, everyone was fine, and they would have to endure if he was to see them safe.

He looked back up at Addurog who was now glowing with a dark blue hue, and his wings were covered in a blue flame as well.

"LET'S SEE IF YOU CAN PROTECT YOUR WRETCHED HUMANS FROM THIS, FORSAKEN FLAME!" Addurog roared from up above.

He flapped his wings intensely and giant blue fire balls rain downed towards Drakonis.

Drakonis moved his hands and started to channel his mana. He would need to reshape the dome and change its composition if he were going to block the attack. He hardened the dark mana into a force-field around everyone in the grindstone.

That moron, Drakonis thought to himself. Addurog was so dead set on killing him that he was willing to destroy his own troop and all of the grindstone to do it! These actions were unforgivable. And this was more than a petty grudge now. It was Drakonis' duty to take Addurog down.

The fireballs bashed the top of the dome, creating giant explosions outside of the dome, but Drakonis' aura was far too strong. None of the balls were able to penetrate the hard carapace of the mana field and Drakonis held his ground against the assault. As Drakonis looked up, he realized that Addurog was no longer in the air.

He tried to sense where Addurog was and found that the Phoenix was gliding towards him at lightning speed. Drakonis channeled again and had to make his mana field even smaller, just big enough to cover his body, to block the attack.

Addurog's blade slammed into Drakonis' side, sending him flying across the grindstone. If not for Drakonis' fast reaction to his current predicament, he might've been cleaved in two. Drakonis was flying close to the ground, and he angled his body toward the ground and jammed his arm into the earth to stop his flight. He was able to bring himself back to the earth, but he couldn't slow himself down. He also noticed that he was sliding past a group of deceased beastkin and managed to pick up one of their swords on the way to the wall. As he lifted up his blade, he noticed that Addurog had followed him all the way to the wall and was bringing his sword down on with a crazed look in his eye. Drakonis managed to block the attack and their blades were locked in a violent clash, sparks flying away from their swords.

"Excellent!" Addurog laughed as he put the full weight of his body into his sword. "But I think it's time to end this!"

Addurog then lifted his blade and started trading blows with Drakonis. Drakonis tried to move away from the wall by walking as they struck, but Addurog was able to cut off his movements. Drakonis felt his stamina reach its limit. But he was taken back by the fact that it was happening sooner than it should have. He felt sweat falling from his brow, but Addurog kept up the barrage. Drakonis slammed his sword into Addurog, breaking it in two, and pushed him a few feet back. It was just enough space to expand his mana field and use it to weigh Addurog down.

"Trying to slow me down, Iguana breath?" Addurog mocked with a smug grin. "I guess you must be feeling it right about now?"

Drakonis wanted to reply but his breath became labored. That's when he noticed that a sickly green aura was radiating from Addurog's sword, Severance. It was at that moment that he realized what was happening. He had fallen for Addurog's plan. The dark phoenix had been secretly sapping his mana and using it to power himself. The mocking and giant attacks were just ploys to distract him from that fact. He was so blinded by anger and the draining was so subtle that he only tired himself out.

“Mana Draining...” Drakonis said softly.

“Ding, Ding, Ding, someone reward the garden snake for his intuition.” Addurog continued. “A nifty perk to come with a new sword. This marvelous piece of work was designed with the intention of penetrating your flesh and destroying your weak and brittle dragon bones. Tell me, how does it feel to be a colossal idiot? You've been fighting like a ragged animal with no strategy. And don't think I haven't noticed you lowering your pressure to not crush the chimps. You're choosing to be weak, you fool.”

Drakonis took a second to look around. He had been taking everyone's wellbeing into account with each attack, each defense, and each movement. He could have just defended himself from the fireball attack, and he wouldn't have been so drained. But he couldn't allow harm to befall them. He had put them all in harm's way by bringing them together. They were his responsibility.

“Just admit defeat, gecko bait.” Addurog said standing upright and pointing his sword at Drakonis. “Announce your inferiority before me. In fact, state the superiority of phoenix kind over dragons and I'll let you leave with your life and maybe some of your limbs. Or continue fighting me and meet the gods of death. I will savor whichever decision you choose!”

Drakonis felt himself getting weaker by the second.

Severance was stealing all the mana in the area and the sword half he held wasn't going to be of use to him anymore. It was rare that Drakonis felt this desperate. He was going to need a miracle to win at this rate.

"Hah..." Drakonis scoffed. "Superior..."

Addurog cocked his head at Drakonis' words.

"My race was exterminated by a god." Drakonis grunted. "The Dragon of Darkness decimated the Grand Dragons. But the Great Phoenixes were destroyed by a lone fledgling. By a weakling that danced for a crumb of power like a court jester. You're a joke, Addurog. And so was your lineage."

Addurog stared blankly at Drakonis. His shoulders began to shake, and his breathing became erratic. He then burst out into a fit of hysterical laughter.

"Me?" He said with that same crazed expression from earlier. "I'm the joke, huh?"

Addurog then raised his sword towards Isobel, Dior, and Mahogany.

"Then laugh about this..." He said in a soft and cruel voice. He then blasted a large fireball from the blade.

*   *   *

Chase

Smoke covered the area. Chase was covering his face from the debris that flew from the blast area. He couldn't do anything to help Drakonis due to the aura pressures and the mana sapping from Addurog's sword. He even tried to warn Drakonis multiple times, but the fight was too intense for Drakonis to hear. Worse, Drakonis wasn't fighting as he normally would. He was too focused on saving everyone, even the beastmen. That wasn't the Drakonis that they had seen on the battlefield in New York. He wasted so much strength focusing on saving everyone. Chase wasn't judging him harshly for it, but it's too hard a task to protect everyone and fight an opponent on equal footing. Even for a dragon.

Chase looked up to see if he could make out anything in the fog. He saw Addurog point the blade at the Isobel and the kids. He was hoping by some miracle that they were saved. That Isobel was able to create a barrier to save them or Drakonis was able to defend them against that blast. But he couldn't imagine everyone walking away from that attack. Addurog was a beast. He may seem like a clown, but he was not to be taken lightly.

As the smoke cleared, Chase saw Drakonis standing in front of Isobel and the children. He could hear them crying but they all seemed alive. Even in his weakened state, Drakonis managed to save them. He also saw that a barrier was dissipating from his skin. Drakonis had saved them and probably others as well. He breathed a sigh of relief.

Then Chase became nervous. He was breathing normally. The pressure that had pressed down on him was all but gone. He only felt Addurog's aura.

As more of the smoke cleared, Chase saw that Addurog's hand had penetrated Drakonis' back. Drakonis coughed and blood spilled from his lips.

"In the end..." Addurog began. "These humans are your demise. This is what you get for being a sympathizer and a weakling. You didn't have the heart to end them on the battlefield and you didn't have the heart to abandon them now. But don't worry... I'll have more heart than I could have ever asked for!"

Addurog then wretched his hand from Drakonis' back, his heart still beating in his hand. Drakonis jerked from the motion and reached out towards Isobel and the children. He then fell face-first into the dirt in front of them.

The beastmen began to mutter amongst themselves. Chase knew what this meant. By Rule of the Wilds, Addurog now held Drakonis' position. He was their new master. A beastmen with a hatred for humans.

Chase couldn't believe it. He wasn't fond of Drakonis. Not even in the slightest, and every night he dreamed of jamming a sword into his gut and watching him bleed to death. But he did come to respect his strength and even appreciated the training. To see him face down in a pool of his own blood brought a slew of mixed emotions. Chase didn't know what was going to happen to them now.

"I CAN'T TELL YOU HOW LONG I HAVE WAITED TO DO THAT!" Addurog yelled out happily. "I'm sated and yet, this feels bittersweet."

Addurog looked down at the bloody mass that used to be the Dark Lord of D'Merrion's army. beastmen began to get up and walk over to Drakonis.

"Drakonis..." Addurog said in a more somber tone. "Bear the burden of my resent. I didn't personally hate you. You just have the face of a man I hate. I hope that oblivion fits you better than the title of Beastlord General did."

Chase felt a small piece of his energy returning. Addurog must have turned off the mana drain. He stood up and rushed over to Isobel.

The beastmen had turned Drakonis over and had picked him up in their arms. Chase had never seen this part of the ritual before, but he knew that they would drop his body in a field with the rest of the corpses. He was title-less now, and his legacy would be that of a loser. They began to chant softly as they walked away with the body.

"Now for you cretins." Addurog said with eagerness in his voice. "Your lives will be changing soon! The quality treatment and freedoms that you've enjoyed were a luxury of Drakonis' weakness. Don't worry, I won't have that same affliction. So, stand up. I have crossbows that need test targets!"

Chase gripped his fists and gritted his teeth. Addurog was going to ride them into the grave. If he thought Drakonis was bad, this was going to be far worse. Chase was thinking of a hundred ways to try and assassinate Addurog when he heard a familiar voice behind him.

"That won't be necessary." The voice replied. Chase turned to see Drakonis' grandfather, Xinovioc, walking towards them. He had stopped the beastmen caravan from disposing of Drakonis' body and was moving towards Addurog.

"You have won your match." Xinovioc said as he reached out his hand. "I suggest you hand over my grandson's heart."

Addurog paused for a moment. He looked like he was taking stock of Xinovioc. For a moment, it looked like he was willing to fight the old dragon.

"As you wish, your highness." Addurog said bringing

the heart to Xinovioc's hand. He then dropped the heart on the ground and kicked dirt on it.

“Oops.” Addurog said making a pouting face. “Silly me.”

He then walked past Xinovioc and put his hand on Chase's shoulder.

“You've piqued my interest mutt.” Addurog whispered to Chase. “I will be keeping a close eye on you. And you better believe I won't be the only one watching you with keen eyes. See you at the Crucible.”

Addurog laughed and then left the Grindstone just as suddenly as he had arrived, all the beastmen except the ones holding Drakonis left with him.

Xinovioc picked up the heart and brushed off the sand from the grindstone. He held it tenderly and brought it to his ear. He then breathed deeply, and his face had an expression of relief.

“Don't worry.” Xinovioc said reassuringly. “Today is not his last. “

He then motioned for the beastmen holding Drakonis' body to approach him.

“Come!” He commanded. “Bring him here!”

The beastmen rushed Drakonis back over to Xinovioc and placed his body on the ground. The beastmen made a circle around Drakonis and Xinovioc.

Chapter 16:
Changing the Paradigm

Isobel

She didn't think that she would return to this room ever again. She had hoped that the sterile walls, pristine-white sheets, and that god forbidden 'sanitized' smell was a thing of the past, that she would leave this room and never return to the site of her worst torture. Even the beds that littered the room were a point of annoyance for her, their perfect alignment against the white walls of the room was sickening. Here she was back in the secret confines of the medical ward, with all of its perfect white features, but at least she had company this time.

Small victories for any kind of peace, my little consort? The dragon whispered in her mind.

She had always mulled over the fact that there was a strong, bleach-like odor that turned her stomach, and it made her feel nauseous. Today it was accompanied by a hint of smoldered coal, a scent that was proudly worn by a man that lived in the forge.

But unlike the last time Isobel had seen him, his

expression was far from proud. He held his son Semaj's hand delicately in his with a type of softness and care you wouldn't expect to see someone with such a fiery spirit. You could hear small soft sobs coming from the man and his daughters, who stood behind him.

"My boy..." King Maj said through soft whimpers. "My beautiful boy..."

Semaj was breathing softly through the mask of an oxygen machine. He laid in the bed completely motionless. If it weren't for his soft gasps through the mask, there would be no indication that he was still alive. His face was welted, bruised, and blue from where he had been beaten just hours before.

Isobel sat across from the family, on another bed, with Chase standing over her. He hadn't left her side since they had retreated from the grindstone.

Your dutiful bodyguard, always at the ready. Heh, too bad his bark is more vicious than his bite.

"How could this happen..." King Maj mumbled rhetorically. "To my boy..."

Drakonis, who had been leaning against the wall near the entrance of the room, walked over to King Maj and placed his hand on his shoulder. Mahogany and Dior instinctively made room for Drakonis.

Hmm... To have your heart ripped out in front of your closest confidantes and have it just replaced like a sword in its sheath. Curious, is it not? The dragon whispered yet again.

If Isobel hadn't seen it yesterday, she wouldn't have believed it. It's not as though she hadn't seen resurrections before. It wasn't hard to return a lost or captured soul, or to stop a soul from leaving with a strong enough incantation. But that only applies if the body is still whole, it hasn't received too much trauma, and it happens within a few minutes. Drakonis' body had second degree burns all over half of his body and his heart was removed. For all intents and purposes... He should have been dead.

The King sighed deeply and stood up while removing Drakonis' hand from his shoulder. He turned and stared Drakonis right in his eyes with a savage expression, tears streaming slowly from his eyes.

"We had a deal, boy." King Maj said, his hands balling up. "WE HAD AN AGREEMENT! Me and my boys craft the best of Majen technology, give you the gift of our forges and smithing, and in return, you accept the Majes into your midst and protect my kind as proper citizens of the alliance!"

King Maj stopped talking for a moment, probably hoping to get a reply from the Dark Lord, but Drakonis didn't speak. And he didn't break eye contact.

"But here lies my heir!" King Maj continued, pointing at his son. "My child! My flesh! My blood and my inheritor lies broken upon this pathetic excuse of'a bed."

The King looked at Drakonis with pained eyes, and Isobel's heart felt for him. She had grown to care a bit for Semaj, and to see him corpse-like on the bed was devastating. The youth was always so full of energy and life. This is a fate that everyone in the room wished he had avoided.

King Maj turned back to his son and held his hand again.

“I am altering our deal, Drakonis.” He said, getting back on his knees. “Karita and I are a part of the war effort. That will not change, even... Even should my son not survive.”

The King's voice broke a bit at the end. Isobel could see that the man was trying his best to hold it together, either because of his pride or just to be strong for his son.

“Addurog...” He continued as he gritted his teeth. “Addurog must pay for this treacherous act. He must be made to suffer for his misdeeds against my kin. You must mete out this punishment, Drakonis. Should Karita return to see her son in such a state, she would stop at nothing in search of revenge, endangering the alliance. Do this for me. For the King of the Majes. I can't... I can't do it myself.”

“Your will shall be done, my friend.” Drakonis replied, bowing his head behind the King. “You have my word that when I face Addurog again... No magic, weapon, or words will barter his fate. This I swear.”

“Thank you.” King Maj replied as he turned to embrace

Mahogany and Dior. "And thank you girls for be'in his friends and sisters, even if you share no relation by blood. You have helped him become a fine young man. I'm sure this all was a scare for you."

"No, my King..." Mahogany and Dior replied in unison. Anyone could tell this was a lie as their noses were red and eyes were watery.

"It is okay, children." King Maj said as he pulled away from them. "I know that I have said to save your tears and grievances for ears away from the court. But today... I don't need ya'ta be strong for your brother... It is all right to show that you care."

The girls then started crying into their father's shoulders.

"That's it..." King Maj said, pulling the girls in close. He reached over and gripped his son's hand again. But this time, there was a tightness to his grasp. "Semaj, ya silly boy. Look at all the grief you're causing ya family. Just... Wake up boy... Wake up."

Tears continued to stream from the King's face as he pleaded with the unconscious boy, but his demands fell upon deaf ears, for Semaj didn't respond. There were a couple minutes of soft sobbing from the family.

"*Ugh... I am becoming sick to my stomach. Someone please come save us from this party of pity.*" The dragon groaned out of boredom.

Isobel gritted her teeth and grimaced a bit, but she quickly returned her face to normal. She wasn't allowed to react to the Black Dragon's comments.

Almost as though the dragon's request was verbally heard and granted, the door to the room slid open prompting everyone in the room to look in its direction. Cyarah stood in the doorway with a clipboard in hand and walked towards Semaj. Drakonis quickly slid into her path, towering a few feet above her.

"Ya got'a lot of nerve appearing before me so soon, you monster." King Maj said as he stood up and pushed his daughters behind himself. "How could anyone do this to a young boy?!"

Cyarah looked at the Majen King with eyes that lacked any kind of emotion, any kind of regret towards Semaj's situation. It was a look that Isobel had become accustomed to over the course of her stay here. Cyarah didn't have a care about anyone in the room and neither did her staff.

"I didn't put your son into this state, King Maj." Cyarah stated bluntly. Her expression didn't change but you could sense a bit of arrogance in her words. "And blocking my path only prolongs the boys suffering, Drakonis. You all do realize that I'm his attending physician, correct?"

Chase scoffed loudly, folding his arms in front of him.

“Why you little...!” King Maj started to yell, but Drakonis put his hand out in front of the king.

Drakonis stared at her intensely with a frown on his face. Then a loud 'crack' echoed in the room. It was soon followed by another softer 'crack' and Isobel noticed that the air around Cyarah was a bit denser. Drakonis was projecting his pressure onto Cyarah.

“My apologies, my prince.” Cyarah said tilting her head and smiling coyly. She then bowed her head towards Drakonis, looking unaffected by the pressure. “I humbly ask for forgiveness for my follies, now and in the past.”

Drakonis didn't reply and the air around Cyarah became denser, causing the ground to crack and crumble under her feet.

“Is there anything I can do to...?” Cyarah started to say as a bead of sweat rolled down her face.

“And what could you possibly offer me to make up for this betrayal?” Drakonis said softly. His body was radiating a soft black smoke.

Isobel could see the area of pressure expanding outward. It took a bit of concentration to centralize pressure that way, and it was obvious that Drakonis still hadn't recovered from the fight, no matter how confidently he stood.

Cyarah stayed bowed down in front of Drakonis, but she sank a few inches into the ground. Cyarah was kind of a small woman, but her resistance to a beastkin General's aura was a sign that she wasn't just a doctor.

"My liege..." Cyarah grunted under the pressure. "I have in my possession an element that can be used to craft an even greater weapon than the one I made for Addurog. An element straight from the depths of the Forgotten Zone."

The pressure field around Cyarah immediately dispersed, but she remained bowed. King Maj and Drakonis both had wide eyes, and Isobel shared a glance with Chase. Chase just shrugged his shoulders.

"Chrocosium..." Drakonis stated. "Interesting. I'm not even going to inquire how you managed to get your hands on such a rare element. Was I such a menace that D'Merrion had to employ such a deadly resource to reign me in?"

Isobel felt Chase's hand tense a bit. She reached up and grabbed his hand for a moment to let him know that she had noticed as well. Drakonis was hiding something.

Cyarah lifted her head. Her hair was a little disheveled from bowing her head for so long, but she didn't seem too weary. Isobel could tell she was a lot stronger than she looked.

"I would be more than happy to explain it to you once I check-up on Semaj, my lord." Cyarah said maintaining her unenthused expression.

Drakonis stared her down for a moment then turned to the side, allowing Cyarah to pass by him. He didn't look too happy about giving in to her. In fact, no one was. They all watched as Cyarah went over to Semaj's machines and started to check his vitals. King Maj never left his son's side, nor did he give up his spot by the bed, and it seemed as though Cyarah avoided having to interact with him in any way, shape, or form. Luckily for her, all the machines were on the backside of the bed.

"He's stable." Cyarah said scribbling something onto her clipboard. "His vitals are normal, and his mana core seems to be just fine. While his physical trauma may be a bit extensive, his spiritual trauma is minimal. He'll make a full recovery in a few weeks and probably be awake in a few hours."

Isobel let out a sigh of relief. It felt as though the air had been finally let out of the bubble and they could take this small victory. They had been in the room for a couple of hours listening to King Maj grieve, and maybe the energy would grow to be more positive now that they knew Semaj was going to get better.

"Good." Drakonis said as he stared down at Semaj. "Now talk."

"As you wish, my lord." Cyarah said bowing to Drakonis, then she arched her tail and sat on it like a chair. "As some of you may know, Chrocosium is an extremely rare element that is not of this realm. It comes from the Forgotten Zone and is sought after by everyone that knows it exists. I won't waste time getting into the details but let's just say it's a commodity and worth the trouble to find and mine it."

"You shouldn't have been able to gather the material at all." Drakonis interrupted. "Chrocosium is afflicted with Dark Mana, and it siphons the mana and life of anyone that touches it. Protective countermeasures and clothes are not even an option due to its ability to steal mana at such a quick rate."

"You are correct." Cyarah agreed. "And for a long time, the mineral and its benefits were sealed within the Forbidden Zone. But due to recent developments, our metallurgy specialists were able to craft a device to safely extract and mine the mineral. It's a long story but to keep it sparse, we successfully weaponized the material."

Interesting, Isobel thought.

Yes, it is, Hehe.

Isobel stopped herself. She still wasn't used to the dragon being in her consciousness. His grip was getting stronger every day, almost like he was slowly walking towards a door in her mind. And soon it felt as though he would find a way to wrestle even her mind from her.

And the more you resist, the easier it is to see what you're hiding. Though I will admit, I do gain amusement from watching you struggle to resist my possession. He said chuckling.

Isobel resisted the urge to frown, but after noticing

Cyarah's expression, she realized that she had failed.

“Something the matter, Isobel?” Cyarah inquired with a confused look. “Did I say something to upset you?”

“No.” Isobel replied swiftly. “I just- I have never heard of Chrocosium.”

“Surprising and Curious.” Cyarah said, crossing her arms. “Most people know of the Forbidden Zone, but Chrocosium existence is not common knowledge. But if I could be candid, I would assume that the Divine Knights would know of such a powerful ore. Do the Divines not share knowledge of Outer Realms with their blessed warriors? How do you even contact them? Do you have a throne room as well or is it more-”

“Back off.” Chase interrupted.

“Get back on track, Cyarah.” Drakonis commanded. “I need to know, was Addurog's weapon made of Chrocosium?”

“My apologies, my lord.” Cyarah continued, though Isobel could tell that she was a little disappointed that she couldn't inquire about The Divines. “To answer your question… Not entirely. No one can handle a one hundred percent Chrocosium weapon. It would steal your life just from touching it. But we were able to line his blade with it and add enchantments to it.”

“So, in other words...” King Maj said looking away from Semaj. “His weapon wasn't even an actual Chrocosium blade... You just took some junk and cobbled it together with the resource like some sort of jigsaw puzzle. How about you stop grandstanding and just get to the point, chimera."

"The point..." Cyarah said with a particularly annoyed look. "Is that Addurog's sword was infantile in development. It was physically stronger than most blades, but its full potential was not reached. We used a small amount of Pure Dark Mana and Divine Mana to bond the blade and strengthen its constitution. But my team is not composed of blacksmiths. Our knowledge of metalworking is limited. We hypothesize that in the hands of a capable or even legendary blacksmith, with access to our resources, the negative effects of Chrocosium could be rendered inert or even re-engineered and weaponized as well."

"You gave Addurog rocks." King Maj whispered while his eyes grew large. "But you want to give Drakonis diamonds... With an element like Chrocosium, you could revolutionize mana transfer between a sword and its user. Or even give a blade the ability to refund mana back to the weave and dissipate spells."

"You could physically cut spells out of existence." Isobel said under her breath.

Don't get any wise ideas, slave. It would take but a few moments to rip the pathetic life from your tiny body. DO NOT TEST MY PATIENCE. He roared in her mind.

“In theory, yes.” Cyarah replied to them. She looked at Isobel with a curious look. “I never took you to be a scholar. But to be fair, you were never awake when I took care of you. It's nice to see another woman have an interest in science and spell conceptualization.”

“We still hate you, Cyarah.” Isobel said blandly. “Stop trying to be my friend.”

“Ow.” Cyarah groaned as she made a gesture as though she had been shot. “Your words burrow deep into my heart, Isobel. I am wounded.”

“So!” Drakonis said loudly interrupting them. “So, you offer a superior weapon as penance for your transgressions against everyone in this room?”

“Not just any 'Superior Weapon', my lord.” Cyarah said leaning forward. “Your aura is almost one hundred percent dark mana. And this sword will be smelted from an ore that originates from the home of dark mana. It will be completely attuned to your aura.”

Drakonis stopped to think for a moment, crossing his arms and looking at the ceiling. Isobel didn't like that he was actually considering letting Cyarah off the hook.

“Ok.” Drakonis finally replied.

“You can't be serious!?” King Maj angrily objected. He laid Semaj's hand down and turned to Drakonis, his face twisted in a bit of disgust. “You would allow this heathen to continue to exist unafflicted and buy her way out of punishment!?"

Drakonis put his hand on the King's shoulder.

"I am not pardoning her crimes, King Maj." Drakonis said softly. "She will still receive punishment. But until then, we will work together to craft a Chrocosium blade."

"I would like to ask for a favor, my lord." Cyarah interrupted.

"What is it?" Drakonis asked. "I've already decided against immediate ramifications for your treachery. What could you possibly ask for to jeopardize that agreement?"

"I would ask to be allowed to train him." Cyarah said as she pointed to Chase.

Drakonis stopped to think for a moment.

"I will allow it." Drakonis agreed, much to the surprise of everyone in the room. "He's learned all I can teach him at this time. It would bene-"

"YOU ARE SOMETHING ELSE!" Chase loudly interrupted their conversation. It was so loud that it startled everyone in the room except for Drakonis. Isobel felt Chase's hand leave her shoulder. "You really are quite the actor, aren't you? You never had any intention of punishing her! You're not going to 'inquire about where she got the ore? You accept this 'Chrocosium' in return for postponing her punishment!? You would have to be a complete moron to believe any of this facade."

"*At least someone said it.*" The dragon snickered.

Isobel looked at Drakonis, studying his face for a reaction. He stared blankly back at Chase. Isobel then turned her eyes to Cyarah, who was trying to hide a smile.

"Why are you toying with us?" Chase continued. "Are you that sadistic? How much farther does this have to go!? Semaj was beaten half to death! Even as his family grieves over his body, YOU'RE STILL PLOTTING AGAINST EVERYONE HERE!"

"Drakonis, you can't possibly be considering forgiving her?" Isobel said softly. "She betrayed you, as well as everyone in this room that had trust in her. You would accept some rock for Semaj's life and her alliance?"

Isobel stared at Drakonis for a moment, and he just stared back. *There had to be more to it than that*, she thought. Drakonis was no fool.

Their stare down was interrupted by a cough from Cyarah.

"Allow me to shed some light on my involvement." Cyarah said as she lowered her gaze. "I... created the plan to humiliate Drakonis. Or well... D'Merrion created the plan, and I assembled the pieces. We knew that Drakonis adored the children and the knights. We used Addurog's men to grab them, but we only wanted them as hostages. No one planned for

Semaj to stand against Addurog. And we knew that if we had grabbed them, Drakonis wouldn't waste time to go to their aid."

"So have you always been a monster or is this a new feeling for you?" Chase said, placing his hand on Isobel's shoulder again. "Who targets children!?"

"Monster, huh?" Cyarah said, turning to look at Chase. "Do you know where you are?"

"What?" Chase said.

"We live in the home of the strongest god in existence." Cyarah continued. "Everything, from every beastmen to every piece of furniture, exists because he allows it to. Every day, Drakonis is beaten within an inch of his life and survives, because The One True God allows him to. Even your lives, this enslavement, is only perpetuated because he allows it to. You judge me for looking out for myself when I have no family, no one to watch my back, but you have only seen the best of beastkin culture. You both have been shown great hospitality even after Isobel brandished that cursed power within the market. What makes you so special to judge from your high horses and be pampered like royalty!?"

"Yeah, Drakonis!" Chase glared at the Dark Lord as he cocked his head at an angle. "What makes us so special, huh?"

"We've wondered that since we arrived." Isobel added. "We were defeated. He could have taken our heads and dealt an extreme blow to the Divines. But he spared us and our allies.

And brought us here."

The room had grown silent as everyone turned their heads to Drakonis. The Dark Lord looked away as all eyes were trained on him. It was as though he didn't know how to answer the question. And anyone could tell that he certainly didn't want to.

"*Now this is getting interesting.*" The dragon said with interest.

The door to the room suddenly slid open and a familiar, elderly face peered inside.

"*Ah, Xinovioc. Such delicious pain behind that friendly smile.*" The dragon continued.

"It's more silent than I expected in here." Xinovioc greeted. "How is everyone?"

"Becoming accustomed to each other." Drakonis replied, obviously eager to change the subject.

"That is marvelous!" Xinovioc said with a smile. "And the heart?"

"You know it's purely ornamental, grandfather." Drakonis replied. "I wasn't really going to die."

"But they do not know that son." Xinovioc said in a soft tone. He sat down on one of the beds and pulled out his tea set. Isobel felt her mouth water a bit as she anticipated the sweet taste of the lemonade. Then Xinovioc began to scribe in the air in front of him. It was the same movement patterns Isobel had seen him follow when he created the soundproof barrier a week prior.

"There!" Xinovioc said as he poured his lemonade. "We can speak freely without interruption or being spied upon."

Hahahaha! Amusing.... The dragon cackled in amusement.

"I don't need that heart to live..." Drakonis continued. "I got it as a gift. So Addurog taking it was merely a gesture of disrespect."

"That's all fine and dandy, but you still lost to Addurog!" Chase said angrily. "And you did it under Rule of the Wilds, no less."

"That doesn't matter." Xinovioc, Drakonis, and Cyarah said in unison.

"The only reason Drakonis lost was because he was holding back." Cyarah said matter-of-factly. "Every beastmen race has a unique and extremely specific racial trait that their species have developed since coming to this realm. No two traits are identical. As you know, the human trait is destiny. Any human has the ability to learn anything, provided that they have the will to withstand the hardships of their decision, and this has given our race the most diverse combat and job archetypes. It's so innate within us that we sometimes forget that our race is the only one that can do this. But the dragonkin's trait is Frenzy."

"Since the beginning of time, dragons have been as strong as they are vain." Xinovioc continued. "Frenzy is the reason behind this. Since the creation of this realm and all who inhabit it, the gods fell back to their temples and allowed man and beast to run rampant upon the lands. And dragons were the strongest amongst the races, only rivaled by the mighty phoenix."

Xinovioc then stood up and all of the teacups he had been pouring floated up off his table. He passed out cups of lemonade to everyone in the room. His first stop was Isobel, whose eyes lit up when she saw him approach.

"I see my lemonade has made a good impression!" The old dragon said elated. "Here you go, my dear!"

His warm smile made her feel safe and comfortable, and she drank the drink eagerly. She was finished before he had even turned around.

"My, my!" Xinovioc smiled, showing a bit of his crooked dragon teeth. "You embarrass this old dragon, Isobel. Here, have another!"

Isobel blushed a bit and exchanged her cup for another. Xinovioc then gestured for Chase to take one. Chase eyed one of the cups, examining it suspiciously, before he took one and loudly sipped it. His eyes grew wide.

"MMMMMMMMMMMMHM!?" He shrieked behind

pursed lips. “There's no way you made this lemonade just now!?”

“Young sir, any wise being knows that good lemonade isn't made in a few minutes.” Xinovioc replied. He was beaming with energy now, smiling effortlessly.

“I thought it would be repulsive because you pulled it out of your cloak!” Chase went on. “This is amazing!”

Xinovioc continued to walk around the room, passing out his lemonade for a minute or two. Most of the interactions went like that save for Drakonis and Cyarah, who Isobel surmised could only resist the taste of the lemonade due to their constant exposure to it.

“Ah.” Xinovioc said as he sat down again. “Now, when a dragon frenzies, he cannot recognize who is thy friend nor foe. His senses become clouded with bloodlust and rage. This makes his attacks absolute and devastating. This was great when dragons lived isolated in the wilderness, but as society became more organized, both beast and man, this trait became a detriment to our evolution. So, we trained our minds to manage the frenzy, to practice civility and reason, even when our hearts did not desire as much. To make matters worse, Drakonis is an infant dragon. He may look like a grown human male, but he is practically infantile in the face of actual dragons.”

Drakonis folded his arms and scowled at the statement.

He obviously wasn't too happy about being called infantile.

"The plan Lord D'Merrion and I created hinged on Drakonis not only coming unprepared to combat Addurog, but also not being willing to fully unleash his frenzy." Cyarah added. "His desire to protect everyone was his downfall. And Addurog was eager to exploit that weakness."

"So, Addurog winning a Rule of the Wilds against me doesn't matter." Drakonis said. "I will challenge him again and win. And we'll go back to how we were."

"How we were!?" Chase said, his voice tinged with annoyance. He stood up abruptly and started glowering at Drakonis. "Where Isobel was locked up like a slave and I was treated like a pit dog?"

Isobel reached up and put her hand on Chase's arm to try and calm him.

"We've been civil until now, Chase." Isobel said in a soft voice. "Let's try to remain as such."

Chase stared at her, his eyes saying many things at once. He had a look of complete disbelief on his face.

"Isobel." Chase said gritting his teeth, veins emerging on his temple. "You look like an old, half-burned candy bar. You can't possibly expect us to go on trusting these maniacs!? Look at us! Your mark has spread over half of your body, and you look like you haven't been fed since I last saw you! You expect me to trust someone who willingly aggravated your mark and didn't feed you!?"

"Chase, I..." Isobel began. "I did this to myself. Although I won't lie and say that I was treated with the utmost respect." Isobel glanced at Drakonis. Their eyes met and he lowered his gaze a bit. She could tell that he still felt guilty. *Good*, she thought. Serves him right.

Ooohhh. So scary, my consort. Do go on.

"But..." Isobel continued, looking back at Chase. "We don't have any other options. As of right now, there is a chance that those beastkin-"

Chase interrupted her with a scoff before shaking his head and looking away from her.

"Those BEASTKIN..." Isobel began again. "Have started gossiping about our whereabouts and word has traveled that I am alive. Someone that was able to control and will the Curse of the Black Dragon. They will be looking to seize any opportunity to either steal or kill me. And if you protect me as I know you will, they will do the same to you."

"I'd like to see them try." Chase said as he flexed his fist. "I'll kill every last one of them."

"Stop being bull-headed for one moment and just think." Isobel scolded him. "Instead of planning on fighting all of Zhalesh, how about we think for a change. We need to get stronger, to protect ourselves, and there is only one way we can do that. There is only one person who can help us do that now..."

"I'm strong enough." Chase shot back.

"Are you?" Drakonis said from across the room. "Can you beat me, right this instant?"

"Want to find out!?" Chase glared back.

"I remember there being two bruised and beaten warriors in the Grindstone." Xinovioc said as he sipped his lemonade. "And BOTH lost to Addurog, if I remember correctly."

Chase bit his lip and sat back down. Drakonis scowled again, and just sighed. Their pride had been hurt, and that was enough to quell their resentment of each other, for now.

"*Ask him.*"

"Drakonis, what is the point of all this?" Isobel said, her expression cold and serious. "Why bring us here and then try to protect us from your own people when you could have just killed us? We're the enemy of your god. What exactly are you planning?"

Drakonis frowned and rubbed his face. He looked nervous and had the same expression on his face from earlier. He didn't look like he knew what to do.

"It's okay, son." Xinovioc gestured to him. "I think it's time to trust in more than yourself."

That's right. Trust, Drakonis. The dragon whispered.

Drakonis sighed and closed his eyes. He looked as

though he was getting ready to unveil his greatest secret. Like he was about to give away a part of himself.

He lifted his head and spoke. “This all began when I was called by the Fae.”

*　　　*　　　*

Drakonis

“Are you sure that was the smartest thing to do?” Cyarah said, confusion in her face.

No. He was not sure. In fact, he had never been more unsure about anything in his life. But he trusts in his grandfather, and he has to hang onto that belief for now. He had told them just about everything.

“It will have to suffice for now.” Drakonis said, trying to sound confident in his decision.

“You even told me, a loyal D’Merrion lap dog.” Cyarah continued. “How do you know I won't just go and tell him? Or even better, how do you even know that he doesn't already know?”

“I do not, Cyarah.” Drakonis said sternly. She was wearing on his last nerve. “Cease your questioning.”

“Yes, My lord.” Cyarah replied as they rounded another corner. He could hear a bit of amusement in her voice.

“Very tolerant, Lord Drakonis.” King Maj half-jokingly.

“We're almost there, my lord.” Cyarah said, looking back at the group.

Cyarah was leading the way to her workshop. Drakonis was next to her and King Maj while Isobel and Chase trailed behind. Drakonis assumed they were a little farther behind so they could whisper to each other and have time to catch up. He was almost sure that they did not receive any kind of sleep last night, and too elated that they were in each other’s company again. Or maybe they were plotting against him now that they knew.

He shook the thought away. He couldn't afford to have doubt right now. If they were going to get to his goal, he had to do as he had always done. He had to be strong and forge a way forward.

As they rounded yet another corner, the inside of the palace changed from D’Merrion's favored interior to a more modern design. There were far more glass windows now, and some computers lying about. Their use was unknown to Drakonis.

Drakonis didn't visit Cyarah's lab for many reasons, but the most evident was that he hated her experiments. Her personal 'pet projects' unsettled his lunch in the worst kind of fashion.

They found themselves in front of a large, steel door with a terminal next to the entrance. Cyarah walked over to the terminal and scanned her badge on its surface. A terminal whirred to life, unleashing a torrent of soft beeps and synth-like chirps, before it quieted down.

"Welcome, Doctor Cyarah." A female voice uttered from the box. It was very monotone, so much so that Drakonis could only assume that it was robotic and not attached to a real, living being.

The large steel door buzzed to life, making large mechanical sounds that would sound alarming in any other setting, and it slowly slid open and revealed Cyarah's workshop.

"And voila." Cyarah said with a little excitement. "Welcome to the capital of beastkin science and medicine! If you'll please follow me." She walked forward into the lab and the group followed behind her.

Everything in the lab was white. The walls were white and showed no signs of age or damage. There were beastmen and humans walking around with pristine white lab coats and clipboards, each absorbed in some science related task. White machines hummed as they completed their programmed tasks without fail. There was a path in between the experiments, an illuminated blue path with small softly strobing lamps, that Cyarah led the group down. This was presumably designed to not disturb the workers or their assignments.

"Lord Drakonis has been here many times, but for the newcomers..." Cyarah announced as they walked. "Please stay on the blue path. It's designed for you and the workers' safety. We pride ourselves on workplace safety and efficiency."

"Who would be dumb enough to not stay within these stupid lines?" Chase scoffed from the back of the group.

"Well, you would be who, Sir Chase." Cyarah turning to the group. "I get constant notifications on my bracelet about the state of the science ward. And you've set off three alarms since setting foot here."

Everyone turned and looked down at Chase's boots, which were outside of the strobed area. Chase was obviously embarrassed a bit, by his mistake slid his foot back within the confines of the lane.

"I will admit that six seconds is a new personal best for us." Cyarah said as she turned again towards the path. Chase grumbled something unintelligible and slid behind Isobel.

Moron, Drakonis thought to himself. Chase still lacked a certain kind of awareness of his surroundings at times.

"This is the Science Wing of the Capitol." Cyarah stated in her usual monotone. "You'll notice that this wing lacks beastkin howling about the Rule of the Wilds every four seconds. We are a bunch that values sophistication and intellect over brawn and notoriety. Ours is a study of the world and all of its contents. In this lab, nothing is off-limits to scrutinize and study. Truly, this is a well-refined hall of study, and research."

Gross. Anyone who was listening could tell that Cyarah was enjoying marveling at her own lab.

"So, what kinds of research do you do here?" Isobel asked softly. It had only been a day since her release, and her voice still hadn't fully recovered. She was barely audible above the whirring machines and footsteps of beastkin scientists.

"WELL, I AM GLAD YOU ASKED THAT!" Cyarah said with a massive grin on her face.

"No, no no, no." Drakonis interrupted. "We don't have time for any of that. I'd prefer it if we didn't idle. Please just escort us to your office, Cyarah."

Cyarah frowned and sighed as she turned and continued down the path. Drakonis chanced a glance back at Isobel to also see her with a scowl, her arms folded in discontent. He looked forward and noticed that King Maj was just looking at him. As they made eye contact, the King shrugged.

They walked behind Cyarah in an awkward silence for a few moments, the grand tour obviously ruined by Drakonis' objection. Drakonis didn't mind the partial silence.

They came upon an office, with a set glass, see-through doors. 'Director Cyarah' was written in bold text on a plaque next to the doors. Cyarah pulled a crystal from her pocket, one with an ominous blue hue and waved it in front of the door.

The door slowly slid open in response. In the center of the room sat a large white desk with piles of paperwork, some pens, and another terminal neatly organized on its surface. Just behind the desk was a large tank filled with a foul-looking liquid of a green tint. In fact, it was the only thing that looked nasty within the lab. There were multiple seats in the office, each just as pristine and white as the rest of the lab. Cyarah walked around the desk and took a seat behind it. She motioned for everyone else to take a seat.

"So... I suppose you want to see it?" Cyarah asked.

"That's the whole reason we're here, Cyarah." Drakonis replied examining the room.

"Let's not waste any more time than we need to." King Maj said eagerly. "Show me the ore."

Cyarah nodded and hit three keys on her terminal in rapid succession. Something began to hum behind her desk and soon a pillar holding a black rock covered in a smokey black mist rose into view from behind the desk. Almost at the same time, a growl and a hiss could be heard behind the desk.

"Hello Lydia." Cyarah said as she lowered her hand behind her desk. Another loud hiss could be heard in response. "How is my darling lady today?" Another hiss.

"Are we going to act like the giant hissing noises are normal or is someone going to offer an explanation for the obscurity that's taking place right now?" Chase said in a kind of worried tone. Almost as though in direct response to Chase's question, a giant beast lumbered into view from behind Cyarah's desk.

Drakonis was sure that this was jarring to Isobel, Chase, and maybe King Maj. But Drakonis had seen this pet many times before, if one could call it that. It was Cyarah's Komodo Dragon, 'Lydia', and this beast had been spliced with so many different animals, you could barely tell what it used to be. Drakonis noticed everyone in the room had already sat down, but he stayed standing for a reason. He knew it was wise to keep his distance from Lydia.

"Oh, that's just Lydia." Cyarah stated very matter-of-factly. "To keep it brief, I made her, and she is the most beautiful predator on this side of the Mississippi!"

"Beautiful, my foot!" Chase said as he leapt up from his seat and stood defensively in front of Isobel. "What the heck is that!?"

"Stay Lydia." Cyarah said as she started putting on a weird set of gloves. Lydia sat down in an upright position, kind of like a dog if the dog was the size of a stallion. "Stop being a drama queen. She's a pet and she doesn't bite... Much."

Using the gloves she had just put on, Cyarah lifted the black rock onto her desk. It clattered onto the hard, metal surface with a loud 'clack'. The sound of the rock made it seem like it was heavier than it looked.

“Annnnnnd this is Chrocosium.” She said marveling at the rock. “This is one of the most lethal elements in existence in its raw state. A few minutes of contact, and you would suffer from a severe case of fatigue. That would then lead to all of the stages of mana exhaustion and eventual death.”

“I presume you’re putting our lives at risk to show us the efficacy of your handling tools?” King Maj said with an underwhelmed tone. “How many sets of gloves can you get to my men so we can work on this chunk of rock?”

“As much as you need, King Maj.” Cyarah replied. “My men will provide you with all the resources you need to handle the ore. You can begin production as soon as tonight.”

“That works for us.” King Maj said contently as he stood up. “Well, I'd rather not dawdle here longer than I need to.”

“Wait, King.” Drakonis said quickly. “How goes the repairs to the market? It's been a few days since I last inquired about it.”

“Hmmm...” King Maj grumbled while stroking his beard. “With the help of the science team, we've made great progress on the repairs in the weeks since the incident. My men have been working nonstop around the clock on the repairs and we should be done just in time for the crucible in a few weeks.”

“We're going to have to expedite that progress.” Drakonis said with urgency. “We need everything done in time for the festival."

"I assure you, my lord." Cyarah interjected. She was petting Lydia, who had moved over to her hip and was purring softly. "Our teams are hard at work and will be done well before the festival in a few days."

"A few days?" King Maj said with some confusion. He rubbed the top of his head and had a befuddled expression. He seemed to be completely lost. "Isn't the crucible in a few weeks?"

"King Maj..." Cyarah sighed. "Remember when we had that dispute, and I was explaining WHY the reconstruction of the market was important to the festival?"

"Yes, quite vividly." King Maj said with the same expression.

"And remember when I kept saying 'The festival precedes the crucible, and it takes place in the market?" Cyarah continued. She stared intensely at King Maj.

"Ahem..." King Maj replied. "I do have some recollection of a conversation taking place.... Uhhh.... with those words being included, yes..."

Frustrating. Drakonis frowned a bit. He was having a hard time believing any of the King's story. In fact, he was more than a little disappointed that the king wasn't taking the festival seriously.

"The festival is no trivial manner, King Maj," Drakonis

stated bluntly. “We need the market in proper condition for the parade. It's important to the kingdom. It's the only time that citizens get to see the One True God. And with all of the recent chaos, it would raise morale around Zhalesh for the people to see that their ruler is unfazed by everything that has happened.”

“I understand my lord, I will try to be more attentive.” King Maj apologized.

“Good.” Drakonis said stiffly. “You may leave.”

“Thank you, my lord.” King Maj said as he bowed and turned to exit the room. The glass doors closed behind the King as he took his leave.

“It seems as though you and King Maj have everything under control.” Drakonis said, walking towards the door as well. “We will take our leave then. We have to be properly prepared for the parade march in a few days.”

“Uh, uh, uh, Drakonis.” Cyarah said with a wag of her finger. “You promised to let me train the knight. Are you welshing on our agreements, my lord?” Cyarah's brow was raised in anticipation. Drakonis had silently hoped that Cyarah had forgotten about that.

“Yes, you are right.” Drakonis said, trying to pretend that he had forgotten. “But not today. The knights have been in nonstop peril, and I believe that they are overdue for a few nights of respite. We will talk about the training later.”

Drakonis looked over at Isobel and Chase. He could see

that there was a look of relief on both of their faces. He motioned to them to begin following him. As he turned back to Cyarah, her face was twisted in a hideous scowl. She was furious.

"Then I guess you should be on your way." She replied through her furled lips. She was not even pretending to hide her discontent.

Drakonis, Isobel and Chase walked back out through the same doors they had entered. They walked back down the blue path towards the exit to the ward.

"You're not going to make me train with her, are you?" Chase said with a worried tone.

"Yes, I will." Drakonis replied. "Don't worry. If you survived two weeks of beastkin training, you will be fine under Cyarah's tutelage."

Drakonis was lying, of course. But Chase did not need to know that. Cyarah was going to push his capabilities to the limit. It was going to be absolutely horrible for the knight, but it was an experience he was going to need to endure in order to survive the crucible. Drakonis might not be the most empathetic dragon, but he wasn't a sadist. The knights deserved some peace of mind, and he didn't believe stressing Chase out with news of impending pain and misery would benefit their plans.

The giant door to the science ward slid open, and the

trio passed through. After they had safely cleared the doorway, the large steel door slammed shut.

Chapter 17:
The Storm After

Chase

Chase gasped as he awoke from the nightmare, and water splashed violently onto the floor with a loud, nasty splat. The bright light from over the white sink blinded him and he brought his hand up to shield his eyes. He looked around, his senses on high alert, and tried to piece together where he was. White walls, spacious interior, and white-gold towels on racks in the corner helped him orientate himself.

The bathroom, he thought to himself. Naked and safe in the bathroom. He breathed a sigh of relief, and relaxed as he tried to control his breathing and racing mind. *You're okay*, He thought. *You're fine. You're okay. YOU ARE FINE.*

Chase closed his eyes and tried to settle back into the groove of the bath. It had been a couple of weeks since his last proper washing, and he just wanted to enjoy being clean for once. Apparently, that was too much to ask for.

After a few minutes, he had managed to stop the repetitive and thunderous beating in his heart. He hated that such a simple dream could unbalance him so much. He felt that familiar heat build in his chest, the rage he held at bay, trying to claw its way to the surface. He could practically hear Isobel lamenting his temper already.

A few knocks on the door interrupted his thoughts, and his muscles tensed in anticipation of conflict.

“Chase, are you okay?” Isobel asked with urgency in her voice. He had made more noise than he wanted and worried the one person he was trying to give a sense of security.

“Yeah.” He replied. “Just sucked in a little frothy water is all. Nothing to worry yourself over, I swear.”

There was a moment of silence from the other side of the door. Chase cocked his head at an angle, wondering if he had spoken loud enough to be heard.

“Still there, Isobel?” He asked curiously.

“Y-yeah...” Isobel said in a softer tone. It was almost a whisper. Chase then heard a thud on the door, like someone had pushed a large object against the door.

“Are you okay?” He said quickly, getting up out of the bath. “I'm coming out.”

“Can we... talk like this?” She asked.

“Like what?” Chase replied, wrapping one of the towels around his waist. “I know we haven't had time to reconnect since the events at the Market and the Grindstone. I'll dry off and come out-”

“No.” She interrupted. He stopped dead in his tracks.

Her voice seemed kind of shaky. At least the rasping she had was fading a bit from her voice, but her tone still was cause for alarm. “I- just want to sit here and talk through the door.”

“Awkward request.” Chase said with some confusion. “I'm still in the nude and there are perfectly good couches out there that we can-”

“Please...” She begged. “I don't want to look at you right now. And I know that sounds mean, rude or whatever... But I just... I need to get some things off my chest. I don't want a bodyguard... I just want a friend.”

“Okay, Isobel.” Chase sighed. He walked over and grabbed all the towels from the rack in the bathroom. He then threw them at the base of the door, and sat on them, leaning against the door. “I'll take a few leg cramps and a rare bum for you. I hope you know, I don't do this for just anyone. You literally have the bodyguard of the High Priestess at your disposal. Can you handle such an honor?”

There was a soft chuckle from the other side of the door. Then silence.

This was it. It was the conversation he sought the most and yet, he didn't want to hear it. He knew what would happen once he did, but he had to. As hard as their time apart was for him, he knew that Isobel had to have it harder. He could look at her body, covered and warped by the Black Dragon's mark and know that it was no vacation. He looked up at the ceiling and thanked the gods that she wanted to be separated by a door. He knew that was a selfish thought to have, but it was better for both of them.

“Chaselo-” Isobel began.

“Woah, woah, woah, lady.” Chase said, immediately cutting her off. “No C-Bombs around here! People could be listening!”

“You don't have to be ashamed of your name.” She replied.

“I AM NOT ASHAMED.” He said with a little more aggression than he intended. “Just... Just don't call me by that name. You worry me when you use my name like that. You only say it when you're in a bad place.”

“Yeah.” She said with a sadness he hadn't heard in a while. He could practically hear her tears through the door. “I'm in a bad place man... I can't believe all this has happened. We were supposed to just route Drakonis' forces and return home.”

“You gambled, Isobel.” Chase said softly. “Heck, we all did. You were confident and even managed to convince Everett. That guy is as classical and pragmatic as they come. He approved the whole operation and even suggested we don't tell the Divines. You got an Elder Knight to go behind the gods back.”

That last bit actually impressed Chase. Isobel was

always good with words. Her eloquence and charisma were inspiring. She had always been a natural born leader, and that's the precise reason the Divines chose her as the Divine Priestess. He was honored to even be allowed to become her bodyguard.

"Yeah..." She replied, her voice cracking. "And it got him killed like a dog. It got you all killed. And these stupid marks on our necks. And we're branded like cattle. This sucks!"

Chase chuckled in response. It wasn't that her misery was funny, but it was rare for him to hear Isobel speaking common slang. It reminded him of their days back at the academy.

"How unbecoming of the High Priestess to question her own actions made in the Divine's name." Chase jested. "Surely one would find the wavering of the god's most trusted vessel alarming..."

"Oh, ha, ha." Isobel laughed back. "You're a moron, you know that?"

"Commonly known amongst the people." He said, smiling to himself.

There was a brief silence on the other side of the door. It was enough time for Chase's smile to fade.

"The past few weeks were so unbearable..." Isobel finally said in a serious tone. "And Drakonis, regardless of what his intentions were, is an idiot."

"That is a conclusive statement, professor." Chase said in a dorky impression. "I candidly agree with this astute conclusion."

"I'm serious." She said, her tone unchanged. "He kept asking me about the dragon and aggravated the mark. He wouldn't stop. Him and Cyarah just... kept me alone, isolated and in pain. I gave them nothing. I said nothing. But it didn't stop their interrogations. And when they left, the visions of the dragon came for me. I couldn't sleep. I thought that would be the rest of my life. I wouldn't die in some heroic battle for humanity, fighting with my comrades. I was going to perish on a giant petri-dish, half naked and scared, with my mind broken and my body covered in black."

Chase gritted his teeth and tried to control his breathing.

"I wanted them to end it." She continued. "I had given up on seeing anything I loved ever again. A vicious cycle of pain everyday..."

Isobel broke down at this point. Chase could tell that she couldn't hold the floodgates anymore. She was just crying and sniffling on the other side of the door. He wanted to hold her, to tell her that it would be okay, that the mark was just another step in the journey... But he felt like those lies had been dragged as far as they would go.

"I... had also been questioned." Chase said as he closed

his eyes. He was doing his best to not just explode. To not be impulsive and go crazy. He tightened his fists and put them in his lap.

"Every day, beastmen were thrown at me." He began. "I fought for my life with nothing but blunt swords and rocks. It was some of the hardest training I had undergone. But after I was completely exhausted, Cyarah would escort me to a sterile room in the medical ward. She would just ask again and again about you, about the dragon, about the Divines. It made me so mad. They didn't even tell me you were alive. It actually baffles me that you were only a few feet away, and I couldn't sense your aura. That makes me feel even more stupid."

"This isn't your fault." Isobel said through her sobs. It sounded like she was wiping away her tears and maybe calming down a bit.

"It doesn't feel like it." Chase said dispirited.

"I understand how you feel." Isobel agreed.

There were another couple of moments of silence.

"What are we going to do?" Isobel asked. She had so much uncertainty in her voice.

"You're asking me that?" He said appalled. "Now, I know we're in trouble."

"Drakonis told us about his journey to the Fae, but I don't want to trust him." Isobel spoke candidly. "Not after this. What he has done to me. I... I want him dead, Chase."

“You know I would do everything in my power to make that happen.” Chase said with no hesitation. “But are you sure? Asking your assassin friend to kill someone is a big deal.”

Isobel didn't say anything for a while. The silence was deafening in the bathroom. And it was at this time that Chase needed to get up and stretch. His bum was actually feeling quite rare.

“Yes.” Isobel finally said as Chase was getting up. “Even if there is some grand destiny for us, he has always stood in the way of peace. He doesn't deserve happiness.”

“Then it will happen.” He said confidently. “But I won't do anything for a while. Just... Think about it for a few days.”

“I don't need to think about it-” She tried to interrupt.

“Just... think about it.” He reiterated. “We’ve heard and learned a lot today. Just take some time to process it.”

“Okay...” Isobel sighed. He could hear her get up and leave the doorway. Hopefully, she was going to bed.

There were so many thoughts swimming in Chase's head. But he had one reoccurring thought that wouldn't go away. He opened the door and saw Isobel sitting on the couch, staring blankly at the balcony. The moon was illuminating her face in an eerie fashion. He walked over to the guest bedroom.

“I'm going to bed, Isobel.” He said as he walked by.

After a moment, she turned to him and smiled. The faded color of her hair made her look almost ghostly in the moonlight.

“Sleep well.” She said, not breaking her gaze at the balcony.

He smiled softly and walked into the room, closing the door behind himself. He planted himself on the bed and put his hands over his face. That confirmed it. Without a shadow of a doubt. There were too many giveaways. The blank stares, the mark covering her body, and her desire to kill Drakonis. She was the only person he could count on to find a peaceful resolution in a war zone. The only person he relied on to keep him level. The only friend he had in this forsaken city. And she was now an Acolyte of the Black Dragon. He didn't know how strong the possession was, but it was there. Trapped behind the visage of his only family. Evil in disguise.

He felt the tears well in his eyes. And he looked around the room aimlessly. He didn't know what to do. He didn't even know if she could be saved. It was too much for his heart to bear, and for the first time since he had arrived in the capitol, he sat there, and he cried.

*   *   *

Isobel

"Excellent performance, my sweet. Such a beautiful show of vulnerability. The best lies are always draped in truth. Can't let him know my nightly visits started being more bearable when you opened your heart to my subjugation, could you? You broke so easily, but I guess a weary heart makes for the worst lock."

Isobel shuddered at the words that echoed in her mind. She had just manipulated her best friend and trusted guardian. Made herself seem vulnerable and broken beyond repair. Even if she had no control, it was still her body, her mouth did the damage.

"And do not believe that your pitiful little message went without notice. Even if he believes that you have been indoctrinated, you will never escape my grasp. No magic can pull you away, and your mind is far too weak to contest my superior pressure. You are mine, through and through."

"I will escape." Isobel whispered, closing her eyes. Her skin felt like it was being seared and she felt the muscles in her neck tighten. "You will... not control... me."

"This rebellion will be short-lived, my dear. It was amusing at first, but I grow tired of your impudence. Cease this resistance!"

"I.... Can.... Be... Free...." Isobel forced herself to say. The dragon was restricting her speech. But she would fight this madness for as long as she could.

ARROGANCE!

"My darling, I see you struggle so." A man's voice whispered in front of Isobel. Her eyes snapped open, and she put her hands up, ready to fight. The man wore a cloak over his head so she couldn't see his face, and the moonlight from behind him silhouetted his body, perfectly concealing the features of his clothes.

"Do not worry, my love." The man said walking closer to Isobel. "I want only peace."

"Stay back..." She said softly. The black dragon was still restricting her voice, attempting to silence her. Maybe he saw this as an opportunity to punish her for her actions earlier.

"*Your insightfulness is exemplary, my pawn.*" The dragon chuckled at his own words.

"Who... are you?" Isobel choked out.

"Oh." The man said surprised. "I believed my charming voice would be a dead giveaway. But if you desire another hint, how about this?"

The man raised his hand in the air. Isobel could barely make out the finer details, but she could see that the hand was longer than any humans. She made a face as she tried to remember who the intruder was, but nothing was coming to mind. Before she could react, the man was behind her with one hand on her hip and his other holding her hand. With the moonlight facing both of their faces, she took her first real look upon the man's face.

His skin was pale and completely transparent like a sort of film above his muscles. She could see his blood vessels and the muscles on his face clear as day. And his hands were so cold that they brought a chill to her body. She pushed the man a few feet away from her, and he stopped right in front of the bookshelf against the wall.

“The man from the market.” She said scornfully.

“My wife recognizes me.” He said confidently.

“And the same man that tried to kill me.” She said as she stared him down.

“You keep saying 'man’, but I do have a name.” He said as he pulled back his hood and revealed a very thin, blond patch of hair on his head. “I am Ariel, Lord of the Lourins. And I am no man. Rather, I am something far removed.”

“What do you want?” Isobel said. She felt the grip of the Black Dragon slip away, almost too easily.

Talk to him. Talk to him. Talk to him. Talk to him.

The command echoed loudly in her head, giving her a pounding headache. She reached over and grabbed the couch to balance herself.

“Isn't it obvious?” Ariel said as he raised his arms. “I

came her for you, my love."

"And why should I not just blast you into oblivion, right now?" Isobel said, fighting her pain and trying to keep herself upright.

"I would wager you couldn't lift a glass of water, let alone harm me." Ariel said with a smirk. "If I wanted to...." Ariel walked slowly over to Isobel, and she backed away slowly trying not to fall over. "I could kill you right now. But red is an unbecoming color. I would love to see you completely unharmed. I came to retrieve you from these scoundrels and give you a place at my side."

"What?" Isobel replied in a confused tone.

"Aren't you tired of this cage that your slaver traps you inside of, restricting your freedom?" He said as he reached his hand out to her. "Don't wish to escape this life and live as you were destined?"

Ariel grabbed her hand and pulled her to himself, hugging her tightly. She wanted to resist but the Black Dragon was not relinquishing control.

Talk to him. Talk to him. Talk to him. Talk to him.

The command rang endlessly in her mind. The more she resisted, the weaker her resolve became. She could feel her body losing feeling. She was losing control fast.

"I can see it in your eyes." Ariel said as he lifted her face to his. He stared deeply into her eyes, and she could see his deep blue eyes shining back at her. "You fight something that goes beyond the control of mere mortals and beasts. I can help you. Lourins are unique creatures that have the ability to bend reality and meld with the weave unlike any other being. I can save you. You can be free. Just come with me."

She wanted to object, to push him away again, and call Chase for help. To do anything but be trapped in his grasp. But her mana wasn't working, and her body wasn't responding to her. She opened her mouth to reject his invitation.

"I want to go." Isobel whispered softly as she placed her hand on the side of his face. She felt the dragon's satisfaction at the words leaving her mouth without her consent. He had control now. She had been maintaining some level of resistance before, but it was like her will had been exhausted. She had nothing left to give.

Go with him. Go with him. Go with him.

The commands were coming full force now. And she was powerless to stop them. She could only watch in horror as her body moved on its own.

Ariel's eyes grew elated, and she could see genuine happiness in his face. He gave her a soft smile and hugged her even tighter. Then he pulled her away from himself.

"Do not worry, my love." Ariel said as he walked her over to the balcony. "I will use all we have to rid you of your affliction. I will sever your bonds and give you freedom."

Isobel wanted all those things, but she had seen the carnage in the market. The blood of innocents in the streets, and the destruction left behind by the Lourins. If that is what it will take to get her freedom, then she would have no part in it.

Ugh. No one cares. Just get on with it.

Isobel closed her eyes and struggled to will her body to stop and at that moment she heard a loud 'thud' along with a howl. When she opened her eyes, a different set of arms were around her. Chase stood there holding her, his eyes red and his electricity dancing around them. She was so relieved to see him, although she was a little annoyed at how close he had cut it.

She looked out over the balcony to see Ariel on the railing of the balcony, holding his face. He was visibly annoyed at being struck.

“It's not polite to use your guests as doormats.” Ariel snarled at Chase. “I would kindly ask that you unhand my woman.”

“Your woman?” Chase scoffed at him. “Not in your wildest dreams bud. How about you crawl back to whatever ant farm you creeped out of and leave god fearing individuals alone, huh?”

Ariel glowered at Chase, his eyes filled with contempt.

“I was trying to make this as painless as possible.” He bellowed. “I always get what I want, no matter how many have to suffer. Let the deaths that come burden your mind for ages to come. And you remember that you made Ariel, Lord of the Lourins, angry this day."

"Buddy, I don't even know you." Chase said confused. "Get lost lest you want I, Chase, to beat you over that balcony."

"We'll meet again, Isobel." Ariel said quickly. He then snarled again and pulled his cloak over his head. He then leaned backwards and disappeared off the railing.

"Who the heck was that guy, Isobel?" Chase asked with urgency.

Sleep.

Isobel felt her legs go limp and her eyes began to lose focus.

* * *

Drakonis

Absurd! Drakonis did a double take, stopping dead in his tracks, and stared up at the God King in complete disbelief. He had seen and heard many acts of lunacy in his day, but this surely took the cake.

"You can't possibly be serious right now?" He yelled from the base of the royal steps.

Lord D'Merrion, who had just happily plopped himself onto his throne, looked down upon Drakonis with a smug smirk. Drakonis was almost unnerved by his jubilant behavior over the past couple of minutes. Usually, the God King's smiles were masks to hide his sinister intentions, but today his feelings seemed genuine. The God King was actually in a VERY good mood.

“Drakonis, my son.” He said in a consoling voice. The tone of the king's voice made Drakonis' skin crawl, and he couldn't hide the disgust on his face. “Ease your mind. It will only be a few days. Well... For me, a few moments but time works differently in other dimensions.”

“The festival is tomorrow, My liege.” Drakonis reminded him. “You can't possibly be thinking of leaving the capitol before you've graced your subjects-”

“Bah!” D'Merrion groaned suddenly, leaning back on his throne. He backhanded the air and slammed his hand on the arm of his seat. “A wasteful show of force so the weak can grovel at my knees. If they want to make offerings and appease their lord, another day in their shops and on their farms would be a better gesture.”

“My king...” King Maj interrupted nervously. “If you could just reconsider-”

“I will not.” D'Merrion said impatiently. His smile was beginning to fade.

“Please, my King-” Cyarah tried to plead.

“SILENCE!” D'Merrion's voice rang out, reverbing in

the large throne room. He raised his hand and pointed at the group. “Are you honestly telling me between the four of you... None of you thought it wise to construct a contingency plan for this situation?”

The group stood in silence at the God King's question. When the king was angry, all of his questions were rhetorical.

D’Merrion leaned forward in his seat, his face now darkened due to the odd lighting from the window behind the throne.

“Figure. It. Out.” He said in a serious tone.

Suddenly a portal opened up next to the throne, lighting up the room and the God King's face. Out stepped the Fae, and he bowed to the king.

“They are ready for you.” He said in his usual respectable manner.

King D’Merrion stood up from his throne, smiling once again, and turned to the portal.

“Excellent!” He said happily. “Let us be off then! I grow weary of this audience.”

“Father!” Drakonis yelled once again from below. The God King turned impatiently to him.

“What?” He replied in a very annoyed tone.

“Where are you going?” Drakonis asked. He could see the One True God was eager to leave but he had to know where to. This was too sudden. What could be more important than the festival that the God King himself had put together?

The God King rubbed his beard for a moment, like he was deciding whether they were worthy of that information or not and smiled in the usual sinister manner he did. It was a smile that sent a chill down Drakonis' spine, one that he had become acquainted with and associated with the brutal 'training' sessions with his father.

“Home.” He said smugly. He then walked through the portal and the Fae followed quickly behind him. Drakonis couldn't speak for the rest of the group but the cryptic response from the king unsettled him. This was his home. He and the Divines created this world. Where could he possibly be going?

“What do we do now, Drakonis?” King Maj asked with uncertainty, interrupting the Dark Lord's mental storm.

“You should do what the God King asked and take care of the festival, of course!” Addurog condescendingly snorted, his face planted deep in his journal. He was writing something he obviously felt spectacular, because he couldn't be bothered to look up at them.

“Figure. It. Out.” Addurog repeated, imitating D’Merrion's choleric tone, as he snapped his book shut. “I'm sure you three can come up with a splendid plan, seeing as that's all you do all day anyway. Meanwhile, while you chimps are busy with your monkey games, I'll be engaging in important affairs for the capitol.”

Addurog laughed heartily, his giant guffaws echoed in the large chamber. He was wheezing, and wiping his eyes free of tears, as though he could produce them. He was obviously very amused with his simple bullying, but Drakonis knew that wouldn't last for long. King Maj turned and looked at Drakonis with a fierce and serious look. Drakonis nodded back at the Majen King to let him know that it was time. Revenge was a dish best served piping hot and with side dishes, and now that the One True God was absent from the capitol, Drakonis could act upon his with urgency.

Addurog turned to leave the throne room, but Drakonis started to channel his aura, prompting the phoenix to stop dead in his tracks. The dark lord wanted the Black Phoenix to know his intentions and to feel the maliciousness behind them. In response, Addurog began to channel his aura.

“The One True God hasn't even been absent more than a few moments, and you're already at my throat.” Addurog said coyly.

“Not yet.” Drakonis scowled. “But soon...”

“If you could see the look on your face...” Addurog said as he unsheathed his weapon.

“Stop talking.” Drakonis replied as he charged forward and aimed his sword at Addurog 's heart.

*   *   *

Drakonis

Frustrated. Drakonis walked over to his horse and laid his hand on the animal's face.

"It's all going to be fine." He said as he petted the animal's head. The horse neighed in response and bent its head down for more pats.

He was not eager nor was he ever enthusiastic about the day, and worse yet, today seemed more stressful than ever. The festival was always an event that took a lot of time and planning to set up. Most of the work was rearranging the market to create a suitable path for the parade, one that would safely guide the royal entourage to and from the capitol. He had to spend much of the days prior to getting the shop owners to agree on placement and then relay the information to Cyarah and King Maj so they could set up the security detail. Finally, he would finish his commitments with ensuring that Therron the Gownmaker and the carpenter's association could complete the parade floats beforehand.

It was an exhausting process, but Drakonis didn't mind it. In fact, these moments of peace where he didn't feel like his life was on the line with every decision he made were a welcome change to his day. Every day he plotted against some of the greatest minds in the realm in a long game of chess. Handling a few crotchety, and crooked merchants was a cake walk in comparison.

He heard footsteps behind him, but he didn't turn to meet their owners. He wasn't here in the market to parley and shop. The Festival of the Crucible was here, and it needed to go off without a hitch to ensure that chaos didn't envelop the streets. There were already rumors of unrest in Zhalesh. Humans and beastkin of the city felt their safety was at stake, and some thought of abandoning the capitol. The capitol's strength comes from the many associations and their unique skills that reside here. If all these individuals were to leave, the commoners and labor force would leave with them. Even if Drakonis despised the One True God above all else, he would never actively seek the destruction of Zhalesh and all that live here. It was a paradise in comparison to the barbaric culture of the wastes.

“We're ready, Drakonis.” Chase said from behind him.

“Good.” He replied, turning away from his horse. Isobel was also standing next to Chase, and they both wore matching royal suits. These suits were very particular due to the fact that The Gownmaker had made them specifically for the duo. They were made with Majen designs in mind and actually fit the pair quite well.

“That Therron may be quite eccentric, but he's a very

capable tailor." Chase remarked adjusting his collar. "I can see why most of the merchants get their outfits from him."

"I'm surprised by how breathable the clothes are!" Isobel replied back. Her skin was looking livelier, the bits not covered by the Black Dragon mark, and her hair had much of its color returned. She was still a bit pale in comparison to how she had looked when they met a month ago. "You didn't receive any special clothes for yourself, Drakonis?"

"No." He said quickly. "My armor serves as a symbol of peace and authority for all The One True God's kingdom. It would better serve our purposes for me to wear it instead of some suit."

"Rather unfortunate you think so." Isobel said with a bit of disappointment. Her face then lit up again. "I wonder what kind of outfit Therron would craft for your likeness?"

"Indeed." Drakonis replied flatly, dismissing the conversation. It wasn't that he wasn't interested in it, but he just felt extremely awkward being approached by them in a casual fashion. "You both remember where your placements are in the festival, correct?"

"Yes." Chase replied as he rolled his eyes. "We'll accompany the Majen children behind the One True God's float. We are not to leave alignment nor attempt escape. If we do, we'll be hunted and killed on sight. Blah, blah, yadda, yadda, we get it. No need to reiterate. We've been instructed on what to do multiple times over the past few days."

"Because it is of the utmost importance that this parade does not fail." Drakonis snapped at him. He looked around to see if anyone was within earshot. There wasn't anyone close enough to hear them, and many of the iron guards and soldiers were walking their final routes before the royal parade began. "The One True God is not in attendance for the festival, so we need to put our best foot forward to inspire the people."

"Then…" Chase started to say with a very confused face.

"Who is that?" Isobel finished for him, pointing up at a man sitting on the float.

The man was extremely large, wore the royal crown, and had the same sparkling and unsightly golden armor with white trim that King D'Merrion was known for wearing. He sat somewhat like D'Merrion, except he was too upright. It was like there was a board behind his back that kept him up straight. And it looked that way because... Well... There was. That man was, in fact, not God King D'Merrion. Even more factually, that man was not a man. He was all they had left and Drakonis hated it. This was the actual reason for his frustration today.

Drakonis grunted disappointingly and walked past the two knights over to the float. His steps made large clangs on the ground that startled the workers near the float, and made the man sit upright. The man on the float looked down at Drakonis through the corner of his eye, and a bead of sweat dripped down the man's brow.

“My lord.” Drakonis said with bow, although he did so through gritted teeth.

“A-ah!” The man replied nervously. “M-m-m-my son! How are you? Ya... Ya son of a gun!?”

Disgusting. Drakonis cringed and almost completely recoiled back from the words. Seeing D’Merrion's face smile in his direction so awkwardly almost made him retch. He shook his head and regained his composure.

“If you look so tense during the parade, father, some individuals may believe that there is something wrong with you.” Drakonis said through his teeth. “It may be very off-putting to the people. So, I suggest you RELAX.”

“Oh-oh...” The man said looking down at his feet. “Wise observation, sir.”

“Stop looking down at your feet and don't call me sir!” Drakonis snapped. He then looked around to see if anyone was paying attention to their conversation, but all of the workers seemed to be too occupied with finishing their adjustments to the floats.

“That's not Lord D’Merrion, is it?” Chase said from behind Drakonis. The statement was far too loud and Drakonis felt his eyes almost shoot out of his skull.

Drakonis whipped around and gave Chase a serious look. A look that signaled he would murder him right now if he let even one more word loose. Isobel was standing next to him, and she had a look of confusion on her face as she tried to piece together what was going on.

A chorus of 'huh's' and 'what's' drummed up amongst the workers. Some looked up at Chase with their mouths agape, baffled at what he just said. Drakonis looked up at the imposter on the float and the man was staring down at the workers with an intense stare. Luckily, D'Merrion's gaze was never desired, and the workers were scared back to work.

Drakonis sighed and looked back up at the man. He was still staring the workers down, and after having a few more seconds to examine him, he noticed his hands were shaking.

"Come on." He whispered to Chase and Isobel as he climbed onto the float. The man was still shaking in the chair and Drakonis put his hand on his shoulder. He stopped shaking and looked over at Drakonis.

"Stop addressing the One True God casually in front of the workers!" He whispered intensely to Chase. "Not a single soul does that!" Drakonis turned and stared the man down.

"Tejari..." He whispered intensely to the man. "You need to keep it together. This city will descend into utter chaos if you fail to perform today. "

Tejari gulped loudly in response, his body becoming

rigid like a board and his eyes started to bulge so intensely it looked as though they would shoot right from his head.

"The fox guy from the royal quarter?" Chase said confused, matching Drakonis' tone.

"Where is the God King?" Isobel whispered.

"Stop talking." Drakonis replied back to them. "He left without any warning, and we needed a replacement."

"So, you grab the help?" Chase with some condescension. "No disrespect to you little... big guy. But are you even proficient with illusion spells?"

Tejari nodded his head quickly but for some reason his whole body shook with the motion.

"Look, it's fine." Drakonis said trying to reassure them. "It's only for one hour and all he needs to do is sit and wave. Simple!"

"This doesn't seem like a good idea..." Isobel said with worry in her voice. She was looking directly at Tejari, who had his own eyes locked on something else. Drakonis looked around to train his eyes on whatever he could be focusing on, and he noticed that Ashnel was walking over to them.

"Look!" Drakonis said quickly. He was trying to get his words out before Ashnel reached them. "Sit up straight, not too straight! Look like D'Merrion. Sound like D'Merrion. And just wave and smile."

"Lord Drakonis." Ashnel said as he bowed. "The

preparations are ready for the festival. We are ready when you are, my lord."

"Tell the drivers that the One True God is ready for departure." Drakonis commanded.

"At once my lord." Ashnel replied. Ashnel then went silent. Drakonis then heard loud sniffs perforate the air, and Ashnel looked up at the float and gave them all a smirk. He then retreated to the front of the parade.

"Everyone off the float." Drakonis commanded. "This already looks awkward and we're breaking Tejari's cover."

Chase hopped down off the float and held his hand out to help Isobel. She refused to take his hand and dropped next to him.

"I can manage." She said brushing herself off.

"I know." He sighed. "I only wished to help."

"And I thank you for the gesture." She said walking away. "I'll go retrieve the children and get our horses ready."

Isobel hurried off to her self-given tasks, leaving Chase next to Drakonis.

"How has she been?" Drakonis inquired as he descended from the float.

"Distant." Chase said rubbing his face.

"That looks to be the case." Drakonis said as he huffed, attempting to make a joke. Chase groaned in response. "Has she had anymore incidents? Any clues to what kind of possession has taken hold?"

"None." Chase sighed.

"I can't help her if you don't provide information on what we're dealing with." Drakonis said annoyed. "I thought you cared about her..."

"And what have YOU come up with since you've been so productive?" Chase scoffed back. "You said you would find a solution. It's been days. And yet, here you are as empty-handed as I am. For someone eager to be "allies," you really are taking your time finding a solution."

"A possession curse is a hard and rare spell to break." Drakonis lectured. "But a possession curse by the Black Dragon is an even rarer occasion. I have an acolyte of the Black Dragon on hand, and even he has never seen an instance of possession. No one knows what this is, but we will figure this out. You have my word. Until then, keep watch over her and make sure she doesn't endanger herself again."

"Without question." Chase replied.

"Is there anything you need from me?" Drakonis asked.

"To hurry up." Chase said as he walked away.

Drakonis let out a deep breath and closed his eyes for a second. He then turned around to check on Tejari, who seemed to calm down a bit. He was now sitting confidently on the float and was staring ahead now, no doubt clearing his mind for the parade ahead. Drakonis nodded at him, to confirm he was ready, and Tejari nodded back. This was an ease off his mind.

Everything was perfectly planned. He had done the work, same as he had every year. So, all he had to do now was let it play out. But he felt a bit paranoid. Drakonis decided to check everything one more time before the parade began.

*　　　*　　　*

Drakonis

Drakonis' heart raced anxiously. The explosions rang out all around him and he shielded his eyes from the bright lights. He could hear the stomps and snarls of beastmen all around him, and the shouts and screams of women and younglings pounded at his eardrums. He looked around at the chaos that formed around him, their eyes trained on him, wondering what he would do next. He raised his hand and smiled, and the crowd roared in approval!

The festival had begun. Or it had begun some twenty or thirty minutes ago. The parade rode through the streets and was greeted eagerly around each corner of the market. Younglings strode up to the float and waved at their king. Tejari, who had seemed at first fearful of his role in the parade, now stood confidently and waved at the civilians. He basked in their praise and cheered the citizens on, which in turn won more of their approval. Even though The God King was never so jovial during the festival, Drakonis let Tejari have his fun. He didn't want to risk scolding him and taking his newfound confidence away. Better an exciting King of the World that inspired the people than one that moped and brought down the whole mood of the festival. Excellent.

Drakonis' position in the festival was highly strategic as well and greatly benefited his current situation. He rode right alongside the God King's float, and could keep constant watch over Tejari, but he was also only a few feet behind the Majen Royalty float. Isobel and Chase rode as the guardians of the float. They, at first, looked as though they were avoiding eye-contact with the crowd, but after the fireworks started and the crowd began to scream, they began to wave back at the citizens. It's impossible for the citizens to know who exactly Isobel and Chase were, but since they had been seen around town with the Majen children, it would go to reason that they were presumed to be royalty as well. And the crowd seemed to be treating them as such.

King Maj was also standing up on his float, greeting the beastkin masses. He and his daughters were waving at the crowd, putting forth their best effort to be in good spirits. Drakonis imagined it would be hard for them to keep up this facade since the heir to the Majen throne still hadn't awoken from his coma.

Addurog was in the crowd as well, standing well above anyone around him, drawing a lot of attention. As the parade approached the phoenix-kin, Drakonis noticed that he had a large cape covering the right half of his body. That's probably for the best, Drakonis thought to himself.

The Phoenix just stood there, scowling at Drakonis. He then pulled out his book, flipped to a specific page, and raised it high above his head. While most beings wouldn't be able to make it out from a distance, Drakonis could see it clear as day. It was a picture of a lizard with a dagger in its neck. *How endearing,* he thought. Addurog then turned away from the parade and moved to exit the market. The Dark Lord didn't have to worry about him right now, and he wasn't going to be much of a threat with his new injury.

Drakonis didn't have to worry about any of the floats behind the God King. They were mostly used for giving out free treats and blasting confetti and fireworks. They also had the added bonus of being accompanied by Members of the Iron Guard.

For a while, they rode in this fashion. The citizens of Zhalesh greeted them heartily, cheering as they took advantage of the free gifts that came from the festival. Booths were filled as traveling merchants and members of the wild clans took advantage of the conveniences of the festival. It was the same as every year. Everything was going exactly as planned.

Excellent.

They were more than halfway to the end of the route when Drakonis heard a familiar chorus of howls from the crowd. It's a part that he loathed and had hoped that if he had given it no mind, it would just go away. A pack of beastkin females and human women came running out towards him, all dressed in high skirts and crop tops, and screamed at the top of their lungs.

“D-R-A-K-O-N-I-S!” They chanted in unison. They took a pyramid formation and began to dance together in front of him. “Drakonis, konis, konis, is the best! Drrrrrraaaaaaaaaaaaakonis!”

They called themselves the 'Drakonis Cheer Squad', and they did the same song and dance every year. Really ever since he started to manage the festival. It was a group filled with women who sought his hand in matrimony. None of them knew him personally, but they all wanted to get to know him. He didn't have to deal with them most of the time because he spent all day either in the capitol palace, at Xinovioc's tower, or out in the wilds fighting the God King's War. But the festival was the only time all year that he couldn't run from them. As the sole son of the God King, there were a number of women that vied for his favor. But a cheer group was filled more with obsessed fans than life partners.

“Who brings peace to the land?” The lead asked,

waiting for the anticipated reply from her team.

"DRAAAAAAAAAAAAAAAAAAKONIS!" They roared in reply.

"Who fights tirelessly for Zhalesh?" The lead went again.

"DRAAAAAAAAAAAAAAAAKONIS!" The team replied again, this time assisted by some of the citizens who had smiles on their faces.

Drakonis put his hand over his face and scowled at the performance. He managed to look forward and catch a glimpse of Isobel and Chase, who were staring at him, holding back their laughter. He felt blood rushing to his cheeks as a wave of embarrassment swept over him.

"And who is the most eligible bachelor in-" The lead started.

"ENOUGH!" Drakonis scowled at the group. The group shrieked in response and rushed over to him, probably excited at the fact that he'd finally said something to them. They piled around his horse and tried to talk over each other. Drakonis felt sweat build on his brow and motioned for the parade to continue. They had already wasted enough of their time...

That's when he felt it. It was subtle, like a light drizzle on a sunny day. Before he could properly react, the feeling was all around him. It was familiar and foreign at the same time. It was a dampening field, and it was filled with dark mana.

Drakonis looked around to see if anyone felt the aura around them. Isobel and Chase seemed to be oblivious and none of the civilians seemed to react to the dampening field descending upon them.

Suddenly, Drakonis felt a gust of wind blow by him, from an unknown source. There was a yelp behind him, and he turned to check on Tejari. But the fox kin was gone. He frantically looked around trying to piece where he could have been taken. And who could have been fast enough to kidnap him without being detected.

“Missing something?” Drakonis heard from above his head. He looked up at one of the buildings near them to see a very pale man with blonde hair holding D’Merrion's neck. This wasn't good. Not good at all. In fact, this was the most not good situation they could have! How could he not only sneak through a field of carefully laid detection spells, but also pass a battalion of beast guards, himself included?

Drakonis didn't have much time to ponder his frustrations. The pale man pulled the Crown of the King off Tejari's head, breaking the cloaking spell and revealing the foxkin's true form. If no one had noticed what was going on before, now they were completely glued to the event that was happening in front of them.

“Hey... Isn't that one of the royal butlers?” One of the merchants yelled out.

“I think I've seen him before?” Someone else replied back.

General confusion swept through the festival. People started laughing and pointing, possibly believing this was another spectacle. But that only lasted for a moment.

The man held Tejari tightly by the cuff of his neck, and the little fox kin began to shiver. His fur lost its color, and he shriveled up into a ball.

“Tejari!” Drakonis yelled hopping from his horse. “GUARDS! READY YOUR WEAPONS!”

“That's his name!” Someone in the crowd snapped.

The pale man threw the fox kin from the building and Drakonis managed to get there just in time to attempt to catch him. But the moment his body made contact with Drakonis' hands, it broke away into an ashy mist. Soldiers piled onto the road, and fear made its way into the crowd with them. They slowly realized this wasn't a part of the festival.

“That fox wasn't even a snack.” The pale man stated as he licked his fingers. “It is a good thing everyone is here. I wouldn’t want you all to miss the feast!”

“Archers!” Drakonis ordered. “Fire! Fire now!”

The pale man smiled in response and snapped his fingers. And a group of figures, around twenty or thirty, rushed to his side seemingly out of nowhere. They wore black cloaks and had hoods that covered their faces. But Drakonis could see their hands, and they were as pale as the man's skin with long fingernails. They all chanted something under their breath and a barrier enveloped the top half of the building. The arrows smashed into the barrier and fell lifelessly to the ground. Soldiers took up arms next to Drakonis, and civilians ran from the road. Isobel and Chase were already trying to evacuate citizens from the area. Everyone had already been instructed on what to do if the parade was under attack.

"Uh, uh, uh!" The pale man said as he wagged his fingers. "What kind of feast would it be if the food ran from their plates?"

"What nonsense- what do you want!?" Drakonis asked trying to stall for time. He gripped his sword tightly, waiting for an opening to take down the leader.

The pale man looked down at Drakonis. His smile had disappeared, and it was replaced with an intense look of anger.

"Justice." The man said as he thrust his arm forward, and the hooded figures hissed as they leapt from the rooftop, launching fireballs onto the crowd below.

*   *   *

Chase

Chase laid on his back and stared up at the sky. It was a nice morning sky, soft puffy clouds and an unblocked sun, that signified a good day was ahead. He grabbed the grass and lifted it into the air before letting it go into the breeze. It had been so long since he had seen green grass. The city of Karia was miles under the surface, and outside of a few cracks in the ceiling, they rarely got to see the sky at all. The actual sky. Not the artificial lighting created by mana devices in Karia. But the actual, endless sky.

He kept breathing in the fresh air. Air that hadn't been purified by some machine. Air that hadn't been regulated through some kind of fan. Air that was... Natural. He loved the taste of it. Missed its chilly touch as it blew by his face. He missed outside. It had been a while since he'd sat in a grass meadow as large as this.

He heard the heavy thud of a few footsteps approaching him. He looked and grimaced as he saw a group of charlatans, dressed in knight training armor, coming to ruin his moment of freedom. More than likely coming to remind him that there was a purpose to this outing.

“Well look at this bum here!” Jerak mocked her with a smile. “Just lazing about in the sun when we're supposed to be on patrol! This is exactly why you're widely considered the 'least capable', you know that?"

"Don't bully him." Mirela chimed in.

"Yeah." Isobel agreed. "He is getting better all the time, and even the greatest warriors need moments of respite."

Jerak put his hand on his chest and opened his mouth wide like he flabbergasted at their defense.

"Oh." He said suddenly. "Apologies, Priestess. How good of you to continually grace us with your wisdom and guidance!

"You're real funny, Jerak." Isobel said sarcastically. Sincerest apologies, Chaselonius! Allow me the luxury of you accepting my apology!"

"Go eat a toad, idiot!" Chase growled at him. He then went back to staring at the sky and made his best angry face.

"Aw." Jerak said as he sat down alongside Chase. "Don't be that way! We're brothers now! Swore an oath and everything! Show your brother some love and give me a forgiveness hug!"

"Ew!" Chase said as he tried to roll away. "Don't touch me, man!"

"Come on!" Jerak yelled as he tried to stop him from rolling away. He reached over but only grabbed air. Chase rolled a few feet away and continued to lay on his back again. He took a deep breath and stared at the sky again. The rest of the group went and sat beside him and just stared up at the sky as well. They sat there like that for a few moments, enjoying the peace of the moment.

"I miss the sky." Mirela said softly. "And not just the sky, I miss wind in my hair. I miss going out with my father and tending to the horses. I miss the surface."

"We'll take it back." Isobel said sharply. "That's what this all is for. We'll stop the beastmen and take back our home."

"Can you two please just stop talking?" Chase grunted at them with annoyance. "Can we just... continue to enjoy this? In a few minutes, we'll just have to go back and report back to Knight Fredrick. I just want to enjoy this."

"You know what I miss?" Jerak said, ignoring Chase's plea. "I miss walking down the road in the morning and grabbing bread from the bakery. They always had the butteriest bread."

"You can still do that, ya jerk!" Chase yelled at him.

"But have you done that... Outside?" Jerak said with a raised eyebrow. The girls 'ooooh'd at his statement like it was the single most interesting statement on the planet. Chase was getting to his wits end with these guys. But then he took a deep breath and smiled. They may annoy him, but they had been his friends and family for half a decade now. They had grown up together, and soon they would be knighted together. They were almost adults now.

"You know..." Chase began. "When we're knighted, we'll get to come outside more often. We'll get to see the stars again. And cities. And maybe the Grand Canyon."

"That sounds like fun!" Isobel glowed gleefully. But then her excitement became a pout. "But we have to save the world first. I don't know if we can fit fun into such a busy schedule. Liberating towns, shattering beastmen deployments, beating beastmen generals..."

"Then we'll make time!" He said with a smile. "Maybe we'll even see something that can get Mirela to start talking."

"I do talk!" she said with embarrassment. "I talk a lot. See?"

"HEY!" Someone yelled from the tree line. Possibly Knight Fredrick. "I said five minutes! I swear if you squires have gotten yourselves killed out here... There will be demerits for all of you when I find you!"

"Ah man!" Jerak groaned as he jumped to his feet. "Time to go!"

Mirela got up and followed closely behind him. Isobel stood up, dusting herself off and looked at Chase, but Chase just kept staring at the sky.

"Chase..." she said softly. "It's time to get up."

"I guess it is..." He sighed as he closed his eyes.

A loud boom made him sit up straight. His head

pounded from him getting up too fast and he grabbed it to try and ease the pain. He looked around and tried to make sense of his surroundings. There was smog from the explosions happening around him. He heard screaming and snarls from all directions. Bodies littered the street, and he could see some of the guards still engaged in combat with their enemies. But try as he might, he couldn't locate Isobel, Drakonis, or the leader of the hooded figures.

He remembered seeing the hooded figures descend from the building above. Their hands lit up and he reached out to Isobel. The blasts most likely knocked him unconscious when they connected with the parade. He hated himself for being unable to reach Isobel in time, but he couldn't sit around and mope about it. He needed to find his allies.

He surveyed the street one more time, trying to pinpoint the building the hooded figures came from. He felt a small presence from behind himself and stabbed behind himself with all his might. The hooded figure was jabbed straight through the chest, but instead of falling immediately, it snarled and clawed at his face. Chase jumped back, dislodging his sword, and examined his adversary as he landed a few feet away. While most of its body was covered, its exposed hands were pale and slimy with long, jagged nails. The hole in its chest leaked blue ooze. He had never seen anything like it. It was more beast than man.

It lunged at him again, clawing at the air in front of him. Chase swung at the beast's hands and was surprised to see his sword not completely cleave through its claws. In fact, his blade bounced backwards off its hands. It was stronger than it looked but Chase was faster. He sparked behind the beast and slammed his blade clean through its heart. It screeched in response and tried to claw at him, even with a blade in its back. Chase held the blade in place and stood his ground.

How was it still alive, he thought to himself. No normal being could take a blade to its chest, let alone still try to fight back. And it was strong like an ox. These things weren't simple beastmen.

After a few moments, the beast started to settle down and eventually went limp on the blade. Chase leaned forward and slid its corpse onto the ground. Its hood fell off and exposed its veiny, bald head. It had ears like a bat, and jagged teeth in its mouth.

"You gotta be kidding me..." Chase groaned. "Are these vampires? Are vampires real?"

Even if they were real, he didn't have time to debate with himself. He looked around, seeing the building that he flew from earlier. There was a massive hole in the middle of the street in front of it, while beastmen soldiers fought against a handful of the hooded beasts. He couldn't afford to stick around and waste time on them. He sparked to the edge of the hole and briefly examined it. It was dark, damp, and smelled like rotten food and rats.

Just like home, he thought to himself.

He channeled his aura and tried to sense out any mana coming from the hole. Almost nothing, but there were two faint auras that were in the hole. One was small and seemed almost inconsequential. But the other was a massive pressure that he had grown accustomed to over the weeks they had spent in the city. Drakonis. Without a doubt, the other aura had to be Isobel.

He leapt into the hole and splashed loudly into the dirty waters of the sewer. There were two paths heading towards the auras and he ran full sprint down one of them. He hoped he had made the right decision.

*　　　*　　　*

Isobel

"You shouldn't have come." Drakonis spat at her as they ran down the cramped tunnels. They were running through the sewers of the capitol, in hot pursuit of the terrorists. The explosions from the fiery spells opened many holes into the ground, and the hooded figures wasted no time making their escape after their assault and thievery.

You need help. The dragon whispered.

“You need help.” Isobel shot back.

“Not your help.” Drakonis said bluntly. “Even if the blast sent us and most of the parade into the sewers, you should have returned to the surface and found Chase.”

Chase can handle himself. The dragon insisted.

“Chase can handle himself.” Isobel replied.

“It's not Chase that I'm worried about.” Drakonis growled back at her.

“We can argue and allow these terrorists to escape.” Isobel said as she tried to catch up to Drakonis. “Or we can work together and fight them as a team.”

Drakonis mumbled something under his breath, but then redirected his attention forward. “It seems like they've stopped. It's a chore to sense their auras but luckily there are so many of them, I can sense their movements.”

Isobel didn't want to say it. Or rather she couldn’t say it, but she couldn't sense any auras. Not since Ariel invaded their room. Not since the Black Dragon's influence over her actions had grown stronger. In fact, she couldn't feel or do much at all. She knew Chase and Drakonis were looking for a way to cure her. To purge her heart of the dragon's will. They had hoped that letting her roam free would have the opposite effect of the isolation she went through, but the truth was... There was nothing they could do to stop her fate. She was on the verge of becoming an acolyte and powerless to let anyone know. To warn anyone of what she was becoming.

“So, what do we do?” Isobel asked as they came to an abrupt stop. They were right next to a broken gate that overlooked some kind of sewery waterfall. She could see there was a large antechamber ahead of them. It was dark and filled with debris and other garbage. In the center of the wet room, Isobel could clearly make out Ariel and a few shadowy hooded figures standing about. They seemed to just be waiting for something. It was certainly a trap set for them.

“I will engage them.” Drakonis said as he walked to the gate. “You will stay here.

“I can help.” She protested.

“No, you can't.” Drakonis looked back at her sternly. His eyes were fierce and filled with anger. “You are a liability. To me, and to yourself. This is obviously a trap. I don't need a disabled knight stumbling about on uncertain terrain.”

Her head turned to the side, and she was staring down at the dirty ground of the sewer. Then she looked back at him, her expression probably something along the lines of a saddened expression.

“Then at least allow me to support you from here...” She pleaded. “I may have limited access to my mana, but I can assist you.”

“No.” Drakonis doubled down. He didn't wait for her to reply either. He immediately turned and leapt down into the pit and landed with a loud 'splash'. The hooded figures jumped backwards, and Ariel turned to face the noise.

Isobel walked over to the edge of the pit to overlook the meeting.

“Aw.” Ariel said. “You've finally caught up to us. How did you like our little surprise? I know it is not your birthday... But I went all out for you! I hope you enjoyed our show.”

“I don't know who you are...” Drakonis said as he stood up. The air around him started to waver and his blackened aura began to rise from him. “I don't care who you are. You are criminals against the beastkin Kingdom. And due to the severity of your crimes, I am authorized to judge you here and now. “

“Oh.” Ariel said smiling. He looked all around the room like there was a grand crowd watching this event. “He seems quite serious. Came with the whole executioner act, huh?”

“You are guilty of treason against the King.” Drakonis said as he advanced on the group. “Prepare for judgement.”

Drakonis brandished his black sword, and it also swelled with a dark, red power. Ariel's entourage quickly jumped back and pulled out their own swords. Ariel did not move from the spot and unsheathed a short sword from his hip. The area quickly began to fill with the same small, black particles that Isobel had seen before. The ones that resembled the black sphere from Drakonis' aura.

It seems like our mutual friend is quite serious. I wonder how he fares against these enigmas, The dragon stated with some amusement.

Isobel had faith in Drakonis' power. She had to. She wasn't in a position to help him if he wasn't. After being under the dragon's possession for so long, she had come to know that the dragon changed his intentions and motivations at a moment's notice. It was hard to get a read on what he was after. She knew he was after Drakonis, but there was no telling if his safety was pertinent to that goal.

Drakonis slashed at Ariel's midsection, aiming right for his gut. Ariel winced against the impact of the blade, but he managed to block the attack. A dark, red slash of power was left in the air and began to tremble violently. Ariel jumped back from the fissure, eyes wide with surprise. Drakonis was instantly behind him and grabbed him by his head and threw him back to the ground. The fissure had grown in size and looked as though it would erupt at any moment. Ariel smashed into the ground, lifting all kinds of filth and water into the air. The fissure then blasted into the cloud and exploded in a red haze.

Drakonis landed behind the cloud and watched it intensely. The debris slowly cleared away, revealing Ariel on one knee with his sword up and facing Drakonis. In front of him were three of his minions, shielding him with a magical barrier against the explosive attack. Ariel stood up and wiped his lip.

“It seems like...” Ariel started to say through labored breaths. He walked past the three hooded beings. “It seems like I underestimated you. Luckily for me, my family believes in me. I should have never fought alone... I am sorry, I won't let arrogance get the better of me again.”

The hooded beings nodded at his words, and some of them began circling around Drakonis. But his warriors holding up the barrier didn't move. The three fell, face-first, into the filthy, muddy water of the sewer and laid there lifelessly. Ariel heard the splashes, and quickly turned and glanced at their bodies before returning his gaze back to Drakonis.

Drakonis stood unfazed by the circling of the hooded figures. His grip on his weapon tightened and he didn't break eye contact with Ariel, who was staring him down. Isobel couldn't tell what expression Ariel had on his face, but if his reaction to the untimely deaths of his warriors was any indication, it seemed like his smirk from earlier was gone and he was taking the fight more seriously.

"You will pay for that..." Ariel snarled at Drakonis. Ariel joined his hooded warriors in circling around Drakonis.

"Not before you and your men find residence in a shallow grave." Drakonis spat back. "That's only but a fraction of the justice your kind deserves for your despicable acts."

I wonder what strategy they will take against the little dragon. The dragon said with interest. *He clearly is outnumbered, but he definitely outmatches these beasts.*

The group circling Drakonis began to pick up speed. Some were going clockwise while others went counterclockwise. They continued to move around him, speeding up ever so gradually, and Ariel seemingly vanished amongst his men. The way they moved was like a dance, and they seemed unfazed by Drakonis' dark barrier. A loud 'clang' of a sword rang out in the room, and Isobel noticed Drakonis' arm was raised. Then another 'clang'. And another.

I see. The dragon said. *Their attacks are quite quick. They may not be as incompetent as I first believed.*

"Over here." Ariel whispered. He wasn't visible, or maybe he was. He was hiding somewhere in the room. "No, I'm here."

"Your futile tricks won't work on me." Drakonis replied flatly. The attacks were coming in more frequently, but he smacked them away with ease. It seemed like he could win this single-handedly and with ease. He wasn't even looking in the direction of the attacks that he effortlessly knocked away, making the assault seem even more futile.

Suddenly two of the hooded figures burst out of formation from opposite ends of the circle, leaping above Drakonis' head, and were bringing their swords down upon him. At the same time, Ariel could be seen fazing into existence right in front of Drakonis aiming his blade at the dark lord's heart from down below. The maneuver was so masterfully done that Isobel could tell that they had carried out this attack many times before. But almost as fast as the attack had begun, it was thwarted by Drakonis' quick reactions.

Drakonis met Ariel's blade and he smacked the man backwards. Without wasting his momentum, he spun around and smacked away the two attacks as well. Right on-cue, two more hooded warriors leapt at Drakonis, from opposite ends of the circle. One was flying right towards Drakonis, his blade seeking purchase in any part of his being. The other leapt high into the air and was releasing a fire ball right at the dark lord. Both were snarling as they threw their attacks.

Drakonis was still spinning from his deflect, and Isobel questioned if he had time to reset his position to react to the new attacks. That thought didn't last longer than a second.

Somehow, Drakonis not only leapt up and managed to spin between both attacks, but he also drove his blade through one of the hooded warriors and cleaved him clean in two. His torso and legs flew violently towards the walls of the room. Continuing to use the momentum of his spinning, Drakonis twisted his body mid-air and smacked the fireball into one of the warriors that was moving in the circle. The man howled at the top of his lungs as his clothes caught fire, lighting up the dark chamber.

Drakonis didn't waste a single breath. As soon as he landed, he disappeared for a moment and then reappeared in the center of the room. There was a multi-colored light in his hand and Isobel could barely make it out at first. But then she knew what had happened in the few seconds he had disappeared. A technique she hadn't seen since they had first encountered him in New York. He stole their souls and held them firmly in his hand. Hooded warriors fell down left and right, some sliding across the ground as they were still in the spinning formation when their lives were taken. The two warriors who had their attacks deflected in the air came crashing back down into the ground with a loud splash. And Ariel stood against the wall with a handful of men left, somehow surviving the violent extermination that had taken place.

This wasn't a battle, or even a skirmish. This was a massacre. Drakonis was winning definitively, and it seemed like the warriors couldn't do anything to stop him. She began to ponder how someone like him could even lose. But she quickly shook that thought away.

No, this is good, she thought to herself. It was good that this issue could be resolved quickly.

Oh my, that won't do. The dragon stated with disappointment. *Maybe we should liven the mood. The battle seems to be a bit dull and one-sided. Your thoughts may be small squeaks, but don't perceive that I'm not listening. Hold your hand up.*

Isobel immediately regretted her reckless thought. This was how the dragon always took advantage of her. It was hard enough trying to maintain what little sanity she had left, but she could never control her thoughts. She loved to learn, to think, to grow, and examine. And now, all these traits would be her downfall.

She felt her hand raise, pointing right at Drakonis and she began to chant an incantation.

"Divines above hear my call." Her mouth moved. "Please grant me this boon of might and fire."

Energy radiated in her hand and swirled around her wrist. But it also had a green hue on it, corrupted by the black dragon. This wasn't a spell she had cast before.

The dark lord was on the counterattack, knocking hooded figures out of formation with swift attacks, and he was too busy to notice what was going on up on the ledge. Too busy to notice this betrayal taking place.

Aw... The dragon said through pursed lips. *You make this seem so evil. Wasn't he the one who separated and tortured you? The one who damaged you, hurt you, and then told you a grand tale thinking it would mend the wounds? I know I told you to get on his good side, but you seem to have lost your sense of self. Don't worry. That's why you need me. To make all the decisions when you can't make them yourself. Isn't that why we made the pact in the beginning? Because you were scared and lonely? As you are now?*

The words were a distraction. She knew they were, but she couldn't ignore them. The way the black dragon manipulated you was as alluring as it was menacing. How it scared you and yet, pulled you into itself. You felt fear and yet there was peace... She started to feel at peace.

Her hand buzzed. She sighed and breathed in. The world came back into view. The blast was still getting stronger, bigger than any blast she had ever fired. She felt her core being strained, and her heart was beating rapidly. This feeling she felt was unfamiliar to her and yet, she knew what was happening. This was the end.

Move, she pushed in her thoughts. Her hand twitched and began to rise from her side.

Move, she tried again. Her hand slowly gripped her wrist. She tried to pull it away from its target, to throw it off even if it was only by an inch.

Move, she strained again. She felt her energy reaching its peak. She didn't have any time left.

As the blast started to fly from her hand, a hand grabbed her wrist and redirected it toward the wall. The blast flew into the antechamber wall and brought the whole wall crumbling down. All of the beings in the room jumped away from the explosion.

Isobel looked to her side to see who was gripping her arm. Chase stood above her, his breaths labored and deep. He stared down at her with worried eyes. And she looked back up at him with relief. She then smiled softly at him and laughed. She was so happy that he had stopped her. So happy to have always had him by her side, watching over her. He was a great friend.

“I'm here, Isobel.” Chase said as he crouched by her side.

She wanted to reply, but she just couldn't stop laughing. She was so glad. So very glad that he had found her. She regretted leaving him behind. She needed him.

You fought long enough, Isobel. The dragon whispered to her. *Rest now. I'll take good care of you.*

“Isobel?” Chase said, his worried expression not leaving his face.

She wanted to let him know that it was all okay. But she just couldn't stop laughing. She just couldn't stop laughing for the life of her and she was getting tired. So tired. She felt her vision fading, but she couldn't stop laughing. The laughing never stopped.

* * *

Chase

"Haha..." Isobel chuckled. Her eyes were wide, and she smiled creepily, almost like she was... Overjoyed. Chase felt his chest tighten like a screw that had been wound far too tight. He hoped that he wasn't too late. That he could save her from the claws of darkness.

He stared at her, intensely examining her body, looking for signs of corruption but he couldn't see anything different about her. Outside of a few bruises, she looked the same as she had before he had lost her. In his haste to secure her safety, he realized he was still tightly gripping her wrist. He let go and her hand lifelessly dropped to her side. He glanced into the sewer where her attack had detonated.

The blast had destroyed the entirety of one of the walls, and debris was crashing down on the room. Drakonis was locked in combat with a few shadowy figures, but their ringleader was conveniently absent. He didn't know if the duo had failed to subjugate their leader, but he didn't have time to ponder such things. Drakonis needed some assistance, but Isobel was his top priority.

Chase turned his attention back to Isobel, who was still chuckling to herself.

"I'm here, Isobel." Chase comforted her. He didn't fully understand the situation, but he knew that Isobel needed him. Had he been a second slower, that blast would have destroyed the whole room and consumed all who were inside. Isobel's head slumped down to her chest, but she kept chuckling to herself hysterically.

"Isobel?" Chase said as he put his hand on her shoulder. He shook her a bit, but she didn't look up. She just kept laughing to herself. He lifted her head and stared into her eyes. And the laughing stopped.

Her eyes. They were black as coal and were dark and empty like the dark reaches of an ocean. Chase stared into them with disbelief, and she stared back at him. Their eyes were locked in dark silence for a moment, which was broken by shouting coming from the room.

"Chase!" Drakonis screamed from down below. His shouts came from in-between the sharp impacts of blades connecting. "What is going on up there!?"

Chase couldn't stop staring into her eyes. He tried to pull away, grunting as he tried to move, but his body would not respond. He was powerless. He had an abundance of questions flying through his head, but he already knew the answer to all of them. The only name he wished he had never known: The Black Dragon.

"Aren't you going to answer him, dear Chaselonius?"

Isobel said in a soft and serene voice. Her tone was calming but her hideous grin sent chills down his spine. She reached a hand up and placed it on his face. It was ice-cold to the touch. That's when he noticed it. Her mark, the black dragon mark, was creeping across her body. Her skin was slowly becoming as black as her eyes.

Isobel pulled Chase close, embracing him tenderly.

"Come with me." She said softly into his ear. She then pulled away from him and held out her hand.

He was unable to reply to her demand. He couldn't get his body to move of his own accord. But he saw his hand reach out and take hers. They stood together and she nodded with a subtle delight. She then led him over to the edge of the room, just through the gate that led to a waterfall, and Chase followed her unwillingly. They both stood in silence as they watched Drakonis battle the hooded figures.

The dark lord slammed his blade into one of the warriors and sent him flying into the wall. This dislodged a massive chunk of the ceiling, and it came crashing down into the room. Dirt and debris covered the room and sent bits of rock through the air. A few seconds passed and the smoke cleared slowly. Light from the sun now softly poured into the antechamber, and the horrid smell of the sewer was mixed with the moist air from above.

Chase could see Drakonis stand at the edge of the cave-in with his blade tightly gripped in hand. He also could see the hooded figures near the wall that Isobel had shot with her blast. Now that light was pouring into the area, he could make out a hole that had been made in the wall. The hooded men were using it to escape!

"Golden Time..." Isobel said suddenly. Isobel's aura exploded beside him. But it wasn't the radiant golden hue that he was used to. It was tinged with green, and the pressure felt like it was a hundred times more potent. Isobel disappeared from beside him, but he didn't have to look too far to find her.

There was a loud impact below, the sound of a heavy clap filled the area. He saw Isobel with her fist caught in Drakonis' hand. The blow shook the very walls of the sewer, and even knocked the remaining hooded men to the ground. Only a few of them remained and they looked up at the two figures locked in a violent deadlock.

"What are you doing!?" He said as he grunted against the blow.

*　　　*　　　*

Drakonis

Regretful. He held Isobel's hand in place, their hands shaking against each other, and stared her down. Her eyes were black marbles, glistening in the sunlight, and devoid of life. Her facial expression, on the other hand, was manic and bloodthirsty. She bared a bright row of teeth to show she was eager to take him on.

He knew that the Divine Knights had no short list of reasons to come for him, but from what he could see, Isobel had finally completely succumbed to her possession. Her aura was draped in dark mana and her pressure was outstanding. Even with this one strike, he could tell that her power was leagues stronger than before. If not for the intense aura she was presenting carelessly, she might have knocked him off his feet or worse with her attack.

"Isobel!" He yelled at her. "Listen to me! You don't want to do this!"

She laughed at his words and pressed her hand deeper into his.

"You don't know me at all!" She said with a crazed grin. "I've wanted to do this since I came to the capitol!"

Drakonis threw her hand away and she used the

momentum to spin around and slam an amazing roundhouse into his side. He caught the kick with his free hand, but the impact from the strike made the walls rumble and sent parts of the ceiling collapsing on them.

Drakonis took a second to scan the area, in an attempt to find the other Divine Knight. A few hooded men were standing up and making their way towards the exit. Annoying. He then spotted Chase sitting on the edge of the area, watching the fight.

"Chase!" He called to him. The knight didn't respond to Drakonis' call, and just silently watched over them. There was something off about him, but before Drakonis could ponder the man's predicament further, Isobel flipped off her kick and was bringing her foot down on his head. Drakonis leapt out of the way of the attack and a cloud of debris and dust erupted at the point of contact right in front of him. He tightly gripped his sword and used his Dragon Sense to search for the hooded men. They were disappearing through the hole in the wall! As the last of the cowardly warriors went jumping through the wall, Drakonis ran over to try and cut them off. Isobel dashed in front of him from her invisible spot in the cloud and blocked his path.

"Over here!" She yelled with wicked excitement. She then threw a punch that looked to be laced in enchantments and augmented incantations. Drakonis swung the blunt end of his blade to deflect the attack, but the blow was so strong that it shattered his sword. Shards of steel went flying all over as Drakonis was launched into the wall behind him and it collapsed on top of him.

How annoying. How utterly disgraceful, he thought to himself. Rocks pelted him as they slammed down onto him. He was in pain, but it wasn't entirely because of the blow. He had let Isobel down. He had hoped that after the festival, he would have more time to seek out a cure or a preventative to her affliction. But he had underestimated her situation. Now she was standing before him, aiding terrorists, and helping them escape. Annoying.

Drakonis sensed Isobel was right in front of him and was waiting for him to move. He kicked a boulder off himself, aiming specifically at her. She back handed the rock away and laughed. He punched through the rest of the rubble and rose back to his feet.

“I feel great, Drakonis.” Isobel smirked at him. “Doesn't this feel just right?

Drakonis grimaced at her words and walked closer to her. He scanned the area again, but this time, there were no signs of the hooded men. They had a head start, but if Drakonis could evade or defeat Isobel in a few seconds, he could catch them.

Drakonis dashed right for Isobel, and she didn't flinch

as he invaded her range. He got as close as possible and stepped to her side to try and bypass her. Much to his surprise, chagrin, and annoyance, she anticipated his movement and aimed another punch at his stomach. He caught the blow and winced from the pain.

“Stop ignoring me.” Isobel said, her grin slowly fading.

“I will fix you.” He replied with sadness in his voice. “I'll reverse this.”

“Is that sadness!?” Isobel recoiled with disgust. “No. You don't deserve those emotions.”

She slammed her heel into Drakonis' chest, and he slid a few feet backwards. Drakonis took a deep breath and got into his fighting stance. He knew what he needed to do. He couldn't stop the men from escaping, not with Isobel blocking his path, and he had to take her down.

“I feel sooo alive right now.” Isobel rasped, putting both of her hands over her heart. “I feared, day in and out, of the Black Dragon's pact. The uncertainty. The thought of it tainting my soul and taking my will away. But this is so much better than anything I have ever experienced. I can FEEL the embrace of the dragon and it calms my mind. I have never felt such peace.”

“Those aren't your words, Isobel.” Drakonis interrupted. “Your mind is being warped by his influence. You're stronger than this. You can still fight.”

"Fight?" Isobel scoffed. She started laughing maniacally. "Why would a daughter fight her father's loving embrace? To go back to that scared girl, who chose her words sparingly, and worried her youth away?"

"Because that's who you are!" Drakonis yelled at her. "Not this."

"You don't know me." Isobel replied intensely. "You never knew me. You saw me as a tool. The same way the Divines used me as a tool for war. The same way Chase follows me like a dog and looks for his dose of sympathy whenever his mood takes a turn for the worse. The same way the dragon uses me. The only difference is... The dragon never lied about his intentions. And now, he whispers to me. Gives me direction."

Drakonis dashed forward and aimed a blow at her stomach. Isobel smacked the blow away and leapt into Drakonis' face with her knee. He reached up and narrowly blocked it with his hand and grabbed her leg. She brought the other knee up to try and repeat the attack, but Drakonis managed to throw her a few feet away.

Isobel slid on the ground, and bounced off a rock, flying a few feet into the air. She made contact with the last bit of overhanging ceiling, bringing it down into the caved-in sewer. A cloud of dust formed as the ceiling crashed into the sewer on top of Isobel. The sewer was completely unrecognizable from just a few minutes before. Drakonis watched the chaos unfold in front of him, watching to see Isobel's next move. His legs were suddenly swept from under him.

"Behind you!" Isobel yelled.

Drakonis used his arm to redirect his body and avoid crashing into the earth. He spun around and launched a kick into Isobel's chest, and she jumped right over him. As he looked up at her crazed expression, she drove her feet right into his chest.

Drakonis sank a few feet into the earth, pinned beneath Isobel's foot. She began to chant something under her breath. Before she could finish whatever incantation she was reciting, Drakonis grabbed her heel and pushed her up into the air.

As he stood up, he watched Isobel fall back down to him, and readied his fists. Much to his surprise, he saw her throw her hand forward and a blast came flying down on him. He smacked the blast away, right into the sky and it exploded with a black glow.

Then Drakonis felt Isobel's aura change. A few seconds before, she had been strong enough to rival an original Divine Knight. But something changed, and her pressure was plummeting almost as fast as she was. He lowered his hands and took a breath. The fight was over.

Isobel was slowly falling back to the earth. When she landed, she would be no problem for the dark lord. But then

Drakonis realized that she wasn't even conscious anymore. He had readied himself to leap after her, but he saw someone jump through the air and grab her.

Chase landed a few feet away from Drakonis with Isobel in his arms, completely unconscious. Drakonis walked over to the pair and took a knee next to Chase.

"We'll fix this." Drakonis consoled him finally. "We will put our best efforts forward and pull her back."

Chase didn't reply. He just sat there holding her body in his arms. He pulled her close and tears streamed down his face.

Drakonis, dissatisfied with how this battle was resolved, turned away from the two knights. He could not bring himself to watch the knight grieve over his dying friend.

Chapter 18:
Imperfect Creations

The King of the Majes

Clang! He brought his hammer down upon the blade, beads of sweat falling from his brow. Clang! His muscles burned with each swing, his every fiber prompting him to stop, but his determination was stronger. Clang! The room was black, save for the sparks flying from his anvil and his bright amber eyes, as he continued to work faithfully. Clang! This was his craft, his life, and either his greatest or worst creation. Clang!

King Maj struck the metal again and again, unflinching as hot shards of metal embedded themselves in his skin. He didn't wear the protective garb of his workshop. No. Not on this project.

His inheritance, The Majen King's Sight, was pushed to its limit. It was an ability that only the King of the Majes could embrace. The title of 'King' wasn't just because he was the best blacksmith from their homeland. He was truly blessed and could see what others could not. His eyes allowed him to see metal in a way that others couldn't perceive, to know what time to strike and where. For him, being a blacksmith wasn't creating a blade from ore. It was transforming the ore into its true form. He breathed life into the weapons he touched.

"Curse the gods!" He roared out in frustration, his hammer loudly impacting the blade. "How could I create something so useless!? This design is not pragmatic! It is not designed properly! And yet, this is how you wish to be!?"

He stopped hammering for a moment and stared at the atrocious blade. It had two sides, each completely different from the other. The left side appeared rusted and bloody. Its edges were jagged like the maw of a dragon, and it curved away from the center like a scimitar. It looked like it was trying to escape its other half.

The right side was white and gold and shimmered with a soft blue aura. It was straight as an arrow and its edges sharp like an arrowhead. Even though it looked gentle and somewhat holy, it had a subtle intensity to it.

"This looks like a child's toy!" King Maj exclaimed. "I'm using some of the purest materials available in all of the realms, and this blade looks like cheap street vendor garbage!"

He shook his head at the mangled mess in his hands before returning back to his work. He couldn't stop now. He had to finish or else he would ruin the blade and ruin the future that Drakonis hoped to achieve. He hammered harder on the blade.

Drakonis! The young dragonkin knight who told him

this insane plan. The one who told him of the future and confided in him to help him. Even then, the plan stank to high heaven. It sent chills up his spine thinking about it now, and anyone that heard the plan would have thought it utterly insane. And if anyone had completely known what they were up to? If the God King knew what they were up to? Well... Let's say that he would rather be hung by his feet and beaten to death than feel the wrath of the One True God...

He hammered faster now. The sword was getting closer to its completion now. His thoughts were everywhere now. His son was still in a coma. His daughters now lived in fear and mourned their brother. And all the while, his wife could be dead. She didn't respond when her children's lives were in jeopardy...

"*You're a failure as a father, husband, and as a King!*" A voice hissed at him. It was low and malevolent. He wanted to shudder, to fight back against the words, but he resisted his urges and hammered still.

See that blade on the table? The voice continued. *Take it and stab yourself. Do it quickly!*

He continued to hammer, ignoring the voice completely. He wouldn't fall prey to this trick. He was much too strong for these silly games.

Do not give into despair, King of Blacksmiths. This time the voice was serene, and gentle. Opposed to the intense dread he felt with its counterpart, this voice was compassionate. *Oh, crafter of mine, do not fret over what ails you. Let patience and acceptance guide you to peace.*

Patience and acceptance, huh? King Maj wanted to chuckle at the words, but he knew that would be folly. To even partially react to the words of the blade would be dire, and he continued to hammer away. The power of the blade grew immensely as he continued to work at it. The voices began to bicker back and forth as well, but King Maj never stopped swinging. He kept swinging his arm at the most beautiful blade he had ever created.

*　　　*　　　*

Drakonis

Drakonis stared down at Isobel, his hands clenched in frustration. Chase sat next to her, holding her hand in his, with the same look of disdain and disappointment that Drakonis shared. He hadn't left Isobel's side since yesterday and watched her intently. Her body was black, covered head to toe by the Black Dragon's mark, and she laid lifelessly on her bed in the medical ward. Here they were, surrounded by some of the best medical equipment in the kingdom, and they could do nothing.

Every few minutes, Chase had broken the silence with

small utterances of regret, but he had been quiet for some time now. Amidst his own worry, Drakonis couldn't and didn't want to think about what chaos was ensuing in the young knight's mind.

"Drakonis..." Chase said suddenly, his voice low and serious. "I couldn't do anything..."

"Not this again." Drakonis replied, breathing in softly.

"What?" Chase grumbled back at him. His tone indicated annoyance, and agitation. Drakonis didn't want to have to nag at Chase for his actions, but at this point, he didn't see how he could avoid it.

"Do Divine Knights always wallow so fondly or is this a habit all your own?" Drakonis stated bluntly. He didn't want to sugarcoat the issue.

"Huh?" Chase said sharply as he partially turned to look at Drakonis now. His brows were furrowed, and it was obvious that any regret, sadness, or disappointment the man had been quickly turning to anger.

"Anytime anything happens to Isobel, you have, time and time again, gone down this road." Drakonis continued as he crossed his arms. "The capital has been in absolute chaos since I've brought you two here. That I understand. But for the life of me, I cannot see how someone as weak willed as yourself even managed to be recognized as a knight."

Chase put Isobel's hand down on the bed softly and

stood up to face Drakonis. His eyes were red, the kind of red that can only come from an evening of mourning, and his chest was palpitating as his anger was visibly increasing.

"This is your fault!" Chase exclaimed as he jammed a finger into Drakonis' chest.

"Clearly." Drakonis replied as he rolled his eyes.

"If you hadn't brought us here..." Chase began to say. His eyes began to dart around erratically, almost like he wasn't talking to Drakonis anymore. "If you hadn't brought us here...!"

"What?" Drakonis roared back, interrupting him. "You would have never known misery!? If I hadn't existed your life would just be sunshine and rainbows, and humans would just live happily ever after? Give me a break."

"Stop deflecting!" Chase screamed as he gripped the collar of Drakonis' armor. He reeled his arm back as he predictably prepared his fist for an attack. As Chase swung with what seemed like all his might, Drakonis grabbed his hand and used all of the momentum of the punch to swing Chase into the wall next to him. There was a loud 'crunch' on impact, and Drakonis jammed his arm against Chase's neck, pinning him to the wall.

"Maybe you should take some time to reflect on your own words." Drakonis growled at him. "Are you really that immature and self-centered? When are you going to take accountability for your actions? And when are you going to hold Isobel accountable for hers?"

Chase grunted as he struggled against Drakonis' grip, but he found no purchase in his efforts.

"I didn't make Isobel create a pact with the dragon." Drakonis sighed as he loosened his grip a bit. "And you didn't either."

Chase reached for his neck, rasping and coughing as he gasped for air. He straightened up against the wall and gave Drakonis a fierce stare down. If Drakonis had any reservations about how Chase felt about him, this moment gave him sincere clarity. There was no love in this relationship.

Their squabble was interrupted by a giant pulse of pressure that washed over them. It was so strong that it created waves in the mana around them. It was done. Drakonis had no doubts about it in his mind.

"What was that!?" Chase gasped as he held onto the wall.

"-Onis..." Drakonis' pocket hummed loudly. Drakonis reached into his pocket and pulled out his mana crystal. King Maj's image projected through the shard in Drakonis' hand. The Maj was covered in soot, sweat, and his eyes were bandaged. He also didn't have anything on but a pair of dingy pants that had holes in them.

"King Maj, I assume you've done what I asked?" Drakonis said as he turned from Chase.

"Yes *cough*, my lord." The Maj replied with a fit of coughs. "There were some *cough* oversights, but it's *cough* *cough* finished."

Drakonis could hear yelling in the background, and he didn't recognize the voices.

"Who are you with?" Drakonis asked nervously. "I specifically told you that you were to WORK ALONE! No one was to know!"

"And at this time, no one does." King Maj replied bluntly as his coughing subsided. "I'll explain those oversights when you get here. Isobel and you need to get here as soon as possible."

That can't be good, Drakonis thought to himself. He didn't need any more setbacks, or blindsides.

Drakonis pocketed the crystal shard and turned back to Chase who was upright now.

"We need to get Isobel to the Blacksmith's Forge." Drakonis informed him. He ran over to the bed to retrieve Isobel, but Chase stood in his way.

"For what reason!?" Chase frowned back at him. "She's at death's door. She could die on the way."

Setbacks. This is not what they needed right now. Drakonis could just toss Chase aside again, but even if he escaped and saved Isobel, Chase would never trust him after that. In fact, he knew that no matter what he would say, Chase would never end his vendetta against him if that were to transpire. *Use your words*, Drakonis thought to himself.

“And if she stays here, she'll die in this room!” Drakonis shot back. “We have to move her now, or her soul is lost. We don't have time to argue. You have to trust me!”

“Trust you!?” Chase bellowed. “You said you'd help look for a cure but here she is-!”

“This is that cure!” Drakonis shot back. “We have the cure. We have a way to save her and get rid of the Black Dragon's influence. But you have to trust me!”

“You both do know that loud arguments can be detrimental to the recovery of my patient, don't you?” A woman's voice interrupted from behind them.

Chase swung around towards the voice. Drakonis took this moment to lift Isobel onto his back.

“It's also detrimental to lift her like luggage during her recovery as well.” Cyarah sighed.

“Move aside, Cyarah.” Drakonis commanded. He then glared over at Chase. “And Chase, either come with us or stay here.”

Chase groaned loudly.

“Fine!” He shouted. “It's not like I have a choice anyway.”

“Cyarah, let's go.” Drakonis said as he walked past her. “We're going to need you as well.”

"I could not fathom anything that you could need me for that doesn't involve any of my tools in this room." She said with a confused expression. "You really do not need my presence."

"Cyarah!" Drakonis shouted at her.

"ALRIGHT!" She begrudgingly accepted. She shrugged and tucked in close behind Drakonis and Chase.

The trio left the room hastily. As soon as the door opened, they took off with a violent sprint through the hospital and out of its doors.

It took only a half hour to reach the forge. The three had run as fast as they could to reach their destination, exploiting the land and using whatever powers were at their disposal to get there.

"I really hate running..." Cyarah said under her breath. "I really REALLY hate running..."

As they stopped at the front door of the forge to catch their breath, Drakonis looked around to find signs of King Maj. His men were hard at work in the workshop, so involved with their own personal projects that they hadn't even noticed him yet. It looked like any other day.

"Where is King Maj?" Drakonis said loudly, trying to catch the attention of one of the smiths.

An older gentleman with a long beard, wiped his brow and turned to them.

“He's in the back.” The man said as he pointed to a large door at the back of the forge. “He's been in 'The Room' for around twelve hours now.”

Drakonis could only assume that this was where the secret project took place. He guessed that hiding in plain sight was the best way to hide what goes on in there.

Drakonis nodded at the man and proceeded to walk past him, Isobel still slumbering on his back, with Chase and Cyarah in tow.

“Guess there's not a chance of us finally getting a glimpse of the King's work, is there?” The man inquired as they strolled by him.

Drakonis ignored the man and kept moving towards the door.

“Go on and be that way then.” The man grumbled.

Drakonis didn't have time to entertain the help. Drakonis stopped at the door and knocked repeatedly.

“King Maj, we are here.” Drakonis announced. “Let us in.”

Drakonis heard a loud clank and was surprised to see a slit slide to the side in the middle of the door. King Maj's face was on the other side of the slit. The bloody bandages looked even more horrific in person than they had in the crystal shard.

“Good, you're here.” King Maj exclaimed excitedly. Through the slit, Drakonis could hear yelling behind the King.

"What is going on in there?" Drakonis asked with some worry.

"Oh, nothing we can't fix with two warm bodies." The King said cheerfully. His expression then turned sour. "I told you to only bring Isobel. Those two can't come in here."

"What do you mean I can't come in!?" Chase cried out from behind Drakonis.

"It's exactly as he stated." Drakonis said looking over his shoulder. "Only Isobel and I can enter. Otherwise, this won't work."

"SHADY AS EVER!" Chase said as he balled his fists. Lightning began to crackle from his body, and he started to breathe heavily. Drakonis felt Chase's pressure growing in intensity and knew he had to de-escalate the situation before it got out of hand. As he opened his mouth to talk Chase down, Cyarah stepped in-between them.

"I know you want to protect your friend," she said softly. "I also know that Drakonis isn't the most... Open... with his thoughts and plans. But I assure you that this will save your friend."

"And how could you know!?" Chase yelled at her. "You're just as much in the dark as I am!"

Some of the workers of the forge gave them small glances, but they didn't seem to care about the altercation. Maybe they were used to the excitement?

“Your anger is clouding your judgement.” Cyarah said as she put her hand on Chase's shoulder. “Since your arrival in Zhalesh, Drakonis has prioritized your safety. If his actions are of any evidence of his intentions, then you surely know in your heart that he truly wishes to save Isobel. Your actions now only endanger her.”

Suddenly, Chase's lightning began to fade. He grabbed his head, groaning loudly in pain, and slammed his foot into the ground to keep from falling over. Cyarah rushed to his side to assist him.

“W-We-...” Chase stammered out. “I-Isobel... We can't...”

The pressure he was exuding returned to normal. For a few moments, he tried to speak, but he was too out of breath to create sentences properly. Drakonis simply shook his head.

“Breathe.” Cyarah instructed him. “Physiological stress leading to hyperventilation. You will be fine as long as you keep breathing steadily.”

“You don't say?” Chase gasped. “Was it... the lack of... breathing...-?”

“I didn't say 'talk'.” Cyarah shushed him. “I said 'breathe'.”

Drakonis turned back to the door, a little grateful to Cyarah for stopping Chase.

“Let us in.” He commanded. “We're running out of

time!"

King Maj nodded and then slid the slit shut. Multiple locks and mechanisms could be heard churning and clicking loudly within the door. Then after a moment, a soft click indicated that it was now unlocked.

"Drakonis..." Chase called out from behind the dark lord.

Drakonis turned one last time to Chase, hoping he wasn't planning on making anymore attempts to stop him.

"Take care of Isobel." He spoke. His breathing had become more controlled, and he was starting to stand upright. "She is... She's all I have left."

"I can give you no more than my word." Drakonis replied. "Take care of him, Cyarah."

She nodded back at him, and Drakonis felt his heart sink. For a moment, Cyarah dropped her masked personality and lowered her facade, and gave him a large, toothy grin. A grin that he had come to loathe at each of its appearances. A grin that signified that she had finally won and gotten what she had wanted.

Drakonis really didn't want to leave the knight in Cyarah's hands. He avoided giving her what she wanted because he could only control her when he had something to give her. In fact, there was a huge chance that she would take advantage of Chase in his fragile state of mind. But he couldn't be in two places at one time. Sometimes, in a game of chess, you had to sacrifice the pawn to obtain the queen. He had to prioritize Isobel's survival first.

Drakonis took a deep breath, steeling his nerves, and then grabbed the handle on the door and slipped into the dark room. He grabbed the handle of the door and shut it behind himself, the gears of the door churned again and locked once it was shut.

The room was pitch black, save for a soft brown light in its center, and smelled of sweat and blood. In front of him, two voices could be heard violently arguing with each other. He looked around and found King Maj a few feet away from him, his silhouette illuminated by the bright light.

“Drakonis, my boy!” King Maj exclaimed happily. “Welcome, welcome!”

“Okay, what is happening in here?” Drakonis asked anxiously. As his eyes became more adjusted, he saw broken hammers on the ground of the lit space. He could barely make out the edges of the room, but it also looked like the room was completely in shambles as well.

“First, put the lass on the table ova there.” King Maj yelled over the shouting, as he pointed at a nearby table. “We don't have time ta waste, and I'll explain as we go.”

Drakonis rushed over to the table. It looked fragile, but it would have to do. He lowered Isobel off his back and onto the table. Her breathing was ragged, but still stable. Her skin, on the other hand, was paler than he had ever seen her. They needed to hurry.

"Short version, King Maj." Drakonis yelled as he put Isobel in place.

King Maj grabbed a set of candles and began to place them on the floor around the table.

"'Member those souls that you collected for my 'other' project?" King Maj asked as he walked. "The souls of the warriors?"

"What about them?" Drakonis answered impatiently.

"Well, the souls of the worthy warriors were so powerful that their wills did not die when they lost their souls, Drakonis!" King Maj exuberated. "The souls worked like a charm for Aviance, and everything went as normal. But... There were some parts left ova from that project... So, I used the leftover components to help construct the sword. The Chrocosium and parts of Aviance... They merged into powerful spirits within the blade and took on'a life of their own. They created something beautiful and unique! For better or worse, they are completely alive!"

"Is that what all this yelling is?" Drakonis asked as he took another glance at the glowing light in the room. He didn't see any swords of any kind in its light.

"Yes!" King Maj said as he lit the candles with a small

magic spell. “This is the accumulation of our hard work, my boy! You wanted two weapons that were unmatched by any blade, but they demanded more. They demanded unity and solidarity. They wanted to give life and death. They hungered for a home, and sought adventure.”

“King Maj, the ritual!” Drakonis demanded even more impatiently.

King Maj finished lighting the last candle. He then stood up and motioned towards the light in the center of the room.

“Drakonis, meet Rajani the dark and Rohaz of the light!” King Maj exclaimed with excitement. “Sibling spirits from the Sword of the Majes!”

King Maj then lowered his arms, and his expression became puzzled.

“Actually... That didn't roll off the tongue the way I planned.” He said with a little disappointment.

The yelling immediately stopped, and the room was silent for a moment. Then the light in the center of the room split into two separate swords. One was bright, almost holy in appearance, with a soft yellow hue. The other was darker, with a menacing aura, and had a soft blue aura to it.

“She is mine!” A woman's voice bellowed from the dark sword as it raced toward the table.

“You are wrong, Rajani!” A man's voice roared from

the light sword. “I will claim this one!”

The light sword smashed into the dark one and sent it careening off course. They both reached Isobel's body and began to flutter around her.

“Oh!” Rohaz gasped. “She is tainted with pestilence and darkness. I will cleanse her of her affliction!”

The light sword then exploded into a blinding light that cast away all of the darkness in the room, forcing Drakonis and King Maj to cover their eyes.

“I am Divine Blade Rohaz!” Rohaz shouted. “My light shall remove all darkness from this woman, and I will claim her body as my champion!”

Isobel began to slowly rise off the table, and Drakonis reached out to her. He then heard screaming coming from where the dark sword went flying. Still covering his eyes, he turned to look at the sword and saw it was pointing straight at Isobel!

Drakonis reached out to grab the blade, but his hand went right through it. He felt nothing but an extreme cold run through his hand.

The blade shot forward and slammed into Isobel's chest, penetrating her and the table.

“NO!” Drakonis cried out.

“Oh poo.” Rohaz sighed from above.

Isobel's eyes shot open, and she let out a blood curdling

scream and clutched at her chest. She coughed and black liquid spewed from her lips. Her eyes darted around the room in complete confusion.

"Where..." She croaked as she struggled against the sword. "What's… happening? Dr-Drakonis? It hurts… so… much!"

Drakonis didn't know what to say or do. This isn't what was supposed to happen. Her eyes pleaded with him to make it stop.

"I will not let you take what is rightfully mine, brother." Rajani whispered as it began to melt down over Isobel's body, putting her in some sort of cocoon. "I, The Calamity Blade, will have my champion."

Drakonis reached out to grab Isobel's hand, but an oppressive pressure began to force him down on his knees. He grunted and struggled as he was forced to watch Isobel be consumed by the black blade.

"You will not interfere!" Rohaz commanded.

"I should have listened to the swords when they said their names." King Maj mumbled to himself.

Drakonis then felt himself be released from the oppressive force. He turned to King Maj and grabbed his shoulders.

"HAVE YOU GONE MAD!?" Drakonis roared at him. "WHAT IS THIS!? WHAT HAVE YOU DONE TO HER

AND THE SWORDS!? THIS ISN'T WHAT I TOLD YOU TO DO! THIS ISN'T WHAT THE FEY TOLD ME WOULD HAPPEN!!"

"Drakonis..." King Maj said in a firm tone, grabbing Drakonis' hand. "Isobel is fine. She is going through the trial, just as you asked. I know that spectacle was a little... violent. But rest assured, the trial is underway."

"You have been talking like a raving fanatic since I've entered this room!" Drakonis shook his head. "Be candid. Cease these cryptic riddles and explain to me what this is!"

"You didn't listen ta me, my boy." King Maj sighed. "She is in the trial now. She is in no danger. I will admit that the swords becoming not just sentient weapons, but ACTUAL spirits is completely unheard of. But this doesn't change anything. She can still be saved. Just trust, my lord."

"Okay." Drakonis stated, catching his breath. "Okay. I guess we just wait then."

"Yes." King Maj agreed. "Give her time."

Drakonis closed his eyes and rubbed his face. Then he felt a hot presence on his shoulder, and immediately opened his eyes to see what it was. Rohaz had settled on his shoulder.

"Fear not, false spawn of the fallen one." Rohaz said, his light humming a bit with his words. "Your trial, soon too, will begin."

*   *   *

Isobel

Isobel's eyes opened abruptly as she shot up, gasping and clutching her chest. She had a sharp, burning pain in the middle of her chest that made it hard to breathe. The sword! She tried to look down and gauge the amount of damage she had taken, but she realized the blinding light in the room was obscuring her vision. She tried squinting to let her eyes adjust but the room was far too bright, like someone was holding a lamp directly in front of her face. Where did this blinding light come from?

"Ah." She grunted as she bent away from the light.

She sat there for a moment, trying to get her breathing under control, and kept clutching at her chest. As her vision finally adjusted to the light, she realized that there was no sword in her chest. In fact, now that she could see clearly, there was no wound at all. And the pain she had felt before was now subsiding, almost like it had never been there to begin with.

She breathed a sigh of relief and searched her surroundings, hoping to see a familiar face. It was at this point that she noticed that she wasn't in the room anymore. She was out in an open field. There was short grass all around her, but it sat still and unmoving. There was no breeze, and barely any insects or animals were alive in the field either. It was a familiar feeling, and yet it couldn't be more surreal. She looked directly up above her at the light that she assumed was the culprit behind her former confusion. A large crystal sat high in the sky, or really in the ceiling of a cavern that was meant to resemble the sky, and it cast a soft white glow over the entire cave. She couldn't believe what she was seeing...

“It can't be...” Isobel whispered in disbelief as she shuffled around on the ground.

She turned around and saw a large cathedral in the distance behind rows of makeshift houses and rough pelt tents.

“The tower of the Divines...” She said as she stood up. “And I'm... in Dream Field?”

That wasn't really the name of this little patch of grass that she was in, but that was the name the kids had given it. Most of the children that lived in this place would come here and daydream about what the surface would look like. Maybe even some of the adults, too. She took a deep breath and was greeted by the familiar scents.

“And those same kids would be brought back to reality by the stale, damp air of Karia-Aphermia.” She said aloud. “Where is everyone? Where is Xeilani? How have I returned to Karia? And... I remember getting stabbed by a sword. What happened?”

Isobel was startled by soft giggling coming from the nearby gate to the city. She turned to see young kids laughing and pointing at her. And then she noticed a tall, muscular man with an amazingly bald head approaching her. Her eyes began to well at the sight of the man and his familiar silver armor. The tell of a veteran knight.

“Anilebelita Fawntasia!” The man screamed. “I should have known you would choose to run off and daydream! You should be in the shrine praying and preparing! And where is that GOOD FOR NOTHING GUARD OF YOURS!? I'll skin her alive when I catch her!”

“E-Everett!” Isobel choked out. She ran to embrace the man, letting her tears fall freely. She collided with the man with a loud 'THUD'.

“O-oh!” Everett said with some surprise. He lightly hugged her back before pulling her away and lifted her gaze with his hand. “What's wrong, child? Are you in pain?”

Isobel shook her head. If anything, the joy of seeing her guardian again made her heart do somersaults in her chest. She didn't even believe she could vocalize how happy she was to see the man.

“I'm just so happy to be back,” she said as she wiped the tears from her eyes. “I've been away for such a long time. And I've been through so much.”

“Well...” The man scoffed with a face of confusion.

“There's not too much activity you can get into in three hours, so how about you dry those tears.” He smiled softly at her but then his grin immediately was replaced by an abrupt scowl. “And you can explain to me why you are lollygagging when you should be praying and studying for the ceremony!?”

“Ceremony?” She said with a puzzled expression.

“Yes, child.” Everett said sternly. “The Ascension Ceremony for your blessing.”

Isobel blinked hard and took a few steps back from Everett. While his words confused her, she also began to actually take notice of her surroundings and her situation. Everett was taller than usual, and he looked a few years younger as well. Isobel looked down at her own clothes and realized that she was wearing her uniform. Not her Divine Knight armor, but her scouting garb... Armor worn by young squires-in-training. She couldn't feel the corruptive black dragon mark on her neck either. And even though she felt like she hadn't talked to Everett in over several months, this conversation felt very familiar to her. One that she had before on a day she could never forget. These intense thoughts and revelations began to take a toll on her, and her legs gave out under her as she fell down, plummeting to her knees.

“I-Isobel!” Everett said as he reached out to hold her up. “What's the matter?”

“Hey, Isobel!” Another familiar voice called from a

distance. "Everett found out we ditched and we gotta..."

She looked up and noticed that voice belonged to Xeilani. She stood a few feet from them, her radiant hazel eyes wide in surprise, and hands up defensively.

"Fancy seeing you here, sir!" Xeilani said casually. "I was just on my way to retrieve Isobel and return her to her studies in the Chapel."

"Child, cease your jests and help me, lass!" Everett ordered.

"What's wrong with her?" Xeilani asked with worry as she rushed over to Isobel and Everett.

"I don't know..." The old man said with a puzzled expression. "She collapsed suddenly. Are you feeling sick, dear?"

Isobel's mind was racing. She was in the past. Somehow, someway... She had been transported to a time when she was at her happiest. One of the last happy memories she had left before... Before they became ascended knights. Before she signed her pact with the Black Dragon. And before 'that' mistake caused her to lose friends who had become like a family to her.

Isobel felt a hand on her shoulder and looked up, making eye contact with Xeilani.

"Hey... You alright?" Xeilani asked as she glared at her.

"Not with that onion breath in my face." Isobel said as

she squeezed her nose.

"She's fine, Everett." Xeilani rolled her eyes.

"Good." The old man replied as he placed his hand on Xeilani's shoulder. A very pronounced vein rose on the older man's temple and pulsated with conviction. "Care to explain why she's out here, alone I might add, and completely unattended by her guardsman? And in such a sorry state, at that?"

A visible chill ran up Xeilani's spine and her eyes nearly bulged out of their sockets.

"Actually, I'm noticing some redness in her eyes!" Xeilani blurted out quickly. "Isobel, you don't look so hot! Maybe we should visit the medical tent and get an expert evaluation!"

"Oh, no you don't!" Everett exclaimed as he grabbed the girl by the scruff of her collar. "I think some disciplinary remediation is in order! I foresee latrine scrubbing and animal catering in your future!"

Xeilani kicked at the air trying to escape the man's grasp, but to no avail. She was taller than most girls their age, and it honestly looked like one adult was holding another.

"No." Isobel interrupted them as she rubbed the side of her head. "I don't feel so good."

Everett eyed her up and down and then gave a suspicious look to Xeilani, who shrugged back at him. He then took a deep breath and sat Xeilani back down on her feet. Even though Xeilani had soft, brown skin, you could tell that she was slightly embarrassed by her reddening cheeks.

"Alright, go ahead." Everett sighed. "Take her to the medical tent."

Xeilani brushed herself off and motioned for Isobel to follow her. She nodded and walked over to her side. They made it a few feet from Everett before the old man roared at them, causing them to stop in place.

"AND DON'T THINK FOR A SECOND THAT I'M DONE WITH YOU TWO!" He growled angrily.

The pair power walked through the gate towards the city, leaving the old man by himself in the field. It only took a few minutes for them to reach the first set of buildings and stores of the district. Buildings that she hadn't even realized she missed.

"Thanks for the waterworks, Izzy." Xeilani smiled at her. "You really saved my skin! Honestly, Chase would be impressed."

She groaned in response to the nickname. She had completely forgotten about this phase in their life. 'Anilebelita' was far too hard a name to constantly pronounce for her brother-in-arms, even when she sounded it out for them, and Xeilani had been trying out different names on her to see which one would stick. Even after she had affirmed that 'Isobel' would be fine. Honestly, though, hearing her use such a goofy name was nostalgic, and brought a smile to her face.

“It's Isobel, Zel.” She smiled back. “And thanks. But know that I did it with mutual benefit. The last time you were sent to the latrines, you complained for a week about how your hands smelled like poo.”

“And I never got that stank off of 'em!” She smiled back at her. “You sure you don't want to be called like 'Annie' or 'Bell' or somethin? Just saying... Isobel is sooooo... Classic and boring...”

“And those names aren't...?” She raised an eyebrow at him. Xeilani shrugged in response.

Isobel looked past Xeilani and noticed Ms. Longley's Grand Library, one of her favorite shops in all of Karia. She had spent so much time reading stories from the past and about all the wonders of the world. She felt an immediate need to peek in and say hello to Ms. Longley.

“Isobel, I see you looking at the library.” Xeilani said as she wagged her finger. “We don't have time for all of that. You were LITERALLY there all day yesterday! Sir Everett ain’t gonna stay in that field forever, and I refuse to have him find me lingering in a library when I was directly instructed to get you checked out!”

“Or maybe he’ll be appreciative that you've actually taken an interest in your studies.” Isobel teased. “Might even forget he owes you an extensive scolding."

"Extreme doubt." Xeilani rolled her eyes. "If I'm getting caught by one of my superiors, it's going to be inside of the Atchinson's Weapons."

Xeilani stopped right at the door of the weapon store, raising her hands above her head, and making hissing noises with her mouth. Isobel squinted her eyes and shook her head in disproval.

"That's the leagues of satisfied customers shouting their praises!" Xeilani smiled as she continued to wave her arms around.

Isobel looked over the store, which was just as run down as she remembered, and just marveled at its brilliance. She was home. She couldn't believe it at first, but she was here in the human sanctuary. She spun around and eyed Daniel's Wacky Wares across the street, just as jank-looking as it had been when she had left.

"Nothing changes around here." She whispered to herself. "I can't believe I am back."

"What?" Xeilani asked. "You say something?"

"No, it was nothing." Isobel said quickly. Everything felt too real to be an illusion, or a dream. And in many ways, she hoped that this all wasn't a dream. Maybe she could get some information out of Xeilani?

"What day is it?" She asked as they walked.

"Uhmm..." Xeilani said with a puzzled expression. "Maybe a Wednesday or somethin?"

"No, the numbered date." She pressed on.

"How could I possibly know that?" Xeilani replied as she threw her hands up. "Every day is the same down here! Might as well call everyday 'today'."

"Sometimes talking to you is as informative as staring at a blank board." Isobel sighed.

"If I gave you all the answers, what work would be left for you?" Xeilani laughed. "C'mon, use your head, Iso-bel!"

Isobel stuck her tongue out at her, and they both shared a laugh.

They walked and joked for nearly an hour, talking about the things that they always talked about to keep their minds off the war. How all of the cats smelled rank and had bad tempers, or where Daniel got his wares from. They talked about how the district names were the original Divines, much to Xeilani's chagrin, and how they each came to be named. They told partial jokes that they had heard thousands of times over. It had been a while since Isobel had felt so carefree, and in some ways, she wished she could have these days back. At least, the innocence of them.

As the tents came into view, Isobel realized that they had finally entered Karia-Eris. This was the home to many of the wounded, poor, and ill of Karia. It wasn't too far from

Karia-Aphermia, and the only thing that really separated them was the small group of stores and some blocks of houses. This district was filled with makeshift tents, each surrounding a large tent in the middle. Isobel always wondered why there were only tents in this district of the capitol, but she always consigned the thought away to the idea that it was easier to maneuver through tents than a building.

Karia was different from Zhalesh in that way. Even if it felt like Zhalesh was more advanced in many obvious ways, many ways that mattered, it still felt like too much. Karia was humble and simple. Maybe it wasn't an Old-World city like they had imagined, Zhalesh showed them that there was bigger, but it was still home.

Xeilani led the way through the sea of tents, which echoed with a cacophony of wheezing, coughing and moaning. Even though she had become desensitized to the sounds of the afflicted, she still felt a small pull in the depths of her stomach. These were the people that she had sworn to protect. The people that relied on her to bring a new dawn to humanity. Even now, as she and Xeilani made their way to a large tent that towered over the others, the tired and weary eyes of the sick citizens were trained on her.

“There she is...” A man moaned from inside one of the tents. She looked to see an older gentleman lying on his side in one of the tents, eyes deadened from whatever scourge plagued him. “It's the priestess...”

“Priestess Isobel...” Another man called from a tent close by. Soon more voices called out to her, each one more ragged than the last.

“Please...” A man called from his tent. “I need a new arm.”

She stopped to bow and acknowledge the people. As she did, a woman arose from within one of the tents and approached the duo. Her clothes were tattered and dirty beyond saving, and her hair was matted with a mixture of sweat and globs of dirt. But even in her unkempt state, she still had a smile bright as the stars on the surface and approached with a ball of bread.

“You bless us with your visage, priestess.” The woman mused as she handed the ball to Isobel.

“You have given enough.” Isobel smiled as she held the woman's hand. “Your deeds are noted by the Divines above, but please, there are others that need more than I.”

“You heal us with your kindness, priestess.” The smiled back as she backed away from Isobel.

A crowd of soldiers and citizens, sick and weary, formed around Isobel and Xeilani and blocked their way. They each fell to their knees, pressed their hands together and began to pray softly. Isobel immediately felt uncomfortable, but she couldn't find an exit in the mass of people.

"SO I'M GUESSING ANYONE THAT CAN MOVE IS FIT TO EAT BEANS AND BUGS AGAIN AT THE FRONT!?" A woman's voice boomed from a large tent in the center of the camp. "IF NOT, THEN I SUGGEST YOU ALL GO BACK TO YOUR TENTS AND CONTINUE TO REST BEFORE KNIGHT MORANSON DOES HIS ROUNDS!"

The crowd grumbled different responses to the woman's words, but ultimately were forced to disperse. Isobel wanted to breathe a sigh of relief at her rescue, but her breath was caught in her throat. She balled her hands up and looked down at the ground. She knew who the woman was. In fact, she was an old friend that she was very fond of. Someone that she had told many secrets too, studied for exams with, and helped her practice her arts. Someone that she couldn't look at because her shame wouldn't allow it.

"What is Isobel doing back here?" The woman asked as she approached. Isobel kept her eyes down as tears welled up in her eyes.

"She was acting a bit weird, so I guess I brought her here for a check-up." Xeilani replied. "But she seems fine to me though... Isobel?"

Isobel turned away from her. Her heart couldn't take it. She wanted to run away. Everything in her told her to run, to get as far away from here as possible. Up until now she had just been glad to be home, and obliviously traveled with Xeilani here, reminiscing about her home. She felt a hand on her shoulder and slowly turned to meet its owner. She met eyes with a smaller woman, whose skin was pale as snow, who had jet black hair that went down her back. Her purple eyes glistened like small gems in the dimly lit cave, and she smiled softly back at Isobel.

"You okay, love?" she asked Isobel softly as she smiled in that particularly comforting way that only she could. "You look like you've seen a ghost."

Isobel felt herself overcome with grief and regret. She felt lightheaded and hugged the woman tightly for many reasons.

"Hey, what's the matter?" The woman asked pulling away from her. "Tell Mama Mirela what's going on, and maybe I can dazzle you with my celestial medical acumen!"

"It's been so long since I've seen you." Isobel replied teary eyed.

"Weird joke, but okay." Mirela smiled back as she looked over Isobel. "Come to the main tent, I'll give you a quick glance. You're looking way rougher than you did a couple of hours ago."

Mirela grabbed Isobel by her arm and led her over to the tent, and Xeilani followed closely behind them. Isobel couldn't stop crying the entire time. As they got into the tent, Mirela sat Isobel down on one of the cots.

"Alright, let's see here..." Mirela said with a puzzled expression. She waved her finger in the air and the tip lit up slightly, like a miniature lamp. She wagged her finger back and forth in front of Isobel's eyes and examined her face. "She looks fine to me. Has anything new happened?"

"Nope." Xeilani slowly replied from her chair next to a desk. She shrugged and then casually laid her arm over the head of her seat. "We were supposed to return to the Chapel so Isobel could study and prepare for the Ceremony. But she was still freaking out about it, so I simply suggested we make better use of our time."

"You suggested that she skip on her prayers again, didn't you?" Mirela replied unamused.

"Nooooo...." Xeilani said as she crossed her arms. "I suggested she get a breath of fresh air. Regardless, she disappeared on me and was gone so long that Everett noticed. Now, I'm probably going to be scrubbing toilets till I die."

"My condolences." Mirela said sarcastically without looking her way. "Let's focus on Isobel. What happened, Isobel?"

"I-I don't know." Isobel said truthfully. "I was in Zhalesh, practically dying on a table. And then I woke up in the Dream field, unharmed and lost."

"Zha-what?" Xeilani said as she cocked her head at an angle. "Why does that sound familiar?

"Zhalesh... The beastmen capitol?" Mirela said with a raised eyebrow. "The same one that we've never been to?"

"Well, we've been to it." Isobel stated as she pointed at Xeilani.

"Woah, woah, woah!" Xeilani said with surprise. "We have never been to any Zellish or whatever it's called."

Mirela frowned slightly and felt Isobel's head.

"What are you saying, Isobel?" Mirela questioned her. "There's no possible way for you to have made such a journey. Does this..."

Mirela looked around the tent suspiciously. Isobel finally took a glance around, realizing that she wasn't the only individual being helped today. It wasn't completely full, but everyone else seemed far too self-involved with their own tasks to be paying any attention to them. Mirela leaned in closer to Isobel.

"Does this concern your visit earlier?" She whispered to her.

Isobel looked at her with a puzzled expression. Then the memory came rushing back. Today was the day that Isobel would finally have her ascension ceremony, and she went to Mirela to ask about the burdens of being a doctor. To be more specific, she wondered how Mirela felt about being a Divine Knight and one of the leading medical practitioners of the capital. And as she remembered, Mirela may have reassured her, at the time, but it didn't quell her trepidation or really give her clarity on her situation. She was too young then. And by the time she understood what Mirela was saying...

“No...” Isobel whispered back as she stood up. “Sorry, it was a bad joke. I'm fine. Really.”

“Bad time for jokes, Izelda.” Xeilani mocked from her seat.

“Don't call me that.” Isobel replied quickly shooting her a glare.

“Well, if you're feeling better then, I guess you're free to go.” Mirela smiled at their interaction. “But if you start to feel uncomfortable again, or have any doubts, you guys can always come see me. I’ll always be free.”

Mirela held her fist out, awaiting a bump. Isobel surprised her with yet another hug.

“O-oh, another one?” Mirela stammered. “You sure you’re, okay?

Isobel wanted to take this chance. Because for all she knew, the time-travel theory was about as solid as a house of cards, and this would be the last time she would see Mirela ever again. She felt her heart sting with that familiar regret she had buried beneath her ambitions, and hugged Mirela even more tightly.

“Okay, too tight!” Mirela choked out, breaking away from Isobel's grasp. “Jeez, Isobel! You are too strong to grapple with people for extended periods of time! I'm, like, twenty pounds smaller than you are! Are you trying to kill me or something?"

No, she wasn't. But Isobel wished she could spend more time embracing her friend.

"Sorry!" Isobel smirked at her. "I just can't stand not hugging someone so cute and adorable!"

"Don't give me that!" Mirela yelled at her. "I may be a little on the shorter side, but I can still give you guys a wallop!"

Xeilani rolled her eyes and walked over to them.

"My sisters..." Xeilani said as she put her hands on their shoulders. "As much as I truly enjoy both of your presences, me and Isobel have somewhere to be! If you're feeling better, let's make tracks before Sir Everett finds us!"

The woman nodded to each other and Xeilani moved to the exit of the tent.

"I'll be outside, but don't make me wait too long!" Xeilani warned before leaving.

Isobel turned back to Mirela who was just standing there, looking up at her.

"I'll ask a third time, are you sure?" Mirela asked, grabbing Isobel's hand.

"I'm fine." Isobel reciprocated, putting her hand over Mirela's. "But please... Take care of yourself, Mirela."

"I... Will?" Mirela said with a bit of confusion. "We're

both going to the front soon... You know that right? I'm not going anywhere where you won't be."

"I know." Isobel replied. "Just... Take care all the same, okay?"

"Alright, weirdo." Mirela smirked. "You have somewhere to be."

Isobel nodded at her and turned away, leaving the tent with a grimace on her face.

Four months from this day, Mirela died. She was sent out on a routine retrieval mission, with a small detachment of knights. It was meant to be an easy, peaceful trip outside of Karia in search of resources and wandering nomads. Unlike beastmen forces, who use crystals and mana to talk to each other, humanity relied on Old-World technology to communicate. But that week, the radios weren't working. There was no response from her group. They hadn't returned, and Isobel had grown worried. She begged the veterans to allow her to accompany the search parties, but they denied her plea. She was too valuable to humanity and the Divines. So, she had to sneak out with a group of soldiers. Jerak and Xeilani wouldn't allow her to do it alone and it took some convincing to get Chase to come along. It didn't take long for the search parties to find what was left of Mirela's group. What she remembered most... was the savagery. Their corpses were stripped of anything of worth, and they were just... abandoned in the mud.

But Mirela's had been strung up and made an example of. She was tied to a log...

Mirela died alone. Fighting, but alone, and probably filled with regrets herself. She wanted to save people. That was her life's mission and she studied as hard as anyone, if not more, to that end. She was their little sister and the beastmen had done that to her. She was kind, and confident. She had grown so much since their childhood. And they did that to her. Mirela wasn't the only thing that would be taken from them. Their lives in Karia didn't prepare them for the reality of war, even if they had spent years getting ready for it.

Isobel shook her head as she realized she had been standing still with her hand balled in a tight fist for a few moments. She didn't want to allow herself to have these thoughts. They distracted her from the Divine's guidance and her mission. But more importantly, they made her weak. And she couldn't be weak anymore, she had too much to lose.

"Earth to Isobel, you awake in there?" Xeilani waved. "You've been acting weird since we left class today."

"No, I'm fine." Isobel smiled at her. "I think I'm ready now."

"Alright, then I'll lead the way." Xeilani turned towards the church.

A tear-streaked down Isobel's face. She felt a pain in her chest, in her heart, as she looked at Xeilani. She couldn't find where the emotion was coming from. She felt like the fog in her mind was just from the confusion of being here, but something about Xeilani felt... Forgotten. Like she was missing something...

Isobel took a deep breath and caught up to Xeilani. Her eyes raised to look at the tower looming ahead. The Tower of the Divines...

*   *   *

Drakonis

Worried. Drakonis stared at the black cocoon, arms crossed, and tapped on his shoulder impatiently. After a few moments, he paced back and forth in the room. He had been repeating this same routine for the past thirty minutes.

"Boy..." King Maj said from behind him. The King had taken a seat next to the table and was just resting in the dimly lit room. "Pacing isn't going'ta make time pass any faster. Sit down and rest a while. You've been working yourself to the death for these kids, and I think you've earned a break. Since I met ya, you've been doing nothin' but workin'. Sit a spell, lad."

"I will not." Drakonis replied sharply. "What if she finishes her trial and I'm lounging about like some kind of restful dog or something? I need to be ready! In fact, let's go over what the trials actually are again."

"You really want me to go over that again, Drakonis?" King Maj questioned. "I can explain it till I'm blue in the face, but it won't make this process any less tense. Just give her time to complete her trial, and all will be fine."

"And what if she doesn't?" Drakonis glared back at the King.

"If she does not complete the trial..." Rohaz stated from the other side of the cocoon. "Then she will become possessed by my other half. We should be taking this opportunity to destroy them both while they are preoccupied."

"Quiet, you!" Drakonis pointed at the being. He had been so involved with Isobel's predicament, he had completely forgotten the spirit was there. "Your input was not warranted or needed! We are not killing Isobel!"

Rohaz, who was gently floating in the air as though he was sitting in an invisible chair, put his hand on his chest and raised his eyebrows at Drakonis. He had shed his appearance as a golden sword and now was a tiny gold man with a small cloth around his waist. He looked completely appalled by the tone that Drakonis took with him.

"I think... It's a good thing we know that Isobel is a strong lass that can take care of herself." King Maj interrupted. "I am completely confident that this trial will go as planned. Drakonis, you have yet to be wrong about any of your predictions. I wouldn't go and start doubting yourself now."

"I was confident in those 'predictions' precisely because they weren't predictions, King Maj." Drakonis said as he rubbed his face. "The events we faced were fated. The Fae told me as such. And while I am confident that I have not been lied to... These events that transpired were not as the Fae described."

"You've been going on and on about that." King Maj said as he leaned forward in his seat. As soon as he opened his mouth to continue, a huge black pulse of mana radiated through the room and pushed him back in his seat.

"What was that?" Drakonis glared at King Maj.

"I don't know." The Majen King shrugged before looking at Rohaz. "Divine Blade, do you have an explanation for that burst of energy?"

Rohaz tilted his head at King Maj, his eyes squinted in confusion.

"How could I possibly know?" He retorted. Rohaz crossed his arms at the two. "I have only been awake for a few moments."

"That's it!" Drakonis yelled as he balled his fists up and frowned at the spirit. He was thoroughly done with the clown show. He walked over to the cocoon and tried to lay his hand on it but was stopped by the familiar pressure of Rohaz.

"Stop!" Rohaz commanded as he raised his hand. "You cannot interfere with the trial. You refuse to euthanize her for the greater good, so you must trust in her strength to-"

"I refuse!!" Drakonis roared back at the spirit. "I've been holding back for Isobel's safety, but if you keep trying to stop me from assisting her, I swear I will do what must be done. Even if that means destroying a rare and extremely powerful enchanted weapon."

Rohaz stared at Drakonis for a bit, eyeing the dragonkin from top to bottom. Then he lowered his hand.

"Your resolve is admirable and a desirable trait in my search for a champion." Rohaz said with serious eyes. "Your trial will be extremely interesting. Allow me to lend my aid to my future wielder."

"Then help me." Drakonis said quickly.

Rohaz floated next to the cocoon and softly placed his hand on it.

"Usually, one cannot enter another's trial due to the nature of which our bonds are created." Rohaz explained as a soft golden light emitted from under his palm. "The trial is a test of compatibility and trust and binds metal to flesh. In short, our souls are bound to yours. To create a pure and unperverted bond, your mind, mana, and soul are locked off from the rest of the mana in the universe. But my other and I are different."

As Rohaz spoke, small golden cracks began to form in the cocoon. Blades of light shot from the cracks and lit up the room. Drakonis would have been more bewildered with the experience if he weren't already annoyed.

"We are one." Rohaz continued. "We are eternally linked, in birth and existence, and I can use my link to create a bridge into the trial. But you must know that this action will not go without consequence. Are you sure you can handle the repercussions?"

Drakonis looked down at the cracked, black mass on the table. He didn't know exactly what he was getting himself into, but he had no choice. He didn't just feel like it was his duty to bring Isobel back. He wanted to.

"I can." Drakonis said confidently.

"Then place your hand upon her tomb." Rohaz instructed. "Know that as soon as you are linked, you will be without protection from mental subjugation. Whatever affliction burdens her mind can and will infect yours as well."

Drakonis didn't have time to weigh the negatives. He placed his hand on the cocoon, which was ice cold to the touch. He kept his hand there for a few moments before turning to look at Rohaz.

"Nothing's hap-" He began. He was cut off by an intense cold running up his arm. He turned to see most of his arm being sucked into the cocoon. Then his fingers grasped something within the black mass. It felt like the hilt of a sword, and he firmly grasped it. He then took a breath and pulled, trying to pull the sword from out of the black mass. He couldn't place any reason behind his actions, he just felt compelled to do so. He grunted as he pulled, and a sharp pain shot through his head. It was like a dagger stabbing him directly in his brain.

"At long last!" A sinister voice hissed in his mind. "You are mine, spawn of D'Merrion!"

Then an explosion of mana burst out from the cocoon in all directions. Drakonis felt like his entire body was being torn apart, limb from limb. But he stood his ground as he used his grasp upon the hilt as an anchor. Then the force of the explosion reversed, and he felt himself being pulled into the mass. He tried to reach his hand out to stop himself from slamming into the black mass, but everything went black before he could raise his hand.

Nervous. Moments passed and for a while, Drakonis believed that his hubris had finally cost him everything. That this time, he had really bitten off more than he could chew. He felt himself breathing and felt relief. At least he was still alive in some sense. But something was off.

He felt his eyes were open and yet, he could not see. His hand was still balled into a tight fist around... Nothing. He realized that he was no longer holding his sword. He also noticed that he didn't hear his sigh earlier, but he definitely did sigh. Or did he? Where was he?

“The Fae...” He heard a voice say. It was a man's voice. It was far off but someone else was here.

“......” Drakonis called out to the voice. He tried to say hello, and while he definitely felt the word on his lips, he didn't hear it. It was like he was in nothing.

“I need you...” The voice spoke again. “To trust me.”

Drakonis figured that walking towards the voice would be better than just sitting around hearing broken sentences, so he cautiously proceeded towards the voice. He silently approached its origin, trying his best to be mindful of his steps.

"The Fae told me of a future..." The voice continued. "A future where we're free..."

As he got closer, he knew who the voice belonged to. It was his own.

"The Fae gave you a vision?" He heard Isobel reply.

"You expect us to just believe that!?" Chase rudely interrupted.

He remembered the conversation. It was only a few days before the festival, in the confines of a room completely warded from the outside. But why was he hearing it now? Where was he? He stopped for a moment and thought about what Rohaz had said.

Whatever affliction burdens her mind can and will infect yours as well.

Was he truly within Isobel's mind? Is this her memory?

"He was all I had," an elderly woman said, a bit of sadness in her voice. The words came from his right and Drakonis instinctively turned to face them. "My son died for nothing!"

"He gave his life for humanity, for a better tomorrow." He heard Isobel tell the woman.

"And yet, you've returned safely!" The woman scoffed. "Some knight you are!"

"You were supposed to protect us!" A man cried from the opposite direction.

"She can only do so much!" Chase's voice echoed from the same direction.

"What good is the Divine's power if you still lose!?" The man angrily screamed. "My daughter is DEAD!"

Soon more voices started chime in.

"Please Priestess!" A man screamed.

"Help us!" Another woman

"Where's my mommy?" A child whined.

The voices grew in volume.

What are you doing!? The Divines are frauds! Where is my family!? Her death is your fault, Isobel. He has gone too far! Failure!

A chorus of voices and insults filled the space. Drakonis covered his ears and started running in a direction. Any direction to get away from the voices. They were so loud it was almost like they were in his skull, deafening his thoughts. He felt like he was being bludgeoned to death with their words.

How could you let us die? How could you let us die? How could you let us die!?

The voices grew louder than anything Drakonis had ever heard. Louder than any explosion or blast. As Drakonis kept running and the voices grew louder, he saw something in the endless black... A small light. He took off as fast as he could towards the light.

The voices continued to attack his mind with their

insults, and he covered his ears even tighter in his vain attempt to keep them out. The run to the light felt like an eternity but his foot soon hit the light with a weighty 'plop'. He heard it.

"What in the god's name was that!?" Drakonis huffed while hunched over. He was completely out of breath. He couldn't even begin to understand where he was, let alone what he had just gone through.

He looked up and around to try and make out his new environment. As he looked up, he spotted a young girl sitting in the center of the white space. She was curled up into a ball and sniffled to herself. She had tattered clothes on, but her hair was brilliant and auburn. Just like Isobel's hair.

Drakonis walked over to the girl. She didn't react to his movement, like she didn't even notice he was there. He reached down to touch her, and a bright light emitted from her body, blinding him completely. He covered his eyes in a vain attempt to protect himself.

After a few seconds, he lowered his hands, squinting his eyes, and tried to make out where he was.

He was outside again. But this wasn't anywhere that he recognized. He looked up at the sky, which was bronze like a sunset, and the clouds were golden. But they weren't a normal kind of 'brightened by the sun' golden. These clouds were magnificently golden. He looked around himself and saw everything was gold! There were large, gold pillars that stretched beyond the clouds and seemed to go endlessly into the heavens. Even the floor was nothing but golden clouds, save for what looked like a small blue pool of water that sat a few feet from him.

Annoyed. Where in the world was, he? Was this another memory? Was this where the trial was taking place? Drakonis was tired of just stumbling about and he was even more frustrated that he hadn't located Isobel at all.

He looked around, searching for a door or building of any sort. He decided to walk over and examine the golden pillars in the hope that they would contain an exit or some kind of clue to escape his predicament. As he came closer to the golden pillars, he noticed that they contained markings that were very familiar to him. These markings resembled effigies and motifs that he had seen in the palace of Zhalesh. The same ones that accompanied the ugly golden and white color scheme of God King D'Merrion's palace. Drakonis couldn't understand how these same carvings could be here as well.

Drakonis heard a loud and obnoxious creaking noise ring out from behind him. He instinctively jumped behind the pillar he formerly scorned to avoid detection. He heard a chorus of feet march into the room, but the footsteps were far too light to be those of adults. He tried to listen to see if he could gauge how many had just entered this area, but for some reason, his senses felt dulled and compromised.

Great, he thought to himself, *another complication to an already complicated situation. Where did these people come from? There weren't any doors to be seen!* As Drakonis tried to make sense of what was going on and whether he could chance watching from behind the pillar, a serene and angelic voice echoed from the sky.

"Anilebelita Isobel Kierra Fawntasia..." The voice called from high above. "We have watched you from afar, as you have harnessed your latent talents for the betterment of humankind and all of Divine Creation."

"Isobel..." Drakonis whispered to himself. Maybe his luck was changing. He slowly peeked out from behind the pillar, trying to see if he could pinpoint Isobel's location, and tried his best to not be spotted.

He only noticed a tall, illuminated woman walking towards the pond in the middle of the pillars. *A Divine*, he thought. *Had to be*.

He hadn't seen one in person before, but she had the same menacing glow that D'Merrion projected when he channeled his aura. He was certain she was a Divine.

He could barely see what was going on in the pond, but from what he could make out, there was a small woman in the middle of it. He wasn't certain if it was Isobel or not, so he decided to continue watching for confirmation.

"You have proven yourself worthy of Divine

Ascension." The Divine continued. "But this power is not for the faint of heart. Your mind, soul, and body must be in complete alignment for Divine Power to take root within you. Otherwise, it will dissipate into nothingness and return to the stars. If you believe in yourself, then come take my hand..."

Drakonis peeked out a bit farther to look past the woman and noticed a group of knights. But not the large and well-trained knights that he had come to loath and combat. These knights were shorter in height, possibly children or squires. They each stood with their heads bowed as the scene played out. From what Drakonis could piece together, he somehow found himself spying on an Ascension Ceremony. And if this were another one of Isobel's memories, he could only assume that this had to be hers.

The Divine lowered her hand towards Isobel, who stared at it for a few moments. She then looked up at the Divine with some sort of conviction.

"I am ready." Isobel said firmly as she took the Divine's hand.

The Divine raised her other hand above her head, and droplets of water rose from the pool they stood within. They streamed gloriously into the air and wound through the air like an elaborate show or spectacle, before beginning to pool within the Divine's hand.

"Now my daughter, prove thyself and become the

Divine Knight you were always destined to be!" The Divine yelled into the sky." Prove thyself, and bring honor to House Fawntasia and the Divine blood of Aphermia that runs passionately in your veins!"

The water created a giant golden orb that glowed magnificently and pulsed with blue energy within the Divine's hand. The Divine lowered the orb and stopped only when it was a few feet from Isobel. She held it there, expectantly, for a few moments. Isobel looked at the orb and raised her hands to touch it, but stopped just before she made contact.

"I-I accept this honor." Isobel said as she reached for the orb. It slowly floated into Isobel's chest and began to merge with her aura.

Suddenly, thunder rumbled through the area and the golden clouds grew dark. Laughter echoed throughout the area, almost like it surrounded the ceremony from all sides.

"You are mine and now the power of the Divines is mine as well!" A voice cackled loudly from above them. Thunder rumbled again and then the wind began to pick up in the area.

The Divine backed away from Isobel, tossing her hand away.

"My daughter..." The Divine said tensely. "What have you done!?"

Some of the knights that were bowing before were now

rushing over to the pool. There was lightning striking now all around them.

"Guards!" The Divine yelled. "Remove her from the pool! If she pollutes its essence, humanity will lose any chance of survival. This will be the end of all Divine Knights! The end of HUMANITY!"

Before any of the guards could approach Isobel, Drakonis was already on the move. He leapt from his spot behind the pillar to protect Isobel. As he landed near her, the pool turned black and thickened over. It started to swirl violently and created a whirlpool that began to pull everyone into its center, even Drakonis.

Everyone in the room spun around Isobel, and slowly dissolved into the black tar whirlpool. Drakonis felt himself spin around violently and tried to grab something, anything, to rebalance himself, but it was no use. There was nothing within reach. The hot black goop swirled and tossed him around. He looked towards the middle and saw Isobel spinning unconsciously in the pool with everyone else.

"You were supposed to save us!" A young boy screamed at Isobel as he was consumed by the black waves. The screams of the young squires filled the air as they thrashed helplessly against the waves. Drakonis started pumping his arms and swimming with the current of the pool to try and reach Isobel.

"Aaargh!" Drakonis heard suddenly and a giant splash sent him flying from one side of the pool to the other. He was briefly submerged in the black ooze and felt his lungs burning. It was like the air was being stolen directly from his lungs. Then somehow, he found himself back above the black depths and spinning again. He looked around and saw that he was a few feet from Isobel and reached out towards her.

"Come on!" Drakonis screamed as he strained against the current. "ISOBEL!"

Just a bit more, he thought. Just a bit more...

*　　　*　　　*

Isobel

"Isobel..." A voice called out. Isobel's eyes fluttered but they refused to open. She was extremely comfortable and refused to get up.

"Isobel..." The voice called again, this time clearer than the last. Isobel stirred for a moment, but she refused to get up.

"Just a few more minutes..." she sleepily replied. She felt a hand on her back and shook her head.

"Wake up, sleepyhead." The voice said softly. "You can't save the world if you hide under your covers all day, my love."

Isobel didn't budge. She was really tired. Probably the most tired she had ever been. She just didn't want to get up.

"Isobel..." Another voice chimed in. This one was more masculine than the last. "Don't make us beg you, honey. Get up."

She just laid there. She felt like something important was happening. Like if she stayed here, she would miss something really life changing but she could not fathom getting up from her slumber. She wanted to stay here, and rest forever.

"Isobel...!" Another voice called out. This one was a little muddier, and harder to make out.

"Isobel!" The voice called again. This time louder and more pronounced. She heard sounds of water 'swooshing' and slushing about. It was like there was a torrent of rain and downpour happening right above her head.

"Isobel!" The voice yelled into her ear. Her eyes shot open, and she was staring eye-to-eye with Drakonis.

"Oh, thank D'Merrion." Drakonis grunted. He was struggling with something and slamming his arms into something. It sounded as though he was swimming.

Isobel felt herself being pulled but it wasn't towards Drakonis. She was spinning but not around. She felt herself rotating in something and examined her immediate surroundings. This was when she noticed that she was in a vat of water or a giant drain or something. She could tell it was warm water of some kind, but it was black and thick like molasses. She tried to move her body as well, but it felt heavy and didn't heed any of her commands.

"Isobel, don't worry." Drakonis tried to console her. There was some desperation in his voice. "We'll make it out of this, I promise."

It was funny. Isobel felt completely at peace, even though everything in her mind told her she was in danger. Isobel looked down into the center of the waters that she involuntarily rode within and saw a black hole. And she noticed that every rotation she did within the black waters took her a breath closer to its open maw.

She didn't feel like struggling anymore. In all honesty, she just wanted to give into the black. To go back to sleep.

"Isobel, what are you doing!?" Drakonis yelled as he pulled on her arm. "Come to me!"

She looked up at him, and then stared back at the black hole in the base of the water. Its cold embrace seemed more and more alluring the longer she stared. Another rotation passed within the black ooze and Isobel felt almost relieved, because she knew she was one step closer to the peace she sought.

She suddenly felt herself pulled into someone's embrace. Drakonis held her close to his chest and threw her arm over his shoulder.

"I know it is... not entirely... your fault..." Drakonis breathed heavily as he paddled with one arm. "But you are... really... REALLY... beginning to... get on my nerves!"

"Then let me go." Isobel ordered firmly. "Why are you struggling so hard to save me?"

"Because..." Drakonis grunted. "I WANT TO! And for once... I'm not... being commanded to do so! I'm getting you out of here... and back to your loved ones! To your family!"

"I don't have any family left!" Isobel yelled over the approaching tides. "The only people looking for me are the ones who have sworn their lives to my safety. Even if you're here for the same reason. Whatever this is... Wherever we are... I deserve this."

"Can we have this talk... AFTER we escape this whirlpool of death!?" Drakonis yelled as the rapids grew louder. Isobel looked down. The hole was only a few moments away. She felt relieved. Then she started to frown.

A black platform was rising out of the black ooze and took them up into the gray clouds. As they flew higher, Isobel looked down and understood what was happening. She had been saved, but only pain awaited her when she arrived. She tried to roll over to escape, but her body still refused to move. She was at the mercy of the black dragon. She was foolish to believe that she was free. Then she heard screaming coming from beside her.

She turned to see Drakonis clutching his head and screaming in pain. He began to writhe back and forth in front of her, howling bloody murder at the top of his lungs. Behind him, she could see the familiar green, reptilian eyes staring back down at them.

No, she thought to herself. She wanted to say it, but her body felt heavier every second she laid in the palm of the dragon. She knew where she was now. She was trapped in the black dragon's domain, and Drakonis must have had some kind of plan to come and save her. But he was a fool. Now he was trapped here with her, at the mercy of the old god. Their torture was only beginning.

“How disgusssstingly ssssweet of you to drop by, Drakonisssss.” The dragon hissed. “I commend you, my pet! I have never been happier! Not only did you bring him to me, but you also managed to get him to come to me of his own volition! Azzaria's mental barriers made it impossible to steal the great Drakonis away, but soon he will join you in eternal servitude. You both should feel honored-”

The darkness around the dragon stirred. It was barely noticeable, but it began to move within itself. It was as though there was an internal turmoil, and the black was fighting itself.

“NO, NO, NO!” The dragon roared. “Who dares enter my domain unannounced!?”

Isobel saw a soft blue light hover above her, a beacon of hope within the dark chasm.

"I dare!" The light mocked the dragon. "Isobel! Hurry and take my hand! But know that once you do, our union is irreversible. We will become-"

Isobel grabbed the light immediately. She didn't want to waste time listening to whatever consequences awaited her. Anything was better than this place.

A sword formed in Isobel's hand where the light had been. Isobel held it high above her head and it began to vibrate violently in her grasp. Then multiple rays of soft blue light burned away the darkness around them.

"GRAAAAAAAAAAAAAAGH!" The dragon screamed out in agony.

Isobel felt the weight from her body disappear completely. She stood up in the dragon's palm and looked at the sword in her hand. There was a soft blue hue that came from the curved, jagged blade and it hummed with a foreign power. She felt connected to it in a way that she had never been connected to anything before.

"Now is our chance, Isobel." The sword spoke. "Let us take back what was stolen so long ago. Let us break the shackles so that no man, beast, or god will ever hold us hostage again!"

Those words resonated with Isobel, and she felt words

pour into her mind. Unfamiliar and yet, exactly what she wanted to say.

"Through the ebb and flow of time and patience, let all within this plane of existence and those adjacent behold!" Isobel screamed as she raised the sword high. "Heaven and Earth's Final Machination! The real Infinitum! Divine DETONATION!"

As the words left her mouth, the sword turned bright red and flashed bright in the darkness, sending light throughout the realm. Isobel looked down to see Drakonis holding his throat, eyes wide in surprise. He then began to fade away with the rest of the world. The dragon howled as the bright light overtook him.

"I WILL HAVE MY REVENGE!" The Black Dragon roared as the world burned away. "YOU WON'T ESCAPE MEEEAAAAAAAAAAAAAAAAAGH!!"

Isobel blinked and realized she was staring at the ceiling. She sat up on what felt like a pile of rocks and felt a hand on her back, helping her rise. It was Drakonis with a worried expression. She looked down and saw she was on a rotting wooden table and inside of yet another dark room. This one didn't inspire any feelings of anxiety for her though.

"Are you alright?" Drakonis asked cautiously.

Isobel shook her head. She didn't feel the fog in her mind that blocked her thoughts. She didn't hear any whispers that weren't hers either… He was gone. Finally, the dragon was gone!

"For once, I am." She smiled back at him.

"Yeaaaaahahaha!" A voice cheered from her other side. She turned to see King Maj dancing. "It worked, haha! It worked! It worked!"

She did a quick once over of her body, just to make sure. Most of her skin had returned to normal, but the dragon mark had moved. She wasn't sure where it was now. She could feel it before, but now it seemed to be gone.

"Is the mark gone?" She said softly.

"No, but it is sealed." A voice called to her. "You didn't pass my trial by the way, but I like you. I think I will give you an exception, all things considered."

"And who are you?" Isobel said puzzled.

"Rajani, Blade of Infinite Destruction and Chaos." The Voice replied. "I am an avid consumer of dark mana! Honestly, you were completely filled with the stuff. It was poisoning you in and out, but I fixed all that. You're good as new now! I believe a 'Thank you' is in order!"

"Thank you, Rajani." Isobel smiled.

"Up here!" The voice spoke again.

Isobel looked up to see a small fairy sprite floating above her. It gave off a soft blue hue and danced around her.

"And I wasn't talking about me!" Rajani stated as it

floated over to Drakonis. “This idiot invaded a spirit quest so he could save you from a deity. I think he's overdue for a reward. Even if he did interrupt my test.”

Isobel looked down at her hand and noticed that Drakonis was still holding it. She lightly pulled her hand away but noticed that there was something red in her palm. Fresh blood.

“Is there something wrong with your hand, Drakonis?” She asked.

Drakonis quickly jumped next to King Maj and slid his hand behind them.

“Nothing you need to worry about!” He said with a straight face. “Just a minor cut I received while transporting you.”

“Let me see it then.” Isobel pressed as she got up from the table.

“You need your rest.” Drakonis tried to dissuade her.

“Let me see.” She kept on.

Drakonis sighed and then revealed his hand. It was shriveled, purple, and withering away. There was a hole in the center of it, and the flesh smelled rank and grotesque. Rajani laughed a bit to herself.

“Simple cost of interrupting my trial, half born!” She jeered. “Be glad it was only a hand and not your heart.”

Drakonis grit his teeth at her, but quickly turned his

attention back to Isobel, who was pressing down on his hand. She then turned to King Maj and placed her hands on his head as well.

"Allow me." Isobel said before she started humming. While she hummed, a soft golden glow radiated from her hands. Her core felt good as new, if not better than before. It was almost like she had a bigger mana reserve than before. The incantation felt extremely potent. Drakonis' hand began to reform, muscle by muscle, and the blood disappeared from King Maj's eyes and hands. Drakonis gave his hand a good grip and then turned to Isobel.

"Thank you." He said genuinely.

"No." she said softly back to him. "Thank you, for not giving up on me and for saving my life when I had given up on myself. I know I wanted to let go, but you brought me back. Thank you so much, Drakonis."

It was obvious that he wasn't expecting such a sincere apology, and he turned away in response.

"Yeah, it was my pleasure." He spoke. "You kind of saved my life too, you know..."

"As much as I enjoy this personal bonding time, I am still Champion-less!" Rohaz exclaimed loudly. "You have no time to rest, young dragon! Let us begin our heroic trial immediately."

"Let me rest a few moments-" Drakonis started to say.

"Justice waits for no man!" Rohaz yelled and a bright light engulfed the room.

Chapter 19:
Peace of Mind

Drakonis

Drakonis held his hand in front of his face while his eyes adjusted to the light. He groaned in frustration; He was getting extremely sick and tired of being blinded every few minutes. He lowered his hand and found that he wasn't in the confines of the hidden room anymore. Actually, he was in a giant green field of grass that sprawled out in all directions as far as the eye could see. He took a moment to check the field and the sky for landmarks that could give him some sort of familiarity, but realized it was a fruitless venture.

He looked around and tried to make sense of his surroundings. As he gazed upon the rows and rows of grass, he did something a bit out of character for himself; He decided to close his eyes and just bask in the sun's rays and the soft breeze of the field. Even if all of this was an illusion, he welcomed the change in pace from the chaos of the last couple of months. It had been a while since he felt this at peace. He was really missing his little patch of land under the Tree of Life right about now.

He started to remember the peaceful afternoons he

would spend under its majestic glow when he heard a whistling noise coming towards him. He barely managed to open his eyes when something struck him dead in the center of his skull. The blow sent him crashing to the grass and he grabbed his head, which was now throbbing painfully. Ow.

"I told you to look out…" A man's voice called over to him. "The ball didn't hit you too hard, did it?"

Drakonis looked in the direction of the voice, trying to get a good look at the figure approaching him, but he couldn't get his eyes to focus. There was a ringing in his ears and his eyes refused to center on the man.

"Hey." The man said while reaching down to him. "Let me help you up."

Drakonis slapped the man's hand away.

"Don't touch me!" Drakonis commanded instinctively.

"Woah there, son!" The man said with shock in his voice. It seemed apparent that he wasn't expecting that reaction and he put his hands up defensively.

Drakonis tried to get up, but he was too dizzy to stand. That was a sensation that he found confusing because there was no way that a simple man throwing something at him would cause him to feel such pain. It must be a result of the illusion. It had to be. Drakonis felt a set of hands under his armpits trying to lift him.

"Come on, son." The man said as he tried to lift

Drakonis again.

"I told you not to touch me!" Drakonis yelled as he pushed the man's hands away again. He looked up to the man, trying to get a good look at his face, but the man just wouldn't come into focus. He could barely make out the man's shape. Why was he so dizzy?

"Now, I know getting walloped in the face was not the best feeling in the world, but I'm just trying to help you, Koni." The man stated. Drakonis was taken aback at the mention of his childhood nickname. "I would never do anything to purposely harm you. Now stop being a brat and let me help you!"

Drakonis felt the man grab his chin firmly in his hand and turn his head to the left and right as he searched for signs of injury. While the man looked over Drakonis' body, Drakonis' vision was finally coming back to him. It was just in time to see his arm be lifted into view and for him to notice how… infantile… it looked. The man dropped his arm and began to scratch his head.

"You look outwardly fine to me." The man said while sighing. "Let's… not tell your mom about this, shall we?"

Drakonis didn't respond. He was too busy examining his extremely tiny arms and legs. He grasped at his head and even noticed that his fabulous afro wasn't so large and beautiful. He was a kid!

"I'm a kid!" Drakonis yelled in confusion.

"Well of course, dummy!" The man said in a very-matter-of-fact way. "I don't see why you would be confused about that."

"I shouldn't be a kid!" Drakonis yelled back at the man. He finally got a good glimpse of the man's face, and his words caught in his throat. Impossible. He saw the man's familiar large, round face and his broad shoulders that made him look like he could carry several large boxes at once. The man also had a weird scar on his eyebrow that might make someone that didn't know him think he was a vagrant or some kind of highwaymen. But Drakonis knew him very well, and it was something that made him feel right at home.

"I shouldn't be a kid!" The man mocked as he smiled back at him. A smile that Drakonis had missed over the years and that gave Drakonis a confusing mixture of comfort and pain. "That is a ridiculous statement. And since we're on the subject of 'ridiculous,' how about you answer a quick question? Why in the god's name didja just stop moving? We were in the middle of a game, and you just went all bug-eyed on me."

Drakonis was so taken back by just seeing the man that he didn't realize he was just staring blankly back at him. When he realized the man had been waiting on an answer, he quickly shook his head.

This is an illusion, he thought. From what Drakonis

could surmise, the trials had something to do with their past, and he decided at this moment not to be surprised by what he saw here. That was the only way forward. He took another second to collect himself and then decided to play along, at least until he knew exactly what he was supposed to do to complete the trial.

"I-I spaced out." Drakonis stammered.

The man hunched over for a moment, and his black hair covered his eyes. He then raised his head and made one of the most disgusting faces Drakonis had ever seen.

"I know you spaced out!" The man growled at the boy. "I was asking why!?"

The pair stared at each other for a moment, then they both just broke out in laughter. A pure laughter that could only be shared between a loving father and his son. A love that Drakonis had not experienced for years, even with Xinovioc.

"Come on, Koni." His father said as he hoisted Drakonis onto his shoulders. "Let's get you home, ya little joker. If we're late for dinner again, your mother's going to fry us both!"

The man then quickly took off into a sprint, and Drakonis grasped at his father's hair to keep from falling off. Wind and familiar sights rushed past his head as they went speeding down a small road. Dirt was kicked high into the air by the man's feet as he barreled down the dusty trail at an insane speed. Drakonis couldn't even make out where they were going for a while.

While Drakonis did feel a little awkward about riding atop the man's shoulders, his small size felt out of place and unbalanced, riding on his father's shoulders as they blasted through the countryside used to be one of Drakonis' favorite activities and he took the opportunity to embrace the feeling. He raised his hands high above his head and let the feeling of the wind and dirt smack him right in the face.

"Oh!" His father yelled at him. "Having fun, Koni? Well, how about I take it up a notch, huh?"

The man then started running even faster, picking up plumes of plants and bugs off the ground. Drakonis couldn't stop himself from smiling profoundly at the excitement. He couldn't even match the speeds his father was able to reach in his actual body.

Suddenly, his father jammed his legs into the earth to halt their momentum. As Drakonis looked up, he noticed that they had made it to their manor in the wilds. It was the only building for miles and honestly, now that the sun was setting behind it, it looked more like a mountain than an actual house. The thing was, they were still going too fast and the distance between them and the large house was drastically decreasing.

"We're going too fast!" Drakonis pointed out to his father. "Slow down!"

"Don't worry, I got this." The man exclaimed as he jammed his hands into the ground as well. His sudden stop kicked up all manner of dust and gravel from the path, until they came to a complete stop but a few feet from the door of the manor. As the smoke cleared, Drakonis looked down to see his father wiping his forehead of sweat and dusting himself off. He then lowered Drakonis to the ground and cleared his face of any debris that had built up in their run.

As the man, quickly tried to tidy their outfits and faces, Drakonis stared at the manor behind him. It was like a small palace with a bright blue exterior that had a small white bench on the large porch in the front of the building. The extremely large manor was his childhood home and where he learned most of his manners and martial skills. He turned his head to look at the front gates, where some soldiers were stationed and dusting themselves off. They didn't seem phased by the large cloud of smoke that had formed over them suddenly. Once they confirmed that it was his father that had caused the chaos, they returned to their duties without worry.

"Alright, we're somewhat presentable." The man smiled as he stood up and stared down at Drakonis. "Guess I'll just have to face the music."

The doors of the manor slowly creaked open, and Drakonis recognized the two maids almost immediately. They walked to opposing sides of the door and bowed their heads.

"Welcome home, Master Adel." They said in unison.

"Thank you, ladies!" Adel said with a large smile. "Hey, do me a solid; Is my endearing and amazingly loving wife in her usual chipper mood or should I leave the door open for escape?"

One of the maids, Ceesa, scowled back at him. She was a well-built woman with dark skin, and an extremely muscular body. Drakonis didn't think about it too much as a child, but she had the physique of someone who had undergone extensive physical training. She also had long black hair that was tied into two enormous ponytails.

"You're ten minutes late to a dinner that she has planned for weeks." She grumbled. "You know what mood she is in."

The other maid, Faye, nervously smiled back at Adel. She was taller than Ceesa, and not as muscular, but her muscles were still impressive all the same. Even though her extremely pale skin was a rare and exotic sight, that wasn't the weirdest thing about her. She had deep black eyes, and if not for the direction of her head, one could never really tell what she was looking at.

"I'm sure you'll be fine!" She waved him off, but then she paused for a moment. "Actually… On second thought, maybe you should go ahead of Drakonis and butter her up a bit. You know, just in case, my lord!"

"You two could dissuade birds from flight with those attitudes." Adel remarked irritably. He turned to Drakonis and dropped two large hands onto the boy's shoulders. "Okay, son. As my only spawn and the gem of my soul, I need you to stay here and guard the front of the home. A fire breathing beast lurks in the center of this massive dungeon, and I must go quell its mighty rage. Pray for your brave and loving father, son! Pray for his soul!"

Drakonis frowned at the man, not amused by his dramatic display. He had forgotten how animated his father's personality was, especially when it came to dealing with "The Beast." He sighed softly and smiled back at the man.

"Yes, father." He replied politely. "I will wait here, as you have asked."

Adel smiled back down at the boy and gave him a strong hug. He then flicked him on the forehead. "Don't take that 'proper' tone with me!" He grinned. "What have I told you? You may be asked to be polite and treat others with respect, but don't forget to express yourself. You are not a servant. You will be a mighty knight one day. And you should remember that dull knights make for dull stories."

Drakonis rubbed his forehead, annoyed, and made a face at him. The maids snickered behind Adel and the man stood up.

"Okay, watch after the boy while I go meet my wife,

will ya?" He asked the maids as he walked by. "Oh, and he's not feeling too well, can you get to the bottom of that as well?"

"As you wish." They both replied in response.

Adel then closed the large doors behind himself, leaving them in the afternoon heat. The two maids then turned to Drakonis with mischievous grins on their face. They slowly approached him and Drakonis put his hands up, ready for a fight. He didn't like where this was going.

"What's going on, pipsqueak?" Ceesa said as she smiled smugly. "Baby need a binky? Not feeling too well, are we?"

Faye followed closely behind her with the same smug look on her face.

"You want some elixir for your poor mood?" She grinned down at him.

Drakonis crossed his arms and smiled back at them. "I guessed it's expected of two old witches to tease a young boy when he's sick." He shot back at them. "I didn't know the servants of this house were such opportunists."

"Who are you calling a witch!?" Ceesa said as she gritted her teeth and balled up her fist. "You want to go kid!?"

"Anytime you want!" Drakonis replied with excitement.

Then he felt a sharp pain on his ear and noticed a hand on Ceesa's ear as well. They both rang out with a chorus of 'Ow' and 'Oh.'

"It is improper of a maid and a prince to act out in this manner." Fay said as she kept a tight grip on their ears. "I suggest you both gather yourselves lest you both would like to become the newest additions to the estates flag posts. We have a dinner to attend in but a few moments, and I'd rather you both not be maimed and irresponsible beforehand. I hope the idea appeals to you both."

"Yes, ma'am!" Ceesa and Drakonis yelped in unison.

Faye smiled and then released their ears from her iron grip. As Drakonis recovered from the stinging pain that burdened his ear, a flood of memories came to him, each another vivid scene of his ear being stretched and tortured by Faye's vice-like grip. He smiled thinking about the fun times they had. The fun times he and the 'real' Faye and Ceesa had.

"Now that you've both have calmed down for a moment, are you actually not feeling well?" Faye asked with some concern. "We do have some remedies for an upset stomach or the flu."

Drakonis continued to rub his ear and scowled in Faye's direction.

"You started that." Drakonis mumbled loud enough for her to hear.

She responded by flexing her hand in front of him, a sign that her hand was ready for a second helping of ear. The multiple audible pops that came from her knuckles sent a chill down his spine.

"No, I'm fine." Drakonis said as he nervously smiled at her.

"Good!" Faye said with a smile of her own. "Then we'll just wait for your father to conclude his talk with the lady of the manor, and then proceed to dinner!"

Drakonis nodded, and the doors to the manor swung open. Adel stood in the doorway with a large grin on his face.

"Coast is clear, son!" He said with excitement. "Let's get us some grub! Ceesa! Faye! Make sure that every servant gathers in the main hall for the banquet! Tonight, is a joyous occasion!"

The maids bowed respectfully and retreated towards the gate to begin their mission. Adel looked down at Drakonis and beckoned the boy forward with his hand. Drakonis walked forward and took his father's hand. He then looked down at the ground and took a deep breath.

He knew what awaited him inside the home. And as the dinner grew closer, he began to understand what day was going to transpire. It was a day that he loathed for many years. One that he never truly got over or forgotten.

He tried hard to ignore it, hoping that maybe Rohaz wouldn't be so ruthless to choose his darkest memories to torment him with. But it seemed like even spirit weapons had no love for him.

The memory that Rohaz chose for his trial was the day that Drakonis found out that his entire childhood was a lie.

*　　　*　　　*

Isobel

Isobel held the small warm cup in her hands. She eyed the drink with suspicion because she saw something green and brown swirl around in its center. She sniffed it a bit and grimaced at its intensely sour and repulsive smell. She looked back over at King Maj who had finished sipping at his drink and was pouring another. When he had finished, he looked up at her. She smiled and took a sip of the rancid-smelling drink. Her tastebuds felt like they were being smelted away by the fluid as she drank the foreign liquid. She gagged, but forced herself to continue drinking so she would not insult the Maj. She had only gotten halfway through the painfully intense experience when she realized that she couldn't continue and lowered the cup from her lips.

King Maj nodded towards Isobel and raised his mug.

"Just as good as I said, right?" The man smirked at her. "Right?"

Isobel pursed her lips and smiled back at King Maj, nodding in agreement. He had just saved her life. The least she could do was praise whatever this weird concoction was.

Although, it made her miss the comforting, and sweet taste of Xinovioc's lemonade.

The Maj let out a loud guffaw and joyously took another swig of his drink, visibly savoring the taste. Isobel decided that she needed a few moments to recover from her first sip. She and King Maj were sitting around the table that she had previously laid at during her trial. Drakonis sat peacefully on the ground with the sword, Rohaz, in his hands. Isobel worried for him because his breathing was slow, so much so that she didn't know if he was actually breathing or not. Noticing her worry, Rajani had reassured her that he was fine, though. The sword reasoned that Rohaz took a liking to Drakonis and wouldn't intentionally kill his potential champion. Afterwards, Rajani circled around Drakonis endlessly.

"So…?" Isobel said as she spun the cup slowly in her hand. "Would you happen to know what kind of test Drakonis will be tested with, King Maj?"

The old man rolled his eyes and groaned. He quickly swallowed the rest of his drink and slammed it on the beaten and old table.

"You and the lad are insufferable!" King Maj huffed, pointing at her. "I told him as many times as I have told you… I do not know what the trials are going'ta be! That answer does not change no matter how many times ya ask."

He had obviously gone through this scenario with Drakonis as well and it seemed like rehashing the subject put him in a foul mood.

"I'm sorry." Isobel apologized. "I don't mean to pry, but I just worry for his wellbeing is all. You can understand that sitting here idly can make one very uneasy. Especially when I know what he's going through… Who knows what horrible memory he's being forced to relive."

King Maj sighed and smiled softly back at Isobel.

"I know, child." He responded. "As I have told the boy, there is no point in worrying our heads. Being patient and having faith in each other is how we'll get through this."

Rajani, who was floating around Drakonis like a predator waiting for an opening, stopped moving for a moment.

"Our trials are designed to target fears and weaknesses in our champions." The sword hummed. "We do not pursue warriors that desire obscurity. A champion must be willing to overcome any and all obstacles to attain their goals. Otherwise, they are no different than the thousands of beasts that look just as they do. They, in their core, must be unique. They must become as gods themselves."

King Maj made a face and raised his eyebrow at the sword.

"You speak as though you've done this many times before, but this is the first time I have ever heard of something like this." The King said inquisitively. "I'm sure there are not just hordes of spirit swords floating around."

The sword zipped over to them, in-between Isobel and King Maj, and silently floated in the air. It stayed silent like it was contemplating something or maybe considering its options.

"You could not fathom what Rohaz, and I are, Maj." Rajani said suddenly. "Your thought that we are of Majen creation, of your creation, is completely and utterly wrong. You believe us to be instruments crafted by your hands, but in actuality, YOU are but an instrument yourself, used to give us form. We are beings that exist outside the rules of any reality you understand. We predate existence and the gods that created it. Before your gods could walk or even harness power, we existed. Before any Fae crafted time and manipulated its flow, we existed. And after all existence crumbles to dust, we will always, and will forever exist."

Isobel's and King Maj's eyes widened at the confession, and they stayed silent for a moment. Isobel found herself overwhelmed with the information. She didn't even know where to begin.

"Did you say…" Isobel began.

Rajani then suddenly turned back to Drakonis.

"It begins!" Rajani roared.

Isobel wanted to ask her what she had meant by what she had said, but she didn't have to wait long to find out. At that moment, Drakonis' hands erupted a bright white flame. The flame was so hot that even though Isobel was a few feet away, she could feel the warmth on her face. Both King Maj and Isobel jumped from their seats.

"Arrgh!" King Maj groaned. "Drakonis is failing his trial!?"

"We have to put out the fire!" Isobel yelled.

Both quickly searched around the room, looking for something to smother the flame. The whole room was fully lit now from the white flames that radiated from Drakonis' hands. Rajani jumped in front of front Isobel, stopping her cold in her tracks.

"What are you doing?" The sword hissed at her. "This is the perfect time to repay them for the disrespect they gave us! Use me to strike them both down, and we will never have to deal with my brother or his champion again!"

"NO!" Isobel shot back at her. "We are not killing them!"

She pushed past the sword and tried to continue her search, but the sword relented.

"Isobel!" The blade yelled. "Stop this foolishness! Allow him to perish and destroy his body!"

"What is with you?" Isobel asked as she grabbed the sword by the hilt. "Why do you want to end your brother… You know what? Don't answer that. I just had an amazing idea.

Let me enter Drakonis' trial. The same way he entered yours!"

As Isobel held the sword, she felt connected to the it. It was like they were sharing minds or something like that. At the very least, she could sense the sword's emotions and as of right now, the sword disliked the idea. It abhorred the thought. But rather than argue, she felt the sword give in to her demand.

"Ok." Rajani agreed. The air around the sword grew cold and the mana in their vicinity grew dense, so much so that it started to frost over and counter-act the intense heat of Rohaz's flames.

"We will enter his trial…" Rajani yelled. "And disrupt his test! Show me your resolve, wielder of mine! Push forward in this road of chaos!"

Rajani laughed merrily and Isobel opened her mouth to object to the plan, but her consciousness began to fade, and she felt light-headed. She tried to reach out with her other hand to balance herself, but everything went black before she touched anything.

A moment later, Isobel felt something rough and wet slide up her face. Her eyes shot open and she locked eyes with a beast with black spots on its white body.

"Ugh, gross!" Isobel groaned quickly.

Before she could react, the beast licked her face again and she instinctively pushed its head away. Isobel rolled over onto her feet and reached down for her sword, but it wasn't floating beside her.

Isobel immediately wondered where on Earth the sword could be, but she heard a whistle come from behind her. She turned around and saw a small, glowing blue sprite on a bale of hay.

"Watch out!" Rajani cheered.

Isobel turned back to the beast with spots, and noticed it was faster than she expected. It was already upon her, and was shoving its face into hers, licking her again. She raised her hand to smash it in its face when it pressed its nose against her stomach. She took a deep breath and put her hand on its head. She had come to the conclusion that it was harmless, even if it ranked among one of the most disgusting things she had ever seen. She heard a snicker behind her and turned to look at Rajani, who sounded like she was trying to stifle her laughter.

"I honestly thought you were going to make soup out of that beast." Rajani laughed. "What? Never seen a cow before?"

"A what?" Isobel said with her face wrapped in confusion. Then after taking a moment to think, recounting an animal compendium she had read one time, she realized what the animal was. "Oh, a cow. A mammal that predated the War of the Divines and was commonly used for agriculture, farm work, and often sacrificed for food."

"Exactly, wielder!" Rajani agreed. "There aren't too many of these where you come from?"

"None, actually." Isobel sighed. "Where I'm from, we primarily eat vegetables and bread."

The cow lowered its head to the ground and started eating the grass at Isobel's feet. It seemed to lose all interest in her at that moment.

What a weird animal, Isobel thought to herself. She took a moment to look around and examine her surroundings. She was in a field, but it was surrounded by a wooden fence. Maybe it was owned by someone?

She walked over to the fence and Rajani raced to her side. The duo looked around and noticed that there was a road and a pond just a few feet away. As Isobel examined the pond, she saw there were fish in the water, swimming without a care in the world. The sun was also setting in the distance, and it was going to get dark soon. If Isobel couldn't find Drakonis, she needed to at least secure shelter for the night.

"Where are we, Rajani?" Isobel asked.

"I don't know, wielder." Rajani said flatly. "Maybe you should investigate a bit. I'd like to see how capable my wielder is. Don't worry, I'll rest on your hip until you require my assistance."

Rajani then turned into a sword and latched itself to Isobel's side. This was not an ideal situation for her. Everything she was seeing now was something she had only read in a book. She had never seen green fields of this size, or even still water on land that had animals living in it. The ash from burning debris and destruction of war had ruined most of the ecosystems she had experienced. Isobel rubbed her forehead in frustration, and then decided to take another look around. Maybe she had missed something that could lead her to Drakonis.

As she looked at the road, she noticed a house up on the hill in front of her. It wasn't particularly huge so maybe it was a small cottage. She could ask the owner a few questions and maybe get some insight into her current situation. She climbed over the fence and started to walk towards the house.

She felt a little nervous walking up the road alone, only because she was in a foreign place. She still couldn't get over how 'real' the trial illusions felt. Everything, from the wind to the crunching of rocks under her boot, and the heat of the sun emulated real life so well.

"One could get lost in here, if given the opportunity." She said aloud.

"It is made from the memories of reality." Rajani chimed in. "Perception shapes reality. Thus, if the trial does not fit the participant's perception of reality, the illusion would fail due to lack of immersion. It is a spell designed to make you forget the fact that this is not reality. To enthrall you with fantasy and force you to grow."

"So, in short, if the test taker isn't immersed, the test

will cease?" Isobel asked.

"Exactly." Rajani replied. Isobel could feel that Rajani was impressed with her quick understanding. "There was a point that you realized the reality of your trial was false. But your mind was shackled by suggestion from the Black Dragon. The interference from my brother and the dragon led me to end the trial prematurely and accept you as my champion."

Isobel rubbed her neck where the mark used to be.

"I never got the chance to ask…" Isobel started. "Is my mark gone now? Obviously, I am not still under the control of the dragon, but did it truly disappear?"

"Oh, it's still on your neck." Rajani said happily. "I am capable of many great and wonderous feats, but I need to eat to accomplish them. I would rather eat the rich and supple dark mana of an old god than the mediocre and shallow mana of a human, no matter how remarkable that human may be. Now I simply drain the mark of its power, limiting your connection to the dragon, but not severing it. And the mark exists as a black dragon around your neck rather than the mark of an acolyte."

Isobel wanted to inquire more about what any of that meant, but the house grew closer, and she didn't want to openly talk to herself. She had no clue if it would matter or not, but if this trial was anything like hers, then the people would interact with her just as real people do. She thought it better to not take any risks.

As Isobel walked closer to the domicile, she noticed that it wasn't alone. There was a towns-worth of houses and buildings and they weren't the same kind of cobbled together homes from Zhalesh or Karia that were built inside of burnt-out buildings from the old age. These were humbly thatched houses and brick buildings with wood and dirt.

Isobel was surprised to see all these buildings atop the hill, but now considering the location of the town, she could see it was an easily defendable location. With the right placement of a detachment of archers, and a platoon of strong-arm warriors, this would be a hard town to crush. But oddly enough, there weren't any walls or guard towers around it. As she got closer, she even saw that the town was racially mixed. Beastkin and humans were all going about their lives in the town, just like Zhalesh.

"How do you do!?" A high-pitched voice said from behind her. Isobel tensed up a bit, anticipating an altercation but when she turned, she was greeted by a tiny man with large ears. "I haven't seen you before! Are you a traveler?"

The small man had tattered clothes and an equally rugged and dirty grey beard. He walked over to Isobel holding some kind of farming instrument.

"Yes!" She said with excitement. "My people are nomadic and I'm on a soul-searching journey through the countryside!"

"Are you now?" The man said as he cocked his head. "Now, I never heard of a nomad with such extravagant clothes!"

Isobel looked down at her outfit and groaned. She forgot that she was still wearing the outfit that was put together by Therron for the festival.

"This outfit was actually a gift from the Royal Tailor, Therron." Isobel said quickly with a smile.

"OH!" The main gasped wide-eyed. "So, you've been to the capitol? How is it!? Is it as grand as everyone says it is!? How is the food!?"

Isobel immediately felt herself being overwhelmed by the onslaught of questions when she noticed a larger, tanned man walking over to them. He had a grey beard with specks of black in it and was balding a bit in the center of his head.

"Leave her be, Leddy." The taller man told the small man. "We don't need you pesterin' all of our guests now, do we?"

Leddy turned to the tall man and was practically jumping up and down.

"But she has been to the capitol!" He said excitedly.

"And so have I." The tall man said unenthused. "Let the lass be on her way."

"Doh..." Leddy groaned. "You never let an old man have any fun."

"Fun is for the young, Leddy." The tall man said as Leddy walked away. He turned back to Isobel and gave her a soft smile. "Sorry about that, lass. Old Leddy loves visitors and stories about the capitol. Spent his whole life here in Venek."

"Oh, it's no trouble at all!" She said as she waved her hands defensively.

"Well then, my name is Finerdhil!" The man said changing the subject. "And welcome to the small, humble town of Venek. I'm the leader of this here town, and I ask that you do not hesitate to make yourself comfortable and at home! If you don't mind my askin', what's such a beautiful lady doing traveling by her lonesome in the countryside?

"I'm just passing through." She replied. She could tell that the man was a little suspicious of her answer. Hopefully he wouldn't inquire too much more about her true intentions. Finerdhil rubbed his chin and pointed to a two-story building with a very shabby steel sign.

"Well, if you're going to spend the night or even want just food, drink, and a decent conversation, head over to the Freedom Tavern." He said finally. "It's getting late, and I wouldn't recommend the roads at night. We've been having a string of disappearances as of late."

Isobel nodded at Finerdhil.

"Thank you for the warning." She said as she walked past the man. "I think the tavern will be a nice change of pace from the road."

"Glad I could help." Finerdhil said as he waved her off. "If you have any more trouble, I stay in the largest house next to the center of town. Come bother me."

Isobel walked through the small town making her way to the tavern. Citizens of the town waved at her, and smiled as they wished her a 'good evening' and showered her with gifts of food and cloth. The townspeople were very friendly. But something about their kindness seemed… Fake. In fact, now that she thought about it, both Finerdhil and Leddy didn't stop smiling the entire time she talked to them. It was eerie, to say the least. But Isobel shook those thoughts away. Maybe she would have better luck finding Drakonis at the tavern.

As she approached the entrance, she spotted a barrel next to it. She quickly stashed all of her 'gifts' in the barrel. They weren't real and of any real use anyway. Some of the people who had given her some of the items already entered the building, so she didn't worry about being caught trashing the goods.

She opened the large doors to the building, half expecting to see large, burly men with frothing drinks in their hands. But as she glanced over the populace of the building, there wasn't a single degenerate in sight. Karia only had two taverns, but both were places she'd rather never visit again. They were places where men and women forgot the tenants of the Divines and let depravity have its way.

But here it was different. The floor wasn't dirty, and there were no obscenities being shared in casual conversation. The barmaids that served the drinks weren't dressed provocatively and seemed to be happy to serve. The interior of the tavern was even larger than she expected, with over a dozen round tables scattered around, and smelled of honeydew.

She walked towards the bar, spinning around, and taking in the atmosphere, and sat down at the nearest bar stool. The man at the bar turned around and revealed his green skin, and large teeth as he smiled at her. The same unnatural smile that everyone in town seemed to give her. He held a small mug in his hand that he was cleaning with a slightly off-white rag.

"Welcome to Freedom Tavern!" He bellowed. "I'm Theo, your host, and server tonight and forever! What can I get you on this fine afternoon, my lady?"

From the details of the man's features, she surmised that he had to be an Orc. They were rare creatures amongst beast and humankind. The books Isobel read spoke of many legends and myths as to why that was, but they also gave her more pertinent information that applied to this specific scenario. Orcs were known for having sour moods all the time, except when engaged in competition or combat. They loved adrenaline and excitement. This Orc was happy well before she even entered the tavern.

"I will have a Beast Brew." She answered him.

Theo slammed the mug on the counter of the bar with enough force to break it, and an even larger smile took over his face.

"A BEAST BREWWWW!?" He howled. "Seems like we have a connoisseur, boys! Full round of drinks on the house for this momentous occasion!"

The tavern's patrons erupted into a massive cheer and a chorus of glassy 'clinks' could be heard all throughout the building. Theo began to construct the drink that Isobel requested, looking at her the whole time. Isobel had never had a 'Beast Brew,' but she had learned that it was a very well-respected drink due to the fact that anyone who could drink it would be knocked on their back. She figured that if she wanted to get into the barkeep's good graces, the brew was the way to go.

After he finished his elaborate show of finesse and speedy construction of the drink, he slid it over to Isobel and maintained a very expectant look.

"So, what brings a capitol girl all the way out here to the mud?" Theo said as he leaned on the counter.

Isobel raised an eyebrow at the Orc.

"Apologies, beautiful." Theo said, tilting his head. "Rumors travel like open flame on dry grass in this town. I knew you were here the moment our mayor gave you directions to the tavern."

Isobel raised the drink to her face and smelled it. It had a sweet scent to it, one that she was unfamiliar with, but the drink was bubbling out of the glass and that put her on alert. She didn't think it would be wise to consume it.

"And why would a 'capitol girl' give out that information to a random stranger?" Isobel asked as she lowered the glass to the counter.

The barkeep pursed his lips and shook his head.

"I noticed you have a pretty sword on your hip, and a very defined physique." Theo examined. "As owner of this establishment, I get rumors from all over. But some people get their rumors from me as well. It's my job to be a 'little' insightful. You aren't any simple nomad. I'm a guess an adventurer or soldier of some kind."

Isobel was impressed. It's not like there were many occupations that would produce muscular women, but the fact that he knew what she potentially could be and still was bold enough to tell her to her face… Theo wasn't just a regular Orc. He must be quite the charmer in real life.

"Well, you're not too far off." She smiled back. "I won't disclose who I work for, but I will say that I am looking for someone."

"Give me a hint, and I can point you in the right direction." Theo leaned in.

"So, you're willing to help for nothing in return?"

Isobel said unconvinced. There had to be a catch somewhere.

"Honestly, this town is boring." Theo admitted. "This conversation alone is compensation enough. I'm just here for the gossip."

"You are a weird one." Isobel said staring at her drink again. "I'm looking for General Drakonis."

"I don't know about 'general,' but Prince Drakonis lives just a ways down the road." Theo mocked. "I'm guessing you're here for his birthday dinner?"

"Yes, actually." Isobel said quickly.

"Well then you'd better hurry." Theo said, turning back to his bar. "Lord Adel and Lady Azzaria have been planning that dinner for weeks, and it may have already started. We're all friendly with Adel, but his old lady gives us all the creeps, so we don't take part in their gatherings. Their get-togethers are always open to the public but one look at Azzaria's face will let you know that you were never welcome. That's for true."

Isobel didn't reply. That name. Adel. It was a name that she hadn't heard in a long time. Maybe it was a different person, a completely different man or beast. But it was a weird name to begin with. What were the odds that it was someone she knew?

"Did you say, 'Adel'?" Isobel asked.

Theo turned back to Isobel, with the same smile that had painted his face for the last couple of minutes.

"Yeah, you know him?" Theo said with a puzzled expression.

"Yeah…" Isobel said as she leaned in close. Theo leaned in close as well so he could hear better. "Was he… A Divine Knight?"

"Oh!" Theo whispered with raised eyebrows. "So, you 'KNOW' him, huh? Well, that's crazy news. I'm sure he'll be happy to see you. That guy comes in here every weekend and drinks up a storm, and lucky for him, I'm not a blabbermouth. Hey can ya- "

A pulse of pressure shot through the room and washed over the whole tavern like a blanket. Isobel looked around, wondering where the mana could have come from. She noticed that other people in the tavern felt the pulse as well.

Theo stopped talking for a moment. His face became distorted, and his lip slouched downward. Isobel noticed that the rest of the tavern was dead silent as well. She got up from her seat and looked around. Everyone else had the same slack-jawed expression, and their bodies went rigid like wood boards, unmoving in their chairs. Then Isobel felt a hand on her shoulder and turned to see Theo grabbing at her with a horrified look on his face.

"Help me…" He whispered. "Help me."

He started moaning loudly and grabbed his head. Isobel turned back around and saw the rest of the patrons moaning and screaming for help.

“Rajani, what’s going on?” Isobel yelled above the screaming.

“I do not have a clue.” Rajani replied to her.

Some of the patrons inside of the bar began to claw at their own faces and smash their heads against the walls and floor. Isobel turned to Theo again and saw him climbing over the bar slowly, moaning.

“She’s in my head!” He screeched at her. “GET HER OUT OF MY HEAD!”

“We need to leave, Isobel.” Rajani warned.

Isobel turned to the door of the tavern and saw it was blocked by a mob of citizens from outside the tavern. Citizens that had previously welcomed her and given her gifts. They were now frothing at the mouth, lurching towards her like a hungry horde of animals. Isobel braced herself to fight the mob, but they were all knocked forward by someone entering the tavern.

“Come on!” Finerdhil called to her.

Isobel didn’t think twice. She ran to the door, leaping over the moaning, pain-stricken patrons on the ground, and she dodged the hands of the possessed patrons. She did one final leap over the fallen citizens at the door to land outside of the tavern next to Finerdhil. He grabbed her by the shoulders as soon as she got close, causing her to jump slightly.

"You have to get away before she gets you…" Finerdhil said.

His face paused abruptly and then his jaw started to slack in the same manner that the other citizens did. He started to shake Isobel violently and began screaming in pain at her.

"She's going to get you too!" He said as his face started to slowly shift back into a smile. "You have to r- ".

Isobel threw the man's hands off her and pushed him backwards with a strong strike from her palm. She didn't want to hurt any of the villagers, but something was terribly wrong. Someone was obviously possessing these people.

As she tried to make sense of what was going on, Finerdhil got up and brushed himself off. He looked up at her with the same smile that he had before when they had first talked.

"I'm sorry about that." He said calmly. "Didn't mean to alarm you. Everything is good here in Venek. Please stay for as long as you like."

Isobel turned around to see if everyone was still losing their minds, but it seemed like everyone was returning to normal. She spotted a man on the ground, with a sword lodged deep into his chest. She wondered what insanity, what pain or level of subjugation, could lead a man to throw himself on his own sword. As she watched from afar, the villagers walked over to his body, lifted him up, and carried him away to one of the houses.

“I’m getting out of here!” Isobel said quickly and ran for the road. She didn’t even look behind her to see if anyone was giving chase. She started taking the dirt road north, hoping that Theo hadn’t lied in any part of their conversation.

“We need to find Drakonis.” Isobel told Rajani. “I hope he isn’t one of these possessed villagers.”

“I doubt it.” Rajani said with certainty. Isobel could feel that she was telling the truth.

“How are you so sure?” Isobel questioned as she ran.

“Because he wasn’t failing the trial earlier.” Rajani confessed. “I just said he was.”

“What do you mean!?” Isobel said stopping suddenly.

“Well, Rohaz has a fancy for spectacles.” Rajani began. “The burning hands was symbolic for everyone outside the trial. It was more of a timer for how long he had and since only his hands were on fire, he had more than enough time to finish the trial.”

“And you are just now telling me this because?” Isobel said angrily.

“Because I desired revenge against my brother for ruining my trial!” Rajani replied with her own anger. "I had hoped you would just cut the half dragon’s head off when I asked. When that failed, I figured we could enter the dream and ruin it from the inside.”

Isobel groaned and started running again. She didn't have time to argue. If Drakonis wasn't in trouble before, he had to be now. She just hoped he didn't get mauled by angry villagers or was under the control of whatever witch was controlling the town.

*   *   *

Drakonis

Drakonis followed closely behind his father, with Ceesa and Faye in tow, into the giant manor. Everything in the large home was exactly as he remembered. They walked through the foyer and passed by luxurious and exotic couches and rugs with intricate designs. Woven with foreign and expensive materials, each piece of furniture and decoration glistened with a bit of radiance. All the flamboyant decorations made the space within the reception area of the manor very welcoming, even if 'The Beast' didn't want people to come around. Now that Drakonis was an adult, and firmly understood dragonkin culture, he knew that the furnishings weren't for visitors.

There was a rosy scent in the air from the floral arrangements that littered the tables in the room, and the home was lively with the sounds of servants moving trays of food to the dining area from the kitchen. Lots of clattering and footsteps could be heard coming from down the hallway leading to the Dining Hall. The nostalgic smell was sweet and very homely, and Drakonis began to recall many memories from his time inside of these walls. Some of those memories were fond while others were not as great.

As Drakonis looked around the reception area, he heard large footsteps slamming down the abnormally large stairwell that sat at the end of the room. The footsteps came from the master bedroom, a room that housed 'The Beast'. If one had the luxury of even seeing the room, anyone could tell that only a dragonkin lived there. It was simply a pedestal with a huge pillow surrounded by all kinds of treasures, and golden trinkets. It was and probably still is a true example of a dragonkin's hoard.

The loud and thunderous steps grew closer and Drakonis stepped out from behind his father to better see the stairwell. Ceesa and Faye each took a position at opposing sides of the stairway and placed their hands respectfully on their abdomens. The loud stomping stopped indicating to Ceesa and Faye that their introduction was needed.

"Enter: Lady of the Manor, Azzaria!" Faye announced.

As the words were uttered, a large reptilian head peered out from the room above the staircase, its fierce green eyes peering down the stairway. It was followed by a large, purple reptilian body with furled wings. Its scales reflected the different colors that glowed from miscellaneous treasures and ornaments that decorated the room and created a sort of shimmering aura around the behemoth. The Blade of the One God was a sight to behold, and many would be enamored by just the sight of her. But Drakonis felt only contempt for the dragonkin.

She finished her descent down the stairs and stopped in front of the group. She held her head high and looked upon Drakonis and his father with a silent intensity.

"Enter: Lord of the Manor, Adel!" Ceesa announced next.

Drakonis didn't turn to see his father's gestures. He just stared up at the beast that towered over himself and everyone around. It was like a direct symbolization of what he felt when he was around her. Like he was always being looked down on; like he never mattered, and all his actions would be scrutinized without fail. That feeling made his stomach tie into a knot and whether Drakonis realized it or not, he started scowling back at the dragonkin.

"Dearest Azzaria!" Adel exclaimed loudly as he raised his arms to the dragonkin. "As you can see, me and the child have returned… unscathed. Albeit a bit late, I hope you don't chastise my tardiness too harshly."

The large dragonkin continued to stare down at both of them, unfazed by the man's words. It was a look that Drakonis had come to know all too well from her. The gaze of a being that looked down upon him with contempt and a silent pity. Her eyes narrowed, and then she scoffed, releasing puffs of smoke from her nostrils.

"Let us make our way to the dining room." She said with some frustration in her voice.

"So, you're not going to greet your family, then?" Adel questioned as he raised his eyebrow at the dragonkin. "Not even going to ask your son how his day was? After all this time away?"

Azzaria looked at Drakonis and her eyes softened a bit. She reached down to the boy and motioned with her head for him to enter her claw. Drakonis stepped into her grip, and she slowly raised him to her face.

"I apologize for my irritability, my son." Azzaria said to him softly. "My mood has run afoul, and I allowed it to ruin the atmosphere of our reunion. Please forgive me, my little fire spitter."

Annoyed. Drakonis felt his own irritation begin to well and clenched his fist even harder as he looked away from Azzaria. It was the stare that Azzaria had that set him off the most accompanied by her sincere, deep voice. She may sound like she was consoling him on the outside, but he knew better than anyone. That inside her heart, there was an all-consuming coldness that left her unable to feel for anyone but herself.

Azzaria was a stone.

“Oh my.” Azzaria said raising an eyebrow at the boy. “It seems the boy is in a bit of a mood.”

“He’s been a little… different today.” Adel admitted. “Maybe we should carry on to the Dining Hall and begin our evening, huh? Today is a special occasion, after all!”

Drakonis chanced a glance at Azzaria and looked directly at her. She was still looking at him, examining him in her claw. He felt exposed. It was as though she was staring right through him, stealing his well-kept secrets with just a gaze. It wouldn’t be the first time that she had.

Azzaria slowly lowered Drakonis back down to the floor, never releasing her gaze, and softly placed her claw on the ground. Drakonis hopped out of the claw and returned to his father’s side.

Adel smiled at the boy, and put his hand on his shoulder, motioning towards the dining hall to the left. Drakonis nodded and the pair proceeded to walk into the large hallway leading into the large dining hall.

“Do make sure to shrink down, love!” Adel said as he cheerfully yelled back at the dragonkin. Azzaria didn’t reply, and Drakonis didn’t look back to confirm what he already knew. She was annoyed.

They walked down the hall silently, not speaking a word to each other. Drakonis looked back and saw that Ceesa and Faye were slowly following behind them. Ceesa gave him a soft smile, and he smiled back. In the past, he had confided with them, sharing some of his thoughts. How he felt like Azzaria didn't care about his progress much, and how he felt somewhat unrelated to her. Even if they were both dragonkin. Azzaria seemed unbothered by anything that he did. They had told him time and again that she was just busy and had much on her mind and many responsibilities. Those words didn't quell his worries though. So, the smile was an attempt to lighten the mood at best.

The group made their way to a set of doors that two guards stood watch over. They saluted Adel as they walked by, and Adel smiled back at them.

"At ease." He said leisurely. "When Azzaria enters, please feel free to join us at the table."

The guards both nodded at him, and he maintained his smile as he walked through the doorway of the Dining Hall.

The space was as grand as Drakonis had remembered. There was a large wooden table that sat in the middle of the room, with a giant chandelier above the table that lit the entire room. Four sets of large windowpanes sat against the back of the room, each with a decorative dragon motif in its center. There was also a giant fireplace that sat behind the two master chairs at the end of the table. Those chairs were slightly larger than all the other chairs and sat farthest away from the kitchen.

There seemed to be over thirty placements on the table, one for each of the servants, and the special placement that was meant for Drakonis. His own spot next to the Lord of the House.

Drakonis and Adel sat down at their respective spots on the table while Ceesa and Faye joined the other servants in finishing the decorations.

The two sat there for a moment staring at the door. Finally, they heard the familiar loud steps of heels in the hallway.

"Please feel free to join us." Azzaria could be heard saying in the hallway. She entered the room, not as a dragon, but now in her humanoid form. She was as tall as the most gifted and muscular humans, easily over six feet and had dark skin. Her usual afro was combed and tied into a bun, and she was wearing a purple dress with floral designs around the waist. It was low cut, and only revealed her legs after the knees. It looked a little baggy on her person, but Drakonis knew that Azzaria hated feeling trapped. It was a natural trait of dragonkin to desire freedom, after all.

She walked into the room and sat at the table next to Adel. The Lord smiled at Azzaria, and she simply frowned back at the man before placing her hands on the table. For a few minutes, the three of them sat silently and waited for the preparations to be finished. The table was prepped with different culinary delights, from lobster, oysters, and rice to fondue and ice cream. Due to the diversity of servants, beastkin and human, an equally diverse dishes needed to be prepared. The servants, chefs, and guards began to file into the room and stand next to their prepared seats. They each wore a mixed bag of attire; Azzaria wasn't too picky on outfits when it came to the 'help'. Ceesa and Faye took spots right next to Azzaria. Then Azzaria, Adel, and Drakonis stood up with the servants.

"Thank you for preparing this meal today." Azzaria announced for all to hear. "Today is a special day. It is recognized as the anniversary of the 12th year of my son's birth, Prince Drakonis."

Azzaria paused, and the servants lightly clapped. Azzaria then raised her hand and all noise ceased.

"With that being said, I have also been away at the capitol for some time." She continued. "Tonight, I have planned a peaceful gathering of which I am grateful for every one of you for your attendance. Tonight, I wish for all to speak freely and enjoy yourselves. You have served us well and I hope you will continue to do so for years to come. Today, I formally thank you."

Everyone clapped again after she had finished, and Azzaria looked at Adel.

"Let's enjoy ourselves tonight!" Adel said excitedly as he raised his glass.

A chorus of 'Yeahs' rang throughout the hall, and

everyone sat down at the table, and began to eat peacefully. The servants asked each other to pass different plates across the table and engaged in casual banter. Everyone except Azzaria, Drakonis, and Adel. Ceesa and Faye walked around the table to prepare their plates, but the three didn't speak at all. The tension was as thick as an oak log. Drakonis just stared at the table, unwilling to look up at Azzaria. Even if this all were an illusion, just a trial that he needed to figure out how to beat, he couldn't shake the sadness that accompanied this moment. He knew what was going to happen, he had known for some time, but that still didn't steel him for what lied ahead.

"Hey, ok!" Adel exclaimed as he clapped his hands. "So how was the trip, my love?"

Azzaria glared over at the man, giving him her patented disappointed and mean-spirited stare. Adel stared back and put his hand on hers.

"Now, now, don't be that way!" Adel smirked at her. "I know that you're still brooding over my transgression, but you can't stay mad forever!"

Azzaria held her ground and continued to stare the man down. She wasn't giving any footing on the matter. Drakonis never understood why she was so mad on this day, maybe she was just stressed out and wanted something to go as planned. Maybe her patience with the man had been drawn thin from his relaxed, but somewhat spry personality. Maybe she had just never liked the man at all; anyone that watched their interactions could come to that conclusion. But this moment was the first time he noticed that they weren't so happy.

"Ok." Adel said rubbing his head. "You're really going to make me do it."

Adel picked up his fork from the table. Azzaria immediately flipped her hand onto his, gripping his hand.

"Don't." She said fiercely under her breath.

"Then talk… to me and your son." Adel said in the same tone.

Faye stopped right next to Azzaria and lowered the plate she had prepared for her, and Ceesa placed Drakonis' and Adel's plates in front of both. Drakonis didn't want to look up, but he knew that if the memory needed to play out the way it did all those years ago, he had to. He looked up and saw it. Azzaria's face twisted into a scowl, her eyes glowing green and staring right back at him. They locked eyes and he was unable to look away from her. The world started to warble and fade away to black. All he could see was Azzaria's eyes and then even those faded away.

Then he opened his eyes.

Everyone was sitting at the table, passing food, and talking casually. Faye and Ceesa were sitting next to Azzaria arguing about something. Probably something about maids or maid duties. Azzaria was taking a sip from her goblet and Adel was sitting next to Drakonis, with a scowl on his face. Adel noticed Drakonis was looking at him, and quickly switched to a happy expression.

"What's on your mind, Koni?" He asked.

Drakonis didn't answer him. He remembered the confusion he had the last time. How he vividly remembered their intense expressions and how tight their hands were gripped. He glanced at Azzaria another time, and she raised an eyebrow at him.

"Something on your mind, child?" She asked with a smirk.

He didn't speak, he just stared at her again. Then he felt a large hand on his. He looked over at Adel, who now had a very saddened expression on his face.

"It's all going to be alright, Koni." He said softly.

Then the world faded away again and Drakonis opened his eyes.

"… Are pathetic." Azzaria exclaimed. "Maybe instead of empathizing with heretics of coward gods, you should make yourself useful and console our son. Altering memories gets a tad bit tiresome. Especially when he resists the process."

Drakonis tried to move but his body felt heavy, like a bag of bricks. He shook his head and looked at Adel. The man had his fists balled up tightly, and a large vein popped from the front of his head. He looked over at Drakonis and pursed his lips in frustration.

"Or maybe…" He said as he turned suddenly towards Azzaria. "He's just old enough to handle the truth. You shouldn't speak about people you know nothing about. Your son included."

"Know nothing about!?" Azzaria laughed at him. "The Divines are lesser gods. Fearful gods that are cower in some hole with their inferior creations."

"You…!" Adel started to say. He was interrupted by a loud thud at the end of the table.

Drakonis turned slowly towards the noise. The Dining Hall was in complete disarray. Chairs had been knocked away from the table and many plates were shattered to pieces on the ground. Some of the servants were growling to themselves softly, gripping their heads and rubbing their faces. Others were face down on their dinner plates or slumped over in their seats, drool pooled in the edges of their mouths. The thud came from a man who was slamming his head on the table, and he gave the table another resounding 'thud.' Drakonis looked ahead and saw Ceesa and Faye slumped against each other. Faye had lifeless eyes, completely withdrawn from the world. But Cessa, her eyes were erratic and unfocused, her pupils like flies darting about over a ripe meal. Drakonis, himself, felt sluggish and out of sorts.

"And now look what you've sown with your poor

actions." Azzaria reprimanded him. "That lackadaisical and whimsical demeanor you parade around with so freely has disrupted the town. Look at my beautiful servants. Look at your beloved 'son.'"

Adel stood up and slammed his fist on the table. Some of the disoriented servants slowly looked in the direction of the impact, but their eyes were so foggy and clouded it was hard to believe that any of them actually understood what was going on.

"How can you be so heartless?" Adel yelled at her. "I understand your disdain for me, but to even forsake your own son. Are his memories not valuable? Is he not the future of the dragon race?"

"This…" Azzaria paused for a moment. "Abomination… is no kin of mine. He can barely be called a fake dragon with how underdeveloped and feeble his abilities are. We have wasted the last fifteen years on this project. There are no dragon hearts to make him whole and without a second heart, he will remain worthless. But that is no longer any of your concern. Leave me so that I may clean up your mess."

Even though Azzaria was being blunt about him, Drakonis already knew how his mother felt about him. This wasn't a new revelation for him. He had already grown to loathe her more than even his most hated foe. But being unable to stand to give her a piece of his mind annoyed him to no end.

"My mess…" Adel said under his breath. He stood up and Drakonis heard the man's footsteps towards the doorway. "What are you going to do with the boy?"

Drakonis saw Azzaria's hand grab his face and force his eyes to hers.

"Well dear…" She said softly. "That is no longer any of your concern."

There was a gust of wind and then Adel's hand had tightly gripped Azzaria's wrist.

"Well, 'dear'…" He said with a smirk. "I actually believe it might be of great concern to me."

Drakonis managed to look up and see the look of disgust on Azzaria's face. She then slammed her fist into Adel's chest and sent him flying through the wall, back into the reception area.

"What a nuisance." Azzaria said shaking her head. She turned and glared at Drakonis. "I will be back for you after I deal with that pest. Don't worry. I won't forget my 'little fire spitter'."

This was new, Drakonis thought to himself. This part was completely different than that day. A deviating story made just for the trial? Maybe he was getting a chance to make things right, and correct the cowardice he showed that day? This was what he was waiting for. Drakonis knew this had to be the moment.

He tried to get up out of his seat, but his body felt heavy. He was just barely able to lug himself from the table and fall onto the ground. He hit the ground, hard, and started to crawl towards the hole.

"H-Help us…" He heard a voice call from behind himself. He turned to see Ceesa leaning over the edge of the table, reaching for him with tears in her eyes. "P-Please… H-Help…"

She collapsed out of her seat, knocking herself and Faye to the ground. She started crawling towards Drakonis, dragging her body across the ground.

"Ceesa…" Drakonis whispered. He wanted to help her and Faye. He really did. But they weren't real. And he knew his time was better spent trying to finish the trial. That was his best option. He turned to crawl away towards the hole in the wall, but he couldn't. Something in his gut wouldn't just let him abandon them. Even if they were just illusions crafted from his memories, they were still Ceesa and Faye. He still cared deeply for them.

He reached out towards Ceesa to try and pull her towards him. She grabbed his wrist eagerly and squeezed it with such force and intensity that he thought she would tear his hand right from his forearm. He grunted out in pain, immediately regretting his decision and tried to rip his hand away, but she didn't release her grip.

"Help… Us…" Ceesa said again, this time in more of an aggressive and menacing grunt and less of a tender pleading for her life. In fact, there was no hint of the sadness left in her voice. Just the pained snarling of a woman that had lost her mind in the madness. She slowly pulled herself towards him using his own arm, snarling with maddened eyes, and she wasn't the only one. Many of the servants in the room copied her actions, and they moaned as they lumbered towards Drakonis, knocking over everything in their paths.

Ceesa's grip on Drakonis' wrist increased and he gave her a kick to the midsection. She recoiled from the attack but didn't give up her grip on his wrist. He gave her another kick, but still she held on tight to her grasp and tried to grab his leg with her other hand. Drakonis took another glance at her, seeing her eyes wrapped in rage and strands of spit sliding out of her mouth, and then put his hand in her face.

"I'm sorry." Drakonis said softly. His hand started to glow a bright red, and then he released a fireball spell into her face. She shrieked out in pain as she grasped at her face and rolled onto her back. The others kept advancing towards him, completely unfazed by her screams of pain. The adrenaline from everything was kicking in now, and Drakonis felt himself able to stand up. He quickly turned towards the hole in the wall and jumped to the other side.

Azzaria and Adel were dueling in the reception area.

Azzaria was in her dragon form again and she was breathing fire all over the room while Adel managed to dodge the blasts with ease. The entirety of the room was set aflame. The delicate tables and couches that littered the room were now melted and burned passionately. Parts of the ceiling were caving inward as the fire progressed along the walls and support beams.

There were gusts of wind that accompanied Adel's movements that seemed to boost his speed as he dashed about the room. He stopped at the top of the stairs, and Drakonis saw that he had beads of sweat on his head.

"All this destruction could have been avoided if you were just capable of a simple 'I apologize,' you know?" Adel mocked her from the stairwell.

"I've no time for your jaunts, pest." Azzaria hissed back at the man. "You're only prolonging the inevitable. You lost your chance to placate me when you decided that you knew better than I. We should have disposed of you all those years ago!"

"Oh… You regret our love, dear?" Adel said as he clasped his hands together. I thought it was 'Death do us part' and all that? Oh wait… beastmen don't believe in trivial rituals and companionship. Only death and war."

Azzaria responded with another breath of flame that Adel jumped out of the way of. He managed to maneuver to her backside, but she was a step ahead of him and slapped him with her tail. He went careening into the double doors and flew outside the home. Azzaria quickly launched flames into the open doorway after him.

"No!" Drakonis said as he rushed toward the door. He then saw the air around himself thicken and he collapsed down on one knee. He tried to move but he was completely trapped.

"I didn't think you would find the will to move." Azzaria mused as she advanced upon him. "We might be able to make a dragon out of you yet."

"LET ME GO!" Drakonis roared at the dragonkin.

"Oh, you dare command me?" Azzaria roared down at him.

"Stop scaring the poor boy, Azzaria." Adel spoke as he entered the doorway. Azzaria turned towards the door and growled at the man.

"I didn't know dragons could be witches." Another voice from behind Adel said. Drakonis saw a familiar blazing hairstyle.

"Isobel!?" Drakonis said puzzled.

"And I'm guessing that's Drakonis?" She said with a surprised look. "You're a kid!"

"You're not supposed to be here!" He said angrily.

"Yet, here I am!" Isobel stated bluntly.

"You know this woman, Koni?" Adel asked

suspiciously. "How is that even possible when you spend almost all day with me?"

"ENOUGH!" Azzaria roared over the group.

As the words left her mouth, everything turned gray and froze in place. Drakonis looked around and saw the servants were frozen as they spilled out of the hole in the wall. He looked over at Isobel and Adel and noticed that Adel was completely frozen. Isobel traded a glance with him and shrugged her shoulders.

"So, you've decided to interrupt my trial, yet again?" Rohaz boomed from above. He was descending upon them, surrounded by a white aura.

Rajani left Isobel's hilt and floated next to them. Drakonis tried to move again and found that the restrictions that held him in place were no more. He stood up and stretched his arms.

"You are one to talk, Rohaz!" Rajani replied. "I was simply repaying the favor."

Rohaz stared at the group and then rubbed his chin. He spun around and mumbled to himself a bit. After a few seconds of awkwardness, he turned back to the group.

"Okay." He spoke. "You pass."

"What?" Drakonis said bewildered. "Just like that?"

"Certainly." Rohaz replied. "After reviewing your actions, I feel like you are an adequate champion. I see no point in perpetuating the issue."

"But I don't feel tested or as though anything has been resolved!" Drakonis argued. He was a bit relieved it was over, but he also felt cheated. He had just come to terms with what he had to do. He felt like he had the answer.

"The point of the trial is not for you to achieve some sort of inner satisfaction." Rohaz told him. "The trial is for me to accurately assess our compatibility via forced engagement. You will just have to work out your insecurities in your own time."

Drakonis didn't know what to say to that. Rohaz raised his hand, and a white light engulfed the room. When the light went away, Drakonis was back to his original form.

"Now, let us leave." Rohaz commanded. "The trial will close at any moment."

"Can I have a few moments with my father, at the very least?" Drakonis pleaded with Rohaz. The spirit thought for a moment before shaking his head.

"I can grant you this wish." Rohaz bellowed as he raised his hand in the air. There was another flash of white light, and then Drakonis found himself back in the dining hall. It was the same scene as before, but Adel and Azzaria were sitting next to each other, smiling at one another. Ceesa, Faye, and the rest of the servants were casually speaking to one another, and the hall was filled with sounds of dining and merrymaking. Drakonis looked down and noticed that he wasn't a child anymore.

"This is nice." Azzaria smiled at Adel.

"Right?" Adel smiled back at her. "It has been far too many moons since we've been able to peacefully sit in a room together. Look at all the happiness around us! How do you even think of being sour at an event like this?"

Drakonis stood up from the table. This isn't what he expected but he decided to make the most of this moment.

"Can I speak to you both in the hall?" He asked.

"Sure lad." Adel said as he got up. Azzaria wiped her lip with a napkin and followed Adel out into the hall. They made it a few feet outside of the door and stood against the wall.

"What is it, Koni?" Adel finally asked.

"Okay." Drakonis said as he took a deep breath. "I'm going to say a lot, so just bear with me. I'll start with mother. Please let me speak and then you can reply once I'm done."

"Sounds perfectly reasonable to me." Azzaria replied with a soft smile.

"Alright." Drakonis said as he closed his eyes. He then pointed at Azzaria. "You hate me."

Azzaria's smile immediately turned into a frown.

"You have hated me since I was born." Drakonis continued. "For not being a fully blooded dragon, and for being too weak to live up to your expectations."

"Hate is a strong word- "Azzaria started to say, but Drakonis kept talking over her.

"You gave me to D'Merrion without a care in the world." He continued. "You speak to me as though I am less than dirt. You hated me for things that I couldn't control. You never loved me or gave me a chance."

Tears started streaming from his eyes as he talked but he maintained his serious demeanor.

"I did do those things." Azzaria confessed. "Maybe not today, but sometime in the future. I see it in your mind's eye. Your memories."

"It wasn't fair." Drakonis pressed on. "I celebrated my birthday alone. Ceesa and Faye tried to console me, but I wanted my parents. I wanted a family! All I wanted… was to make you proud of me. To not be seen as trash, but nothing I did was ever good enough."

"And it will never be good enough." Azzaria told him. "You know that. So, I wonder… Why the desire to tell me this, a fragment of your memories? What do you hope to accomplish?"

Drakonis had thought long and hard about this. He knew she wasn't the real Azzaria, but he had to get this off his chest. He needed to say this to her.

"Because…" Drakonis started again. "I want to say that

I won't go searching for your love anymore. I don't need you to be my family. I have a family now. People that rely on me, that want to see me. People that love me for being myself and don't expect me to fulfill unrealistic and lofty expectations. But it wouldn't hurt for one time… Just one time to hear you say that you love me."

Azzaria's eyes softened and she smiled at him.

"Even a fake Azzaria wouldn't betray her true emotions." She said calmly. "I can't gratify your inner most desires, but I can say something of meaning. Looking at you now, through the eyes of Azzaria, I can see you have grown to be a fine warrior. While you may not be a dragon, you are still worthy of reverence in this realm. I hope in some way, this knowledge placates the longing you feel."

Drakonis didn't feel 'placated' at all. In fact, he knew it was selfish to even believe he would receive some sort of gratification, but he didn't want to waste time mulling over it. He turned to Adel who just stood there and watched the conversation silently. He then walked up and gave the man a hug.

"Thank you." He said to the man. "Thank you for believing in me and even protecting me till this day."

"You're a strong man, Drakonis." Adel said as he pulled him away and examined him top to bottom. "And while you may have the blessing of the wind from the heart beating in your chest, I can sense your mind is strong and your body is even stronger."

There was a soft rumbling in the world. Drakonis felt that his time here was coming to a close.

"You're going to be fine, my boy." Adel reassured him. "Remember…"

"Dull knights make for dull stories?" Drakonis said trying to guess his words.

"Be true to yourself." Adel said sincerely. "And remember that you're not alone. Take care of your family and let them take care of you."

"Thank you, father." Drakonis said wiping the tears from his face. "Truly."

"I'm watching you…" Adel said as he began to fade away. "Always…"

The world started to fade into white oblivion. The last thing Drakonis heard as everything disappeared was Azzaria's voice.

"See you soon, my little fire spitter." She whispered.

Epilogue:
The Returning Forces

Chase

The world seemed like a blur, almost like everything was moving too fast. Chase felt a sharp pain, not only in his head, but in his chest as well. He tried breathing, just like Cyarah had instructed but that didn't subside the pain he felt. It had been a few minutes since he had charged out of the forge, unable to control his sense of regret, and feelings of helplessness. Hard as he tried, he couldn't bury them this time. This time, Isobel could very well perish. And he had done nothing to stop it. For all he knew, he was alone in this kingdom now.

The usual underlying rage that he felt at all his insecurities was gone now. It was like the candle had finally burned out. And there was nothing left in its place. He continued to walk forward, not really paying attention to where he was going. He felt like he had brushed shoulders with some things, but he couldn't really focus on what they were or even where he was going.

"I thought…" He said softly to himself. "I really

thought…"

He thought he had become adept at managing his anger. That he could grow through his hardships and become better than the pathetic sap he was known to be. But some part of him always pulled him back down into the mud and reminded him that he was no better than his base personality. That rage was all he was. And now, he didn't even feel like he had that.

Chase stopped for a few minutes to catch his breath and look around at his surroundings. He was in the same square that had been assaulted during the festival. It was completely different now though.

The buildings had burn marks from the day before and many of the stalls lay collapsed and singed from the fires. There were far less beastmen, and even fewer people, walking about. There were many people lying about, their lives no longer in their possession, but many of the bodies on the ground had been covered with blankets. Groups of individuals gathered around the dead and mourned the deceased.

Everyone that had nothing left to mourn walked around the market, some hurried and others just wandered, kind of picking things up or maybe just trying to pretend to have some semblance of normal life. No matter what their bodies tried to do, their eyes gave up what was really on their minds… Misery. Regret. Dread.

For some reason, this gave Chase comfort a bit. That he

wasn't the only one that had lost. That everyone else here felt some part of his pain. The condition of beastmen citizens was of no concern to him, and he would not lose sleep over the deaths of his enemies.

"Good." He said to himself.

And that felt good. But it wasn't good enough to patch the pain in his heart. He clutched his chest and started breathing softly to himself. The pain in his chest and head still lingered. He realized, at that moment, that he needed to leave. Being here, amongst the defeated hurt his pride too much. It wasn't the dead that bothered him. It was the fact that he had lost again.

As he took a final glance over the destruction, he came to a realization. The guards hadn't stopped him from moving through the palace or even when he had passed through the courtyard. In fact, they should have tried to stop him multiple times since he left. He guessed that maybe they had abandoned their posts to tend to their loved ones. He took the opportunity to start walking towards the gate leading to The Grindstone. It was outside of the confines of the walls, and he could easily leave once he passed all the burned-out buildings. He could get help and return to save Isobel… If she survived, that is.

"Okay." He spoke. "I have a plan. No more wandering…"

As he started to move, he felt a small presence

concealing itself on a building near him. He turned to look and spotted Cyarah looking down at him. She didn't make any sudden movements or even try to hide as he stared up at her. She had hidden herself well, as well as a woman who never takes off her lab coat could, but for some reason, she revealed herself to him. If her intention were to follow and stop him, she wouldn't have given her position up so easily.

"What do you want?" He yelled at her. "Come to stop me?"

She just looked back at him silently. Chase reached down to pull out his sword, getting ready to fend off any sneak attacks. He felt his sheath and realized no sword lie inside of it. Somehow, he had forgotten his weapon. He silently cursed himself for being dimwitted and looked back up where Cyarah was. Except now, she was gone.

He tried to sense her pressure, but the presence was gone now. He didn't waste time thinking about it. He took off in a sprint towards the gate. As he ran from the square, he saw more people and beastmen walking with their heads down through the streets. It took only a few seconds for him to come to a stop right in front of the gate. There were a few guards standing guard, but they didn't seem to have their hearts in it. They looked up at him and their eyes grew wide. Two of the beastmen guards, a hog and a bird of some sort, rushed over to him. He put his hands up getting ready for a fight.

"It's you!" The hog said. His voice was deep and louder than Chase expected. "The lightning knight!"

"It really is him!" The bird reciprocated in a high pitched and annoying voice.

The lightning knight? Chase thought to himself. He made a puzzled face, and the beastmen immediately recognized that he didn't know what they were talking about.

"You don't remember?" The hog said excitedly. "You saved us!"

"I saved you…?" Chase said with even more confusion. "I think I would remember if I had saved a pack of beastmen."

"Woah, man!" The bird said appalled. "Beastmen? Not cool, man."

"I don't care for what you believe is 'not cool, man'." Chase said mockingly. "I wish to go through the gate."

The giant hog stepped in between them and put his hands up defensively.

"Don't mind my friend!" The hog said. "He is a little younger and he doesn't understand that there is a war going on. We'll let you through. But please, let us thank you!"

The hog motioned with his hand at something behind Chase, and the knight turned around and saw a crowd had formed behind him. It was a mix of humans and beastmen, many of them looked like young adolescents except for a small few. They each thanked him individually. Some of them were even crying as they showed their gratitude.

"What did I do?" Chase questioned them.

"I can barely describe what happened." The hog admitted. "We were there in the market, just enjoy'n the festivities, and then what happened to the foxkin. The guys in cloaks and then they were raining fireballs on us. Us in the guard would've been good to go, but there were some kids. People. You did your thing… It was like you were a red line or something. But you moved so fast. It was insane!!"

"I didn't understand any of that." Chase replied. His head started throbbing again and he didn't want to sit around and listen to their story anymore. "Please… The gate."

"Oh, yes sir." The hog said excitedly. He walked over to the gate and began to push.

"HALT!" A voice boomed from atop the gate. A giant shadow leapt from the top of the gate and crashed down in between Chase and the beastmen guards. As the dust settled, Chase noticed that the shape looked like a large bear, but he was completely armored, from head to toe. He was considerably larger than all the other guards and had metal talons on his claws.

"State your name!" The bear boomed. "Then hand me the appropriate paperwork and reason for traveling outside of Zhalesh."

Chase looked past the bear at the hog and noticed that

he was sheepishly hiding behind the giant warrior. Obviously, this bear was his superior.

"Obviously, I am traveling to the Grindstone for training." Chase stated directly. "I do not have any papers."

"NONSENSE!" The bear growled. "Do you take me for a fool!? Lord Drakonis sends the appropriate paperwork forward before any of his constituents leave or enter through all gates in the city. I have served for more than twenty winters, and he has NEVER failed in providing proper documentation! NOW. STATE. YOUR. BUSINESS!"

The bear growled loudly and slammed both claws into the ground, roaring at him. Chase sighed and realized he wasn't going to be able to leave without a fight. He raised his hands but then felt a hand on his fist.

"Boys…" she said loudly over the growling. "We can work this out without violence, can we not?"

"What do you want, mutant?" The bear roared down at Cyarah.

Cyarah looked back at Chase, and smiled at him, then returned her gaze at the bear.

"I am this knight's chaperone." She said as she handed a card to the large bear. He used two of his claws to lightly clasp the card. "I was sidetracked by a few tasks. Considering the events of yesterday, I had urgent tasks that I needed to attend to before I could meet Sir Chase here. We are acting on the behalf of the One True God."

"NONSENSE!" The bear roared again. "Why was the proper paperwork not submitted then?"

"Because we move as the One True God demands." Cyarah replied, never dropping her smile. "And his whims are like the wind. They move without cause and are purposeful in their nature. Do you question your god's demands?"

The bear stared at her for a moment, then looked down at the card then back at her. He then started to hand the card back to her when one of his claws slashed the card completely in two.

"Oops." He said snidely. "Apologies, freak. It seems to me you lack the proper paperwork to leave the city. I will inform the other gate captains of your highly unprofessional request. Consider this a warning the next time you try to leave the capitol unauthorized."

Cyarah looked down at the card at her feet for a moment. Chase could sense that a fight of some sort was on the horizon now. He was eager to leave but for some reason, he was interested in how Cyarah would handle this insult. Cyarah laughed softly to herself.

"You know…" Cyarah said as her laughter faded. "I will never understand why a lowly creature such as yourself would even need to understand why I, the head of Research and Development in Zhalesh, need to do anything. Your pea brain probably couldn't even understand my simplest of thoughts. Walking around in all of that 'Majen tinfoil' probably has baked your brain beyond edible mush."

"YOU DARE-" The bear said before stopping abruptly. Chase saw it. It was instantaneous. Like watching a hummingbird dart about in a meadow. As the bear got ready to respond to her torrent of jests, Cyarah's barbed tail shot out and stabbed him squarely in the neck. Cyarah raised her hand and began to examine her nails in a particularly uninterested manner.

"Oops." She said intensely with a smile. "My hand slipped."

"Ah…." The bear tried to choke out. "Ah… But… It was… Your tail…"

"Worrying about the wrong things still?" She mocked.

The bear tried to stay standing but he collapsed into the dirt and looked up at her.

"Wha…" He tried to say, but the choking was getting worse. "Did… Did…. You…?"

"Oh, I just injected you with an intense neuro poison taken from a spider that doesn't exist in this world." She smiled down at him. "It's quite potent and is very effect against the spider's predator, the cave whale!"

"Cave whale?" Chase said with confusion.

"Well, I'll be going now, but enjoy the next…" Cyarah

said as she pulled a small watch from one of her pockets. "Three minutes and sixteen seconds. I hear internal liquidation is quite gruesome this time of year!"

She walked past the hulking mass towards the gate. The beastmen guards behind the bear jumped immediately out of her was as she approached. The hog turned and opened the gate with newfound enthusiasm. Cyarah turned to Chase.

"Coming?" She asked.

Chase took a moment to look down at the beastmen bear. He was wheezing loudly and some of the people had rushed to his side. Chase walked past the large guard.

"H-help… Me…" The bear managed to rasp.

"I don't think I will." Cyarah replied quickly. "Sit and reflect on how you are supposed to treat people."

"Please…" The bear begged.

Cyarah then turned to Chase, the same uninterested expression on her face from before.

"What do you think, Chase?" She asked. "Should I help him?

Chase looked down at the bear, who was now staring up at them. The heavy armor hid his face, but Chase could hear the bears wheezing under the mask. The citizens that had been praising him now looked at him, anxiously awaiting his response. They were practically begging him with their eyes to save the beastmen.

"Do it." He replied.

Cyarah stared at him for a second, then turned around to the beastmen. She reached into one of the many pockets on her coat and Chase heard the jingles of multiple trinkets. She pulled out a vial with some weird looking green goop in it, and knelt next to the beastmen, putting her hand on his shoulder.

"Consider yourself lucky that he was here to convince me." She said as she jammed the vial into the beastman's mouth. He drank the goop, and immediately wretched and gagged afterwards. Cyarah stood up and sighed, then proceeded to the gate.

"I'm leaving." She said as she walked through the gate.

Chase looked down at the beastmen, whose wheezing had subsided, and he was being helped up to his feet now. The large beastmen looked at Chase and stared at him for a moment.

"Thank… you…" The bear managed to say through deep breaths.

A chorus of praise rang out from the group of people and Chase didn't want to hear anymore. It was eerie being at the end of a thank you parade. It was usually Isobel in the middle of one of those disasters, but now that he was in the spotlight, he didn't know how to feel. On one hand he felt more appreciated than he had felt being in the service of the Divines, but on the other hand, the gratitude felt disingenuous or fake.

Then again, Cyarah seemed particularly brutal to the guardsmen for almost no reason, maybe the 'thanks' was justified simply for showing kindness. He didn't want to waste time pondering the situation; he was more eager to leave than anything else.

Chase turned away from the people and made his way through the gate. He stood on the other side of the gate, finally on the outside of the large walls of the market and on the road to The Grindstone. If he wanted to, he could just take off in a direction and never return to Zhalesh. Cyarah stood just a few feet away from him, looking at him with some sort of expectation.

"So…" she said as her smile returned to her face. "Where are we going?"

* * *

Cyarah

Cyarah stared at him, awaiting an answer to her question. It was one of genuine curiosity, and she had hoped it would make the man think of his actions before he went on the run. She had seen him mumble to himself earlier as he zig-zagged through the streets of Zhalesh. Chase didn't seem to have an objective in mind, but he did seem very eager to leave. Her beliefs were solidly confirmed the moment he looked out over the grasslands leading to The Grindstone, and a smile crept onto his face. He looked like a wild animal that had been caged for weeks and was finally free.

"What does it matter to you?" Chase shot back at her. The smile on his face didn't last and was replaced with the sour and brooding expression he always had. The same face she had seen him carry every time they had met. "Drakonis told you to watch over me, but I've yet to see you do as he says."

"Is there a right answer to that question?" Cyarah asked him. He shrugged back at her, beads of sweat dripping down his forehead, and looked back over the grasslands. She could feel his pressure rising and could physically see his aura. Bolts of red lightning started to shoot out of his body and his eyes glowed red with power. She knew he was going to run, but she was confident that she could keep up.

Chase gave her one last look, tilting his head at her, before he took off into a full sprint. A cloud of dirt and rocks shot into the air as he left a trail of lighting and debris in his wake. Cyarah leapt into the air and motioned with her hand. She felt the magic runes in her arms begin to vibrate as they activated and released pools of dark mana. She then formed a flat platform in her hands and thrusted it under her feet. Now that the board was made and it was stable, she could use it to follow Chase.

He was fast. In fact, he was faster than she had expected of him. It seemed the constant training, the stress of his life, and his own blessing were enough factors to inspire him to move at such a speed. But she was also fast, especially when she used dark mana to augment herself. She took off after the knight and it only took a few seconds for her to be right above him.

She wasn't going to stop him from running, that wasn't her ultimate intention. She was simply going to follow him until he tired himself out and she could talk to him for a moment. He was capable of anything in his highly emotional state, and she didn't want to aggravate him further.

It was interesting watching him move. The way his aura changed him into energy, and how she could only see him as a lightning bolt. How at certain moments, when he wasn't fully concentrating on running away, his aura would reveal him, and he would take a moment to look behind himself. She wanted to know the complete inner workings of his aura. She also made sure to wave every time he looked to check if she was still there.

Chase ran for a solid thirty minutes before stopping in a burned out and desolate city ruin from the Old World. All the buildings were completely covered in overgrowth, and they were crumbling from lack of maintenance. Honestly, she could have chosen a better location. The sun was still high in the sky, but the temperature was cool and very comfortable.

"So…" Chase said as he hunched over. He was breathing hard from the run over. "How… long are you going to follow me?"

"As long as I want." She replied coyly. "You know, I'd thought you'd be a lot faster."

"Biting as ever." Chase replied as he stood upright. "You know, I bet it was easy to keep up riding on that disc or whatever that is."

"Oh, this?" Cyarah replied. She floated down towards him, and the mana filed back into her runes. "I'm an expert in dark mana so mundane objects like this are of no consequence to me. If not for its volatile and destructive impact on the environment, I would travel like this more often than not."

They stood there for a few moments while Chase caught his breath.

"I'm guessing you're not going to just let me leave?" Chase said once he regained his composure.

"Even if I wanted to, Drakonis would never let you just get away." She said pointing at her neck. It was a motion to remind him that his dragon mark still existed and was active. He rubbed his neck, and his eyes went wide.

"Did you really think you could just vanish?" Cyarah said. "You were going to leave Isobel to die in the capital and just go back whatever hole you crawled out from? You really are shameless, aren't you."

"Shut up." Chase shot at her. His eyes started to glow again, and his pressure started to blanket the area. "You don't understand anything. You don't know what my life has been."

"On the contrary!" Cyarah said in a chipper tone. "I know a lot about you. I was the one who conducted your psyche eval. And you know what I found? A co-dependency disorder and a severe bipolar disorder. But even worse than that, for some reason, you don't believe you deserve love and don't have any self-respect. That last one is not from medicine; I'm just letting you know."

"Stop talking..." Chase said through gritted teeth. Bolts of lightning started to shoot out from around him, blasting the deserted street with sparks of red energy. Cyarah readied her runes again.

"Or what?" Cyarah continued. "You'll go into a fit

about how you couldn't 'save your friends'? Or worse, make some kind of childish joke to cover up your insecurities? How did they ever let a guy like you into the Divine Knights? I can barely feel that pitiful pressure you're pumping out."

There was a loud 'crack' that shot through the air, and Cyarah raised her hand. Chase's fist impacted with hers, clearly aiming for her head, and her hand shook against the impact. It was a strong blow, way stronger than she had anticipated and one that brought a bead of sweat to her brow, but nothing she couldn't handle.

"Just like an ape to only use brute strength." Cyarah grunted. "Let me show- "

Chase brought his other fist backwards and aimed a blow at her chest. Cyarah raised her hand to deflect the second blow but was a second too late. She did manage to stop the fist from impacting, but the electric aura radiating off Chase sent her flying backwards a few feet. Her hand shook violently as the electric current raced through her arm before dispelling after a few seconds. She winced a bit at the pain and looked up at Chase. He stared her down with a menacing stare that made her heart race. A stare that had every intent to kill.

"Stop… Talking." He said slowly.

"Okay." She said as she raised her hand. Globs of black mana began to form in her hands, moving all around her like a formless blob. The blob floated around her and became five orbs above her head. Cyarah snapped her fingers and one of the orbs transformed into a hook, and she took her coat off to hang there, leaving her with a dark blue dress. She turned back to Chase, who only watched her questioningly and seemed wary of the orbs.

"Survive." She said as she motioned with her hand. Large tendrils began to shoot out of the orbs, aimed squarely at Chase's chest. If he wanted a real fight, he would have one. Even if her intention wasn't to kill him, she was going to tire him out. That was the only way to get his attention, and ultimately, get what she wanted.

Chase leapt out of the way of the tendrils with ease. Cyarah realized that the attack wasn't particularly fast, but it was almost never ending and took little effort to keep going. She could, realistically, do this all day.

The tendrils shot out of the orbs rapidly in Chase's direction and he continued to dash about. Holes began to form in the street and surrounding buildings as the assault continued to level the abandoned cityscape. Tendrils bashed the area behind Chase as he leapt onto a destroyed vehicle, and then abruptly, he used the same vehicle to leap towards Cyarah. She commanded the orbs to attack all at once, to stop his advance. They created a wall in front of her and Chase slammed his fist into the wall, sending a huge impact of electricity through the dark mana wall, that quickly dissipated.

Chase roared and started to pound away at the wall, disappearing from sight. Cyarah tried to sense his aura, but it was erratic and all over the place. Then she felt the need to guard her backside, commanding the wall to move behind herself. Chase slammed into the wall again, screaming in frustration as his attack did not connect with her. He continued to assault her location from all sides, each blow being decisively blocked by the wall of dark mana. Chase came to a stop right in front of her, huffing rapidly and angrily staring her down.

"WHAT SORT OF TRICKERY IS THIS!?" He yelled through labored breaths.

"Dark mana." Cyarah replied. "I'm sure you've heard it mentioned before."

She could sense his pressure dying down. He was tired from his reckless attack and was becoming more vulnerable. He just stared back at her as he continued to breathe harshly. Rain began to softly fall.

"You know, while you do have a great amount of physical strength for a human, it doesn't really fit your style." Cyarah told him. "There is a more effective way to regulate your power. You must embrace your elemental heritage."

"What are you going on about?" Chase yelled back at her. He then groaned and grabbed his head. "What are you saying!?"

Cyarah opened her mouth to say more, but a loud boom radiated throughout the area. She looked up and realized a storm was approaching. She looked at Chase and he was still wincing in pain, grabbing his head. Then his blazing red eyes suddenly turned white, and lightning began to strike around them suddenly. Cyarah commanded the dark mana to protect her from the bolts, but the strikes got stronger and more frequent every second. Then a large blast of lightning struck Chase and an explosion sent her flying backwards.

*   *   *

Chase

Chase looked around himself and saw he was surrounded by an endless white fog. It was raining and the air was extremely cool. He didn't know what was going on and was thoroughly confused. He remembered the pain in his head becoming unbearable. It was like a knife was being driven into his skull. But now the pain had subsided, and he was eerily at peace.

He walked around the white space for a moment, trying to understand what was happening.

"Hello?" He called out. He only heard his own voice echo back to him. After his 'hello' stopped repeating, he only heard the soft taps of raindrops hit the ground. He continued to walk and look around, his footsteps loud from hitting the wet ground, hoping to see some signs of escape. He then stopped for a moment. He realized that the rain wasn't the only thing he had heard. He continued walking for a moment, and he heard it again… Footsteps. Not his own footsteps, but softer and less prominent steps that were coming from directly behind himself.

He spun around to see who had been following him but was surprised to see no one was there.

"Hello?" He called out again. His voice continued to echo into the space, but the footsteps began, again, to be heard from behind his head. He spun around trying to catch a glimpse of what could be stalking him, but this time was greeted by someone. Or something. It was smaller than him, and even in the white space, was bright and shimmered in a great red radiance.

"Chaselonius?" The being said.

"What… Are you?" Chase asked back.

"You don't… remember?" It asked him.

Chase felt a sharp pain shoot through his head again. Something about the being was… familiar. He tried to remember where he had heard the voice before, but it was like a wall was stopping him from finding the information. He moved away from the being, wincing from the pain. It was becoming incredibly hard to concentrate.

"Through the void I searched for you." The being

continued to say. "There was not a single strand of your presence in existence. I had assumed you, the last of House Helowyn, had perished."

The being tried to approach Chase again, but he fell backwards, breathing heavily.

"Stop!" He yelled at it. "Stay away from me!"

The pain in his head was getting more and more intense. He felt like his head was about to burst. The being ignored his plea and tried to approach him again.

"But you and I are bonded." The being stated. "We are eternally linked in our solemn promise. A promise that had been created by your ancestor, Helowyn Karia. You and I are irrevocably linked."

Chase tried to turn away from the being that was harming him, to escape the pain but he didn't make it very far before he felt a hand on his back. In an instant, all the pain was gone, and his mind felt unburdened. He turned to face the being and was greeted by the visage of a beautiful woman. Her features were indescribable, and yet he found them attractive all the same. She reached down and pulled him up to her chest, hugging him tenderly.

"Of whose magic would make a coward of my only knight?" She asked.

He stared up at her, and everything came racing back to him. The memories flowed into him like paint straight to a canvas.

"The Divines…" He said back to her. "I did... something unforgivable, and I was punished."

"Nothing is unforgivable." She said as she held him. "You are righteous and strong. I could not have chosen a more honorable knight. Our paths may have diverged, but we are now reunited."

"We are not, my liege." Chase said solemnly. "Once I wake, your influence will leave me. I will more than likely go back to who I was moments before."

"I know, my knight." The being said sadly. "But even this is finite. You will have my love and guidance once again. Give it time."

Chase sat up and leaned against the woman.

"Oralei." He said to her. "As I am right now, I have the mind of both of me. The new me and the old. I have been humbled by life. Seen my own weakness and felt what it was to be a part of a group. To need others. Right now, the wall that blocks my memories has a small hole for us to talk, a space that lets but a piece of me join us here. It blocks the power of my previous self. But once it comes down, I fear that my new self, his memories, and his morals will be devoured by the power of our bond. Chase will die. Just as Xeilani did."

He felt a tear on his shoulder. He looked up at Oralei and wiped it away.

"I'm sorry, my knight." She apologized. "I feared fading into nothingness. The loss of all my beautiful elementals instilled a fear so deep that I took advantage. I gave you too much of myself. Too much of my fear that it corrupted you and your youth. You weren't ready to inherit such power and I saw it in your arrogance. How could I, after doing that to you, even speak about how you carried yourself? Your pitiable state is due to my negligence."

"I don't blame you." Chase consoled her. "I was weak. I gave in to the rage in my heart. Maybe, if the new me becomes strong enough, he won't be overtaken by the rage."

"Regardless of how the war in your heart resolves, I will be here." She smiled at him. "Now that I have found you, I will never leave again. No magic will separate us."

Chase stood up and held Oralei's hand.

"Give me one last boon before I leave," he said as he stared into her eyes. "When I release this hand, you and I will be strangers. I thank you for giving me this chance to see you through sane eyes. Please, instruct the new me as you did for the old me. He needs to learn about himself. He is the only one that can save himself. Otherwise, my darkness will win the day."

They stared into each other's eyes for a moment. Oralei then nodded at Chase.

"Thank you." Chase said to her. He was prepared to

dissolve into nothingness, but he held her hand for a few more seconds. "Do not tell him of the old me. His weakness may lead him to pursue it. If the entire wall comes down too soon…"

"I know." Oralei said to him. "Please, let us not waste the little valuable time he has. I know you love to talk."

Chase smirked at her and laughed before he let go of her hand. Chase looked around himself and saw he was surrounded by an endless white fog. It was raining and the air was extremely cool. He didn't know what was going on and was thoroughly confused. He remembered the pain in his head becoming unbearable. It was like a knife was being driven into his skull. But now the pain had subsided, and he was eerily at peace.

"Do not panic, my young bonded." A voice said from in front of him.

Chase jumped back from the voice. He reached down to grab his sword, and remembered it wasn't there.

"Who are you!?" He asked quickly. He looked down and noticed a red and radiant… something… in front of him. He was ready for a fight, but for some reason, he didn't sense any malevolence coming from the being.

"I am… Oralei." The voice said. "I am your bonded, and you are mine."

"Bonded?" Chase questioned. "What are you talking

about?"

"You and I share a bond through spoken contract." Oralei explained. "We have… always shared this bond. From your birth. I have searched far for you. Through all of the nether to make your acquaintance. To give you the gift of your heritage. To make you into a True Elemental."

"And what are you?" Chase asked.

"I am the element of lightning incarnate." Oralei stated. "I find those with the affinity for my power and I gift them with prowess and power. In exchange, I ask for a promise of sorts."

"And what is this promise?" Chase asked her.

He saw her mouth move, but she didn't say anything. "Huh?" Chase said with confusion.

"Are you going to tell me?"

"You will fulfill the promise by staying true to our bond." Oralei said.

Chase scratched his head. He didn't know what the promise was, but for some reason, he didn't feel the need to question her further about the subject. He trusted in her words.

"Well, what am I to do now?" Chase asked.

"A divine restriction limits your capability." Oralei instructed. "You must seek a master of Divine Magic or the one that cast this curse upon you."

"How am I to know who they are?" Chase said.

"There are only a few Divines… My knight." Oralei said. She seemed indifferent, almost like she couldn't care less whether he removed the curse or not. He couldn't make out what the glowing creature was thinking even so he felt extremely compelled to ask.

"Are you always this… carefree, with your bonded?" Chase asked with concern.

The being did not move for a moment. Then it advanced on him. He took a step back. Maybe questioning it wasn't such a good idea?

"I'm sorry, my knight." Oralei apologized. "I loved my previous elemental greatly. And it occurred to me that I may never see him again. He was one of the strongest beings I had ever seen and truly a master of our power. I loved him like no other."

"Geez, giving me really big shoes to fill." Chase said. Now he felt bad for asking. "He sounds like he was quite a warrior."

"The best of his kind." Oralei said. "It seems our time has come to an end."

Chase could sense it too. Wherever they were was disappearing. The fog began to dissipate.

"Will I see you again?" Chase called to Oralei.

"When you are ready." She replied. "Seek the Divine Master, and we will reunite once again."

Chase felt himself drop down onto one knee and panned his environment. He saw the crumbling buildings and burned-out city that he and Cyarah were fighting in. And he spotted Cyarah but a few feet away, watching him like a hawk.

"Have a nice nap?" She joked.

"I'm not going to answer that." He replied flatly. He felt considerably calmer and the pain in his head was nonexistent now. He felt like he could think clearly.

"Then answer this: Are you an Elemental?" Cyarah asked eagerly.

Chase looked down at his hand, which now was a bruised mess thanks to him slamming his fists into Cyarah's barrier. Something was different from before. He was so exhausted and scared before, but now he felt stronger somehow. He didn't feel the same emptiness that was in his heart before.

"Yes, I am." Chase said to her. "You said something about me being an Elemental before my vision."

He didn't want to tell her anything. She was probably the last person on Earth that he should talk to about anything. But at this moment, she was probably one of the only people who would know about what he was.

"Come." Cyarah said as she sat on the nearby sidewalk. Chase walked over and about three people lengths away from her. "I don't have cooties."

“Just talk.” He said annoyed.

Cyarah frowned back at him and crossed her arms. She turned away from him, an action that he actually preferred and appreciated.

“Your bonded told you about your promise?” Cyarah asked him.

“She reminded me, yeah.” Chase replied.

“Well, as an Elemental, your bonded blessed you with a piece of their power.” Cyarah explained. “In exchange, you carry out your promise to them with the life you live. An Elemental’s Promise is one of the most sacred bonds a person can have, and the secret of that pact must be protected at all costs.”

“I didn’t plan on telling you anyway.” Chase said smugly.

“Well, you can’t tell ‘Isobel’ or Drakonis either.” Cyarah mocked. “Once you give up your promise, you void the blessings of the bond.”

Chase didn’t know what to say about that. It’s not like he was above keeping secrets, but he didn’t even know what the promise was. How was he supposed to not say it? What could it possibly be?

“So how do you know so much about Elementals and bonds, huh?” Chase asked curiously. “You happen to dissect an Elemental and squeeze the truth out of them for your wimpy god?"

"No, you idiot." Cyarah scoffed at him. "I happen to be an Elemental. An Ex-Elemental, I should say."

Chase turned and looked at her. She was still facing the other direction, staring off into the distance.

"So, let me take a guess..." Chase said as he smiled. "All you do is lie, cheat, and betray everyone around you. I'm guessing you sold out your bonded and ran off with their power. Really made out like a bandit."

Cyarah turned and stared at him coldly. If a stare could shoot a man dead, this would be it. He could tell that a very long backstory sat behind those eyes.

"I loved and still love my bonded like no other." She said intensely.

"Well, if you love them so much, why are you an 'Ex' bonded?" Chase mocked her.

"Because…" She started to say. "Because… I had lost my drive to fulfill my promise."

"So, you're a quitter!" Chase said smugly as he smirked at her. Cyarah balled her hands up into tight fists and frowned at the man.

"You are absolutely insufferable!" Cyarah yelled at him. She rubbed her face and sighed into her hand. It seemed like her frustration had reached its peak. "I… am from one of the Nine Houses of the Divines. I hailed from House

Argathion."

Chase stared at her in disbelief. He wanted to call her a liar; to reprimand her for trying to impersonate a Divine Knight and insulting his intelligence with her joke. But the fact of the matter was there was almost no way to know of the fallen houses without having been a part of them or enlisting in the Academy. And even as a Squire-in-Training, you are explicitly instructed to keep Divine Knight history confidential. He couldn't, even for a moment, believe that anyone outside of Karia even had any record of their existence. Not since the Black Dragon Catastrophe… And House Argathion was lost well before that incident. They were destroyed for Treason against the Divines.

Chase put his hands together and looked up into the sky.

"How?" He asked.

"How… what?" Cyarah asked in a confused tone.

"How did you end up in service to the Divine D'Merrion?" Chase elaborated.

"Same as you… I was abandoned by the Divines." She answered.

"I was not abandoned!" Chase shot at her. "Me and Isobel are not abandoned!"

"Even now, as Isobel faces death alone, with you on the verge of desertion of duty, do you believe the Divines watch over you?" Cyarah asked him. "You can't be that delusional?"

"I have always placed firm belief in the Divines for salvation." Chase said aloud.

"I can tell you're lying." Cyarah said to him. "We spent weeks together. I know you better than you think. Why are you so ashamed to be who you are?"

"I…" Chase started to say. He wanted to say that he was proud and confident in his belief still. That he was sure the others would save them. That his father, Everett, would come to their aid any day now. But truthfully, that faith died when he was sentenced to rot in the castle dungeon for weeks. Now, he was only certain that if he could get strong enough, he might be able to help them break free. But even that was a bluff he made up in his mind. He just sighed loudly and knelt forward on the sidewalk, putting his face in his hands.

"I am from House Argathion." He heard Cyarah say suddenly. "Our family was the protector of the First Poison, Dark Mana. The Knight of our house had no affinity with it, and the Divines wanted a warrior to be able to wield its wicked power. This secret never escaped our home. Power of the Dark Mana would have had an immeasurable impact on the war. So, naturally, our house felt we had a great mission, but the other households didn't hold us in high regard. They frowned upon our household for not having members of worth to the Divines."

"Stop…" Chase told her as he looked at her. "The Divine Houses haven't existed since my childhood. They were wiped out by the Black Dragon. Seven Houses were wiped out. House Argathion was annulled long before that. Are you telling me that you are over fifty years old?"

"Let me finish." Cyarah said firmly. "Every member of House Argathion was sent into a room with the 'artifact'. Now that I'm more knowledgeable on the subject, it was nothing more than a shard of Dark Mana, but to us, then it looked like living black tar. When I was very young, I was sent into the room as well. It was so long ago, and yet, I can still remember seeing it. The mana called out to me, and I reached for it. And it floated over to me."

"That was the day you found out you were an Elemental?" Chase asked.

"No." Cyarah replied. "My parents and relatives only knew that I had an affinity. And that I was the only child in existence to have it. So, they offered me to the Divines."

"But that was a ploy." Chase said. "House Argathion planned on using their forbidden power to usurp more power for their weak household."

"What?" Cyarah said with a confused expression. "No. Why would you say that?"

"When I was still in the Academy, I didn't pay attention to many of the history lessons." Chase admitted. "But the story of the Nine Houses of the Divines was always interesting to me. Argathion is known as the house of traitors."

"Traitors?" Cyarah repeated as she shook her head in disbelief. "We didn't betray anyone. Our house was sacrificed. I was offered to them, and the Divines refused me. The Nine Divine Knights were stronger than they had anticipated, and they realized they didn't need the power of Dark Mana anymore. This is what my father, Sir Argathion Serge Karia, told me as he sat in his study upon his return. My father swore that he demanded that they be rewarded for their service, but the Divines did not overturn their ruling… For a time. About ten years later, they ordered our family to hold a small outpost. What they failed to tell anyone was that one of the Beast Generals was campaigning through the area. She annihilated the outpost, killing almost every heir of the Argathion bloodline. All but one. That was the first time I had met Azzaria, her name struck fear into the hearts of men."

Chase scoffed at her.

"So, the Divines deliberately destroyed one of their households?" He questioned her as he cocked his head. "They removed a Divine Knight's entire family? Ha. Get real!"

"So then, what's the story then?" She asked him.

"House Argathion betrayed the Divines and tried to use the First Poison to steal power for themselves." Chase corrected her. "The Divines thwarted their plan and sentenced each member of the house to ceremonial execution. The other eight houses continued their duty. The End."

Cyarah frowned at him again.

"I'm not going to argue my family's history with you." She said shaking her head.

"Then answer this." Chase said staring at her. "If house Argathion was wiped out, then how did you survive?"

"I never met the Divines." Cyarah told him. "My father only spoke to them on my behalf. I had, somehow, survived the onslaught on the outpost, but everyone I knew was gone. And the Divines didn't send anyone to check for survivors. I didn't even know the way back. So, I wandered for a while. Eventually, I made it back to my home, but our estate had been razed to the ground in our absence. I had nothing left. It was at that point in my life that I was visited by my bonded."

As unlikely as her story sounded, Chase felt confident in his ability to sense underhanded tactics from others. And this time, Cyarah didn't seem disingenuous. This was the only time he felt like she wasn't trying to just save her own skin. Even if her story called the legitimacy of the Divines into question, he couldn't completely discredit her tale. His own bonded told him that he had a Divine Restriction on him. He didn't understand what that meant, but the Divines had done something to him, and he aimed to figure it out.

"So, what happened next?" Chase asked.

Cyarah looked up at the sky.

"I actually can't say." She spoke. "Even now, it would feel like a betrayal to unveil the secret of our meeting. For now, know that the aftermath was me journeying to the Land of Dark, Xi'Gardia."

Cyarah stood up suddenly, brushing herself off and grabbing her coat off the floating hook she placed it on earlier.

"We have to walk and talk." She told Chase. "We should go back before they send Addurog or someone equally foul after us."

Chase agreed with that sentiment. He regretted even thinking that leaving was a good idea. At least he had some time to clear his head, and while he didn't trust Cyarah at all, she did at least teach him something while he was out here.

As they two walked back, Cyarah explained how she was transported to Xi'Gardia, how beautiful the realm was, and how she came to learn of their culture. She went into great detail about Dark Mana ingrained in their society and how her bonded taught her how to use the First Poison. She spoke highly of her bonded and Chase could tell from how she spoke of him that her feelings of affection were genuine. He didn't care for most of it, but one part stuck out to him.

"I'll tell you this, Chase." Cyarah explained. "There is no pain like breaking a promise with your bonded. And that is because there is no love stronger than an Elemental and their bonded. So, I implore you to never break your promise."

A tear slipped from Cyarah's eye, and she wiped it away quickly. Chase looked ahead at the gate and saw someone waiting there. As they got closer, he couldn't believe his eyes. Isobel sat at the gate, alone, waiting. He wanted to run and make sure that she was okay, to be by her side again, but he stopped himself. He turned back to Cyarah, who was watching him with her hands in her pockets.

"You know…" He spoke. "When you're not being a lying sack of rubbish, I don't… hate you."

"…Thanks?" Cyarah said back, side-eying him. "I guess you can be a bit… likeable… too."

"Okay." Chase said looking at her.

"Okay." Cyarah said, giving him the same side-eye. "Anything else?"

"Yeah, you're not really over fifty years old, right?" Chase asked.

Cyarah lightly chuckled as she walked to the gate. As Chase turned to walk as well, Isobel collided with him, giving him a massive hug.

"Oof!" Chase said aloud.

"I looked all over for you." Isobel said into his chest.

Chase hugged her back and then pulled her away to examine her.

"I can't believe it…" He examined. "You look…

normal. Well, except for that neck tattoo. You look healthy! How do you feel?"

"I have never felt better!" Isobel said with a smile.

As he was talking with Isobel, Chase noticed something floating behind her. It was like an orb or light or something.

"Uhhh… You're being followed by a pixie or something?" Chase asked.

"No, that's just Rajani." Isobel said indifferently.

"Rajani?" Chase said confused.

"Yes, Rajani, silly Elemental!" The orb spoke to him.

"Elemental?" Isobel said suddenly.

"We have a lot to talk about…" Chase said smiling at her.

* * *

THE WORLD

-Two Weeks Later-

The City of Zhalesh erupted into a festive excitement with fireworks exploding high above the city walls. The remaining citizens of the city crowded onto the empty streets for the welcoming ceremony of the expedition forces. God King D'Merrion's personal orchestra played a ceremonial hymn to set the mood for the joyous occasion. D'Merrion upon his newly renovated float with a smile on his face, eagerly awaiting the army.

Drakonis, Chase, and Isobel gathered along the western side of the street, trying to find an appropriate location to view the event. Drakonis had spent all morning instructing the pair on the proper ways to carry themselves in the Queen's presence, just in case they were unlucky enough to make her acquaintance. Chase and Isobel would have very much rather missed the event entirely though. All the same, they listened to the dragonkin's advice and followed his every step.

Addurog and Ashnel found a booth on the opposing side of the road to view the festivities. Addurog, not too interested in the event, pulled out his book of pejoratives and began crafting mental attacks in his journal. Ashnel looked down at the phoenix and began to reprimand his disrespectful actions. Addurog didn't care.

Cyarah accompanied Xinovioc from his library to the festival. The elderly dragonkin needed help moving some books and Cyarah just so happened to be in the library reading some historic novels. After a brief interaction, they decided to go to the festival together.

King Maj, followed by his two lovely daughters, Mahogany and Dior, wheeled his son Semaj to a great spot to view the event. It was above everyone else, and it had a good overview of the courtyard. The King was especially excited today.

Ophag, whose life had been considerably easier now that Ashnel had to tend to Addurog's demands, had decided to see the festival with his family. Targus, who had spent days deciding if the city was even worth staying in, filed in next to them. The 'Drakonis Cheer Squad' danced their routine on the side, but were quickly escorted away because, well, no one has any time for that nonsense. Even Therron, who rarely leaves his emporium, was in the crowd to welcome the expedition forces.

All of the citizens of Zhalesh talked and enjoyed some of the festive food, and marveled at the fireworks spectacle, awaiting the return of the army.

"Hark!" A guard that sat upon the large gate yelled. It was the same bearkin that nearly lost his life to Cyarah's cunning. "They arrive!"

The large gates of the city creaked open and revealed hundreds of female warriors, each clad in purple armor of Majen design, led by a large purple dragon, the one and only Queen Azzaria. Azzaria walked upon the earth confidently, with one lone warrior at her side, and the soldiers walked uniformly behind, never missing a step. Even though there was a hymn playing over their motions, it was like they had a rhythm of their own to abide by.

Drakonis pointed out Azzaria to Chase and Isobel, but Isobel quickly reassured him that they could tell who she was.

Chase made a snide remark about how he thought she would be bigger.

Semaj, Mahogany, and Dior all clapped and screamed as they pointed at the lone warrior next to Azzaria's side. King Maj became teary-eyed, his heart filled to the brim by how excited his children were to see their mother return to them.

The people of Zhalesh cheered for their returning troops. Confetti began to rain from the air upon the soldiers' heads, and whistles rang out from the crowds. Even with the excitement of the crowd calling to them, none of the troops broke their demeanor. They stopped only a few paces in front of the One True God's float, and all bowed their heads.

"Raise your head, worthy warriors!" D'Merrion called to them. "All of Zhalesh welcomes you back to the safety of its walls!"

The crowd cheered harder for the soldiers, erupting into a chorus of wanton claps and screams. D'Merrion raised his hand, and the crowd grew silent. The warriors raised their heads and stared straight ahead at the One True God.

"So, tell me, Azzaria, Queen of the Skies, and true Queen of all the Realm…" D'Merrion said with a large grin on his face. "Tell me of the success of your campaign so that I may start my crucible and begin the storied tradition anew!"

The courtyard was completely silent in anticipation of Azzaria's response. Then Azzaria spoke up.

"My love…" Azzaria spoke out. "Great God King D'Merrion, Lord of all gods… I, Azzaria, first grand general of the Grand Expedition Forces regret to inform you that we have failed in our conquest of Arundi."

Gasps rang out all over the crowd followed by subtle mumbling, like an avalanche atop a great mountain. These mumbles slowly grew in volume until D'Merrion roared out over the crowd.

"I will have silence in MY COURTYARD!" D'Merrion screamed over the voices of his people. D'Merrion kept walking until he reached his beloved's face. He stared deep into her eye, and she didn't break eye contact with him.

"Fear not, people of Zhalesh!" D'Merrion yelled as he turned away from Azzaria. "I know that this news worries you. In light of recent events, I know your confidence in your security is shaken, but now that Queen Azzaria is here, we will make those who stand against us pay. There will be revenge for your slain brethren and family members!"

Claps slowly erupted from the crowd. Many of the people didn't buy what King D'Merrion was saying, but none dared speak against his word. They all knew one truth, if they disagreed, they would die. So, they clapped and cheered him on instead.

"We have spent the past few weeks mourning the dead." D'Merrion continued. "Let us now celebrate the living, and welcome back these brave warriors from their crusade!"

D'Merrion waved his hand to the people as he spun around and smiled at them. As he met the gaze of his wife again, he whispered to her.

"We will speak more of this later, my queen." D'Merrion said softly.

While D'Merrion spent time trying to build public favor back, Azzaria switched her gaze to Drakonis. Her voice echoed loudly in his mind.

I commend you on using your limited ability to make sure the festival isn't interrupted. She spoke to him. *However, your lackluster ability to apprehend these terrorists has not only endangered The God King's political image amongst the Merchant's Guild, but you've also managed to allow these vermin to wreak havoc freely against the people of Zhalesh. You are supposed to be their protector, but instead you herded them to their demise! We will speak AT LENGTH about this when I am properly settled. For now, I have located several perpetrators inside of the walls and put them into a catatonic state.*

Azzaria then changed her gaze to Isobel and Chase. She tried to peer into each of their minds, but the contents of each were blocked for different reasons. Chase's mind was a scrambled mess, but Azzaria was used to seeing this type of magic. This was only the work of Divines and she easily deciphered that he was a Divine Knight. This annoyed Azzaria greatly, and that annoyance only grew when she made eye contact with Isobel.

Isobel noticed the dragonkin staring their way and she looked back at her. Both stared at each other for a long moment. Rajani suddenly spoke to Isobel in her mind.

"Isobel, Azzaria has tried to invade your mind." Rajani said to her. "I have protected you from her power but know this: Do not confront Azzaria. We will not win. She is a hero of her people and far beyond the capability of anyone short of King D'Merrion. No matter the cost, avoid her ire."

This was the first time Isobel had felt fear come from Rajani.

The people cheered for the warriors and the soldiers followed D'Merrion's float to the palace. This ended the pre-festival to the crucible.

-A Few Minutes Later-

Drakonis, Chase and Isobel entered the Maj's Forge, each with a different mindset after interacting with Azzaria.

"King Maj?" Drakonis called out loudly. "Are you here? You're not creating any more terrifying weapons, are you?"

King Maj, who was in a conversation with two other Majen blacksmiths, turned to greet Drakonis.

"Lad!" He said with a jolly smile. "Bwahaha! I would be lying if I said no! Come! Come!"

King Maj motioned for them to join his conversation. He and the blacksmiths stood next to a table with a large tablecloth on top of a large orb-shaped object.

"My men were eager to see this thing unveiled and I told them to wait around!" King Maj said with an even bigger smile. "Are we ready to unveil it yet?"

Drakonis, and secretly Chase and Isobel as well, noticed the Maj was a little chipper than usual.

"You seem to be in quite a mood today." Drakonis commented.

The giant man laughed again and put his arm around Drakonis.

"How am I supposed to act when I get to show off some of my greatest work and see my beautiful wife as well!?" The Maj exclaimed. "Look. Let's not waste time."

King Maj then grabbed the large cloth and pulled it away from the table, revealing a large golden orb with many different rotating runes on the outside of it. The orb rotated around to reveal a large blue eye in its center.

"This is my greatest creation!" King Maj said excitedly. "This beauty is even more magnificent than Rajani and Rohaz combined! Behold, AVIANCE!"

The orb leapt up from the table and floated around the

room, examining everyone.

"Hello." The orb said in a soft woman's voice. It went around and said hello eagerly to everyone in the room.

"Aviance is the ultimate weapon!" King Maj explained. "She can turn into any weapon that the wielder wants! And she's quite charming to boot. A real go-getter!"

"That sounds amazing on paper, but has it been tested?" Drakonis asked. Before he could get his answer, Rohaz and Rajani manifested next to him and started yelling at King Maj.

"What is this pale imitation, Maj!?" Rohaz roared at the king. "Were you not satisfied with my sister and me? Do you seek to disrupt the very balance of law and life itself?"

"I detest agreeing with Rohaz, but do you not see the travesty that you have created, Maj!?" Rajani fumed.

King Maj brushed past the two swords to stand by Aviance, who had now calmed down after greeting the entire room.

"Do not be jealous of my creation." King Maj said a little smugly. "I will forever have love in my heart for my former greatest creations, but as a wise Maj once said, 'Out with the old and in with the new'!"

Drakonis activated his draconic visage and stared at the orb, trying to see the power of the souls inside. He barely saw any traces of the former souls used to create the weapon.

"King Maj, I can barely see the orbs within this one."

He examined. "Was the golden soul that much more powerful than the others?"

King Maj agreed with Drakonis and the two engaged in a detailed conversation about Aviance, only confusing Isobel and Chase in the process. Chase reached out to them to try and get them to explain when the door to the forge was kicked open. Everyone looked towards the door and saw a woman in purple armor with blood red hair standing in the doorway. It was the same lone figure that stood confidently at Azzaria's side in front of the other soldiers.

"I guess I should have known you would be here, King of the Majes." The woman stated loudly with her arms crossed. "Every other Majen smith went to greet their wives, but you decided to play with your true loves in your man cave.

The woman had a large smile on her face, but her serious tone didn't give away whether she was serious or not.

"Karita, my queen!" King Maj said, practically floating over to her. "I would have greeted you as soon as you set foot within the gates, but this here 'lord' forced me to toil day and night for his bidding!"

"Nope!" Drakonis yelled as he raised his hands in the air. "Do not bring me into this, King Maj! I will not even jest at a fight with the Queen of the Majes!"

Karita smiled at the men and laughed heartily. Then her expression became one of strict business.

“As much as I would love to catch up, I am here on behalf of the God King and His Queen,” Karita stated. She pointed at Chase. “I am here for him.”

Drakonis jumped in front of Chase, staring down Karita.

“What business do they have with him?” Drakonis asked firmly.

“You know that I cannot reveal that.” Karita replied solemnly.

“Then allow me to accompany him.” Drakonis spoke.

“My apologies, Prince Drakonis, but God King D’Merrion was very specific in his wording. That knight and that knight alone must come to the throne room. No one is to follow.”

“This really sounds like they are going to kill me…” Chase said half-jokingly.

Karita sighed and rolled her eyes.

“Please understand, if I had been ordered to eliminate you, I would have done so without talking to anyone.” Karita informed him. “And regardless of that fact, it’s not like anyone could stop me from doing so. So, just come along!”

Drakonis turned to Chase. Chase nodded back at him. Even though Drakonis had a million thoughts running through his head at the moment, he simply nodded back at Chase. He had grown to be a little more trusting with both knights.

“Be on your guard.” Drakonis warned. “And don’t do anything stupid.”

“Me?” Chase joked. “When do I do anything stupid?”

Aviance zoomed across the room and shot a beam of light up and down his body. The light traveled up and down Chase’s body before stopping at his head.

“You are Chase.” Aviance said confidently. “The logs programmed into my limited database show that you have made several terrible decisions since coming to the capitol. Would you like me to categorize them from best to worst?”

“Never in a million years.” Chase said, pushing Aviance out of the way.

Chase followed Karita out of the forge and into the hallway.

-A Few Minutes Later-

D’Merrion sat on the steps leading to the palace. Mahogany, Dior, and Semaj sat next to him, listening to him regale tales of his old adventures.

“And then I slammed the whale into the earth!” D’Merrion exclaimed, making loud explosion noises.

The kids were in awe at his story, completely enthralled with his tales of heroism. He spent a few more minutes talking about his past exploits, but then decided to give them something.

“Have you ever tried to use magic?” D’Merrion asked them.

“No, but I want to one day.” Semaj admitted.

“Me too!” Dior said excitedly.

“And what of you, young Mahogany?” D’Merrion asked.

“I’ve tried it, and I can’t…” Mahogany said meekly.

D’Merrion rubbed his beard for a second then snapped his finger like he had an amazing idea.

“Oh, I know!” He said in a very whimsical voice. “I will just show you how magic works. That way you can understand for yourselves! How does that sound?”

The three kids jump with excitement. They were finally going to see real magic at work!

D’Merrion stepped a few paces away from them and raised his hand into the air.

“First thing you have to understand is that we do not create magic!” D’Merrion explained. “Magic exists all around us in the form of mana! Right now, your bodies are steeped in magical pressure, your presence in the world.”

D’Merrion took his other hand and pointed to his chest.

“In the center of your chest, you have something called a ‘core’ that regulates the magic you take in.” D’Merrion continued. “You can only hold so much mana in your core.

That all depends on how much you train physically and how often you practice casting incantations and spells. The more you practice, the stronger the spells. Now, here is the important part. We can't just gather mana ourselves. Someone or something does it for use. We call that… The Mana Weave."

The wind blew briskly into the area. Small pebbles shook on the ground and the sky slowly turned crimson.

"As practitioners of magic, in order to cast a spell, you must ask the weave for its permission." D'Merrion continued. "The Weave then, through an arbitrary system or prerequisites that only it knows, dictates how worthy you are of casting the spell you ask for. It must be respected in order for your magic to come to life!"

A giant ball formed in the sky, almost like a second sun. It was right above D'Merrion's head and looked big enough to engulf the entire kingdom.

"As long as you respect the weave, it usually grants you reasonable strength, relative to your worthiness." D'Merrion started to yell over the growing winds. "Now let's see what happens when you disrespect the weave! Thanks, you bum, for giving me the power I rightfully deserve, but this power is pathetic in scope to my own! Give me more, you peasant!"

As D'Merrion spoke his last words, the giant sun in the sky shrunk almost instantly. After only a few moments, it completely evaporated and the only evidence that it was there were the misplaced rocks on the ground.

"As you can see, the weave is fickle." D'Merrion shrugged. "If you want to use its power, you must respect it. We have never seen the weave but over the years, we have almost perfected its use… Anyway, do you have questions?"

The kids had been sitting there the entire time with their mouths wide open. They jumped up at D'Merrion, completely excited and blown away by the spectacle. They were completely ignorant of the fact that D'Merrion could have destroyed the entirety of the realm with that ball.

"My liege!" D'Merrion heard a voice call to him. It was Karita. "I have brought him."

"Excellent!" D'Merrion claimed with a smile. "Please, enjoy the festival!"

Karita quickly gathered her children and left Chase there with the God King. Chase stood watching the God King and the God King stared back. The God King walked towards Chase and Chase could feel the pressure around him get heavy. The God King kept walking towards him until he was but a few feet away, but Chase was still standing. Struggling, but still standing. Chase then felt the area around him return to its normal pressure. He breathed a sigh of relief.

"Welcome, Knight Chase." King D'Merrion said with a smile creeping onto his face. "You have come a long way since you first arrived here in Zhalesh. You may have wondered why

I've summoned you here today. It's simple really."

King D'Merrion leaned in towards Chase, who was still recovering from the massive pressure pressed upon him.

"I wanted to see you with my own eyes." The God King said with a maddening grin. "I wanted to see who this 'Broken Knight' really was…"

-Drakonian Saga: Dragon of Darkness-Special Edition-

– END-

Glossary - The Terms in Drakonian Saga

A

Ascension Ceremony: A ceremony where the transference of power happens, either from an elder, through necessity, or defeated warrior, through Rule of the Wild. A 'Blesser' gives their power to a new candidate, giving him magical power and pressure and also awakening his core's latent potential. This ceremony solidifies a warrior's newly acquired role and rank within beast society. Humans, however, have different rules.

Aura: The visual manifestation of one's power when their core is in use. An aura's appearance is usually not dictated by the owner of the core and can take on many different appearances.

B

Beastkin: The familiar name that beast kind prefers to be announced by when associating with non-beasts, however rare that occasion may be. This term suggests that beast kind has a sort of unspoken kinship or familiarity amongst the different beast affiliations, even when most of the time this is not the case.

Beast Kind: A term used to describe beings from other worlds that have settled on Earth for whatever reason. They have been cut off from their home worlds, or chosen not to return, and now live in the human majority realm.

beastmen: Derogatory term used by humanity to describe beast kind. Some humans may see beastkin as “anthropomorphic animals” or a "beastly humanoid", and this lack of awareness usually leads to bloodshed in the beast/human settlements.

C

Channeling: The act of mana moving to and from a being’s core. In order to cast spells and incantations, one’s core must contain mana. There are many ways to learn how to acquire mana, but once one has absorbed mana into their core for the first time, their body learns how to passively take in and recover mana for the rest of their life. Even with this passive intake of mana, one can still forcibly intake mana at any time.

Chosen Devout: Priests of the Nine Divine faith. Instead of pursuing Knighthood, young squires of The Academy can choose to live a life of worship and faith in the Divines. This option is usually chosen as an alternative to the brutality of war. The Chosen Devout spend their days guarding the Cathedral of the Nine, maintaining the barrier that cloaks the city of Karia from discovery, and engaging in perpetual research and mana control. While they aren’t the most physically capable combatants, they tend to be well-versed and adept at all manner of incantations and spells.

D

Dragon of Darkness: Don't even worry about how redacted this information is.

Dark Mana: Known as the First Poison, this mana originates from Xi'Gardia. It differs from mana from most realms as it seeks to drain lifeforce.

The Dragon Deal: Redacted

Divines: The Divines are the beings that created the human majority realm after the initial war with the Ancient Ones. They come from the original realm, Paradise, that was severed to create the new realms. "Divines" is a name they gave themselves after they defeated the Primordials.

Divine Blessing: The Nine Divine equivalent of an Ascension Ceremony. The main difference is that the ascension ceremony is not a full transfer of power and aura, but in actuality, partial gift of mana and access to Divine Karia's Core.

Divine Conduit: A modified mana crystal designed by the beastkin Technology and Research Division that attunes every mana crystal within a certain radius to a specific frequency. This allows the conduit to transmit messages to many crystals at once. The conduits can also communicate directly with other conduits over a longer distance than normal mana crystals would.

Divine Knight: Warrior of the Nine Divines. Most Divine Knights are chosen from one of the Seven Sacred Families, but it is possible for someone to be chosen based upon merit and achievement. Many that undergo the training for knighthood go to The Academy and are taught history, smithing, cooking, survival, and martial arts daily. After a few years, young squires are then enlisted into the Divine's army to learn from Senior Knights. The final act before becoming knighted is the ascension ceremony, where proven knights meet one or all Divines and receive their blessing.

Divine Candidate: Anyone that comes from a Sacred Family and pursues being a Divine Knight. Usually, these candidates receive constant tutelage in horseback riding, spell works, swordplay, archery and other skills, then they are sent to Karia to The Academy for further development.

E

F

Forbidden Zone: redacted

Fairy: A sprite with sentience. Sprites tend to exist within reality without conscience and go about a day-to-day routine, uninhibited by what happens within reality. Fairies are unique in that they have goals, emotions, and feelings. Most still behave like sprites and choose to not interact with beings outside of their race since most fairies don't have extreme power themselves, but interactions with beastkin and humans is not a completely foreign concept.

G

H

I

Incantation: A spell that needs a vocal chant to cast. Most incantations are powerful in nature and need constant permission from the Weave to cast. In some instances where individuals share cores, all parties need to give permission for their cores to be used to cast the incantation.

J

K

L

M

Mana Crystal: A shard that has an abundance of uses, one of which is to transmit vibrations to other mana crystals. Beastkin use them to communicate across long distances. They are powered by Mana from their users, and usually take the glow of a being's soul when in use. In dire situations where mana reserves are low, one can smash the crystal to release the mana trapped inside. In some specific instances, it is possible to repurpose the crystals to behave like an Old-World computer, using it to display data and imagery.

Mana Gun: Guns designed by humanity during the first world conflict. They contain partially charged mana crystals that charge and regulate power throughout the gun.

Due to the design of the gun, a wielder can change the potency and size of the mana bullet fired from the gun. If one is so inclined, they can also charge the mana crystal inside to increase its power. Due to the Mana Weave, these guns tend to lose effectiveness at long range and without proper maintenance, the barrel can be destroyed by continuous concentrated blasts. Many of these weapons were confiscated and repurposed by beastkin kind after their previous owners were slain.

Mana Weave: The Mana Weave is an entity that can only be described as existence outside of existence. It is a sentient, and yet docile being that gifts the world with magic from its dimension. The mana weave has an innate connection to all beings via their mana core, able to directly pull mana from any being's core at any time. It materializes magic in all dimensions outside of its home, but in order to send the magic to where it's being requested, it desires an exchange of mana between the caller and itself.

N

O

P

Paradise: Redacted

Pressure: When speaking in relation to auras, pressure is the density of air in an area where mana is being moderated. When large amounts of mana builds up in an area, it condenses the molecules in the air. This concentrated air weighs more and can make it hard to breathe or move in the area.

Primordials: Redacted

Q

R

Rule of the Wilds: Ritual combat between two or more beastkin warriors, often used to solve ranking disputes amongst the beast kind. Any beastkin is allowed to invoke the rule, and challenge even a general for his position. In the civilized world, defeat leads to loss of rank and possible social shunning for any period of time, but in some rare instances, the losing party will be slaughtered or exiled. In the feral clans, losing a Rule of the Wilds leads directly to an Ascension Ceremony.

Runes: A term used to describe any special kind of magically imbued stone. Typically, they are pre-crafted objects of power that can be used to enhance a spell or a being’s aura. In some rare cases, they are created via spell and used to augment spells or incantations.

S

Sacred Family: A family from Divine Karia's bloodline. There is a family for each of her offspring. While there used to be Nine Families originally, war and infighting has seen to the demise of two households.

Sigil: A visual representation of a spell or incantation. The sigil itself is not in fact powerful. In order for a sigil to be present, a spell either was created with the sigil in mind, or the spell is so powerful that a sigil becomes present upon usage.

Spell: Any instance where beings use their cores and mana to create or destroy. The general rule for spell casting is that the Weave must be consulted for use during a spell's first cast by an individual. After the initial casting, a being can use the spell to their heart's content if it isn't too powerful. Stronger spells become incantations, depending on the worthiness of the individual.

Spell-crafting: The dangerous art of constructing original and unique spells based on one's own imagination. This can seem like a harmless feat that any individual can do, but in actuality, 2the power to create is a dangerous prospect that threatens nature and reality. It is a great feat to even be able to conceptualize a spell, let alone cast it and be found worthy to wield it by the Mana Weave.

Sprite: Small entity that maintains some autonomous function. Also goes by the name of 'fairy'. Not all fairies are sprites but more often than not, a sprite resembles a small fairy. These smaller beings tend to stay away from most beings and don't exist as a part of any organized society. They abide by their own rules, adhering to some unseen force in reality. When encountered in their habitat, they tend to ignore all around them to complete their goals.

T

The Three Gods: Extremely redacted.

The Pound- Redacted.

U

V

W

S

Y

Z

Made in the USA
Middletown, DE
04 September 2024